Two mysteries:

DEATH IS THE COOL NIGHT

and

LOST TO THE WORLD

by

Edgar-nominated author
Libby Sternberg

Copyright 2016 Libby Sternberg

ISBN-13: 978-1530400355
ISBN-10: 153040035X

These are revised editions of the original novels of the same titles by Libby Sternberg, published in 2010.

Death Is the Cool Night

A mystery

by Libby Sternberg

Prologue

1942

Dearest,

If you sign the papers and return them to my lawyer, that is sufficient. In the meantime, I am grateful for your letters, which are a welcome thread to the "outside" world. All I seem to be capable of doing is waiting . . .

There are many injuries of one sort or another here, and I feel the need to hide my hands – they are a mark of carelessness, not heroism. The other men might think I "earned" them in some way.

My sacrifice – a future as a concert pianist – seems small compared to that of others. It seems so silly here, to have a dream of anything except reprieve.

I explain that my hands were injured years ago, and I always say it was my fault. That puts an end to it. I don't want pity.

I'm tired and hungry most of the time. I'm sick of lots of things. But not of hearing from you, my darling. I hope you don't mind if I call you that. Other men have sweethearts outside. Let us pretend you are mine.

Write again soon. Write every day. Every hour. When many letters come at once, it feels like Christmas morning . . .

Yours,
Gregory

Chapter One

"HE'S DEAD. I don't know how yet. Just got the call this morning."

You would think I could have kept a straight face at such news — the death of the conservatory's opera conductor, Ivan Roustakoff. You'd think I could have managed a pang of regret. Instead I found my lips curling up into a smile and my breath easy, as if news of a disaster being averted had just reached my ears.

Ivan, the bastard who made my life as rehearsal pianist miserable, was dead. *Well, well, well.*

I cleared my throat. "So sorry," I managed to murmur, looking down. I'd had a quick shot of gin to fortify myself for the day and didn't want my breath giving it away.

"It's terrible, of course. He has a sister — she's a wonderful supporter of the conservatory. And that fiancé of his — "

"Renee," I said, providing the name to the conservatory dean.

Not Renee. Renata. But she, like many singers, had changed her name to appear as if she were a refugee from a more sympathetic country. Aggressor names were unfashionable. Despite a thick German accent, the tenor singing Calaf was Hank Miller. Teutonic blonde hair and shining blue eyes, and a father who served in the *Freikorps*, beating back forces of rebellion in Berlin. Hank! Hans was more likely.

Dean Whiley stubbed out a cigarette with perfectly manicured fingernails. He wore a suit so neatly tailored and pressed that someone might have finished the last seam just that morning. His thick gray hair needed no pomade to stay in place. His blue eyes reflected the color of his bloodline. He sat behind an ornately carved desk, probably some gift from a philanthropist's trip to Europe. The desk was too large for most rooms, but the dean's office was spacious, with arched windows nearly to the ceiling letting in the cold light of morning.

"You want me to notify the cast and orchestra of the cancellation?" I asked.

We had been rehearsing Puccini's *Turandot,* an overly ambitious piece for student performers. But Roustakoff himself had been consumed with ambition. His plan had been to entice the great Rosa Ponselle, retired and living at Villa Pace outside Baltimore, to his production, and to so mightily impress her with his ability to squeeze something sweet from these sour lumps of students that she would lend her grand name to an opera company he wanted to start. He hadn't been stupid, though. He'd known he might be able to coax beautiful performances from chorus and comprimario players, but he wouldn't risk the leads on neophytes—thus the contract players Renata and Hans—nor would he allow students to bumble around the stage, demonstrating their lack of acting ability. It wasn't a staged production. It was opera in concert.

"Not a cancellation. A change in plans." Dean Whiley let a flicker of a grimace cross his face, telegraphing this was a decision with which he didn't agree.

"You have conducting experience," he said, looking me straight in the eyes. The gaze said something else. It said "you're not up to this."

"Yes," I said, countering his assessment. Conducting didn't require supple hands.

"Davidson is on some tour," he explained, referring to the other conservatory conductor. "And, of course, the rehearsal schedule is unusually long—several months, I believe. You'd have more than adequate time. And if you need more than what's already planned, I'm sure we can fit other practice days on the schedule."

"I can do it." Even if I couldn't, I'd not admit it to him. "I know the score. I'm ready. I knew I'd have to fill in if Maestro Roustakoff were ill. So I'm ready."

He looked surprised, as if I'd violated a rule of etiquette, talking about how capable I was.

"All right. I suggest we make the announcement at rehearsal. We'll compensate you, of course. Teaching assistant level, most likely." He waved the air as if these details weren't important. But they were crucial to me. My pantry was bare. I didn't wear tailored suits.

I knew not to press. These moneyed people thought talking about money was crass. I'd work that out with some paymaster in the basement.

He stood, and I followed his lead, holding out my hand as a gentleman, an equal. He smiled and nodded and reached for my hand to shake on this deal.

And for one second, or a sliver of a second, I saw him hesitate, just the tiniest retraction, the smallest revulsion. But who wouldn't be repelled by the gruesome mitt poking from beneath my frayed cuff? It looked like something raw, caught in a meat grinder, a bulging red and purple scar covering the top, and white ridges on the palm. I was lucky I could feed myself, let alone play a piano at all.

"Good luck, Gregory," he said, hardly gripping my hand. He shouldn't have been afraid of hurting it. I'd grown used to the constant ache.

❧❧

I spent the rest of the morning studying the score in a corner of the library—the big Peabody library with its four stories of wrought-iron balconies lining the walls. My hands floated in the air in my shadowed nook as I looked at each page, stopping to make notes on entrances, interpretation. I didn't need food. Puccini's glorious last opera sated me, playing in my mind's ear at a volume that kept the rest of the world in muted darkness. Only this creative burst glowed deep. From time to time, I sipped from my flask, letting the liquor burn my throat and clear my inner vision.

This all would have been ecstasy except for an occasional pinch of pain. Not pain in my hands—I was numbing that with the alcohol—but pain of remembrance. Or rather, lack thereof. I had lapses, you see, starting with the time after my accident when medicine and liquor combined to erase whole mornings, afternoons, and evenings from my history.

Now I struggled to conjure up memories of the last time I'd seen Ivan. At a practice with the leads. In the big hall on the second floor. He'd abused me as usual. And then. . .

What exactly had I been doing last night, the night Ivan died? Where had I been—oh yes, the practice building down the street with its four floors of studios. I'd been there. That was it. I could breathe.

❧❧

From salvation to jeopardy, all in one day.

As soon as I entered the cavernous rehearsal hall that afternoon, a brown-suited man with pasty complexion touched me on the sleeve and asked for a word. I noticed he glanced at my hands but didn't comment on them. He must have been told by someone to look for the one with the damaged paws.

In the corner, by the door, he introduced himself.

"Sean Reilly." He flashed a badge. "Can we go somewhere not so noisy?"

Optimistic—that's what this Sean fellow was, if his suit was any indication. It pulled at the buttons and cramped his shoulders. Maybe he hoped to fit it one day. I nodded to the hallway, and we stepped outside.

"Where were you last night?" he asked after asking my name.

Funny—I'd been pondering that question all throughout the day. I thought I had enough detail to stand up to scrutiny. I'd soon find out.

Somehow I'd already guessed that Ivan wasn't just dead. He had been killed. How, I wondered, glad to be able to wonder. If I didn't know. . .

"Home." Yes, I'd gone home after sitting in the studio. That recollection was clear.

"Anyone with you?"

"No, I was alone."

Damn but I wanted a smoke. I wondered if I had time for one before rehearsal. I didn't want to light it and let it go to waste. And maybe lighting up a cigarette made one look guilty?

"You weren't here for the practice?"

So he knew about the practice, a private affair that had made me so angry I'd drank myself to sleep after walking half the way home through misty rain.

Ivan had been there with his two stars—Renata and Hans—and that simpering vocal student Laura, who turned pages for me.

Ivan had told me to meet him at the conservatory at five and we'd all "get to know each other." I'd assumed he'd take us out to dinner. I'd counted on it. He'd made it sound so festive, so gay. But no, once at the conservatory, he'd immediately mocked me. I'd been dressed in my best jacket, and he noticed. And when I'd divulged the reason—my assumption we were dining out—he'd guffawed. *This early, my boy? Oh that's right, you're used to sitting down to supper once the afternoon shift's over, I imagine.*

Nothing was too obvious or too low for Ivan, yet everyone laughed because they assumed he was clever. He forced them to believe it.

Here, hold this, will you? His blasted cola, his constant drink during rehearsals. Sometimes it smelled of rum, which didn't bother me, a fellow boozer, but made me envious of his ability to hide it so well. He joked about satisfying his sweet tooth, about it being his peculiar American vice. But it wasn't his only vice. My god, you only needed to look at Renata to see the other—he introduced her as his fiancé! Or the besotted Laura, who was nervous as a bird around him.

And so for more than an hour we'd pounded out *Turandot*. My hands, already sore from an afternoon of play at my friend Salvatore's house where I'd entertained his sisters with the latest popular tunes, rebelled. After too many octaves—that score wasn't made for piano, dammit, it was for orchestra—a pain shot through my wrist and up my arm like a knife sluicing through the skin. I'd cried out and retracted my hand, holding the wrist and sucking in my lips.

And Ivan—he must have seen the look of pity in Laura's and Renata's eyes—he quickly doused their sympathy with lightheartedness, making a joke about how it was time to stop and put them *all* out of their misery. He knew his audience well. People don't like to think of my suffering. So he'd provided them with the distraction from those unpleasant thoughts, turning compassion into mere camaraderie. How he forced people to love him!

But that Laura girl, she didn't succumb. Not that evening. She'd asked me after the rehearsal if I was all right. I'd said yes, seething with anger. My hand shaking from anguish and rage, I couldn't even light my cigarette. She lit it for me. And later, I noticed her heading to the practice rooms in the building down the street. I followed her there—for what? For nothing.

I ended up in a studio alone, watching the rain fall on the city, listening to random voices in the stairwell, wondering what they meant. I don't remember how long I was there. It was a black swath of time with intermittent memories. And here was one:

Before sitting there alone, I'd had my own encounter with Ivan on the stairs. Away from his audience, he didn't sweeten his cruelty. *You're not up to the task. It will only get harder. I can use Chalmers to play instead.*

He'd fired me.

And then I'd gone home, poured myself a whisky, and fallen asleep at my kitchen table in the basement of my Baltimore row house, a far cry from the expansive homes that Ivan and Whiley and even that Laura girl lived in.

All this—without detail, especially the one involving the firing—I told the detective. He wrote notes in a small pad he kept in his jacket pocket. He thanked me, asked me where to find a few folks, like Renata and Hans who were not on the schedule today, and stepped out of the way, as if looking for others whose names he didn't want to divulge.

Laura arrived and scanned the growing crowd as well. She was met by the detective. Someone must have described her to hi, too—golden hair, porcelain face, green eyes. She was a beauty. She shook her head. She nodded. She said things too low to hear. He let her go, and she immediately approached me.

"Maestro Silensky," she said.

"Please, call me Gregory."

"I just told the detective that we were in the practice studios last night. I hope you don't mind."

Yes, but I'd not known she'd noticed me.

"Of course." Now, however, I'd have to amend my story with the detective, letting him know I'd seen Laura there, implying perhaps, as she'd implied, that we'd actually been in a room together. Or had we? Had she visited me—had I visited her? Each other's alibi. Was it a kindness she'd done for me, or one I was doing for her?

I was already uneasy—I didn't want to make a fool of myself before the musicians—and now the smallest tentacle of another kind of fear began curling its way up my spine.

I shook it away and entered the rehearsal room. This was where I belonged. This, at last, was payment for my suffering.

✧

I stood at the podium, baton at my side twitching out an unheard beat while with my right hand I flipped through the pages of the opera score.

Once a sculpture gallery, the hall was vast in proportions, its walls reaching up nearly two stories and its windows large enough for a crowd to stand in comfortably. In an attempt to dampen the room's overly-live acoustics, some long-forgotten administrator had hung a large, faded tapestry on one wall. But still the room reverberated with sound. Students joked that they could sing duets with themselves in it.

At that moment, I wished I could sing. Immersing myself in the score had restored my equilibrium. Now Puccini's glorious music filled my mind again, pushing out all other anxiety, framing bad memories as operatic scenes to be felt from an emotional distance.

Last evening in this hall, Roustakoff had humiliated me. The detective's questions had brought back more memory, and I now filled in the history.

Once in the hall, Roustakoff had lost no time, immediately calling out "The second act," as if the room had been full of adoring students. He'd waved the downbeat, and I had played the B flat minor chord that signaled the start of the section in which Turandot poses her three riddles to Calaf.

And as soon as my hands had found the first chords, I knew it would be a disaster for me, that I'd be soaking my hands all night because of the stinging pain.

The Reed girl had fed my irritation. She had stared at my hands when she thought I wasn't looking. As soon as she sensed my gaze, she looked away.

"*Straniero, ascolta!*" Renata had sung into the empty hall yesterday. *Stranger, listen!* Her voice—dark and large, but a fast vibrato that made it warm, not sloppy.

As she sang the first riddle—"everyone invokes it, everyone implores it, but this phantom vanishes at dawn and is born again in every heart"—I had to reach up to turn the page myself because Laura was staring slack-jawed at Renata—no, not Renata, at Turandot herself, cold, bitter, yet eerily sympathetic, someone who had been branded by pain so deep that she struck out at those around her.

Then it had been Hans's turn. As Calaf, the tenor had sung the line repeating the riddle, and victoriously rose to the answer, his voice growing tremulous with anticipation as he sang the high last line with the solution—"hope!" His voice was clear and bright, a honeyed texture rounding it out. So bewitched was Laura by his magnificent singing that she leaned back, her hands in her lap as Roustakoff whispered the chorus's reply—"*la speranza,*" *hope.*

Roustakoff had dropped his hands at his sides. "*Bene!*" He beamed at the singers, then frowned at me. "Even without the help of artful accompaniment."

Of course my playing hadn't been "artful." My hands had tormented me before I'd even sat at the piano, cramping where the skin pulled tight across the palm and between index finger and thumb. I'd reflexively rubbed my hands on my trousers to ease the pain, staring accusingly at the keyboard, once my comfort, now an instrument of torture, wishing I could risk a drink from my ever-present flask.

"Five bars before letter 'G'," announced Roustakoff, referring to the rehearsal cues on the singers' scores. Lifting his hands in the air like a bear ready to pounce, the conductor swiftly gave the downbeat, and I tried to lose myself in the lush music, biting my lower lip when I felt a cramp start in my right hand. Just as Renata was about to enter with her part, the hand twitched uncontrollably. I pulled away from the keyboard as if it were a scalding hot iron and waited for the inevitable curse from the conductor. It didn't take long.

And that had been the moment when Roustakoff had poised the sword over my head ready to fall.

"Damn it, boy! If it's beyond you, get someone else to play it!" Roustakoff turned back to Renata and assumed his position, hands poised in the air. "Again!"

Gritting my teeth, I took in a breath and held it. I closed my eyes, having memorized the passage after many repetitions.

The first time Roustakoff had abused me in front of others, I had discovered a sad truth. People pitied me, that was true. But in pity is the seed of disgust. And when Roustakoff chastised me, the conductor was tacitly giving them all permission to feel comfortable with their disgust. Of course, they rarely showed it by looking at my hands. No, instead I noticed them quietly disapproving of my unfashionable clothes, disheveled hair, or run-down shoes. We wouldn't mind his hands so much, their looks seemed to say, if he took better care of himself. They kept their distance.

Another half hour the conductor worked us. We accomplished little in the extra time, except a renewed appreciation for Roustakoff's sarcasm. I matched his sneering with my own, even whispering a comment—now forgotten—to Laura at one point.

"Silence!" Roustakoff's voice boomed into the space, and I heard in my mind's ear the chorus as they sang the hissing "*Silenzio.*"

Roustakoff didn't take his eyes off me. "You have used the breaks as an opportunity to mock me and other teachers here. I will not tolerate your insults during my rehearsal."

He'd turned back to the podium and begun again, but by then my hand decided to punish me as well. The slicing pain, the electric shock of abused muscle, sinew, and skin. I could play no longer. And that was when he'd won the day, with his "putting us out of our misery" comment, making my misery no more nor no less than that of the singers or even little Laura Reed turning pages beside me.

What a bastard.

Now Roustakoff was dead and I was alive, claiming his moment of victory. I could not resist feeling vindicated, no matter what troubles awaited me.

Noise in the hall grew exponentially as instrumentalists took their places and began tuning and practicing difficult passages. Choristers meandered to the chairs set up behind the orchestra while the men who would sing the roles of Ping, Pang, and Pong—providing comic relief in the otherwise serious opera—were in place in front, as was the soprano who was singing the slave girl, Liu, and the bass who was singing Timur.

I turned, spotting the college president speaking with a petite dark-haired woman in the back of the hall. Ponselle. The great singer herself was here.

When the president came forward with Ponselle, I stepped down from the platform and smiled at the diva, taking her offered hand. Quick introductions followed, and then I returned to the podium and tapped my baton on the edge of the music stand—the age-old signal that the rehearsal was about to begin.

The room slowly hushed as all eyes turned to me. I was surprised that my voice trembled as I welcomed everyone, then introduced the "special visitors."

The president, a stately man impeccably dressed, moved forward and gracefully extolled the virtues of Miss Ponselle's career, her phenomenal scope, how fortunate they were to have her in this city and in this conservatory as an honored guest, and then led the room in a round of genuine, sustained applause. Ponselle nodded her head and smiled in acknowledgement.

The room hushed again.

"I am sorry to report," the president said, holding his hands in front of him, "that your esteemed conductor, Maestro Roustakoff, will not be with you for this opera."

The room seemed to grow quieter still as he went on. "He has passed away unexpectedly. Our sincere condolences go out to his loved ones."

There were a few gasps in the room, a whispered "oh, no."

But from the middle of the soprano section, I heard a faint gurgle of laughter. It was soft—but the hall amplified everything, and my keen ears picked up its timbre, hanging in the air like the first tones of a wind chime blown by a spring breeze. My gaze darted around as the president began an impromptu eulogy, summarizing Roustakoff's accomplishments as conductor and composer and how he would want the opera to continue.

At last, I found the source of the laughter—Laura Reed. Her face rosy from blush, she was smiling now, and her eyes were closed as if in rapture. And then—as if on cue—she fainted dead away, sliding to the ground with a reverberating thud.

More gasps and fluster. Choristers moved away, another soprano bent over Laura and fanned her face. The president's mouth fell open, and he said, "Well now" before ordering someone to call for a doctor.

Now the head of this troupe, I assumed the role of leader and pushed through the instrumentalists and singers, kneeling down beside her prone figure. Her golden hair splayed around her like a halo, and my first inclination was a selfish one—to touch this cloud while I had the chance, but I stayed my hand and instead felt her forehead. It was clammy. Her eyes fluttered, then opened. They were shimmering green.

"Dead," she whispered, smiling.

"Be quiet," I said. "They've gone to fetch a doctor. Have you been ill?"

Her brows creased. "A little. I'm better now."

She raised her head slowly, and I ended up cradling her against my chest. Her hair smelled like roses, just as it had yesterday. When I looked up at the crowd, I saw admiration in the eyes of many of the choristers and instinctually felt myself puff up with bravado.

"Clear out," I said in a firm voice to the group. "I think we should postpone rehearsal. Same time tomorrow—be prepared to stay longer." I issued this last command with a touch of impatience. I was Roustakoff now.

As the singers and instrumentalists wandered away, the hall filled with noise once more. From the corner of my eye, I saw the president standing nearby with Miss Ponselle, his hands in his pockets as if unsure what to do. Once again, I took charge.

"Miss Ponselle, I apologize," I said, still on the floor with Laura. "But I think you should probably go. I hope you can return tomorrow."

She smiled and nodded, and the president looked grateful for the opportunity to lead her from the room.

"The nurse is on her way," he said gesturing to the door where a white uniformed woman hurried into the hall carrying a black bag.

When this little tugboat of medical efficiency came in, I was pushed out of the way. I heard hushed conversations and could tell the nurse was asking Laura about "female" things, so I discreetly stepped to the window and pulled out a smoke, quickly lighting it while I looked over the park and toward the townhomes where Roustakoff lived. Had lived.

Someone must have loved him. His fiancé, his family, the German tenor who'd come to America at his bidding—they would be mourning. For them, I could feel some measure of sadness, reassured as this more natural response washed over me.

In a few moments' time, Laura was on her feet, and the nurse was snapping closed her case. I turned and walked back to the scene.

"Is there something I can do?"

Laura was pale—no bloom of rose painted her cheeks. But somehow this made her even lovelier. She looked like one would imagine angels appearing— her skin almost translucent, her eyes bright.

"I think she's fine," the nurse said. "Didn't eat anything for breakfast or lunch. Girls today are foolish about such things." She turned to Laura.

"Do you have a way of getting home, dear?"

"I have my car."

"It would be better if someone could escort you." The nurse turned to me.

I had hoped to study the score.

"I don't want to be a burden," Laura said, not looking at me. "I'll find a way."

The nurse harrumphed and probed her further, but Laura kept insisting she'd be fine, she'd get someone to take her home, or have her mother drive in to town to fetch her. Satisfied at last, the nurse left.

But the more Laura had protested to the nurse, the more I now wanted to escort her after all. I couldn't help wondering if Laura was so quick to dismiss the nurse's suggestion because I wasn't part of that crowd, the landed gentry of this very divided city. Even that cad Roustakoff would be more welcome in her neighborhood. Would she be embarrassed to have me accompany her home, afraid to show up at her comfortable house with a ragtag musician with mottled hands?

"If you have your car, I will drive you," I said firmly. "It's no trouble, really."

She looked a bit surprised at first and ready to protest further, but she merely smiled, a little self-satisfied, too. "Thanks. You already know where my home is."

One Year Earlier

Dear Hans,

I was thinking, with both gratitude and some regret, of the time you took me to the Katakombe cabaret with your friends, and we laughed so hard at Werner Klink that my side ached and I thought I had burst my appendix. Do you remember? Those were happier times, nights in the Kurfeurstendamm, in the jazz clubs and dance halls, coming home in the gray light of dawn, and then the grueling practice during the day. I believe it can be that way again some day.

You introduced me to so many pleasures, my friend, that I cannot help but return the favor. I'm doing all I can to book safe passage for you. After Fontainebleau, you will need to get to Spain. You should be able to flee from there to Morocco and then to the United States. I'm preparing for several concert operas in the coming year, if I can convince the turtles at the conservatory to see things my way. There is so much to be had here – I'm entering that composition I showed you last summer into the Kliegman and have high hopes.

Now, my dear friend, I must ask a favor of you, one I hope does not cause you too much trouble. My travels took me to Milan, as you know. There I met the most entrancing spinto, really a dark lyric, a voice like honey. I fell in love with both her voice and her spirit. And she, like you, is a refugee, tossed about by the forces of the day, over which she has no control. I will marry her. Together, you can both travel to America, my fiancé and her guardian. I've sent her a telegram and given her your name. She'll join you in France and then you both should head south.

I need not tell you what she looks like. Just think of Prosper Merimee's tale of the gypsy – "dark hair, erotic scent, her red skirt over white silk stockings, her shoes of red morocco tied with flame-colored ribbon, a lacy mantilla over her shoulders and cassia flowers in her chemise." She may not wear a mantilla, nor put cassia flowers in her hair, but Renata is every bit Carmen. You will love her, too, I am sure.

Your dear friend,
Ivan

Chapter Two

"IT WAS YOUR FIRST TIME," Laura said. "You'll be more comfortable tomorrow."

She was comforting me? I bristled, gripping the big wheel of her family Packard. I didn't get to drive much and was shifting gears clumsily, so I already was in a foul mood. Now she was trying to tell me that my leadership of the ensemble was adequate for a "first time."

I studied her when I had the chance. Classic features, perfectly done face, Revlon lips, a pale blue cashmere sweater over gray skirt, black shoes unmarred by scuffs, gray gloves, a black tam. Everything about her looked expensive. Why had she laughed at the announcement of Roustakoff's death? Better yet—why had she fainted? She already knew, from the detective's questioning, that he was gone.

"Do you know how he died?" I asked, tapping a cigarette against my knee at a traffic light, fighting the urge to smoke. It was my last one.

She shrugged. "The policeman said that part was pending."

"Why do they think it's worth investigating?" I probed.

Again a shrug. "All unexpected deaths, I guess, get this treatment."

At her direction, I turned on to Roland Avenue, driving us through a tree-lined boulevard of old homes and old families. Baltimore was such a snobbish little town pretending to be more important than it was, with its neat segregation of ethnic types—old money families to the north, its scrambling ethnics to the east and south, its Jews neatly tucked in the west. And the Negroes getting whatever was left. Even my neighborhood was divided, with Italians on some blocks, Germans and Poles on others, Cechs on others still.

"And his sister would want a thorough investigation. Do you know Louise Ruxton Watts?" she asked. "She's DAR with my mother."

Ruxton. That had been Roustakoff's real name, until he'd traced his bloodlines back to Russian and French royalty. My god, his family must have steamed over that, Anglicans all, with a great-aunt ensconced in some British estate. But in the music world, foreign ruled. It was the mirror image of this society, where too many vowels in a name had you knocking at the servant's entrance.

And we were there, at her home with its own servant's entrance, a Tudor-style thing on a corner with trees and a garden with a drive around the back.

And then we were walking up a path that led back around to the front door, and now I remembered how I knew her. I'd played for a party here.

Like all such forgotten memories, it unsettled me, igniting once again the fear that I'd lost some time last night. Those lapses gave retrieved memory a frightening aspect as I struggled to recall if this was a lost time, or simply a normal forgetfulness.

Last spring I'd been hired by a family to play for a party celebrating their son's graduation from the Naval Academy. This had been the home.

As we walked up to the door, I remembered. Large home, decorated with nonchalant wealth. A Boesendorfer piano by French windows near the terrace. The house trapping the still, sinister warmth of a spring heat wave. But I had been near the windows during the party, where fresher air had touched my cheek as my renditions of the latest popular tunes competed with the tinkling of glasses and conversation. As the partygoers had laughed in the humid air, the men's faces had glistened with sweat— they'd stood there in their suit jackets and ties, moving slowly, talking in low tones, making the world operate at their pace. I remembered. I'd gone to the movies later that night, and smiled at Abbott and Costello's antics in *Buck Privates*.

Laura Reed wasn't the type who'd have to turn in milk bottles for the dime ticket to the cinema.

No, but she'd been kind to me. She had appeared from the party crush just as my hands had betrayed me. Sitting on the cushioned piano stool, I'd rubbed them on my trouser legs as I had on Sunday. She'd startled me, noiselessly approaching from behind, offering a drink of iced tea. Yes, roses. She'd had the same scent of roses then and worn rose, too— a short-sleeved dress that had made her look girlish. I'd thought of her as too young and out of reach for me, thanked her for the drink, and resumed playing.

"Mother!" she now called as she opened the door and let us both in. "I'm home!" She took off her hat and gloves, and I took off my own hat, holding it in front of me. Now that I'd seen her safely home, I'd leave, find a bus, go.

Her mother appeared in the hallway, coming from the back of the house. Walking slowly as if even the queen would have to wait for her, Mrs. Reed didn't take her gaze off me. She was sizing me up, deciding whether I was suitable for the servants' or the family table. Her eyes didn't give away her decision.

"Welcome home, dear. Who is your friend?" she asked.

"Gregory Silensky, this is my mother, Amanda Reed. You've met. At Rick's party. Gregory played."

A Negro maid in gray uniform and white apron appeared behind Mrs. Reed. Silently, she took Laura's things and hung them up.

"Thank you, Gertrude," Mrs. Reed said, without looking at her.

"Did we interrupt you? We won't bother you, will we?" Laura asked. She gave her mother a quick kiss on the cheek.

"No, not at all." But she sounded insincere. "Gertrude and I were just going over the week's menus," Mrs. Reed said, smiling. Her smile didn't move while she talked. "I'm asking the Smalls to dinner some time soon. And we're meeting them at the club, too, later this week. You know their son—Tom."

Laura froze. "Did Carol mention him to you?"

"As a matter of fact, she did. She and Daniel will join us at the club." Mrs. Reed's smile faded, and she tilted her head to one side. "Is there a problem, Laura?"

"No, no, not at all," Laura said. She turned and stopped at the door. "I just wish you'd talk to me first before filling my calendar."

As interesting as this domestic drama was, I had to be going.

"I'll be on my way, now that I know you're all right," I said.

Mrs. Reed's mouth opened. "Is something wrong, Laura?"

"She passed out at practice," I said.

"It was nothing! I hadn't eaten much for breakfast."

"And she'd had a shock. We all did."

"Ivan Roustakoff died," Laura said, as casually as if she'd told her mother the newspaper was here.

"The conductor . . ." Mrs. Reed seemed more unsettled than Laura herself.

"Yes. Dreadful man." Laura turned to me. "Look, you shouldn't rush off. Let me get you some tea or something. You can play our piano."

So it was an honor for me to play their piano, rather than an honor for them to hear me play.

"No, I should go."

"I insist," Laura said, taking my hat from me and handing it to Gertrude. "We'll have a bite to eat, and then I'll drive you home—fully recovered!"

"Does Mr. Silensky live nearby?"

"Near the harbor."

"So far. Your father can drive him."

"I can take a bus."

"Nonsense," Laura said. "C'mon, Gregory. You can play for me. I have some songs I'd like to show you." She pulled my hand into the living room, and I ended up taking off my coat and giving it to the dutiful Gertrude.

As we walked through the living room, I remembered it. The house was deceptively large. While a long living room stretched nearly the length of the house to the right of the foyer, beyond it was a smaller room that seemed to serve as a combined study and music room. Here, the

Boesendorfer sat next to the terrace doors, now closed against the autumn chill.

"Who in your family knew enough to buy this thing?" I asked, sliding on to the bench and fingering the glossy ivory keys. Although Boesendorfers enjoyed the highest reputation for quality, most non-musicians assumed Steinway was the ultimate piano. The Reeds' Boesendorfer had a rich, mellow sound, and the keyboard action was just right—not too stiff and not too easy.

"My grandfather," Laura said, leafing through a Schubert album until she found the Serenade. "He bought it on a trip to Austria, I think. Had it shipped here on the Titanic's sister ship."

"Is he a musician—does he play?" I asked, lightly fingering through the Schubert even though she still held the album.

"He's not alive anymore," Laura said. "Funny. But I don't know if he ever played. He died before I was born."

I imagined him—prim, wealthy, collecting pianos like horses and art.

"My mother plays a little," she continued. "Some Schubert waltzes. Clementi. Even a little Chopin," Laura said, almost defensively, as if she had to justify why her family would have such a fine instrument.

"Does she play well?"

"I—I suppose. I don't know. She doesn't play much," Laura said. "She's too busy with the household."

I said nothing, but wondered how busy could a woman be who had a paid helper and grown children.

"Look, I don't want you to think you have to play for me," she said. "It was just an excuse so my mother wouldn't send you packing right away. I can get Gertrude to make us some tea."

Even when she tried to be nice, it came out patronizing. Why should her mother send me packing when I'd done her daughter a kindness?

But I couldn't be angry with her. How could you be mad at such a childlike angel? And that was how she looked in the warm glow of the lamps on a gray afternoon. The color was back in her cheeks, and her gold-red hair brushed her shoulders, her cherub lips settled into a smile. She'd showered affection and attention on Roustakoff—I remembered her admiring gaze at practice—and now she was bestowing it on me. I'd not refuse.

"All right," I said, falling into playing Dorsey's "I'll Never Smile Again," something I'd play at the country club on Saturday nights when they didn't have a band.

"I don't sing that sort of thing," she said.

"Oh, really?" I asked, amused at her tone. My gaze didn't leave hers as I let my fingers gently glide from the popular song into the guitar-like strumming of Schubert's *Ständchen*, moving so smoothly from one to the other that she didn't notice at first that I'd shifted from a Frank Sinatra

19

tune to a German lied.

"So, you are clever," she said, as if it were a sad trait to possess.

"No, just tired of—" But I stopped, unable to think of what tired me. Arrogance, pomposity, being poor?

I turned on the bench to face her. "Actually, I'm tired of cleverness," I said at last. "There's nothing wrong with Tommy Dorsey or Glenn Miller's tunes. There's nothing wrong with their orchestrations. Some of them are quite good, and some of them are as elegant as a Schubert song. They might require a different kind of skill to deliver, but they're beautiful works."

I thought back to how Ivan had sneered at the work I did at the country club, the dance tunes I played. His own compositions were angular twelve-tone pieces with no discernable melody. You could play them backwards and no one would be the wiser. Yet his was the stuff that impressed the cognoscenti of the music world.

He'd won the prestigious Kliegman with his latest piece, and it would be performed and broadcast, now posthumously, by the New York Philharmonic. I'd entered, too, and had received a meaningless second-place, with nothing but a certificate and my name to go in a program to mark my victory.

"It seems to me that as more people get to enjoy our so-called classical music, the more clever it becomes, with people like Schoenberg pushing it just one step beyond what the average guy can get," I continued, warming to my lecture. "Can't have the common man enjoying it, too, can we? Then it's not so exclusive anymore."

She looked at me, perplexed and even a little hurt, the Schubert book clasped to her bosom, the very picture of the kind of music-lover I despised. She'd never embrace Dorsey or Ellington like that, because she'd learned they were beneath her.

"I love to sing Schubert," she said, her lip trembling.

Poor thing wasn't used to being hurt, and I'd offended her.

"Then sing it you shall!" I grabbed the book and began the introduction in earnest. She moved to the curve of the instrument, her hands overlapping each other on the piano lid, and when she opened her mouth to sing, she closed her eyes, and the sound was . . .

Sweet. Pure. Boy-soprano-like, angelic, innocent, the higher notes so straight and clean they sounded almost instrumental. When she sang *"Liebchen, komm zu mir,"* she sounded like a child calling to a dear friend. But when she came to the end of the song, beseeching her lover to make her happy—*beglücke mich*—a tiny vibrato colored her tone, making the plea heartbreaking and desperate. I was moved.

"You have a lovely voice."

She smiled. "At least you didn't say 'pretty.' All my teachers say it's pretty."

"It is."

"But not operatic."

"Not everyone needs to sing opera."

"I do."

No, I thought, you need to *be* operatic, giggling at the announcement of Roustakoff's death, fainting a moment later. Perhaps she felt trapped here in this beautiful home. Perhaps that's why she sang. That's why she had fallen for Ivan. Poor child.

"Let's do it again," I said to her. "And this time, just sing it a little louder. Push more breath out."

So again she sang, and this time, steadying herself by holding on to the piano lid, her delicate fingers draped over the wooden lip, her eyes shut tight, her mouth open and round, the smooth voice created images in my mind — silk, roses enveloping me, downy soft and pure.

Now, Schubert reached out through the ages, whispering intensely, *This is what young love is, this is how it feels, afraid and confident, hungry and satisfied, and forever on the razor's edge of both disappointment and fulfillment. Feel it with me, touch it with me. Come along. Beglücke mich.*

"*Komm, beglükke mich!*" — she sang, and I felt as if she were singing just to me.

Come, make me happy! I wanted to answer: "yes."

I played the final D major chord and said nothing. She opened her eyes.

"It was too timid," she said. "Let me try it again. Madame wants me to be fearless . . . ."

"No," I said softly, looking up at her. "It was perfect."

I wasn't flattering her. It *had* been perfect, and, as always in the presence of perfection, both sadness and joy overcame me, combining to make an imperfect emotion — envy. I would never be perfect again.

"Sing it like that for your teacher and she will be pleased. What else do you have?" Now I wanted to play, to hear this angel sing. It soothed me and my hands, too. They didn't ache when I played for her.

"What other Schubert are you learning?" I asked as she flipped through another book to find the page of her next piece.

"Nothing. Madame has not told me to," she said, placing Mimi's aria from *La Boheme* in front of me.

"You are too obedient, Laura," I chided her. "Don't you want to explore music on your own? Have you always just sung what your teachers have told you to?"

"Why, yes," she said, looking surprised at the question.

"You should be striking out on your own, experimenting. Look at *Gretchen am Spinnrade*, and *Heidenröslein*. They would be good for your voice. Especially the Faust," I said, referring to the Goethe work that provided the poem for the "Gretchen" song. I'd love to hear her sing that, with its more operatic flair that would perhaps bring the woman out from this girl. From memory, I began playing the rocking spinning-wheel accompaniment to "Gretchen," hearing in my mind's ear the opening lines – *meine ruhe ist hin, mein Herz ist schwer* – *my peace is gone, my heart is heavy.* "And French music would be good for you. Do you sing any?"

"I know 'The Jewel Song,'" she said.

Taking my hands off the keyboard, I groaned. Of course she would love that, with its syrupy trills, Gounod's interpretation of Goethe's ill-fated heroine.

"Let me give you some advice," I said. "Don't bring that into your lesson. Madame Gertschak will lecture you on how deficient Gounod's telling of the Faust tale is. Did you know that in some areas of Germany, they bill his opera as *Marguerite* rather than *Faust*?"

"No," she said.

"His opera centers too much on the heroine's betrayal rather than on Faust's bargain with the devil," I offered. "But this reminds me—Madame is a wonderful teacher. But she's not good for French music. Don't forget, despite her insistence on being called 'Madame,' her name is Gertschak."

"Then, what should I do?"

"Start looking for some yourself and learning it on your own," I said. "I can help you. Do you have any?"

She turned toward the shelves behind the piano and pointed.

"I don't know. I might. I've collected things over the years. When I was thirteen, we went to Europe and I bought music as souvenirs. I didn't even know what I was buying half the time."

What luxury that would be—to buy music at random, without even knowing what you were buying.

I rose and went around to the shelves, reading the names on the spines of the scores. Some of it was junk—leftovers from the Romantic era, sappy love songs that weren't even as refined as what Sinatra and Crosby sang on the radio nowadays. But in the midst of these weeds, I found a rare bloom, a thin collection of songs by Claude Debussy.

"Here!" I said triumphantly, quickly turning to face her with my find. As I did so, I caught a whiff of her perfume again.

For a second, I paused, looking into her emerald eyes, and suddenly, unexpectedly, I wanted to kiss her. She was beautiful. And she had been kind to me. And I heard the end of the Schubert—*beglükke mich*. Yes, she could make me happy.

"This," I said, swallowing hard, "is a find. Something you should try."

I cleared my throat, hesitated, and walked back to the piano bench. She followed me, to stand over my shoulder for a view of the music. I felt her warm body so close to mine. She must have felt it, too, because she cautiously but deliberately placed her left hand on my right shoulder.

"Show me," she said in a whisper. "Teach me."

It was impossible not to want her. With disappointment, I realized this was what Roustakoff had felt. It sullied me.

I straightened, took my hands from the keyboard, and flipped through the pages of the book, talking about Debussy, about Fauré, about their interpretations of the same poems, how Fauré set *Claire de lune* as if it were a little music box where the characters twirled and danced, and Debussy set the same poem as if it were recitative.

But here, too, was seductive peril as I glanced at Paul Verlaine's poem *Green* and thought of what both composers' settings meant to me—Fauré's all eager and pleading as the lover sings of the fruits, flowers, branches he bestows on his beloved. You can hear in those relentless rhythms, those ascending and climactic melodies, precisely what he wants, what physical happiness he desires. But Debussy—he set the poem as if their love had been consummated and they lay together enjoying a languid afternoon. Both settings were portraits of desire—its ache and its release.

I closed the book, handing it back to her, standing.

"Learn the *Fetes Galantes*. They're quite lovely." I moved away from her and her enchantment.

She laughed. "Like my voice."

"Your voice would be perfect for them. I think French *mélodies* require your tone. Too many singers approach them as if they were *lieder* or, worse yet, operatic arias." I rubbed my hands together, which now began to throb.

"I should go."

"I'll drive you."

"No. I can get a bus."

"Nonsense."

"It's silly—I accompanied you home because you fainted. You shouldn't be driving me back."

"But I'm better now—rested. Let me at least take you back to the conservatory."

She walked to the hallway, retrieving our things. I followed.

After we'd put our coats and hats back on, she called out to her mother that she'd be back before dinner, and we left.

On the ride into town, Debussy's version of *Claire de lune* played in my head, with its softly building desperation.

Tout en chantant, sur le mode mineur
L'amour vainqueur et la vie opportune.

They all sing in the minor key,
Of vanquished love and the opportune life.

Chapter Three

"HE WAS POISONED! And that *poliziotto*—that *mostro*—he thinks I did it."

Renata erupted into a string of Italian profanities, her arms waving as she paced the practice room. I waited for the storm to pass, my hands on my legs.

Even though I had conducted two rehearsals, revised the schedule for the next six weeks, worked with the orchestra, gone over the printed program with the House manager, and met with the dean again to arrange other Ponselle visits, I was still acting as coach for the singers, like some lowly *répétiteur*. When I sorted out the payment schedule for my work, I'd learned the damned conservatory was paying me little more than what a graduate teaching assistant would make. Far less than whatever the great Roustakoff had received, I was sure. When I had asked the dean about this, he'd suggested my coaching salary could be added to the amount—assuming I would be doing the coaching. Of course I would. I needed the cash.

"How do you know Ivan was poisoned?" I asked.

Renata's anger masked no grief over her fiancé's passing. It had been clear to me from the first meeting that she was not in love with the conductor. She'd used him to get to America and launch her career here. And he'd used her as well, I had no doubt.

"His witch of a sister told me. Oh, how she hates me! She thinks her brother was making a poor match with me." More Italian cursing before she settled into the curve of the piano. "She says the person who looks at these things—"

"The coroner."

"This person has given some kind of report—not the last report, but something—"

"Preliminary."

"And this says he was poisoned! Hah! If *I* were to kill *a man*, I would not do it like this, in secret. Oh, he would know I was the killer. I would look into his eyes and shoot him or stab him with a knife!" She demonstrated, shoving her closed fist forward above the piano.

"Renata." I chuckled. "You are charming."

"*Grazie.* Let's sing." She leafed through the music in front of her, looking for a score, continuing to talk.

"They say it is in the drink."

"What?"

"The drink—the one you carried into the room for him. The poison was in the bottle. Something to take for the pain. But too much, it makes the heart slow, *andante* to *lento* to *fermata*. Laudanum. Medicine for the pain." She stopped her music search, looked up, and barked out a laugh. "Hah! You will be the next person the *poliziotto* comes to see. I will be free and you will be the one—"

"Charged."

Laudanum. Medicine for "the pain." Yes, just as I'd taken it for my pain after my accident. A shiver coursed up my spine. Dammit.

I closed my eyes, trying to remember that night again, trying to account for every second of it. In the studio. Alone. Was I? For how long?

My hands trembled. I placed them on the keyboard and hit a muted chord as I breathed out a frustrated sigh. Roustakoff would torture me even from the grave. The detective would be back, asking more questions. I was sure of it. My mind raced through possible answers. I was in the studios that evening.

But so was Ivan. I'd overheard him in the stairwell, talking to Hans. Flashes returned. Their voices. Arguing?

"The poison," I said, trying to sound casual. "When was it put in the bottle?"

Renata found the music she was looking for and pulled it out.

"Louise, his sister, she tells me they do not know. Probably after the *Turandot* we sang. He was a *mostro* himself, eh? He was drinking later—whiskey—that made it worse!"

So Ivan went to the practice building, talked to Hans, and some time during that conversation when he was away from his things, someone put poison in his cola.

"Are they sure he didn't do it himself?"

"Killed himself?" She paused, considering this. "I do not know. If I were the detective, I would look at this. But his witch of a sister says he had plans, so this is not the possible thing. But I do not know . . .he was a *mostro*, like I said."

"Where was he found?"

"At his house on the Mount Vernon *Piazza*, the big house." She thought for a moment. "I was still practicing. I came upon him later."

"I didn't know." How horrible. I'd assumed someone else had discovered him.

She shuddered. "I thought he'd fallen asleep," she said softly, her bravado gone. "I shook him to wake him. I slapped his face, thinking he was drinking too much. 'Ivan, Ivan,' I shouted."

Now, true emotion played over her face, as she sucked in her lips and stifled a cry. "I called the doctor. It was too late."

To console her, I suggested that no one should suspect her if she were the one to call for help.

"Good thought, my friend," she said to me, a smile returning. "I will be all *innocente*."

But I would not.

As my anxiety increased, I remembered something that consoled me. Laura, after talking to the detective, had said to me that she'd told him we were together. Yes, we'd been in the building together, but not in each other's company—as far as I knew. I'd not yet corrected the detective's possible misperception. Now I wouldn't. Thank god—an alibi!

Renata walked around to me, placing music on the stand before me.

An alibi—for Laura, as well as for me. Was that the reason she'd laughed at the news of his death? She knew she had succeeded . . . no, I couldn't bear to think of that. Such a pure creature. Roustakoff couldn't have ruined her so much that...

"This is not Turandot," I said, turning my attention to the score.

Not Puccini at all. Roustakoff's name was on it, there in the upper right. How could that be—even without playing it I could tell it wasn't his usual fare. My hands found the chords, lush and vibrant, even romantic, a love song of some kind. Renata began to sing in her clumsy accent:

In the halls of Fontainebleau
Perfumed ladies go
Their demure looks and down-turned eyes a silent rebuke
To those, like us, who love more boldly.
Do not leave me here
Alone.
Do not leave me here
My love.
Do not leave me.
Do not leave me.

Haunting, dream-like, with a subtle nod to folk-like tunes, the music reminded me of recent British compositions, the vocal line rising out of the harmony to the climactic last syllable, creating the bright major third in what otherwise could have been a sad minor chord.

A chill shook me. This was his last piece, the piece that won the Kliegman. And it was good, dammit. It was wonderful. I wished I had written it.

"Your voice isn't quite right for this," I said.

"What? Of course it is right for it. He wrote it for me—his fiancé, his love! I will sing it in New York, as he intended."

"It's for a man's voice."

"It is—like all art song—for a woman or a man." Her dark eyes narrowed. "But it is for me. Look at the dedication."

To my only true love, it read, hardly evidence of Ivan's intent. He'd had many loves.

As if reading my mind, she said, "I was his fiancée. His only fiancée."

"But . . ."

The night of Ivan's death—his murder—returned. Thank god—more memories.

I'd been sitting at a piano, watching the rain. I'd opened the window to let in fresh air. I'd finished the liquor in my flask. I'd heard their voices in the stairwell nearby, its tall arched windows opened to the evening air, as well.

"You can not stand in our way, Ivan," Hans had said. "Please."

"Begging is beneath you," Roustakoff replied. His voice was tired, and there was something in it I hadn't heard before, something human and afraid. But maybe it was the rain muffling Roustakoff's usual sharpness.

"Hans, how many times have you thought you were in love?" Roustakoff continued. "Why should this time be any different?"

"She is not a thing that you own," Hans had said more strongly, but with a hint of a tremolo coloring the perfect tenor. "We want to be together. We will not make it difficult for you. As soon as this is over—the opera—we will go quietly and get married."

"Renata isn't going to stick with you, my boy," Roustakoff said, sounding as if he were giving the tenor fatherly advice. "You don't know her the way I do. If I offered her the Kliegman solo, she'd leave you without so much as a second thought. Don't fool yourself."

"You wrote that piece for my voice!" Hans exclaimed, hurt. "I was just practicing it!" His voice trembled even more with shock and pain.

A rush of rain drowned out all sound, and I'd thought they'd gone away. But then, Hans's whimpering voice spoke, as if he were fighting back tears. "You promised me."

"Don't talk to me about promises."

"But that piece, it was for me, for my voice. You said—" Hans pleaded.

"I *did* write that piece for a voice like yours, but if you won't believe me when I tell you how false Renata is, I will . . ."

I'd been so used to thinking of Roustakoff as a cold son of a bitch that it hadn't moved me one way or another to hear him threaten to break Hans's heart. Poor sap, in love with Renata. I'd seen that in his eyes the first night, too, and rumors had flown around the conservatory before our first encounter. About Hans's family, about Renata and Hans, about Roustakoff's dalliance with a young singer.

Laura.

He was heartless. Just like his music. All of it except this one piece.

"Will you get out of her life?" Roustakoff had demanded.

Why had he been so cruel to Hans—Ivan only wanted Renata because someone else wanted her more.

"Ivan, you don't love her really." Hans had pleaded. I could have sworn the man was crying. "She is—*gemütlich*—comfortable for me to be with. My family would love her. My father . . ."

"Your father is a goose-stepping fascist. Do you think he'll be happy with a dark-haired wop for a daughter-in-law? Oh, no, my dear. He'll want someone of pure blood." Roustakoff had laughed, but it was artificial, as if he were doing it just to hurt Hans. Then his voice changed, so much so that I'd thought at first that Hans was speaking again. It was flat and resigned, almost tender.

Rain covered the beginning of the rest of the conversation. Then: "You'll get over her. You'll sing my piece. And become famous. The Met will want you. Ponselle will come to *Turandot* and help launch your career. Everything will work out. Your life will be filled with treasure beyond belief. Artistic acclaim. Financial reward. Peace. Even love. You'll see."

The rain had intensified, muffling their voices beyond comprehension.

Maybe I should have told the detective about that conversation. But I couldn't now, without telling Laura first, so she could say she'd heard it, too, in the practice room we'd supposedly shared.

I looked up at Renata. Perhaps Ivan had told her, too, she'd sing the piece. It wasn't my place to get in the middle of that love triangle, even if one of its members was dead.

"I'm sure you'll do a fine job, Renata. Just sing the lines with less vibrato, more like a boy soprano, perhaps."

❧

You couldn't not stop and listen.

After my practice with Renata, I stood in the hallway, brightened by the yellow light of afternoon sun, hearing the honeyed tenor voice climbing up the melody, softer, softer until, with a penetrating purity, he sang the last line on that shimmering major third: *Do not leave me now.*

Silence.

And then, the sound of muffled weeping.

I found the studio and knocked on the heavy door. When he didn't answer, I pushed it open.

He sat at the piano, his arms crossed and his head down.

"Hans?"

His gaze flew up. He sat up straight and composed himself. His face was red. He pulled a handkerchief from his pocket and blew his nose.

"I am sorry," he said, standing. "Do you have this room now?" He gathered his things together, winding a knit scarf around his neck.

"That was beautiful," I said, pointing to the one piece of music still on the piano. Ivan's piece.

Flustered, he gathered it into a leather satchel. "*Ja*, it is a good piece."

"I meant you sounded beautiful singing it. It's perfect for you."

He looked up, those blue eyes blazing with gratitude. "*Danke*. I will add it to my repertoire. I am sure it will be a very big piece, much sung."

But he would not sing its debut. Renata had arranged that, as she had pointed out to me just a little earlier. What a shame—Hans's voice was more suitable.

"Renata will sing it. She doesn't do it nearly as well," I probed.

"No, no, she does it very well," he insisted, not looking at me. "She has the perfect sound for it. It is her piece. I am very happy for her."

"Does she know Ivan was going to let you sing it?" I asked.

His head shot up, his eyes didn't blink. "She will sing it, and it will be beautiful. And I will be happy."

I couldn't help myself. I laughed. "You say that as if you have to force yourself to be happy about it, Hans."

At first surprised by my lightheartedness, he paused, then relaxed into a smile. "*Nein*, I do not force. The detective asked me the same thing."

I leaned on the piano.

"When did he talk to you?"

"Two times," he answered. "First right after the death. Then a little later."

So Reilly was still doggedly pursuing the case. I wondered if and when he'd talk to me again.

"What did he ask you?"

"Not many things. The same things. Where was I, who will sing the Kliegman, and, about Renata, *ja*."

"He knows about you and Renata?"

Hans looked down, nodding. "*Ja*." With great sadness, he murmured, "She tells him."

Renata had told the detective she and Hans had been lovers. So sure of herself, so confident she was "all *innocente*." She didn't care who knew about her affairs. She was fearless.

Four months earlier

Dear, dear Ivan,

My sweetest, most darling one! If you don't see me on Tuesday, I think I'll die. You promised me I could come to your home, your maid would be out and it would be a liaison dangereuse.

I have been practicing the Boheme, but Madame is not so sure it is for me. I told her that you had suggested it, and she was silenced.

Oh, my sweet, when I heard the Grieg in the hallway the other day, my knees went weak. I knew it was you, so ferocious at the keyboard, but so elegant. No one plays like you. Or conducts like you. Or writes like you.

I think you are the one teacher who can really make me sing.

I will leave this billet doux *at your door. You must find me. I have so many things to tell you, my love, that will make you unbelievably happy . . .*

Your only true love,
Laura

Chapter Four

THE DETECTIVE DID FIND ME AGAIN, this time at my home on Potomac Street, a brick row house with marble steps, basement kitchen, living room and bedroom on the first floor. I usually rented the top floor, but my last tenant had moved out in the summer after getting married and needing a home for his new bride. I missed that money.

"Mr. Silensky," Reilly said, standing on my stoop on a Saturday morning over a week after the murder. "May I have a few words?"

Crap. I thought it had faded away. I'd been so busy with rehearsals, with making money. With drinking.

"Sure." I rubbed my stubbly chin and blinked my eyes. Last night I'd stayed up late with Sal. We'd gone drinking. I'd flirted with his sister Brigitta afterward. Sal thinks I should ask her out or stop flirting. And then I'd had a tortured sleep where a parade of nightmares ripped open my gut, dreams of my accident—that I was used to—but another dream of killing Ivan.

But of course I'd dream of that. I loathed him.

I ushered Reilly into my living room, gesturing to a worn Victorian-style settee in an ugly olive green, and seeing the room through a visitor's eyes. An old Victrola stood in the corner opposite the sofa. The floor was covered with a thin, threadbare carpet of indeterminate hues. A battered upright was crammed next to the Victrola, and bumping up to this was a small half-moon table on wobbly legs, covered with unopened mail—bills I didn't want to see—and some music. The walls themselves were papered in a pale blue print with vertical rows of faded roses. A picture of the Sacred Heart of Jesus graced the wall above the table. My mother used to make a shrine there, with flowers and candles.

This room represented the cheap dreams, sentimental musings, and superstitions of Old World peasants trying to be something they were not, trying to imitate the very aristocrats they loathed and envied. But Reilly, with his too-tight suit and ruddy face, he knew this world. I didn't need to apologize to him.

He sat, poised on the edge of the sofa, hands between his knees, holding his notepad.

"Working the weekend?" I asked him.

He gave one nod and smiled.

"I need to go over the events of the night Mr. Roustakoff died." He looked at his notes. "You were with him in the big building?"

"The conservatory, yes."

"And afterward—maybe two hours later—you went down the street."

"To the practice studios." I pulled a creaking straight-back chair from a corner and slumped in it. "Look, you don't need to ask me for fingerprints. I will tell you right now that I handled the cola bottle. I understand the poison was in it."

Half his mouth curled up. "Yeah."

"He asked me to take it into the rehearsal for him. But that's all I did with it."

"You're directing this show now, aren't you?"

"What?"

"The rehearsals and all. For the show."

"The opera. Yes, I've been asked to step in for him."

"That's kind of a big break for you?"

"It's not much money, if that's what you mean."

But it wasn't what he meant, and I knew it.

"What about this prize . . ." He looked at his notes. "The Kliegman. You're second place, so you must be excited about your piece being played now."

"No, that's not how it works."

"Says so in the rules."

"What?"

"If the winner don't show up for the radio broadcast, he can't claim it."

"I didn't know." I tensed. I wanted to be happy, but I couldn't, not in front of him. "I'm sure they'll make an exception. Ivan can't help it that he's dead."

Reilly didn't react to that, but consulted his notes once again.

"You went from the big building to the practice building," he said. "And you were there with the Reed girl. What were you doing?"

"Practicing." The lie came so easily.

"What kinds of stuff—the opera?"

"Schubert songs." Another easy lie.

"How'd you hurt your hands?"

"An accident at Bethlehem Steel."

He winced. "My cousin works there. It ain't easy."

"No, it isn't."

"Why'd you work there if you play the piano?"

Play the piano—that's how my family had referred to my obsession. As if there were only one piano in the entire world and their talented Grygor its fortunate player. My fellow musicians said "play piano." Or, "I am a pianist." "Tickle the ivories," my Dad used to say, so proud to have learned such an American phrase. But therein lies the problem. Mine was not a family of musicians, even though my mother had once dreamed of singing when she was young. They were a family of laborers, workers with their hands. The kind of work that raises calluses and builds muscles. Beth Steel down by the river in Baltimore.

"My father and brother worked there. They got me a job one summer. To make money." The summer before I was to enter Peabody on a full scholarship.

"Times are tough," he said with genuine appreciation.

My mother had loved to hear me play. My father — he wondered if so much music made me soft, made me girlish. When he'd offered me the chance to prove him wrong, I'd taken it. My mother had died the year before, too late to hear of my success with the conservatory scholarship, and was no longer around to defend my artistic sensibilities, so, in trying to please my father, I made one devastating mistake. I followed in his footsteps, working the line one summer, letting him smile at his friends as he looked at his big, strong strapping sons.

Work that took my brother and burned my hands. And a year later, after burying my dreams of becoming a serious pianist, I buried my father, a broken soul after losing his oldest son, sick and tired of life.

"Yes, money's tight," I concurred, irritated to have to remember this history.

"Your hands bother you much?"

"Constantly." I rubbed them on my legs, staring him in the eyes.

"What you take for the pain?"

"I drink." I laughed, and he chuckled with me.

"But the docs, they must've given you something."

I stopped breathing. Yes, they had. Laudanum. The same thing that had killed Ivan. My breath stopped. I couldn't let him see, I had to stay calm.

Where was the bottle? Still on my kitchen sink. Why had I kept it when it had tortured me so? I'd not used it in years, but hadn't thrown it away, figuring one day, the pain might be bad enough. Its presence burned a hole in the ceiling, the floor below, the air.

Dammit. It had been in my dream. I'd grabbed Ivan by the throat and forced open his mouth. I'd poured a whole bottle down and laughed.

"I don't take anything for it except the occasional shot of whiskey." No more laudanum. Not after I'd discovered how it strangled my senses and made me lose track of time, even more than the alcohol.

"What makes you think Ivan was murdered? Maybe he killed himself."

Reilly looked amused. He shook his head. "Not likely. He'd set up some meetings and stuff for that week. He had a lot to live for." He locked his gaze on me. "Unless you know something got him worked up?"

The conversation in the stairwell returned. Hans in love with Renata, Ivan breaking up the romance by bribing her with the solo in his Kliegman.

"His fiancée," I began, wondering how much to say, whether I'd look suspicious for not revealing this earlier. "I overheard Ivan talking to Hans—Hank—about his fiancé. There might have been something going on."

Reilly nodded—he knew about Renata and Hans—and jotted a note.

I told him in the barest detail about the conversation I'd heard that night, feeling guilty for making others sound guilty.

"You didn't say nothing about this when I saw you the first time."

"I didn't see any significance in it."

"You think Mr. Roustakoff was broken up about his girl betraying him?"

"I honestly don't know."

"The girl don't think he cared."

"Renata is full of bluster."

"She said he pretty much gave her his blessing."

"All I can say is what I heard that night. And it sounded to me like Ivan was upset with Hans for stealing his girl."

Reilly said nothing, as if evaluating whether this was true. Eventually, he stood.

"You mind if I look around?" He glanced toward the French doors that separated the living room from my bedroom. The bed was rumpled, like me, and clothes draped over a chair.

"Actually, I do. I have to get going. A gig," I lied, standing also.

His eyes crinkled, his mouth lifted. He knew evasion.

"All right. Another time then."

He left, and I leaned against the door for a full minute, catching my breath and my thoughts.

The Kliegman, like the opera, was mine. I'd wanted them both. But I wouldn't kill for them. I hadn't even known of the Kliegman rule. No, surely I had known. I'd read all the papers when I'd entered my piece. I'd just forgotten.

Oh Jesus.

I ran my fingers through my hair. I paced. I thought of my dream. Ivan. The laudanum. Was it laudanum in my dream? No, some unmarked poison. What color had the bottle been? Oh Jesus. Why couldn't I remember?

I raced downstairs to the kitchen. I grabbed the bottle on the sink, uncapped it, looked inside. Held it up to the light. A tiny bit left.

Christ—how much had been in there before? Surely, if I'd been using it to do evil, I'd have used it all.

I threw it away.

༺❧

"Sallie, you there?" I tapped on the window abutting the pavement, then paced in the sunshine, my hands shoved into my pockets. I'd thrown on clothes as soon as the detective had left and raced to my friend's house.

A few seconds later, the front door creaked open. Salvatore Sabataso appeared, rubbing his unshaven jaw, still hung over from the night before when we'd sat in his living room and I'd impressed his sisters with my piano playing and singing. Yes, I'd sung. I think I had.

"What? This is my only day to sleep in, you shit." Sal worked in his mother's market, and at his insistence she gave him off one Saturday morning a month. There was no Mr. Sabataso. I was never quite sure what happened to him—if he'd not come to America with the mother, or if he was dead, or he'd run away. The Sabatasos seemed happy enough.

Another face appeared behind him, that of dark-haired voluptuous Brigitta, the sister who batted her eyelashes at me and liked to sit on my lap. She smiled.

"Can you get your car?" I asked Sal. With seven kids, all of them now earning money in one way or another, the Sabatasos had been able to afford an old Ford.

"I dunno."

Brigitta pushed him aside. "The car is available. I could drive you somewhere, Greggie."

"Holy Moses, Brigitta, you cannot drive that thing." Sal glared at her and she flounced away. He turned back toward me. "Sure, I can get it."

"Right away. I gotta be someplace."

༺❧

In a half hour, I was sitting with Sal in front of Laura Reed's house. I could have called her, using the Sabataso telephone—another luxury I could not afford in my own household—but I needed to see her in person. On the drive in, I'd explained what I could to Sal, all except my dream and the deep fear that went with it—that I wasn't remembering everything that went on that night, and what I didn't remember was bad. Sympathetic, he'd offered to talk to a second cousin, who was starting as a beat cop this month, to see what he knew about Reilly and the case.

Why was this going on, when so many other things in my life were going right? It was as if I couldn't hold on to anything good without something nasty coming along to smack me down.

"I'll wait here. Go on," Sal said to me.

But I hesitated. I looked around, wishing I knew what kind of car Sean Reilly drove. Was he here, too? How would it look if I came up to the Reed house on a Saturday morning just after the detective had questioned me?

I reassured myself by a quick glance at the automobiles within view.

35

They were good-looking machines. Reilly would probably own something more like the Sabatasos' dusty Ford.

After sprinting across the street, I knocked with a confidence I didn't feel on the front door.

The maid answered, and when I asked for Laura, she disappeared, leaving me standing on the porch by the half-open door.

A few moments later, Laura appeared. She wore a long pink chenille robe that cinched her waist, and her hair looked like spun gold in the sunlight. Her face, devoid of powder or lipstick, was pale as parchment. As she blinked at me, she rubbed her arms.

"Did Detective Reilly come to see you?" I blurted.

"Yes."

"What did you tell him?"

"Nothing. My mother wouldn't let him come in. I was still in bed."

I blessed Mrs. Reed's protectiveness.

"He came to see me this morning."

She tilted her head, confused.

"I told him what you'd told him, Laura. That we were in the practice studio together."

She exhaled and nodded.

"I told him we practiced Schubert."

"Yes, we did," she said, remembering the afternoon in her home. How easily she merged these memories, just as I had. Jittery, I shifted from one foot to the next, my hands balled in fists at my side, my muscles tense.

I had to know. Dammit, I had to know. . .I'd come here wanting the answer to one question. I had to ask it, no matter how awful it sounded.

"Laura," I said, looking into her eyes. "Did you do it?"

Hard, yes. But I was beyond reason, worried that my dream had been real, that my hands had done the ugly deed. I *wanted* to hear she'd done it. I would place no judgment on her if she had. I'd have protected her with all my being—I didn't care about her guilt—but I needed to know that I . . .that I . . .

"What?" She stepped back. Her eyes widened, shimmering with unshed tears. "How could you think that?"

"No one would blame you. After what Ivan did." Here I was assuming, but her reaction confirmed my worst imaginings.

She slumped against the doorjamb. I thought she'd faint again, but she just shook her head. She chewed on her lower lip.

She placed her hands over her face and cried.

After a while, we both heard voices behind her in the house. I saw Mrs. Reed's shadow. It disappeared into the kitchen.

"You can't tell anyone," she whispered to me, her hands dropping by her sides as she stepped farther out onto the porch. "I took care of it all alone. All by myself. It was horrible."

She shook. More sobs engulfed her. If she didn't control herself soon, her parents would come out and find out this terrible secret.

I put my arm around her, and she crumpled into my embrace, hysterical with grief. I stroked her hair. I kissed her sweet head. Poor, poor girl. What had Ivan done to her? Poor darling.

And even as I caressed her, something inside me rejoiced. No need to worry about lost memories. I'd not done it. *I'd not done it.*

But, as if to pay for that uncommitted sin, I resolved to help her. Somehow.

At last, she composed herself and stepped back, her face now mottled and streaked. I handed her a handkerchief.

"We should get our stories straight," I said.

"I can meet you at the conservatory."

We set a time, and I left, having Sal drop me at the music school on his way back home.

Three months earlier

Dear Laura,
As promised, here is the name and number of the doctor I mentioned. He is a bit of
a Bolshevik, so be prepared for a treatise on Marxism. He is safe and reasonable.
He knows to send me the bill . . .
Yours,
Ivan R.

Chapter Five

IVAN HAD NOT JUST RUINED HER. He'd gotten her pregnant. And sent her to an abortionist.

This was what she'd meant when she'd said she'd taken care of it "all alone." I wasn't in the clear.

As she told me this story in a practice room two hours later, I'd frozen, unable to think, only to fear. She'd not meant to give me the impression she'd killed Ivan.

She'd suffered. Physical pain, she told me, as well as spiritual anguish.

My own anxiety over an unknown deed faded in the recitation of this very real act—her pleas with Ivan, his assurance that he loved her, but that he was expecting his fiancée any day, and Laura needed to take care of this problem on her own.

At that moment I wished it was true that I had killed Ivan. I wished I could do it as Renata had claimed she would have—staring him in the eye as I sank the dagger into his heart.

Worse still, Laura had figured out from Ivan's note that his trade with this "doctor" was regular. How many other poor souls had suffered this fate?

"There, there," I cooed, not knowing what else to say as she leaned into my chest gulping for air as she sobbed. We sat side by side on the piano bench, the Schubert open before us, but untouched, merely a prop in this second alibi, the reason for our meeting.

"I was gla-a-a-d," she hiccuped. "Glad he was dead."

Yes, glad just as I had been. I shivered. Again, I thought of the detective's questioning, the laudanum, my dream, my worries.

No, not that. I couldn't think—

I couldn't—

No, I didn't—

Too cowardly.

She felt soft and comfortable in my arms. Although she must have dressed in haste, she looked wonderful. A white silk blouse and a green plaid pleated skirt fit her as if she'd donned them for a fashion magazine. Her arms trembled in my embrace. She still smelled of roses. The scent intoxicated me. I kissed her hair and then her forehead.

"Thank you," she said, at last. "For not thinking me a monster."

"We're both monsters—I lost no sleep over his death."

She smiled.

I pushed a stray hair from her face and peered into her stormy eyes. "Who do you think did it?" I asked.

She shrugged. "He could have done it himself. It would be the cruelest kind of trick, don't you think? Everyone being blamed for his death—he has a lot of enemies."

A lot of former lovers, she meant.

"The detective said he had everything to live for," I said, uneasy.

"Maybe it was the German. Everyone says he loves Ivan's fiancée. She stays with him now, you know."

Yes, I did know. But if Hans loved Renata, it wasn't clear to me that she returned the affection to the same degree. In rehearsals the past week, she'd pulled away from Hans and looked sour and out-of-sorts when they arrived and left together. If anything, Renata had been more loving toward me. I now held the power to help her, and it would only be amplified when she learned my composition would be played instead of Ivan's by the Philharmonic.

Her reference to Hans made me remember the conversation I'd overheard. I gave her a quick summary of that incident, telling her that if Detective Reilly should ask about it, she could tell him she'd not heard it so clearly because she'd been studying her music.

At this, she laughed. "You mean just looking at the music?"

"Yes, you could say you were memorizing it, preparing to sing it."

"All right." She relaxed into my arms again. So quickly we'd become comfortable with each other, and I didn't doubt for a second that I deserved it. She'd been with Ivan, a malevolent creature, and now was me. I was a step up.

"Do you want to sing?" I asked.

"Yes, I'd like that." She sat up. "I looked at the Debussy you showed me."

And so we spent a glorious hour as she let me hear Mozart, Schubert, Debussy, and Purcell speak across the centuries through her unblemished voice. My hands didn't ache when I played for her. They felt whole again.

Is it any wonder that I fell so quickly in love?

Late that afternoon, I lounged at Sal's house, my thoughts on Laura and Ivan. When we'd parted, Laura had invited me for dinner at her house some time soon. I'd accepted. Could I wait that long? I was on fire for her now.

Did I want her because Ivan had had her? Did I want her because I knew she'd longed to see him dead—did that soften my own guilt? Oh God, I didn't know, I didn't know.

"His sister's kicking up a big fuss," Sal said, filling me in on what his cousin had told him about the investigation of Ivan's death. My friend had not wasted any time. He'd contacted his cousin as soon as he'd dropped me at the conservatory that morning. "Calls the station every day, has the attorney general on the horn, thinks they should be working no case but this one. Everybody's supposed to be on the look-out."

"Look-out for what?"

"Whoever did him in."

Brigitta came into the room with two brown bottles of National Bohemian. She gave one to her brother and shyly offered the other to me.

"Mama wants to know if you'll play something for her while she cooks," Brigitta said, smiling at me. "She says to tell you it's payment for her good meal." The girl blushed.

"I can't stay for any meal. I'm playing at the club tonight."

"You still doin' that?" Sal asked. "I thought you had this opera job now."

I stood and walked to the upright in their bright dining room, letting the cold bottle of beer chill any pains from my hands.

"I'll play something for you, Mrs. Sabataso," I called out. "But I can't stay for dinner!"

Sal just shook his head as Brigitta scurried back to the kitchen. He took a long gulp of his beer and wiped his mouth with the back of his hand.

"Better watch out or my sister will be dragging you down the aisle before you know what's good for you."

"I thought you said I should take her out," I said softly.

"Yeah, well, I'd been drinking."

I chuckled, doodling at the keyboard, drifting into the familiar chords of popular songs.

Sal's house was closer to the harbor than mine, and with the windows open to the fall breeze, I could smell the salt-tainted air of seawater. Here in this friend's house, the memory of Laura in my arms, our alibis secure, I felt lighthearted. I quickly pounded out a medley of tunes—Me and My Gal. I'll Take You Home Again, Irene. Let Me Call You Sweetheart.

Until finally, Mrs. Sabataso came out of the kitchen, clucking her tongue and waving a spoon at me.

"Why you play that, Greggie? Why you not play the good songs?"

And without missing a beat, beaming a huge grin at her standing in the doorway, I changed the last chord of Take Me Out to the Ball Game into the first chord of the drinking song from *La Traviata*, and enjoyed watching her face contort as she wondered whether to be pleased or offended.

"You are too good for your own good!" she said after a few bars. But then she laughed and puttered off to the kitchen.

I looked over at Sal who was lighting a cigarette and picking up the evening paper in the living room.

"You want me to stop so you can listen to the radio?" I asked, knowing the Sabatasos had just bought a new floor model displayed proudly in the corner of the living room.

"Nope," Sal said. "The girls listen to that Stella Dallas thing. It's not on now, thank God. Only thing I really like is the Shadow."

Brigitta came into the dining room, setting plates on the table, "We'll listen to The Shadow if you want to come over one night."

Sal laughed. "What I tell you, Greggie?"

Brigitta scowled at her brother and left the room.

The Sabataso household was warm and hospitable, and I was spending too much time playing there. But I liked making Mrs. Sabataso smile, and I often fooled her by hiding a popular melody in an inner voice of an old Italian classic, slowly peeling away each outer line until nothing but the pop song was left. As I did that now, I talked to Sal.

"You were telling me about Roustakoff," I said, letting my left hand take over the melody while my right grasped the beer bottle so I could drink.

"Yeah, well. Like I said, the guy's sister is making a stink about it. She should let sleeping dogs lie. The guy was no saint. Reilly's got a list he found in some opera score of broads the guy had."

"*Don Giovanni…*" I murmured.

"Say, how'd you know — yeah, that's the opera."

Of course Ivan would put the list there. Leporello's list — the names of Don Juan's conquests — was a part of the opera. Would Laura's name be on it?

"Anyways, the list has names of girls he knocked up. Reilly's going down it. Already talked to a few. One's dead."

"What?"

"Killed herself, poor sap."

I stopped playing. I thought of Laura, how fragile she was, how close to the edge of collapse. I closed my eyes. Thank God she'd not gone down that road.

"That girl's family could have wanted revenge," I said at last.

"No dice, yet," Sal told me. "My cousin says Reilly's like a machine with this stuff, checking and rechecking. He's already cleared most all of them."

All except Laura. He'd not spoken with her yet. Her mother had interfered.

Her mother — was she a vengeful family member?

"Don't you worry, pal," my friend told me. "You've got an alibi like gold. Even if you did do it, you're safe."

"I didn't do it." It felt good to say it out loud. It had to be true. The full memory of the evening would return eventually. I'd sat in the studio. I'd heard the voices.

But already, after making up an alibi with Laura, I was beginning to imagine that scene instead, as if it were real. Laura in my studio. Schubert. The rain. Maybe it was real.

Sal laughed. "Do you think I care?"

I stood.

"I gotta go get ready for the club. Takes me a while to get there on Saturdays. Not so many buses are running."

Sal stood, too. "I can take a hint. Let me grab the keys. I'll drive ya."

Dear Ronald,

As you know, my brother was murdered recently. I am sorry to inform you that I have been less than pleased with the handling of the investigation of his death. As attorney general, you should be aware that the police have treated this matter with a casual interest that is at best an example of shoddy workmanship and at worst an offensive insult to the bereaved. I am deeply grieved by my brother's passing and how his untimely death has been investigated.

Would you please use your considerable influence to right this situation? As you know, in all the time I have known you and supported your career, I have never asked any favors in return. In fact, it isn't so much a favor I request of you now, but rather, an attention to the duties of your position. I would hate to think that other mourning families' concerns are treated with the same disdain as mine have been. I want my brother's killer brought to justice.
Sincerely,
Louise Ruxton Watts

Chapter Six

I NEEDED TO KNOW.

I needed to know if I'd done it, if she'd done it.

On that latter question, I'd made no progress. After her tearful confessions earlier in the day, how could I have asked her again the accusatory question—did you kill this loathsome creature, Laura, this beast who needed so desperately to be "put down?" Are you lying to me?

Poison, after all, was a woman's weapon. Hah! That was my one consolation, when I became unable to move from thought to thought, stuck on the notion that my dream of killing Ivan might have been grounded in reality. Poison wouldn't have been my weapon.

How would I have killed Ivan? Would it surprise you to learn that I actually took a considerable amount of pleasure in thinking how I would have *liked* to kill him?

Here was my scenario: I confronted him in a studio at the practice building. I poured on him all the rage I'd stored, giving full voice to my fury. I screamed and shouted and he was cowed. I even, in this mixed-up dream of revenge, slapped him for Laura's sake. And then I dragged him by the scruff of the neck to the top of the five story stairwell and kicked him ignominiously down the steps, following at each landing to make sure his neck was broken.

Yes, officer, it was awful—I tried to break his fall, but it all happened so fast.

This daydream gave me comfort. It allowed me to believe I didn't poison him. Poison—it was a woman's weapon.

But this daydream did not completely stave off the flow of horror-filled worries. Did Laura do it? Or did we do it together? She was, after all, as muddled as I was, as transfixed by anger and pain.

When Sal drove me to the Brentwood Club that Saturday night, I even interrogated him about my mood the night of the murder.

"When we sat around drinking that night, what did I say?"

Sal shot me a quick look. "I dunno. Lots of stuff. Mostly about playing and all."

"About Roustakoff?"

"Yeah. Like usual. When weren't you complaining about him?"

"Did I tell you about the rehearsal that afternoon?"

"You said he was a son of a bitch." Sal laughed. "You said that a lot,

Greggie."

"Did I tell you what I did that evening?"

Sal thought. He'd been drinking, too, that night, so his memory would be fuzzy, as well.

"You said the bastard yelled at you in front of the singers. And your hands hurt more than usual — say, you sounded just as mad at your hands, come to think of it — and then he stopped rehearsal and made it seem like it was your fault or something."

"And then what?"

Sal looked at me again. "What, you want me to give you a play by play? I didn't take no notes on that night, you know."

"Whatever you remember, pal."

He exhaled sharply. "You said something about going to practice after but that was dumb because you couldn't practice when your damn hands hurt." He laughed again. "And then you said no matter how much they hurt, you'd love to use 'em to strangle the bastard."

Strangle him? Yes, strangle, kick him, shoot him — but not poison. That was a woman's weapon.

These uncomfortable thoughts plagued me as I sat eating a steak sandwich in the kitchen of the Brentwood Club that night, an exclusive golf and country club just north of the city where the neat homes of Laura Reed's set gave way to more open land. Compounding my anxiety was resentment. I was conducting an opera during the week, for God's sake. Why should I still have to play at the club on weekends?

Although it wasn't part of my pay arrangement, the cooks often fed me when I arrived early for the job. It was always bland food. The first time I'd asked if they ever fixed spaghetti, Rufus, the large Negro cook, had let out a huge belly laugh. "No, suh, no spaghetti here. That's a fer'in dish. Just steak, fish, pork and potatoes and terrapin soup. And rice pudding. That's all we got here."

So steak it was. Or a nice pork chop. Or sometimes a rockfish. I had been playing at the Brentwood for the entire two years I'd been at Peabody. Saturdays. Sometimes on Sunday afternoons. Sometimes on Friday nights. Soft ballads, old hits, some Gershwin, and a waltz or two. About every two months, the club would hire a band, and I'd get the weekend off.

"Rufus, how's the crowd tonight?" I asked, munching on my sandwich in the corner of the large kitchen.

"Small, not much, not much," said the chef in front of the gas-heated stoves, blue flames licking the underside of pots and pans there. "Ever since the war talk, people haven't been much for going out. More and more uniforms out there. Nice lookin' boys too. It's a shame, a cryin' shame," he said shaking his head. "I don't care what Mister Franklin Roosevelt said. We're gonna be in this thing sooner than later. You mark my words."

As if the conversation made him think of it, Rufus went to a nearby table and flipped on the radio. The remaining sounds of the *Vagabond Quartet* show crackled into the kitchen. Rufus turned down the volume so the broadcast wouldn't spill beyond the room.

"Good evening, Mr. and Mrs. North and South America," I said, mimicking the rapid-fire delivery of Walter Winchell, "and all the ships at sea!"

Rufus laughed. "He ain't on now."

"No news at all this early."

"Never know, never know. They might break in with somethin' if it happens," Rufus said. "I got two boys, you know. Two fine boys."

I didn't pay much attention to the war talk. I had my own war to fight. Stepping in for Roustakoff hadn't made my paltry salary for accompanying go up much. In fact, I was surprised the conservatory didn't think to talk to me about cutting my salary since I wasn't actually playing for the rehearsals. In typical aristocratic fashion, the administration might assume that the honor of moving into Roustakoff's position would be payment enough.

Having finished my sandwich, I took off my jacket and removed a sweater vest, straightening my tie before putting the jacket back on. The owners didn't think much of my college look. They'd told me "jacket and tie or suit." I wore the vest because it was warm. Running my fingers through my hair to neaten it, I realized I needed a haircut. No money for turning up the heat, no money for a trip to the barber. I placed my plate in the industrial-size sink near the stove.

"Guess it's time to face the music," I said to Rufus, who laughed at my little joke. "Do you mind if I take a drink with me—some vodka on the rocks?" Vodka looked like water and wouldn't offend anyone's sensibilities. And it would calm my nerves.

"Go right ahead. You know where it is."

As I filled my glass, the door to the kitchen swung open and a black-suited waiter appeared, placing a dinner order on a clip above the counter near the stove. Rufus turned and scrutinized it quickly, then turned back to the stove and stirred a pot.

"I'll see ya on your break, Mister G," Rufus called after me as I followed the waiter out the door into the club dining room.

The sleek, black baby grand piano was in the corner across from the kitchen door. It sat on the edge of the polished wood dance floor, now empty as patrons finished their meals at white-draped tables beyond. The warm murmur of dozens of conversations filled the room as I strolled over to the piano, flipping open the lid to the bright keyboard. I cupped my hands around my icy glass, hoping to numb the ache that lingered in my fingers from goofing around at Sal's house.

Before beginning, I took a swig of the strong vodka and sat down. To my right was a tall window through which I could see the neatly clipped lawns of the golf course, like lime green velvet snug over the hills and up to the edges of the sand traps.

Despite my resentment of the Brentwood crowd, I always felt a sense of peace when I sat at the Brentwood's piano. For five hours, with ten minute breaks every two hours, I'd lose myself in anonymous music, my eyes fed by the pastoral view as the day's light waned, my soul sustained by the unseen wall around me, the kind that Brentwood clientele understood and respected — no fraternizing with outsiders.

I started with "Someone to Watch Over Me" and followed with a medley of Gershwin tunes, even managing to pound out the first few pages of *Rhapsody in Blue* before letting it mutate into an improvisation. No one would know. Often I just played the first page or so of a well-known "classical" piece and followed with my own riffs on the themes. No one ever complained.

All they remembered were the familiar parts, not the long, tortured middle sections, where the composers died a thousand deaths weaving melody and harmony together into a continuous journey. Roustakoff's winning piece had had an elegant middle, something memorable, with inner lines playing a familiar, folk-like tune. What was that tune? My fingers scrambled for it, a lilting thing just out of reach of memory.

By seven-fifty, I was on my second Hit Parade medley and my glass of vodka was two-thirds empty. Whether it was the liquor or my own self-control, my hands only ached intermittently. Good thing, I thought as I finished a rendition of "Chattanooga Choo Choo." I hated playing that song, but knew it was expected. Miller's scoring, with its octave pairings of clarinet and horn, was exactly what the driving melody called for — not the percussive beat of the piano. Nonetheless, a smattering of applause greeted me as I pulled my hands off the keyboard at the end of the popular song. I smiled and nodded to the half-full room, then took a long draw from my glass. Time for a break. I would head back to the kitchen for a refill, stretch my legs . . .

"A request," a waiter said, quickly handing me a slip of paper before rushing off to the kitchen to fill a dinner order.

I sighed. All right. I'd play the request, then take a break. Unfolding the paper, I wondered if I'd know the tune. Sometimes, people tried to stump me. I was pretty unflappable, though, with a huge phonographic memory and an equally large learned repertoire of popular and classical tunes.

"The White Cliffs of Dover," the note read in sloping, feminine handwriting.

The Boesendorfer by the terrace. The sweet spring air. The offered glass of tea. My mother would like to hear The White Cliffs of Dover . . .

The scent of roses. The rose dress. The spun gold hair.

I closed my eyes, remembering.

I looked up, but a pillar blocked my view of the entire room. I saw no one glancing over with anticipation, waiting for the song. I started to play, straining to see over the piano and beyond the pillar. As my fingers found the easy chords for the sentimental song, I motioned with my head to the waiter who'd given me the note.

"Who made the request, Joe?" I asked in a low voice. The waiter straightened and nodded toward the dance floor.

"The woman heading to the floor now. In the white dress," Joe said, and left with his round tray for the station near the wall with cutlery and linens.

I waited for the woman to come into view. When she did, my fingers slipped, and I hit a wrong chord, quickly correcting before the crowd could tell.

It was Laura, her hand draped on the shoulder of a tall, good-looking young man with blond hair parted in the middle with excruciating neatness. The white dress she wore wrapped around her sensuous little body and floated about her knees. A simple gold bracelet glistened on her wrist. She smiled at her dancing companion and leaned into his broad frame.

Of course! I could never be anything to a woman like that. I was mutilated, beneath her. This other man was her kind. He looked clean and tidy, with a bright future and no scars.

But maybe I'd misremembered my talk with Laura earlier. Maybe we'd made no connection. Maybe she hadn't leaned into my shoulders and let me embrace her. Or maybe she had—but for the sole reason of hiding her crime. Or our crime. *Sweet Jesus — was that it?*

I came to the end of the song. Normally, I'd play a reprise, repeating the lines just before the high point and slowing the ending to prolong the audience's enjoyment of the simple tune. But this time, I ended the song where it ended, not extending it one second beyond its composed setting, watching intently as the dancers stopped and separated, noting that Laura Reed did not linger in the arms of her companion.

As the audience applauded, she looked over at me, seeming to notice me for the first time. Her neck and face turned red as she brought her hands together to clap for my performance. Before she could even think of approaching me, I left the piano and went into the kitchen for my break, taking the now-empty glass with me.

"Nice job," Rufus said as I thundered through the door. The cook was chopping scallions on a cutting board, sitting on a stool at a long wooden table along the wall. "That last song was pretty."

"Sentimental mush," I muttered, heading for the freezer for some ice and vodka. "Someone requested it." I refilled my glass and strolled to the door leading to the outside. "Gonna get some fresh air," I said, taking a swig of vodka and walking out to the lawn.

An autumn rain had drenched the city the day before, but now only the scent of it lingered, the damp, musty smell of a good soaking. In the distance, I detected wood smoke. And underlying it all was the sickeningly sweet smell of death—the rotting leaves of early autumn. They would all turn soon and coat the earth. It matched my mood.

I strolled further into the night and stood on the edge of the silent golf course. Behind me, I could hear the muted clatter of the kitchen staff as they rushed to fill orders. In the distance, I could barely make out the line where the dark trees that rimmed the course met the blue-black sky. No moonlight cut through the cloud cover. I raised the glass to my mouth and drank again, letting the fiery alcohol burn away my senses.

Vodka had been my father's drink. He'd swig it back, his face red from the liquor and the heat in the basement kitchen, and he'd look at me and ask me, "Grygor, what you do with your life?" This usually came after a piano lesson, when Mother would be so proud.

My brother, Michael, a year older than me, had picked up on Dad's implicit scorn, calling me a sissy and a chicken whenever he got the chance, whenever he saw me running from a schoolyard fight because I didn't want to damage my hands.

When I got the news that Peabody was willing to give me money to go to school, I thought that would quiet them both. I'd wept when I read the letter—my mother would have been so pleased. But she had been in the earth a year by then.

That letter—that was a reprieve for me. It meant no time spent in the prison of shift work after high school. I'd managed to avoid it up to that point by working in Sal's family's store during the summers and on Saturdays. That summer before school began, though, they couldn't afford extra help. Enough Sabatasos were of an age to handle all that was needed. What harm could one summer at Bethlehem Steel do? It would bring harmony to our household. It would have made my mother proud, just like that letter from Peabody, to know I was trying to please Dad.

What harm could it do . . .

I took another drink.

"Wodka," my father would call it, and he'd goosestep around the kitchen, making fun of the Russian soldiers who'd marched through his home town in Poland. My mother would shush him as if they were still out there ready to rampage, and that would make him angry, but not at her, at me. He would squint at me and he'd say, "What, you want me to sing like those records you buy for Grygor? You want me to wail like that?" And he'd mimic the gusty roar of Caruso belting out "*La donna e mobile*" from *Rigoletto*. But when my father sang it, it sounded like "Laddin hey moby lah," as he imitated the florid lyricism of the great singer, and then it would deteriorate into a taunt—"la-de-dah-de-dah-de-dah."

"La-de-dah. La-de-dah. You teach him nothing but la-de-dah. Wait till he is older. I will teach him. He will be a real man. He will work at the factory with me. La-de-dah then, young man. La-de-dah will be over for you then."

Why could I remember that so clearly, and yet the night of Ivan's death is as blurry as this evening's sky?

La-de-dah.

～♥～

"Aren't you cold out here?" Laura Reed's voice came from a thousand years away.

I turned to see her silhouetted against the lights of the club, her hair a soft halo, the white dress a smear of brightness in the gloom.

"What are you doing out here?"

"I came out to see you!" She was breathless from excitement and the walk outside. "I didn't realize you were playing."

"I play every week."

"I don't come to the Brentwood often." She crossed her hands over her chest in the cold evening air. "Haven't been in a long time."

Seeing her shiver, I set my glass on the ground, took off my jacket, and placed it around her shoulders. I was proving that I was a gentleman, as good as that la-de-dah man she'd danced with.

"Next time, bring a coat out with you," I said, letting my hands linger on her shoulders. How could they not linger? I wanted to do more than rest my hands on her shoulders. But the vodka was mixing with my fatigue by then, a potion that gave me courage.

"Gregory, is something wrong?" she sounded uneasy.

"Why'd you send in a request—so I'd see you were here with another fellow?"

Even in the shadows, I could see her shoulders slump and hear her sigh.

"My mother wanted to hear it," she said.

She came to me and folded her arms around my waist, leaning her head on my chest, just as she'd done in the practice room earlier today. It felt so comfortable. Had we embraced like this before today? I kissed her head, as if to test our relationship. She didn't pull away. She seemed to feel, as I did, that we needed each other now.

"Why are you being so cruel to me, Gregory?"

"I'm not."

"Don't be like Ivan. Please."

Always his name.

"Laura."

"Yes, my love?"

"Do you remember the night Ivan died—*did* you come to my practice studio? I mean, really, truthfully? Did we talk?"

"What does it matter?"

"It matters a great deal."

"If you want me to say I did, I will. I told the policeman we were there together."

"I remember." I stroked her hair. "But were we?"

She looked up at me as if trying to determine what I wanted her to say, her eyes glistening in the light from the club.

"We were in the building together."

Maybe she didn't want to know, or didn't want me to know. All right, maybe I shouldn't want to know either.

"We were in the building together," I repeated, lifting her chin so that I could kiss her fully on the mouth.

She was very beautiful, maybe even more beautiful in the ash-gray light of evening when shadows carved her perfect features into bold relief—the slim nose, the even wide eyes, the bud-like mouth. And the hair, a mass of softness even my rough hands could feel.

Ivan Roustakoff must have exulted to have such a beautiful woman, and now I had her.

"Who is that boy you're with?" I asked her, pulling away before my longing got the best of me.

"He's a friend of the family," she said. "He doesn't mean anything to me, Gregory. My friend, Carol, has been trying to get us together. She arranged it with my mother." Her voice trembled. I felt a surge of power. She was beautiful, and she didn't want to upset me.

"I'll go back now and tell him I want to go home." She turned to go, but I pulled her to me again and kissed her in the twilight.

Lah-de-dah, I thought. Lah-de-dah.

TO: Chief of Police
FROM: Sean Reilly, detective, Third Precinct
RE: Ivan Roostakof death

My notes on the investigation of Ivan Rustakof's death are enclosed, just as requested. We don't have enough to bring in anybody. I am not sure the man was even killed. I will continue to interview suspects.

Chapter Seven

THE NEXT DAY I WENT TO MASS. I lit four candles—one each for my brother and mother and father's souls, and one for myself. I knelt at the altar and hoped God could snatch the prayers from my soul, because I articulated nothing but a general sense of longing.

At that point, I wanted only a few things, but they were all big—I wanted Laura, most of all. And I wanted innocence.

In the afternoon, I held a rehearsal with the leads. Laura was there, to turn pages for the accompanist, but her eyes were on me now.

Hans sang poorly, his voice cracking on the high notes, and his spirit missing from the opera's signature aria, *Nessun Dorma*. How could anyone sing that aria without feeling it?

When I told the singers to take a break, Renata explained Hans's mood as he walked outside for "fresh air."

"The *poliziotto* speaks to him. Twice, maybe more times." She shrugged, throwing a fur over her shoulders in the drafty room.

"Why are they after him?" I asked this question almost hopefully. Hans as culprit would exonerate me. And Laura.

"Hans speak to Ivan that night. They had the fight."

The fight—the discussion I'd overheard was hardly a fight, more like a disagreement. So Reilly had used the information I'd provided to gain more from Hans. Hans must have told him they'd argued.

"About the Kliegman," I said, prompting her to tell me more.

Her face came up, and she straightened.

"*Si*. The silly boy thinks Ivan wanted him to sing it. I, of course, will sing it." She pulled her fur tighter.

So, even though Hans had insisted to me he was happy with Renata singing it, he still yearned to have his voice showcased. I couldn't blame him. The piece was more for his timbre than Renata's. But I couldn't imagine him killing for that. Nor for Renata's hand, either.

But this explained why Hans and Renata no longer seemed close. She hadn't walked in with him for the practice. In fact, she'd been accompanied by another man, a short, balding fellow who was vaguely familiar. She introduced him as a member of Peabody's board. So she had a new "sponsor." Hans was being pushed to the background.

"My piece is in the running now, you know," I told her, amused to watch her expression change, first to fear, then to anger, then to confidence.

"Yes, I have heard that the second place can be played. But you and I know they will use Ivan's piece, *si*? Of course they will." She smiled. "And if the orchestra, they play your piece and not Ivan's, think how guilty that makes you look, Maestro!"

She sauntered away, grabbing her new sponsor by the arm and leading him from the hall just as Hans returned, watching her, pining for her. He sat in a chair and studied his score.

Laura, meanwhile, came over to me.

"She's a temptress," she said simply and softly, placing her beautiful hand on my scarred one.

I smiled at her. "You're jealous!"

She looked down. "I think the police should look at her," she said with unusual vehemence. "She had a lot to gain from Ivan's death."

"But more from his life, don't you think?"

When she didn't respond, I continued. "Renata lived luxuriously with Ivan. He was placing her in his operas. She is singing his composition with the Philharmonic—"

"Hans was supposed to sing it!" Laura interrupted, speaking so loudly that Hans's face came up. She looked at him.

"You were supposed to sing the Kliegman piece, Ivan's composition, weren't you?"

His face reddened.

"I do not care to sing it."

"But it suits your voice. I heard you sing it," she persisted.

Had Hans been singing it so often that she'd overheard it at the practice studios, too?

"You sing it beautifully," she added.

"*Danke.*" He looked down. "It is beautiful. I do my best."

But not today. Today he'd sung poorly.

Why was he pretending not to want to sing it now, when Renata clearly believed he did want it?

"Hans," I said, "Renata seems to have the silly idea that you were trying to steal the solo from her."

His color deepened, and he shook his head vigorously. "*Nein.* She is wrong. I do not care if I sing it. I only care that the piece is performed! That is all I try to do—to make sure the piece is played. It is too good not to be played. It is the winner!"

As if realizing that would mean bumping my composition from the program, he softened his tone, looking straight at me. "I am sure you have written a very fine composition, *Herr* Silensky. But Ivan's piece was the winner, and he could not, is not to be blamed for, for . . ."

"Dying," Laura said.

"*Ja*," Hans agreed. "His piece should be on the program. Maybe," he said, looking at me again, "they will play your piece, too."

I smiled. "Perhaps if you persuade them."

He frowned. "We should practice," he said, looking at his watch.

Renata's laugh carried into the room. He looked over his shoulder, his eyes wrinkling with hurt. She strolled back in, on the arm of the board member, who was clearly as smitten as Hans.

Hans stood, placing his hands on his hips.

"Renata, you make us late. Do not do such things, or you make us angry, *ja*?" he snapped at her.

Both Laura and I exchanged glances, surprised by this uncharacteristic outburst, which I fully expected to be rebuffed by the fiery Renata.

Instead, she took her arm from the board member and walked meekly to the music stands, taking her place and opening her score.

When Hans stood by her side, she finally glared at him. "You make me unhappy, Hans. You do not like to see me unhappy."

"*Nein, meine liebchen*," he murmured. "I would do anything to keep you happy, as you know."

She stretched, the fur dropping to the floor. He retrieved it, placing it around her shoulders with a provocative possessiveness.

"Your back, it hurts you, *meine liebchen*?"

Her face flamed, and she stood rock still, not looking at him, staring at the score.

"No," she said on a whisper. "I am fine."

Hans smiled at me, as if he'd achieved some victory.

"Renata, she had an accident many years ago. A horse threw her." He looked at her, but she still didn't look up. "Isn't that right?"

"*Si*. But let's not talk about it. Let's practice. You are so eager to sing. Let's sing!"

⁂

At the end of another hour, my hands ached, and the singers were incapable of producing anything worthwhile. Why should my hands hurt when I wasn't using them at the keyboard? This was an unforeseen betrayal. I rubbed them together, Laura quick to come to my side, placing her own warm hands over them.

Hans had sung better for the last hour, but both of them were less than their best, Renata's warm tones devolving into near-screeches on the high notes. When I'd told her to soften them, to stop "screaming," Hans had come to her defense, telling me she was tired, and he thought her voice was beautiful. Perhaps I, as a mere conductor, did not appreciate it. He grew in boldness throughout the rehearsal because Renata's paramour had to leave, clearing the field for him.

Hans had his comeuppance, though.

Just as we were leaving the hall, the dark shadow of Detective Reilly spilled into the doorway.

My first reaction was to push Laura behind me, to hide her from his gaze. My second was to belligerently ask what he wanted now.

He glowered at me, took a drag on a cigarette, and stubbed it out on the conservatory's polished oak floor.

"I need to talk to the German," he said.

Renata, her eyes wide with worry, looked at Hans. He squeezed her lightly on the arm.

"You go home, Renata. I will take care of this. Do not worry."

≪≫

"Let's go see him now." I paced Sal's living room an hour later, while Mrs. Sabataso cooked and Brigitta loitered in the doorway, watching me.

"See who?" she asked, wiping a platter clean.

"Larry," Sallie told her. When she looked confused, he added, "the one who's the cop."

She disappeared into the kitchen to help her mother, as I continued to pester Sal.

"I thought things had died down, and then Reilly shows up at practice this afternoon!"

After Reilly had cornered Hans, I'd stepped back into the rehearsal hall as if I'd forgotten something. But it was really to escort Laura down the stairwell beyond the room's far corner, so that she'd not have to brush past the detective, drawing his gaze. Instinctively, I'd wanted to protect her. And, yes, maybe protect myself as well. Let him go after Hans and leave us alone.

"And what about that list—did they get hold of all the girls on it?"

Sal patted his pockets looking for a cigarette.

"I don't talk to Larry every day." He pulled out a smoke and lit it. "He ain't my favorite cousin."

"Well, can we go see him?"

"That's not a good idea, you know. Larry wants to move up. He'd grill you for information to pass along to Reilly."

I sank into a chair, lighting my own cigarette. "When you asked him about it before, did you mention me?" I glanced around. "You got anything to drink around here?"

He went into the dining room and poured me some wine from an open carafe. "I said I'd read about it in the papers." He handed me the glass.

"Then just check up on it—you haven't heard or seen nothing and you want to know." I stared at him.

He looked at his watch.

"Where you going?" I asked.

"To Larry's. Dinner's in an hour and it's good to have an excuse to get away from him. He's a gabber." He grabbed a jacket off a nearby chair. "You stay here and talk to Brigitta."

ᶜᵛᵍ

He was back just in time for dinner, so he had no chance then to give me what he knew. Brigitta, who'd been more than happy to entertain me while her brother took a walk, laughed a little too loud, obviously trying to keep my attention. But my mind was on one thing—finishing dinner so I could hear what Sal's cousin had had to say. I endured pasta, meat, salad, and dessert and coffee before we were able to push away from the table.

"You go help Ma clean up, Briggie," Sal said to his sister. "Greg and I have man talk." He motioned to the front door. We both lit cigarettes as we shrugged into jackets against the evening chill and stepped outside. The wine had not been strong enough to soothe my hands, but I had whiskey at home that I'd break into later.

"Larry says it's still the sister driving this thing," he said as we walked around the block, smoking. "He says Reilly and all of them think the fellow was just a doper who messed up and accidently done himself in. If it was anybody else, they'd have closed the books on it. In fact, they pretty much had closed the books on it. But the sister raised a stink."

Laura and Renata had been right about this. The sister was keeping it alive.

"Is that why Reilly was out seeing Hans today, because of the sister wanting something to happen?"

"Maybe. I don't like to ask too many questions. I let Larry tell the story." Sal blew out a plume of smoke. "He said they like the German because he's got a lot to gain from Ivan's death."

"The fiancée, the big solo."

"He just mentioned the girl."

"She's not interested in him anymore, though."

"Don't matter. If he thought offing her lover was the way to her heart, it don't matter what she's interested in." Sal steered me past the church and around another block.

"I guess not." Poor Hans. If he had killed Ivan, it was all for naught.

"What about the list of girls?"

"That was tricky, my friend. I had to pretend it just came to me— remembering him mentioning that. And I had to kind of casual-like bring it up, like I was real curious."

"I'm sure you gave a stunning performance."

He laughed. "It was good enough. He said the list was hard because the girls' names weren't their real names. The victim gave them opera names, and he wrote some descriptions. So they had to kind of piece together who was who."

"But they found some."

"Yeah. And they stopped when they figured he was a doper gone bad."

That meant they could continue down the list, getting to Laura eventually — what name had Ivan used for her? As far as I knew, Reilly had yet to talk to her again about the night in the practice building. The first time he spoke with her, he probably hadn't known she was on the list. He was questioning her like me, someone who was there the night it happened. I would have to warn her about the list, something I'd yet to do.

"What's it gonna take to get them to stop investigating?" I asked Sal.

"Short of a photograph of the guy poisoning himself, I don't know. Larry seems to think Reilly's just waiting for the sister to calm down and is just fitting in this investigation around real ones he's got going. If it leads to something, it's a good grade for him. If not, he's got other things moving."

Maybe it would all be over soon.

That's what I told myself later that night, a half bottle of whiskey gone, my hands not throbbing any longer.

TO: Detective Sean Reilly
FROM: Office of Chief of Police, Baltimore City
RE: Death of Ivan Rustakov
CC: Precinct Captain Jacobs

We believe there are adequate grounds to continue the investigation. We believe you should move with all speed to bring this case to a close. If you cannot handle it on your own, we will provide extra personnel as needed. The murderer must be brought to justice.

Chapter Eight

TWO DAYS LATER, Laura drove me home after a particularly long and tiring practice. She wanted me to come to dinner at her house the next night. She'd asked before and I'd foolishly agreed. But the more I fell for her, the more I'd put off the dinner. She was sure I'd like her mother and father. She was sure they would like me. I wasn't. She was such a sweet child.

We talked about music she should learn. She wanted to sing Mahler, but I told her it was too heavy for her. She insisted, however, and I told her I had the *Songs of a Wayfarer*. She parked the car and stopped in. I offered her a drink. She declined. I had one.

I played them for her, and I learned several things.

I learned that hearing a different voice interpret a composer gives you new insight into the meaning of the piece.

I learned that I loved her.

We became lovers that afternoon, her stockings draped over my chair with my wrinkled clothes, our limbs entwining on my mussed sheets, my fingers through her magnificent mane of hair.

I told her about Ivan's "Leporello's List" and she cried in my arms.

What opera name would he have given you, beloved?

Without hesitation, she answered, "Lucia."

Lucia, the mad woman who murdered her husband on their wedding night, so hostile was she to the union.

"He always said there was something crazy about me. Something mad that he loved."

Oh Laura.

Meine Süsse Liebchen,

You know I will not hurt you. I will protect you to the death. I will not say a word about your medicine for the back pain. I want only to help you and to keep you by my side.

I am so sorry, my sweetest Renata, my darling one. I am so sorry. Please forgive me. I never would hurt you. Oh, my darling, I do not care if you sing it. I want you to sing it. I do not want to sing it at all. It is far from my mind! The only thing I think of is you. Please, liebchen, forgive me. Please do not turn your bright face from me. I cannot bear it. Again, I wait for you to come to the door, but you do not answer. Again, I leave you this little note. Please answer me. I cannot bear your silence.

Your only true love,
Hans

Chapter Nine

THE LAST CHORDS DRIFTED AWAY.

"Bravo!" a voice boomed from the doorway, followed by applause. A tall, stocky man stood there in a navy blue pinstripe suit, with round spectacles on the end of his nose. He had thin brown hair, parted on the side, thick lips and small eyes.

"Father," Laura said. "How long have you been standing there?"

"Not long," Jack Reed said.

I stood, awaiting the inevitable introduction. After it was over, Laura turned back to her father.

"Do you want me to fix you a drink?" she asked obediently.

"That's all right," he said. "You stay put." He walked over to a small cabinet by the window opposite the piano and pulled out a decanter of golden liquid, splashing an inch into the bottom of a thick, squat glass. Turning back to us, he looked at me.

"Would you like some? Scotch. Single malt."

"Yes, please," I responded. Laura had already given me one, so I handed over the now-empty glass to have it refreshed.

"Dinner should be ready any minute," Jack Reed said, sipping at the drink. "We'll talk more, then." He left the room, calling his wife's name.

Laura had driven me here, to her home, after practice today. I wasn't keen on the dinner idea. Her parents had hardly had time to get used to the notion that we were interested in each other. But she'd insisted. And when she looked at me with those doe eyes, I could hardly resist anything she asked.

I'd fortified myself with a vodka from my flask before arriving, but she'd suggested I suck on a candy to keep the odor of alcohol from offending her mother. I'd countered with a better suggestion—that she offer me a drink as soon as we arrived. She had.

Mrs. Reed had made the smallest of small talk when Laura had dragged me in, like some mangy cat, and offered a suggestion of her own—that I accompany Laura. She "so loved" to hear her daughter sing. She'd listen while finishing dinner.

Finishing dinner—what did that mean? Sitting in the kitchen

watching Gertrude prepare it?

My nerves and resentment subsided once I sat at the keyboard. Laura had learned the Fauré and Debussy I'd recommended by then, as well as some new Schubert. As always, playing for her soothed both my soul and my hands.

A half hour into our serenade, her father had returned. She'd warned me he liked to talk politics and asked me to be "understanding," by which I knew she meant "silent."

↭

"Why was anyone shocked when he pledged our aid to those Bolshevik savages?" Jack Reed was saying, his fork poised in midair in the Reed dining room. "Roosevelt's always been partial to the Communist way of thought. Half his cabinet thinks that way. And his wife is practically a member of the Party."

I saw Mrs. Reed look at me and quickly look away. That had been the pattern throughout the meal. At first, it had annoyed me. But then I began to enjoy it, taking great pleasure in smiling at her whenever her glance traveled to me, to my hands in particular. I made sure to let them show, resting my hands on the clean tablecloth, spreading out the fingers. *Yes, look at them. They're ugly. Look at them.* After several glasses of wine, I was having fun imagining the thoughts coursing through her mind as she took me in.

Scallywag.

Ruffian.

Why does Laura think he's appropriate?

Once, when I smiled at her, I made sure to stretch my arm so she could see the frayed cuffs and admire my threadbare jacket.

"This is my favorite room in the house," she said, breaking the flow of her husband's political tirade. "I can see the irises blooming from here in the spring." She motioned to the bay window opposite that bumped out over the side garden, now dried and sere.

"Amanda, I think you say that every time we have guests," Jack said, smiling at his wife. Then he turned to me.

"Why don't you tell me a little bit about yourself, Gregory? What are your plans?"

"He's going to be a famous conductor and composer!" Laura said, with great pride in her voice.

Mr. Reed grimaced. "The man can talk for himself, dear."

"Yes, I can." I cleared my throat as if about to make an oration. "Now that I've taken over the opera from Mr. Roustakoff, I hope to receive the attention of Miss Ponselle and perhaps interest her in hiring me to run her new opera company."

This was nonsense, a plan I'd concocted on the spot. I took another sip of wine and nodded, as if settling things.

"Roustakoff," Mr. Reed said. "That fellow who died."

"Was murdered," Laura interjected, with her usual glee whenever Ivan's death came up.

"Laura! That's hardly a suitable tone when talking about a death, let alone one caused by a crime.

But Laura would not be deterred. Looking straight at me, as if we were conspirators, she said, "Maestro Roustakoff was a tyrant. And the world is better off without tyrants, as we are all learning on the world's stage."

"Well said," I responded, holding my glass up to her.

"Tyrants," Mr. Reed said, taking up his political theme again. "Let them fight it out amongst themselves. The Huns have always been barbarians."

"You mean Huns like Beethoven, Brahms, Bach?" Laura chided.

"Music is supposed to be a civilizing force," I added, egging her on.

"But it had no such effect on our dear departed friend, Ivan, now, did it?" She giggled.

But Mrs. Reed saw nothing amusing in our little dialogue.

"Laura, I do think your nerves are bothering you again."

"Mother, you always say that whenever I disagree with you."

"You should go see Doctor Milton."

"Really, Mother."

"He could give you more medicine. Have you finished what you have?"

Mr. Reed looked at me. "Women are always having one ailment or another."

"What medicine would that be?" I asked, forcing a smile to my face.

"I don't even know its name," Laura said, irritated at this line of questioning.

"Laudanum," Mrs. Reed replied. "It has amazing powers. We used it when you and Richard were babies, to help soothe you to sleep."

Laudanum. Had I said that or thought it?

"Laudanum," I whispered.

"What's that, boy?" Jack Reed asked, spearing another piece of roast.

"Laudanum's what killed Ivan Roustakoff."

Mrs. Reed's mouth opened. She grabbed her water glass and swallowed a few hasty gulps.

"I didn't know," she said at last. "I . . .I assumed. . . well, I don't know what I thought."

Like me, she'd probably imagined a more gruesome death, perhaps in her case something involving a pearl-handled pistol.

"I . . . I . . .thought you liked the conductor, Laura" she added in a subdued tone.

But between those sentences, I knew what had occurred. Troubled by her daughter's nonchalant attitude about Roustakoff's death, she now had learned that he had died by a medicine her daughter had taken. She'd made the leap.

So I wasn't losing my mind to have made the leap myself.

My cheer left me, replaced by a sick feeling. I'd gone from wanting to know I'd not done it myself to wanting to know Laura had not done it either. I needed more wine. I reached for the carafe, careful to expose the most damaged part of my hand to Mrs. Reed.

"It's his sister who's pressing the investigation," I said.

"What?" Mr. Reed was not following our unvoiced conversation.

I turned to him.

"Louise Ruxton Watts is her name. The police think Ivan just – excuse me for saying this in polite company—was a dope fiend. And he accidentally mixed too much with liquor."

Mr. Reed snorted his judgment. "So he killed himself."

I was aware that Mrs. Reed's gaze had not left mine. She hung on every word I uttered.

"The police think that. But Ivan's sister—Louise—refuses to accept their verdict. She's been calling the district attorney, the police chief, all to get them to bring in some unlucky soul as the murderer."

"I know Louise," Mrs. Reed said.

"Through DAR?" I asked, as if my own mother had belonged.

"Yes."

"The police were nosing around about it. They interviewed me." Laura seemed to enjoy making her mother uncomfortable.

"Why would they interview you?" Amanda asked.

"They interviewed a lot of people who saw him that night," I offered.

"What does it matter?" Laura said. She wiped her mouth with her napkin and placed it by her plate. "Both Gregory and I were in a studio together that night. I could care less what Louise or the police think about the whole mess."

Mrs. Reed looked at me, almost in desperation.

"Silensky. Are you related to Victoria and Bertrand by any chance?"

Jack Reed chuckled. "Their name is Siles, darling. Nowhere near . . .'"

"People changed their names when they came here," I said. "But my father kept his."

"When did he come over?" Mrs. Reed asked, with real warmth in her voice now.

"In 1919, with my mother," I answered. "But they're gone now."

"I'm so sorry," Mrs. Reed said. "Do you have any siblings?"

"No," I answered truthfully.

"Well, you did," Laura said. I'd told her about Michael.

"Yes," I said, looking at my hands. "He's deceased as well."

"Oh, dear," Mrs. Reed interjected.

Laura stood. "Come on, Gregory. We can sing some more—unless you'd like dessert."

"No, I'd love to play for you." I stood, too.

As I left the room, I noticed Mrs. Reed watching me, her attitude a far cry from what she'd exhibited at the outset of the dinner. She now seemed to like me, her stare soft and sympathetic.

Two days later

Dear Tom,
Thank you so much for answering my questions about "spousal privilege." I really shouldn't read so many of these silly murder mysteries. I'm going to give them up and devote my time to more worthy endeavors.

You are so knowledgeable. I'm sure your father is rightly proud to have you a member of his firm. I expect to hear great things of you.

Please, give my love to your mother and father.
Sincerely,
Amanda D. Reed

❧❧

Dear Gregory,

I enjoyed meeting you and thank you for your polite note after our dinner. We would like to see more of you.

I have some urgent issues I would like to discuss concerning Laura and your future. I understand there is a coffee shop a block from the Conservatory that is open on Sundays. I will be at the coffee shop at eleven o'clock in the morning two Sundays hence. I do hope you can be there, too.
Sincerely,
Amanda D. Reed

Chapter Ten

REHEARSALS AND LAURA consumed me now. Because this was a student production, the practice schedule Roustakoff had constructed was very generous, with many sessions to help the chorus master the difficult score, a full two months and more before the performance. He'd insisted they memorize it, just as they would in a staged performance. Much of my time was spent as drill master, going over and over sequences, deferring to Renata to help them refine the pronunciation.

Renata—I couldn't help but smile at her maneuvering. Some time in the past week and a half, she managed to produce a marriage certificate from Italy demonstrating that she and Ivan had been married in secret—*Il Matrimonio Segreto*—and therefore she was entitled to live in his grand house once again, and not in the small student apartment that Hans was renting. She explained that she'd not wanted to reveal the marriage during everyone's grief, and had waited a decent amount of time in order to let us all give vent to our sorrow. She must have been desperate to get away from Hans to offer this weak story.

Where had she gotten the certificate, I wondered. Had she brought a blank one with her, just in case, or telegraphed a friend asking for help?

She didn't wait for a judge to validate her marriage—as Louise Ruxton Watts insisted. She just picked up her things and moved back to the big home on the corner of Mount Vernon Place across from the conservatory. Poor Hans was crestfallen, his pale blue eyes a window on his inner pain.

I sympathized with him. He was as besotted with Renata as I was with Laura by now. When I went to bed at night, I dreamed of her, the scent of her soft golden hair still in my head, the touch of her skin, the childlike dependency on me all arousing in me a deeper desire than I'd ever known.

She was a magnificent lover, carefree and impetuous, eager to please me in any way I required. I'd have spent all my time making love with her had it not been for my music schedule, my conservatory jobs, and the Brentwood.

One item removed from that schedule was practicing for the

Kliegman. Just as Renata had produced a fake marriage certificate, she engaged in a very public effort to champion the playing of Ivan's piece in New York. In this crusade Renata was joined by conservatory notables and music world doyens, with even the music critic of the *Baltimore Sun* chiming in the effort, writing a column about what a travesty it would be for the deceased's composition to be ignored just because he'd had the misfortune to die. I'd provided a quote for his piece, full of understanding and agreement. What else could I have said — I couldn't even argue mine was the better composition. I knew by now it wasn't.

Ivan's piece would be played. I was relegated to second-best once again.

But I didn't mind. Jesus — I was relieved! I'd not benefited, at least in this regard, from Ivan's death.

I had his opera, his girl, but not that.

And I didn't need it. Laura made up for so many other things. With her, my hands didn't ache — she showered them with kisses when we were together, telling me they were beautiful because they created loving music and love itself, as I ran my fingers through her voluptuous hair and cupped her breasts, calling her my angel. With her, nightmares of Ivan's death and my possible role in it receded. With her, I felt normal.

This was a mirage, of course. But then, when I was so beset by demons from all sides — the relentless pace of the rehearsals, the doubts over my abilities, the worries over money, the fear of what had happened that night at the conservatory, the continual pain in my hands, the constant struggle to hide my drinking — Laura was an island away from all these cares.

Yes, I asked her about the laudanum shortly after the dinner at her parents. She explained that during her affair with Ivan, her nerves were frayed, and her mother had insisted she see a doctor, who'd given her the poison. Yes, she actually said poison. But her dose had been gone long ago. Gertrude had thrown the bottle away that summer.

Did I truly love her?

A better question is: Did she truly love me? She was a child, knowing only what she wanted, what she liked, wanting people to like her. Her smile came easily with me. Her beauty became transcendent, a glow of gold and rose and warmth when she appeared before me. We started making plans. I would have to do everything for her, take care of her, provide for her, keep her safe. She didn't know how to do those things on her own. It made me feel like the man my father had wanted me to be.

As confidence in our love affair increased, I was hit by a blow. The conservatory would not use me to conduct the other opera Roustakoff had planned, Bizet's *Carmen*. I'd started counting on that money, too, now that I had a girl I liked to take out. Instead, they handed the job and its money to Chalmers, the pianist and conductor Ivan had threatened to give

Turandot to when my hands had failed me.

I wasn't able to benefit from *Carmen*, and neither was Renata, proving how much more she would have gained had Ivan lived. She would sing the role of pure Micaela, hardly a good match given her conniving spirit. She was unhappy being relegated to a supporting part and complained to the conservatory president, even to Rosa Ponselle herself, with whom Renata had started a tentative friendship. Ivan had promised her Carmen, she wailed. No one was moved.

She must have felt very confident to pull the secret marriage out of her hat. It could have made her look guilty to benefit so mightily from Ivan's death. But by then, suspicion was being centered almost entirely on Hans, poor, downcast Hans, whose affair with Renata cast him in a guilty light. At least the attention was off of Laura and me.

I knew Laura's mother was not as confident, however. I'd seen her looks at dinner when Laura had acted so nonchalant about Ivan's death.

Hans was the suspect. Hans was the one who looked guilty.

Maybe, I thought with an enormous exhale of relief, Hans *was* guilty. Maybe none of us — me, Laura, her mother — had anything to worry about.

๙๖

I stood when I saw her. She walked quickly to the booth in the back where I sat, her arms tightly clutching a black leather purse in front of her, as if she were afraid of coming into contact with anything in the coffee shop.

"Thank you for meeting me," she said, managing a smile.

"Let me get your coat," I offered.

She looked quickly around. Seeing the coat hooks at the side of the booth, she turned her back to me, allowing me to slip her light raincoat from her shoulders and hang it up. Underneath, she wore a stylish suit of deep blue, a scarf tucked around her collar, a simple hat with little ornamentation, and plain leather gloves, which she slowly removed. She could have been decked out for a funeral.

When she sat down, I studied her more closely and saw the strong resemblance to Laura, the delicate features, the green eyes — although hers were paler — the reddish hues in her chestnut hair, cut short and neatly curled behind her ears. Had she been a flapper in her youth? Had she done wild and passionate things — is that why she suspected such action from her daughter?

"Let me get you something," I said, looking for the waitress.

"No, nothing. I'm fine, really. I just want to talk." She removed her gloves and set them on the table.

"You want to tell me to stop seeing your daughter." I had decided on my way into town that this was probably the main reason for this meeting. I was ready for it, having fortified myself with a sip or two from my flask. I would listen, maybe argue a little, and then maybe even promise her I'd do as she wished. But I wouldn't make up my mind about that. I'd let that simmer for awhile to see how I felt about having Laura snatched away from me.

I pulled out a cigarette and stuck it in my mouth. She stared at my hands. "Do you mind if I smoke?" I asked. "Or does it make you uncomfortable?"

She immediately shook her head, blushing, and looked down.

"Go right ahead." She folded her hands over one another.

"I'm not here to tell you to stop seeing Laura."

So she figured I'd assume that. Smart lady. She waited while I lit a match and then the cigarette.

"But I am here to suggest that you be. . . discreet and allow me to help you."

She looked up at me. "Of course, I'm assuming you do want to continue seeing Laura."

My eyes widened. This was not what I'd expected.

"Yes, very much so."

She started talking in a calm, reasonable way about her husband, about how he loved his "little girl" and would have a hard time seeing her with someone, about how this was a "formidable obstacle," about how she could help in that regard if I was "serious" about Laura. And also about how "concerned and worried" she'd been when she suspected Laura had been involved in a "romance" with Ivan.

Here, at last, was the reason for the visit. As she prattled on, I looked at her. She seemed serene on the surface, but her eyes gave away her anguish. She couldn't stop them from narrowing into a fretful frown, and by sheer force of will, she occasionally calmed her gaze by blinking fast to open her eyes into a more restful pose.

She was convinced her daughter had killed her former lover.

That's what I heard when she talked about Laura's "nervous disposition," about Laura's need for a "settled and calm world." That's what I heard, a drumbeat under everything else she said, when she confided in me that Laura had always been "high strung," and that's why they'd not stood in the way of her music ambitions, even though she would have preferred if Laura had gone to finishing school like all her friends.

She was convinced her daughter had killed her former lover.

That's what I heard when she talked more about Jack Reed and the need for her to prepare him for any "future plans" Laura would make with a "young man." That's what I heard when she mentioned that whatever young man Laura chose, the family would, of course, help set up the couple.

At the end of this recitation, I tapped the last ash from my cigarette and stubbed it out.

"I *have* envisioned a future with your daughter, Mrs. Reed," I said. "And I'm glad you approve. I would appreciate your help with any family obstacles."

"Laura has a trust fund. I'm sure she's told you."

"No, she hasn't." I sipped my coffee, wishing I could reach for my flask and a dash of whiskey.

"When she marries, she—and her husband, of course—can take the money in a lump sum or live off the interest."

"Well, that's wonderful. But I'm sure you know I'm not interested in Laura for her money." I knew she'd want to hear that, and it held truth. I'd not known about a trust fund, about the Reeds' desire to help Laura's husband.

"If Laura's father doesn't approve, he could tie up the fund for years, maybe even forever," Mrs. Reed said with real regret. "So it's very important, you see, to proceed with caution. *You* may not want the money, Mister Silensky—"

"Please call me Gregory."

"—Gregory, but Laura shouldn't be denied what is rightfully hers. I'm sure you'll agree."

She looked down at her perfectly manicured hands with their buffed nails and smooth skin the color of pale pink roses.

"What are you suggesting?" I asked. I thought I knew, but I wanted to hear it clearly.

She looked up and smiled.

"Well, Gregory, I don't think I need to tell a young man how to court a lady." She laughed, but it sounded artificial and I could tell she knew it. She cleared her throat.

"If you assure me you are serious . . . " she leaned into the table, "I will do everything in my power to convince Mr. Reed that it is in Laura's best interests to pursue a relationship with you. I would suggest, however, that you make your intentions known quickly—your honorable intentions, of course—so that Mr. Reed doesn't think you are taking advantage."

She paused and stared at me.

"Is that what you will do, Gregory—make your honorable intentions known to Laura?"

She was asking me if I intended to marry her daughter. When I didn't respond immediately, she went on.

"In addition to Laura's trust fund, we would, of course, secure an apartment for you. And I have some friends on the boards of various schools—St. Paul's, Friends, Gilman—and would make inquiries for you for teaching positions."

"My intentions are most honorable," I said, sounding like an English barrister. "And I will be making them known very soon. Should I approach Mr. Reed?"

She smiled and shook her head.

"I will do that. I will tell him you wanted to talk to him, but spoke with me instead. He would be far more willing to accept a *fait accompli*, you see. That is, if you've already asked for Laura's hand, he would be more willing to accept that than you actually telling him you were going to do so. I'll make sure he understands, though, that you were courteous and approached me. And then, of course, we would plan something quick and quiet, but very elegant. Oh dear, Gregory, I don't mean to offend or even to rush you. I'm so sorry to put it this way. My husband is a good man. He wants the best for his daughter. And I'm sure he imagined she'd marry a man like those in our club. It's only natural, you see, to want those things for your children—to want what you think is the best. It would break my heart if Laura were cut off from us. But if you were to ask Laura for her hand, he wouldn't be inclined to be so strict if I prepared him in advance, and we didn't make a big fuss about things. So you see, Gregory, if it's handled the right way, it could benefit everyone, not just Laura. It would save this mother's heart. Where is your mother, Gregory? I'm sure she'd understand."

"My mother passed away about eight years ago," I said.

"I'm so sorry."

"I thought I'd mentioned it already."

"Oh . . . well then, I apologize for not remembering."

She brought her purse up on to the table, and for a moment, I thought she was getting ready to leave. Instead, she drew out a handkerchief and dabbed her eyes. This must have been hard for her.

"What do you want to do with your life?" she asked gently.

"Compose."

"Have you been having any success?"

"I won second place in the Kliegman."

When she looked confused, I explained.

"And that allows you to make a living—composing? she asked.

"Hardly anyone makes a living just at that. Teaching, conducting are part of the life. Unless you go to Hollywood, of course."

"What do you mean?"

"Some serious composers—like Erich Korngold—write music for the cinema. They make decent money from what I hear. But then they find it hard to be taken seriously by their colleagues. By the Roustakoffs of the world." I felt my breast pocket for another cigarette but didn't pull one out. I also felt my flask there. I sipped coffee again. "He's the one who won the Kliegman, by the way. He'll get the notoriety and the money—too late."

Mentioning the dead man made Amanda Reed uneasy. She fidgeted in her seat. "Talent finds a way to succeed," she murmured.

I laughed. "Tell that to Mozart, who died young and poor."

Her head shot up at his sarcasm. "That's why it's so important to be careful with Laura. Making sure she's not cut off, that is. And, as I said, we could help you with securing a decent position. Maybe even something permanent at the conservatory itself — if that's what you'd like to do?"

"I wouldn't do anything to hurt Laura."

She fidgeted again. She wanted to say more but was having a hard time with it. What else did she want from me?

"This Roustakoff death is quite the scandal," she said casually. "I spoke with some friends who know his sister well. She will not rest until someone is brought to justice."

"But he might have killed himself — accidentally, of course."

"Louise is ferocious in her quest. She won't stop until her brother's killer is caught."

"There might not be a killer."

She gave me a quick smile that faded as soon as it lifted her lips. "Louise always felt the need to defend her brother's choices in life," she said. "I imagine she feels this is her last chance to make sure his name isn't sullied."

"Then perhaps someone should set her right."

"At the very first opportunity, I intend to try my hand at consoling her and offering her some advice. In the meantime, people could get hurt. Innocent people." She stared at me. "You said the police had talked to you and Laura?"

I nodded. "Police have talked to me twice."

She sat stock still. "Are they talking with everyone?"

"Everyone who knew him, I guess."

"Lucky for you Laura was with you." She laughed lightly, again artificially. So this is what she really wanted to talk about.

"Not that it matters, but she only walked with me to the rehearsal hall that night. She can't vouch for me after that, nor me for her."

She swallowed, sucked in her lips, composed herself again.

"One more reason why a marriage would be so beneficial." She grimaced slightly. "Not that you need it," she said in a rush, "but once you are married, you can't testify against each other. That will be a blessing for someone like Laura, who is so easily upset. Knowing she won't be badgered by the police, that is."

"The police think we were in a studio together, and I have no intention of correcting them," I said steadily.

She smiled, this time more genuinely. She pulled on her gloves, and then opened her purse again, grasping from it a small envelope. She handed it over to me.

"I have absolute faith that you will do the right thing, Gregory. But I know there are many expenses in planning a wedding, even a small one. I thought perhaps you could use a gift to help you get started."

When she left, I looked inside the envelope and counted the money. She'd given me a thousand dollars.

Dear Sis,

I wished I could have talked longer when I called last week. Mom says you are serious about a guy and I'd like to hear more about him. She seemed to think you might be moving fast with things, due to all the war talk.

Whatever happened to that conductor fellow you were so taken with last year? If things didn't work out there, it's only natural you'd want to take up with someone else. But sometimes that can be the wrong thing to do. Let your heart mend, little girl.

I'll write more later. Even though I'm bored most of the time out here, there's always something I have to do.

Your loving brother,

Richard D. Reed, Ens., U.S.N.

U.S.S. Arizona

Pearl Harbor, Hawaii

Chapter Eleven

"LAURA, MY SWEET, I think we should get married."

"Oh darling, yes! Yes, yes, my love!" And she asked, in that innocent, beguiling way of hers, how I'd like to make love to her, spooning her body's curves into mine, her shapely posterior settled against me. I took her as she presented herself.

≈≈

It wasn't as if a short engagement was unheard of. It wasn't as if people didn't run off and get married and live happily the rest of their lives.

I'd not given much thought to how I'd ultimately propose to a girl. But what became clear to me after my meeting with Amanda Reed was that I'd be a fool not to grab a chance with Laura—a phenomenal beauty, an uninhibited lover, a woman of means.

So I broke it to Sal that week and asked if he'd stand up for me. I expected him to be surprised, but not so passionately opposed.

We were sitting at a tavern near the harbor on one of the few afternoons I had free—no rehearsals, and, since Laura had a lesson that afternoon, no tryst.

We'd had a few beers,and I'd just ordered a gin and lit a cigarette when I told Sal I was going to marry the girl.

"Holy shit, Greg, you're pulling my leg now!"

"No, I'm not. I love her. She loves me. Her mother approves."

"Just her mother? Don't she have an old man?"

"Her mother is going to bring him around."

"How you gonna support her—ain't she got money?"

"Yes, she does." I explained about the trust fund, the connections, the family's desire to help us get started. I didn't tell him about the thousand.

He took a long drag on his cigarette and blew a plume of smoke over my shoulder.

"You knock her up?"

I laughed. "Not that I know of."

He took a different tack. "What's going on with the case?"

"You tell me. You're the one with the cousin on the force."

"Didn't you tell me that Laura girl was knocked up by the murdered guy?"

So Sal was putting pieces together. And why shouldn't he, I thought as I sipped at my gin. He was a smart fellow.

"Yeah. But that was over before the guy died."

He tapped embers into the tin ashtray between us and slowly shook his head.

"It don't smell right to me," he said at last. "And I'll bet you she'll want out eventually, after all the drama's over."

"Thanks for the confidence in me, pal."

"Nothing against you. I'm just thinking she's the kind who'll want the finer things."

"You've not even met her." I drank again. "And besides, we will have the finer things."

"Where you gonna live?"

"An apartment near the university."

"You bring her round sometime, and Mamma will cook her a nice meal." He slapped me on the back, but it was artificial cheer. He knew that such an image—the refined Laura Reed at the Sabataso dinner table— would tell me all I needed to know about how wrong my dream was.

With the help of another gin, I pushed doubts aside. I paid for a couple rounds, and by the time we left the bar a few hours later, we were the same pair of friends we'd always been, laughing and singing as we walked home. He agreed he'd stand up for me. I needed only to tell him the day and the hour.

"Greggie, my sister ain't never gonna forgive you," he said when we reached my home.

❧❧

I learned in the next few days just how powerful an old monied family could be. Amanda Reed produced in short order: a hurried marriage license (is this how Renata had done it?), an appointment with a judge at City Hall, a small celebratory dinner at the Chesapeake Restaurant on Charles Street, a convinced if grudging Jack Reed, and a new "trousseau" for her only daughter.

She also furnished our apartment, in a beautiful new building on Charles and University, on the third floor. As soon as the opera was over, I'd sell my old place in Sal's neighborhood.

In the week after the wedding, I had Sal stop over, and he was appropriately impressed with the tall windows and high ceilings, the spacious living and dining rooms, the large kitchen and equally grand bedrooms—there were two—as well as the marble in the bathroom and the prints on the walls.

Holy shit, he'd exclaimed, as he toured the place. Laura winced at the curse, but offered him tea. I was glad he declined. She'd not yet mastered much in the kitchen.

I found out soon enough, in fact, that my new bride could barely boil water or tend to her own wardrobe, let alone perform the usual household duties of a loving spouse. She didn't know how to make coffee, nor cook much beside boiled eggs and a special cake that required so many ingredients it used up all our food budget.

Even with the Reeds' assistance, we went through money as quickly as it entered our bank account. My thousand was gone in record time. I'd spent some on our rings, some more on a pearl necklace I gave her as a wedding gift—Mrs. Reed's suggestion—and blew the rest on clothes and food and liquor and I don't even know. I think I gave some to Sal, too, as a gift for being best man. He didn't ask me how I came by it.

That first week, after the wedding at city hall, was a rough one, getting used to having someone depend on me. I drank more than usual, which was saying a lot.

The ceremony itself was a blur, and not just because of our nerves. In fact, to calm myself, I'd started drinking rather early that day, whiskey shots with my coffee, gin mid morning, and on and on. Laura told me later my breath smelled like mint vodka. I'd sucked on quite a few hard candies before showing up in my rented suit. Mrs. Reed cried. Some friend of Laura's—Carol—cried. Mr. Reed and Sal both managed to look equally sour.

Then we went for a luncheon where I polished off a bottle of wine all by myself, Mr. Reed scowling at me, Laura aflutter.

Our "honeymoon" was one night at the Belvedere hotel where we were told to hush by the front desk when our lovemaking became too raucous. She was a tigress unleashed once she had that ring on her finger. No man could have asked for more.

"What do you love about me most?" she asked me that night, lying snug in my arms.

I smelled the intoxicating scent of her hair. "This," I said, letting her locks fall through my mottled fingers. She turned on her side and slowly, slowly brushed her hair against the length of my body from head to toe, an erotic swoosh that had me craving her again by the time she was finished.

Now that I had my own decent flat and clothes and all the rest, I took a less cynical view of those who had money. I talked on the telephone with a couple of Mrs. Reed's friends about the various schools she'd mentioned. There were no openings yet, but a few good possibilities. I also spoke with the conservatory dean, and this time I didn't feel funny or "less than" when I sat across the desk from him. With the Reed money in my pocket, I was as good as him. He told me a few changes were coming with Ivan gone, but nothing would be settled until after the operas were over.

I was on my way. And all it had taken was marrying the right girl.

Dear Rick,

I know this will come as big news to you, but your baby sister is married. The fellow she has been seeing, Gregory, swept her off her feet, and they were wed in a lovely ceremony at City Hall just a week ago. Gregory is a conductor and composer with quite a future ahead of him, and I am so pleased that Laura has found someone with whom she can share eine bessre Welt — *a better world. You do remember that Schubert song that you loved to hear her sing?*

They are living in an apartment near University Parkway, so I can see her quite often. Gregory takes wonderful care of her. He is very talented, and I am sure he will go far. One of his compositions placed in a national competition and was slated to be played by the New York Philharmonic, but some complicated circumstances interfered. I am sure we will all be hearing his name in music circles before long.

The important thing is you are not to worry. Your sister is well cared for with this young man. He is dedicated to her safety, comfort, and well-being. As you know, I've worried about Laura's nervous disposition, and she is much calmer now.

Keep yourself safe, darling. And do call when you can. We love to hear your cheerful voice.

All my love,
Mother

P.S. If you'd like to send a wedding gift, you need not be lavish. Laura and Gregory are quite well set up. A sweet trinket from the islands would be sufficient.

Chapter Twelve

FOR A BRIEF PERIOD—a whisper of time—all was calm. Rehearsals for *Turandot* and *Carmen* continued. I battled with Chalmers over practice schedules—since we shared singers and instrumentalists—but that was the extent of the drama in our lives.

I began to wonder, in fact, if Mrs. Reed hadn't reacted too quickly on her suspicions about Laura's part in Ivan's murder. Hans was the one who looked guiltiest now.

I'm ashamed to admit that I was just glad I didn't need to think of my own memories of that night. Drinking kept most of them at bay. As long as I didn't remember and as long as suspicion fell on someone else, I could breathe freely.

We had dinner with her parents on Sundays, and I started smoking a pipe at Mr. Reed's suggestion. I dropped the Brentwood job entirely, kept my clothes neat and my hair cut, and I saw Sal less often. My liquor cabinet was stocked with only the finest now, and I sampled it frequently. Laura began to chide me about this, sulking when I didn't listen.

We were an old married couple already.

کویہ

"Hans, you cry just like a girl. Here, take my handkerchief! *Basta!* I do not tolerate this. Do you think I would not find out? Do you think I do not know you betrayed me? *My only true love*—you disgust me!"

Thus raged Renata to Hans in the cavernous practice hall before anyone arrived, her voice carrying to the door where I entered, coughing as I stepped over the threshold, so they'd know their conversation was interrupted. I didn't need to know more. I'd already heard the story.

Hans was guilty all right, guilty of trying to sing the Kliegman. His protests to the contrary, his declarations of support for Renata—they were as false as praise at the conservatory. Renata had learned that he'd managed to run up to New York by train to sing the piece for the contest judges. He claimed it was merely to persuade them from disqualifying Ivan's piece. I wanted to believe that was true, but by this time, I found so much comfort in a guilty Hans that any guilt at all would do.

I'd learned of his betrayal from Chalmers in a conversation two days ago after ironing out scheduling conflicts. Chalmers had gone with Hans to accompany him. And even Chalmers believed that Hans had really wanted to show off how well he sang the composition.

Gossip of that sort never stayed under wraps at a place like the conservatory. By the time Renata heard the story, I'd heard it twice over, with several embellishments, including other auditions he'd done for the Met, for a regional opera company, for a touring opera company up from Florida, for every impresario under the sun.

His little excursion certainly didn't help heal the rupture with Renata.

Hans was a lost soul now, which caused me considerable irritation during that rehearsal and subsequent ones where his listless, sloppy singing discouraged everyone. He assured me he was only saving his voice for the big moment, but I had my doubts. I berated him more than any of the other singers, while praising Renata out of proportion, just to goad him into doing better.

Praising Renata, however, caused problems for me. Laura resented this, pointing out Renata's flaws, how she missed a beat or sang a wrong note or was slightly off pitch. Her jealousy amused me most of the time. I enjoyed coaxing her out of her mood and into bed later.

Mrs. Reed visited often, but usually when I wasn't home. After one such visit, I came home to find we had the telephone as well as a cleaning woman who came once a week.

The phone proved handy. On it, Laura could talk to her mother almost nightly, which meant she wasn't pining to visit her parents or nagging me about my drinking or complaining about my attention to Renata. It also meant Mrs. Reed could talk to me, which she did one Thursday evening shortly before the opera entered its final week of rehearsals.

"Gregory, is there any way you can persuade that Italian woman to move out of Mr. Ruxton's house?"

"Who?" Then I remembered—Roustakoff's name had originally been Ruxton. She was talking about Renata living in Ivan's home.

"Why?" I asked.

"I finally managed to see Louise Watts. The poor dear is still grieving over her brother. She feels that no one takes her seriously, that everyone thinks her brother was a cad and he got his . . . well, just deserts."

How true.

"The Italian woman who claims to have been his wife—which Louise says is absolutely false—causes Louise considerable pain."

"I don't know what I can do about Renata. She's difficult to manage."

"Well, do try, will you? I think if this Renata woman is out of Louise's brother's home, she won't feel so abused. I think it will calm her down. And then that whole dreadful episode would be over."

And Laura would no longer be in jeopardy. That's what she was really saying.

"The police seem to be focusing on the German tenor," I told her.

She paused. "That's all well and good," she said. "But still, I think Louise would be less excitable if the Italian were gone."

I might have been numbed by drink, but it hit me like a boulder sometimes how awful it would be to have a mother who thought you capable of murder. But then again, if Mrs. Reed knew what Roustakoff had done to her daughter, she might have wanted to murder him herself. So I'd see what I could do about Renata, knowing it was a useless expedition.

As long as Louise was upset, she'd keep pressing the police. The detective could swoop in at any time, making our lives miserable once again.

I had another reason to help. I'd dreamed of Roustakoff several times in the past week, and all of them involved his murder at my hands. Never poison, mind you, but always me with my hands around his neck or with a gun to his heart. I'd even confessed these dreams to Laura, who, with childish trust, had put her hand over mine and smiled. *But I've dreamed that, too,* she said.

The investigation had to close.

❧❧

"Renata, could I see you, please, for a *momento?*"

The practice was over, my hands throbbed, I needed a drink, and a drenching rain had given me a blasted headache.

Well, maybe it wasn't the rain. Maybe it was too much liquor. Sal and I had gone to a bar the night before, for old time's sake. I'd not returned until two, upsetting Laura.

I saw Laura shoot me a glance as she marched off the risers. We were in the last days of rehearsals and everyone was on edge, particularly me. Although Mrs. Reed had promised to talk to a friend of hers at St. Paul's school about a music department chairmanship, I'd not heard a word about that. And I certainly didn't want to risk it falling through with bad notices about my conducting debut. A lot was riding on this opera.

My guess was that Mrs. Reed was waiting to hear from me—on my progress trying to convince Renata to back off her insistence she was Ivan's widow.

Widow—she even used that designation to advantage, wearing glamorous black dresses to every rehearsal, complicated hats with seductive netting touching her brows, sleek dark gloves up her arms. I suspected she was using Ivan's credit at various stores to upholster herself so well, another annoyance to Ivan's sister, to be sure. Amanda Reed was right. This had to stop. And if it did, maybe the investigation would as well.

"*Si, Maestro?*" Renata stepped my way, preceded by her heady musky perfume. She looked particularly beautiful today, her curvy body encased in a dark black silk cut low to reveal her perfect bosom. Her massive weight of black-brown hair was cinched at the nape of her neck, exploding in a burst of curl beyond a gold clip, with seductive tendrils tickling her cheeks. Her wide eyes blinked at me.

"I need to talk to you about some. . . upcoming productions. Do you have some time?"

She sized me up. She looked at a diamond-encrusted watch.

"In an hour perhaps. Come to my home. I will be happy to talk about singing more with you, Maestro!" She grabbed both my hands and quickly kissed me on both cheeks before leaving.

Laura came up behind me.

"Why do you need to talk to her?" she asked, holding her coat out for me to help her with.

"The conservatory wants to see if she'll sing a *Butterfly*," I lied. "It's just an idea. My guess is it won't happen." I held the trench coat up, and she slipped into it, quickly tying the belt and putting on a fedora-style hat.

"I was going to go shopping this afternoon. I don't want to have to wait for you."

"You take the car, darling. I can catch a bus."

"What time will you be home?" She pulled on gloves, not looking at me.

"By dinner, I'm sure." I kissed her on the head to reassure her. "Or even earlier. I'll take care of this meeting and tidy up some things with the orchestra." Another lie, but I was trying to sound businesslike. "I'm sure I'll be home in time. Are you cooking or shall we dine out?" I knew what the answer would be, but wanted to remind her she did fall short in some wifely duties.

She pouted. "I was going to try to make an omelet. Mother is going to send me to some cooking school. She's had Gertrude come over to show me how to do a few things."

I hadn't known. I wondered what Gertrude thought of fast marriage.

"Then I'll be sure to rush home, my sweet, as soon as I'm finished."

≈≈

I didn't rush home. I ended up spending far too much time with Renata.

When the appointed hour arrived, I raced across the plaza, past the Washington monument and the marble balustrades around the green, and knocked on the door of the Roustakoff manse. It was brown and muddy-looking in the rain, its rounded corner and spire-like roof making one think of a church instead of an individual residence.

Renata answered the door herself, ushering me into Ivan's spacious living room. Music was playing on the phonograph, a recording of Renata herself singing Carmen. She wasn't subtle—she was still angling for that role. Even though it was a mezzo part, she had the dark timbre and lower range to handle it. Ponselle had sung it.

"Do you want something to drink?" She headed to a liquor cabinet and poured me a Scotch when I said yes.

She'd exchanged her widow's weeds for something more colorful and comfortable—a burgundy lounging set with a top that wrapped around her body and satiny trousers from which sandal-clad feet peeked.

"Tell me about my singing for you," she said, handing me the drink.

My plan had been to flatter her first, so I rushed forward with it effortlessly. I complimented her Turandot, pointing out specific places where she shone in the role, I talked about how "regretful" it was she was doing Micaela and not Carmen herself, and how I hoped to change that with my influence over the authorities.

"You can get them to let go that cow who is singing it now?" She slid on to the sofa next to me.

I laughed. "She doesn't sing like a cow!" The mezzo-soprano the conservatory was using was, however, built like one, with broad shoulders and hips, and disturbingly large eyes that often fixed in a dull stare.

"Carmen must be a woman of passion, Maestro. Like me!" She raised her glass to me—she was drinking wine—and sloshed some on my pants leg. This was followed by much apologizing and cooing and fussing. She retrieved a towel from the kitchen and proceeded to sop up the offending stain, but her touch was too light and provocative to do any good in that department. It succeeded in others.

"You are so serious," she whispered close to my ear. "Is it this that makes you so serious?" She lifted one of my mangled paws and kissed it, looking at me through dark lashes.

The Scotch relaxed me. I asked for another. She complied. I talked about how I doubted I could get her Carmen, but I'd be damned if she didn't get something like a *Butterfly* in the spring. She sat very close.

"*Bene*," she said. "I will go to New York, right after the last performance of *Carmen*. I leave that night. I sing his piece." She gestured to Ivan's things. "I sing for some important people in New York. But I be happy to come back to you, Maestro. Will *Signorina* Ponselle start the opera company?"

"She's thinking about it."

"And you will be its Maestro?"

"I'm going to try." I'd talked to her several times, and I knew Mrs. Reed would help me.

"Then I will be your diva. People will want to come hear me!" She laughed and stroked the back of my head. "I know people will want to come to me. People like me, Gregory. Not just my singing."

She leaned back, and the top she wore, not securely cinched at the waist, tugged open, revealing breasts encased in a black lacey chemise.

Everything she did—her purring voice, her cat-like actions, her offers of liquor, her hand on my leg, on my arm, her little pecks turned to molten kisses—were aimed at seducing me. And, dammit, I enjoyed it. She made me feel like I deserved this distraction, from such hard work, from the pain in my hands. She made me feel like she herself was a gift and I'd be a fool to turn it down.

After my third Scotch, I was ready to move from petting to lovemaking. I was tugging at the buttons on my pants with her help, in fact, when someone knocked at the door. She growled out her frustration and went to answer it, retying her belt as she cried out, "I am coming!"

I couldn't see who was there, but I could hear him. Detective Reilly.

Chapter Thirteen

"I AM BUSY," Renata said as soon as he asked to come in. "So, no talking today." Then she spoke in Italian.

I smiled as I gathered myself, tucking in my shirttails, neatening my hair, grabbing my jacket. I fled to the kitchen, ready to spring for the door. I waited and listened.

"I only have a question or two."

"I only have a second or two."

"Why didn't you tell me earlier that your lover, the Kraut, was slated to sing that big solo in New York?"

"What? The Kliegman Prize? But I am singing it. What is this? I am no longer singing it?" More Italian, what sounded like a string of curses.

"He says he was supposed to sing it."

Her tone changed. I heard a smile in her voice. "*Si*, but he is not singing it. I am. He made the mistake and it is no more the mistake."

The detective's voice, muffled, sounded frustrated. "When did you learn this?"

"I do not remember." Then she laughed. "You think I would kill my dear Ivan because Hans was singing his piece? But I would kill Hans to do that! And if I were to murder the singers in my way, there would be a long line of them, *Signor*. There is a soprano singing Carmen now, a part that I want. Go look for her dead body. It is the body of a cow. If you think I kill for parts, she is the first on my list. And now, I must go. *Ciao*." She closed the door and came looking for me, calling my name. I appeared from the hallway.

"He is gone," she said with disgust. "Let us go back—"

"I need to leave."

"Are you afraid of the *politziotto*? Or of me?"

"He's not going to stop, you know," I said, at last coming to the point of my meeting. "Ivan's sister is pushing the police to keep the investigation open. It would be closed if it weren't for her. They'd probably call it as a doper doing himself in accidentally."

She tilted her head as if trying to comprehend what I'd just said.

"His sister is—"

"Very sad," I said. "Why do you make her sadder?"

"How you think that?"

I gestured around. "Why don't you get out of his life, move from this house?"

She crossed her arms over her chest. "It is my house. I am his widow."

I couldn't help myself. I snorted out a chuckle. "Renata, you know they will find out eventually that there is something wrong with the marriage. You know you cannot keep this."

She heaved her shoulders in a sigh. "But where am I to go?"

"Move back with Hans."

She shook her head. "No! He and I are done!"

"He loves you."

"I do not love him."

"But you did — once."

"Once. Not for very long."

Long enough to get to America safely, I thought. How long would she have stayed with Ivan?

"Find another place to stay — the Belvedere."

"Perhaps with you?"

I smiled. "I'm married now, Renata."

"Oh yes. I forget. It is easy to forget your wife."

Yes, Renata, you are right. I was all too quick to forget her this afternoon. It won't happen again.

"Maybe a hotel? Another apartment? What about that gentleman, the board member?"

"He is married, the poor man."

"Get him to pay for a place for you to stay."

"*Turandot* is in a few days. And then after that, I sing Micaela. And then I leave for New York. Maybe I will not return to sing for you and *Signorina* Ponselle."

So she'd be in the place for maybe a month longer. *Carmen* was already in rehearsal and would play two weeks after *Turandot*.

"Once you leave, don't make any claims on Ivan's property. It would only cause trouble."

She squinted at me, as if evaluating.

"I make no claims on anyone, *Signor*. I only take what I need to live."

❧❧

On the bus ride home, I let my guilt punish me. It was the booze, I told myself. I shouldn't have drunk so much. I had to get a grip on that. If I had become Renata's lover, I'd have lost Laura for good. There was no way Renata would have kept a liaison to herself.

For one horrifying moment I even wondered if we *had* made love. But I convinced myself Renata was not a woman I'd forget if I'd had her.

It was the booze. That was the problem. Laura was right. I needed to cut back.

But when I drank—I'd conducted some of my best practices after a few early gins. I'd written my Kliegman entry while under the influence of some cheap whiskey. I'd played with virtually no pain some of the bravura pieces I used to handle with ease after downing so much vodka I'd lost track.

So it wasn't as though I were using the stuff to forget. I was using it to create, and creation is a form of remembrance, isn't it?

I closed my eyes. My mouth was dry. Would I smell of her perfume? So what if I did. I'd been in her house. I could explain that.

I needed another drink. The last one had worn off, the Scotch—or brandy or whatever it had been—she'd given me was fading. Only that dry, sour taste was left, and the clicking gears of a headache a'borning.

Offer it up, Greggie. That's what my very religious mother would say to any pain, large or small. Offer it up.

All right. I imagined lifting an imaginary glass to heaven. Here's to you, Lord. Here's my pain, my suffering. Is it enough to let me off?

The nurses in the hospital had always been impressed by my stoic face, my grim, teeth-gritting silence when they'd tended my wounds, unwrapping the bandages to reveal the mottled mess of moist and rotting flesh. "Mister Silensky," they would say, "some men have been known to cry when we do this. You are so brave."

It hadn't been courage that had silenced me. It had been resignation. And it had been fear of God.

Shortly after awakening from the anesthesia and painkillers, I had been visited by Father Warshevsky, my parish priest. He'd offered Communion, but I had refused. How can I take Communion, I'd asked the priest, when my heart is not pure. So, Father Warshevsky had offered Confession. I had started to say the familiar words, "Father, forgive me for I have sinned…" but began to cry.

The tears had run down my face like a waterfall, and I was ashamed. More so when my father stepped into the room, his sympathy turning to embarrassment. His son crying. His surviving son. I'd killed the other, hadn't I? With my neglect, with my carelessness?

Father Warshevsky had blessed me. He had anointed me with Holy Water. He had sat on the edge of the bed with the low angle of the bright evening sun on his back, its intense light bleaching the color from everything—even the white sheets and walls of the sterile hospital room—and he had looked at my father and offered empty condolences. He'd told him, "At least your Grygor survived." My father had nodded, then tilted his chin in the air, and looked away. When he sat by my bedside, I wondered if he'd rather be elsewhere.

But of course he had. He wanted to be in the cemetery with Michael. He joined him soon enough, drinking himself into an early grave.

I opened my eyes and stared at my hands. Sometimes, in a certain light, the purplish scars made them look as if I had blood running through my fingers. They looked that way tonight.

⁂

When I got home, I was drenched. The bus stop was a good four blocks from my door.

Laura had the table set with a linen cloth, candles glowing, and something fragrant on the stove. She served me with a sort of determined affection, and after our last sip of wine and my last—and sincere—compliment, she came over to me, grabbed my hand, and led me to bed, making me forget whatever I'd hoped to do with Renata that afternoon.

⁂

Later, after she was asleep, I slipped back to the kitchen. I cleaned up the dishes and pots and pans—good lord, she'd used virtually every one we had—and then I placed a quiet call to Mrs. Reed.

She answered on the third ring.

"I talked to Renata," I told her. "She'll be gone in a month. And I don't think she'll be going after any of Ivan's estate."

"A month," she breathed into the phone. "Louise is a determined woman."

"Tell her that Renata will be gone—tell her you heard some gossip through Laura."

"I don't want Laura's name mentioned in connection with that cad's murder!"

I sighed. Enough of these coded conversations, everything a secret, nothing said outright.

"Why do you think Laura did it?" I asked.

Silence ensued. We'd never said what we both knew she was thinking, what I myself had thought. When she spoke, her voice trembled.

"My daughter is a very sweet and vulnerable child who has chosen you to bestow her love. I know that she was taken advantage of before she met you. I know she was in the vicinity of the murder. And I know that the murderer was cruel to her. I know that. . ." She paused.

"Yes?"

"That is all I know, Gregory, but it is enough to make me want to do all in my power to keep that . . . that . . . creature from hurting her."

"Then talk to your friend Louise and let her know that the Italian will be gone soon. Look—say you heard it through Peabody. Renata's singing in *Carmen* after *Turandot*, and then she's off to New York."

Mary,

I won't be home for dinner tonight, so don't be waiting up for me. I didn't wake you this morning because you were finally resting so peaceful, and I know the baby's been giving you grief, even with months to be born. Be sure to telephone me if you need help. Don't worry about bothering me.

I hope this is the last of the late nights. I'll be wrapping up one of my cases — the one that's been going on for weeks now.

I promise not to be too late.

Love,
Sean

Chapter Fourteen

A DAY BEFORE the performance and all hell broke loose. First, Hans disappeared. He didn't show up for the dress rehearsal the afternoon before the big night, and no one knew where he was. Renata coldly suggested I find another tenor to take his place.

Another tenor — to sing Calaf — on twenty-four hours' notice? She was crazed.

But find one I must. The conservatory helped in this regard, placing calls to Rosa Ponselle for recommendations, the dean meeting with me to go over "contingencies" — one suggestion was to have several talented students sing the role in pieces, another was to have someone declaim it. Declaim *Nessun Dorm?!* I laughed to think of it.

Upon questioning, Renata suggested that Hans had left because the police were closing in on him. Detective Reilly had been to see him again, she told me in a surly conversation just before our practice.

"He is so *stupido*," she told me, looking at her nails. She'd given up her black and had moved on to wearing dark green, a shimmering iridescent dress that looked like it was woven of fish scales. "Running away — of course they will think he did it!"

Then, Laura started to go to pieces. It turned out Reilly had been to see her, too. He'd found her at our new apartment that morning before she'd joined me at the conservatory. He'd asked her a lot of questions about her relationship with Ivan. He knew she was "Lucia," she told me, a desperate shine in her eyes as she tugged at my jacket sleeve.

"Gregory, you have to talk to him. Tell him again we were together. Gregory, please. Can you call him now — before the practice?"

I had to excuse her from the rehearsal. She wouldn't let me be. She was beside herself. I feared a scene. And I myself was late as I made several calls, sitting in the conservatory's telephone booth in the studio building.

I called Amanda Reed.

"Didn't you talk to Louise? Didn't you tell her to back off — Renata's going, for God's sake. Can't she be patient?" I explained how Reilly had visited Laura.

"My God," she said. I almost thought she'd fainted, the silence lasted so long.

"Mrs. Reed . . ."

"I'm here. I'm . . . I'm thinking. Perhaps you should take her away."

"I have the opera. Besides," I said, remembering Renata's words, "taking her away makes her look guilty. It makes us both look guilty."

And we weren't, were we?

"Hans is the focus. . ." I murmured into the phone, pressing it against my ear.

But I didn't believe he'd done it. Not really. I'd only hoped the detective would focus on him long enough to take the heat off everyone else.

What did I think really happened? I wanted to believe Ivan had accidentally killed himself. Somewhere deep inside, I'd settled on that explanation. And I'd been able to push aside, using booze and my newfound satisfaction as Laura's husband, other possibilities.

I slumped on the hard bench.

"Are you still there, Gregory?"

"Yes."

"I'm going to take Laura away."

"You shouldn't do that."

"She's had a nervous disposition. I told you that. She's always been high—"

"High strung." A euphemism for what—willful, childish, insane?

"Where is she now?" she demanded.

"I sent her home."

"The detective might look for her there again."

"I doubt it."

But I wasn't sure. What if he decided to drag in "Lucia" for questioning? What if he was as angry with the Reed and Watts set as I had been before marrying into it? What if he would enjoy bagging "one of their own" as a suspect? God help me, but I would have, had I been him.

"I'll go fetch her. I'll have the doctor come look at her." Her voice grew stronger.

"She was quite upset," I said. "Look, I know someone who might be able to find out what's going on. Let me see what I can dig up. I'll call you again."

We hung up. I looked at my watch. Rehearsal should have started ten minutes ago. Quickly, I dialed Sal. He wasn't in. I left a message with Brigitta for him to call me, telling her it was urgent.

I hung up, reached in my pocket and downed the last of the vodka left in my flask. Squaring my shoulders, I went off to rehearsal.

At least there, a problem had been solved. Miss Ponselle, I learned in a note from the dean, had contacted an old friend, a retired tenor she'd sung with at the Met. He was taking the train from New York and would sing Calaf, a role he'd handled dozens of times. He would be available to meet with me to go over the score in the morning. I could give him any special instructions at that time.

Somehow, I made it through the rehearsal. It quickly became a blank to me. Several choristers asked me about Laura. I told them she was ill but would be fine. Renata asked, too, but in a snide way, as if to imply that my wife was not as strong as she. She asked me if I'd join her for a drink, but I declined.

I checked on a few things and went home, taking the bus. Laura had the car. I was in a daze, numb.

She wasn't there when I arrived. I expected as much. The car was parked out front of the building, though. So Mrs. Reed must have come and taken her away.

I was about to telephone their house when the phone rang.

"Greggie, I know why you called." Sal's voice sounded low. I heard the radio in the background. He was trying to keep his family from overhearing.

"That detective chased away my tenor."

"It ain't the tenor he's after."

My heart sank. I slipped into a chair.

"Yeah?"

"Some student's alibied him. Heard him singing or something the night of the murder."

"But he was. . ." In the stairwell with Ivan. Obviously, they'd discounted my story.

"So they're after Laura?" I whispered.

"They don't care, my friend. Laura or you. Just somebody to get that Ruxton bitch off their backs. Reilly's sick of being pushed around by his captain. He's got a wife about ready to give birth, it turns out. And he just wants to wind all this up so he can get back to his other stuff."

Why hadn't I been more insistent with Renata? If she'd moved out of Ivan's home, maybe Louise wouldn't be so agitated. Maybe she would have given up. Maybe Reilly would have been able to tend to his wife.

"Why's he coming after us?"

"Cause you both had motive, opportunity—"

I heard someone in the background ask who he was talking to.

"Look, I gotta go. Just be careful. Don't say nothin' to nobody. Stay away from that detective, if you can. I'll call you later."

I got off and dialed the Reed residence.

"Laura's resting," Mrs. Reed said. "Dr. Milton came to see her and has given her a sedative."

"Laudanum, perhaps?" I couldn't resist asking.

"No! Something different."

"When will she be back?"

"I'm not sure."

Suddenly, I wanted her. I wanted my wife. Not to make love to her, but to cry on her shoulder, to have her comfort me. I wanted her to tell me it would be fine. I wanted to hold on to her.

"Has the detective called?"

"Yes."

My god. I'd expected a "no."

"What did you say?"

"I said she was sick and under a doctor's care and wouldn't be available."

"Did he ask about me?"

She said nothing.

"Did he ask about me?" I repeated, more intensely.

"Yes. He wanted to know if I knew where you were. I said you were probably at the conservatory, but I wasn't sure."

"We were together that night," I reminded her. "Laura and I— together in a studio. We can vouch for each other, remember?" That was the bargain she'd struck, dammit, and she had to live up to it.

"We may take Laura away—to a sanitarium."

"I'd like to see her!"

She was my wife! I needed her. They couldn't just abduct her like this. I was responsible for her, not them.

"You could stop by," she said uneasily. "But I'm not sure if that detective isn't hovering. I thought I saw his car earlier."

"How will you get Laura out?"

"I—I will think of something. Jack will."

Jack would call in a brigade of lawyers. And what about me?

"We were together that night," I repeated. "We're each other's alibis."

"Yes. That's a good thing. An excellent thing."

"And we can't say anything against each other anyway, now that we're married."

"Yes. Exactly."

"So we're safe."

"I certainly hope so."

There was no point in saying more. I got off the phone.

I paced.

I screamed.

I drank.

I packed my bag. Detective Reilly might come nosing around here again if he didn't find me at the conservatory. I wrote up a note and posted it on the door so the detective would see it.

I left, making my way back to my old house on Potomac Street, which was now as cold and dark as a tomb.

Dear Cloverland Dairy Delivery Man,
I'll be in New York for the next few days. Leave milk with the neighbor. I'll pay
you when I return.
Sincerely,
Gregory Silensky

Chapter Fifteen

I STAYED IN BALTIMORE, but I hid, like a fugitive, calculating where Reilly would look for me, what he'd ask. I nearly avoided him. Nearly.

Did I meet with the tenor from New York the next morning?

My notes on the score tell me I did. But I don't remember his name.

Did I go over house light cues with the stage manager?

I remember snagging my sleeve on a metal bracket. But that's all I recall.

Did I try to call Laura?

Yes. And this I remember — Gertrude answering the phone, telling me that "Mrs. Reed and Miss Reed" — she'd not called her Mrs. Silensky — "are unavailable due to illness." A very rehearsed line.

I started drinking as soon as I woke up that day, swigging vodka like water, lacing my coffee with bourbon. Sure, the performance was that night. But alcohol was my muse, now that my wife had been ripped from my side.

Had she found out about me and Renata?

No, I hadn't done anything with Renata. I hadn't, had I?

I stumbled through a haze, always on the move, to the conservatory, to my Potomac Street house, to the cleaners for my tuxedo, to the bar for a bite to eat and more drink, to the park, to the harbor, to somewhere, always somewhere that was away from . . . here.

And everywhere I walked, I had this feeling of inevitability, as if a bill long overdue cried out for attention now. It was time to pay.

I actually saw Reilly once during the day, rushing up the steps of the conservatory after I'd left by the stage door in the back. I hurried home after that, walked more, did things. I don't know. I don't remember. I drank more. I slept a little, in a chair in the near empty apartment on my second floor Potomac Street home. At some point I roused myself and drank some more. I showered, shaved, dressed in my tux. I left by the back door, walked down the alleys with my score and baton under my arm as if out for a late afternoon stroll. I made my way to Conkling and grabbed a taxi.

Once at the conservatory, I let myself into the hushed cream-and-gold hall, looked at the stage crammed tight with risers, chairs, and music stands, barely room for the conductor's podium, and stood there imagining how it would feel once the audience filled the house. *Fortes* would have to be *fortissimo, pianos, mezzo-piano.* The hall wouldn't be so "alive" with so many bodies in it cushioning the sound.

I strode—or stumbled—to the stage, stepping up to the podium, placing my score down, lifting my baton. My god but my hands looked awful in the buttery light there. I laughed. Let the audience gasp. I'd show 'em.

"Ivan, you bastard," I said to the empty hall. And then, under my breath, "Did I kill you?"

৵৽

After locking the door and turning out the lights so no one would know I was there, I fell asleep in my dressing room. I don't know how long I slept. When I awoke, I heard voices in the hall outside, singers arriving and making their way upstairs to the classrooms where the student chorus and orchestra members would gather. Renata and the other leads occupied the few rooms below the stage on either side of mine. I could hear her warming up, humming scales, singing passages, engaging in various vocal acrobatics. The Calaf had also arrived. I heard a few bars of *Nessun Dorma* on the opposite side.

I stood and flicked on a light, looking at myself in the mirror. My face was ashen, my eyes bloodshot, my lips pale. I looked like a ghost.

"Appropriate," I mumbled. *Turandot* had been Puccini's last opera. He had died before it was finished, another composer, Franco Alfano, writing the last bits. Those parts of the opera were not considered nearly as good. During one performance the great Toscanini had stopped conducting the opera at that point, turning to the audience and telling them, *this is where the master laid down his baton.*

And here I was, second-best, like Alfano, not the great Ivan Roustakoff who had planned this production, hired its lead singers, brought the chorus and orchestra together, convinced the conservatory to underwrite the performance and Rosa Ponselle to bless it with her presence. She would be here tonight.

But to compare Roustakoff to Puccini was a disservice to the great composer who, as far as I knew, was not the cruel tyrant Ivan had been.

No, but Ivan had brought all this together, whereas I . . .what had he accused me of? Yes, mocking him and other teachers from the wings. And I had done that. I was good at that.

"Not at this," I said to myself, rubbing my hands over my face, trying to bring some color back in.

I heard a key in the lock to my door. The stage manager opened it and looked startled to see me.

"Sorry, Maestro. I didn't know you were here. Do you need anything, sir?"

"No, nothing. Just . . .no visitors, please."

"Yes, sir." He closed the door, leaving me alone.

I'd conduct the opera, and then what? I didn't know. My mind still fogged from all the drinking I'd done that day, I could barely concentrate on the score. I glanced at it now, allowing myself to become lost in its lush and savage instrumentation that played in my mind, even as more noise—singers humming, greeting one another, instrumentalists tuning and practicing in the studios above—rained around me like sparks.

For a half hour I stayed almost motionless, my mouth and hands moving a bit now and then as I became lost in that beautiful music within.

So immersed was I in the ecstasy of the music that I didn't notice at first when a figure approached behind me, his shadow appearing in the mirror.

I smiled. Sal.

"I'm impressed. You came."

"I've been trying to reach you all day, buddy," Sal said with irritation, just as a soprano trilled past the closed door. He looked over his shoulder. "I'm not sure you should even be here."

"Do you want to be alone?" the stage manager asked, his hand on my half-open door.

"Just close the door. I'm fine. Thanks." I turned to Sal.

"I have to conduct this opera."

"Yeah, well, I guess it does make you look less guilty you not running away."

I took a deep breath.

"I am not guilty." There, I'd said it. Did I believe it? I didn't know.

"Reilly thinks you are. At least he thinks you and the dame might be guilty, and he doesn't care which one."

"What about Hans?"

"I told you—somebody's giving him an alibi. Some other student heard him singing that night."

"But he was talking to Ivan—he wasn't in a studio all night!"

"Don't matter. They got other stuff now." Sal looked down, a grimace flicking across his face. "They searched your place. The place on University."

"So?"

"Fifteen minutes to places," the stage manager said in the hallway. Instrumentalists were warming up on stage now. Their muted sounds drifted into the room.

He looked me straight in the eye. "So they found the laudanum, bub. They found it and more."

But I'd tossed my old vial weeks ago after hearing of its implications in the murder. My mouth fell open. Sal continued.

"Apparently, Your Little Miss High and Mighty had it prescribed to her—"

"I know!" But she'd told me she'd used it all up, that it was gone.

"—after her abortion. Once Reilly figured out she was one of the dames knocked up, they checked with the abortionist, found out his whole modus operandi, including the fact that he gave the girls laudanum to 'dull their pain' he says after the thing was over."

I reached out for a chair and sank into it, my elbows on my knees, my head in my hands. So she'd had more laudanum she hadn't told me about.

"Where'd they find it?"

"I don't know exactly, man. In your place is all I know."

The faraway sound of the opera preparations grew. More instrumental tones floated down, a baritone competed with a soprano as they both flew through scales, humming exercises, arpeggios. It was moving too fast. Everything. From the moment I'd met Laura until now, it had all raced by so fast that I hadn't had a chance to grasp it, to understand.

"That ain't all," Sal said.

"What else?" I murmured.

"They found some piece of music, something with a note to her on it, something he wrote for her."

My heart raced. I looked up. "The Kliegman." It had been dedicated to "my only true love." Was Laura that to him? No, Ivan was callous, insensitive, rude. He didn't love. He took.

"Anyways, it said he wanted her to sing it."

Too fast. I'd grabbed her too fast, afraid something good would slip through these clumsy fingers of mine. I should have known.

The pieces jumbled one over another. I couldn't think straight. I couldn't keep two thoughts together. Sal did the solving for me.

"So they thinks she would have been better off with him alive."

"But he was going to let Renata sing the piece!" I stood, pacing. "Or Hans! He told them both at different times . . .Jesus! Are the cops that stupid?" I growled.

What did it matter?

A swell of laughter passed by the door, singers' laughter, all silver and gold and flashes of light.

"Look, I'm just telling you what they've got. And what they've got is you and Laura, involved way back last year."

"Jesus, I just played for her brother's graduation party then. That's all!"

"Don't matter. They got you two together. They figure you started an affair."

"That's crazy!"

"They figure you started something with her, got ripped apart when she took up with Ivan, and then did him in so you could have his girl. And his job, too. And other stuff."

The prize—even though Ivan's piece would still be played, it looked as if I'd tried to snag that as well.

I could hear orchestra members going to the stage; some already there tuning their instruments. A hum of activity rushed by outside the door as the stage manager went through and knocked, calling out, "Five minutes, maestro. Five minutes."

I grabbed Sal by the shoulders. "What is Laura saying?"

"Nothing. She's locked up tight in the family home, probably with an army of lawyers around her, too."

"But I'm her alibi and she's mine. If she says she wasn't in the studio with me that night, she'll look guilty."

Sal barked out a cynical laugh. "No, my friend. She'll look like she's given up covering for her wicked husband."

"Christ almighty." I paced to the windows, but nothing but blackness greeted me there. Nothing but blackness anywhere. Nothing. Nothing. Nothing. I was a fool. The biggest fool in the universe.

"What will he do now?" I asked, not looking at Sal.

"Reilly will pull you in for questioning."

"When?"

"Don't know. They're watching you, though. So you don't flee."

"You mean cops?" I turned around.

Sal nodded. "My cousin Larry's in a car outside."

"What should I do?" I practically whispered it.

He fixed a steady gaze on me. "You leave. Brigitta's in the Ford. I made sure my cousin saw me come in. You take my jacket, comb your hair for crissake, and jump in my car. It's right out on Charles, near the stage door. You'll see it first thing. Brigitta will drive you to the train station. I'll stay here and wait for her to get back. They'll think you're me."

He pulled something from his pocket, an envelope filled with cash.

"Here, this should see you through a few days. You call me when you get somewhere, and I'll let you know when things settle down. I still think the guy was a doper who overdid it. The sister will back off at some point."

I held the envelope in my hands before me. It was heavy. Sal wasn't rich. He must have gotten all his family to chip in. I couldn't take this.

"I have to conduct the opera," I said, low and flat.

"Jesus, Greggie, you gotta get free and clear! Ain't that more important?"

But I'd never be free and clear. Sal might not know it, but I knew it. Louise Ruxton Watts wasn't going to back down. Things weren't going to "settle down." The only one going down was me.

"No, I have to do this," I said, more strongly, so he'd not feel bad leaving. I didn't want him to see me go down. "I have to. It's been my dream."

Yes, it had, and why shouldn't I grasp at least a piece of it when I was on the verge of losing every dream I'd ever hope to have? One last burst of pleasure.

"I won't leave until I've conducted the opera." I pushed the money back at him.

He shook his head back and forth and cursed in disgust.

"Holy shit, but you are a stupid son of a bitch!" He shoved the envelope back in his pocket and glowered at me, red-faced.

"You wanna spend the rest of your life in jail? Or worse—you wanna fry? Cause that's what they'll do to you. They won't care if the evidence ain't all there, pal. They've got a great story here—jealous low-life from the wrong side of town trying to steal what ain't his from the rich. Hell, even I'd believe it if I read it in the papers. Some jury might find it convincing, too. You're willing to risk your life for this?" He swung his arm around the dressing room. "For one fucking opera?"

Not for one opera. For whatever I could take from that opera, before the world closed in.

"They're going to get me one way or another," I said, resigned. "If not here, somewhere else. I don't think they'll let it go, Sal."

He exhaled a long sigh and rocked on his heels.

"They'll come get you in here, you know. Reilly's been looking for you, and once they figure you're in here, they'll just come in and take you."

"On stage?" I asked, incredulous.

Sal shrugged. "I don't think Reilly would care."

"Do they know I'm in here?"

"If they don't now, they will soon—figure it out, that is."

Now I sighed. We both stood without speaking, the raucous noises of the opera preparation growing with every second.

"One minute to places," the stage manager said in the hallway outside my door.

"I can get you a lawyer, a good guy some folks in the family have used."

"Thanks."

Another voice reached us, something in the distance, a man's voice asking where "Gregory Silensky" was.

I looked at Sal, panicked. I'd not even get a chance to conduct the opera. They'd come get me now!

Sal rushed to the door and locked it. He looked me up and down.

"Take off your fancy jacket," he said, shrugging out of his dark suit coat.

"What? I'm not going to—"

"Take it off, man! There ain't time to argue."

I slipped out of my tails and handed him the coat while he exchanged his with mine.

After he put it on, he bent to the mirror and mussed his hair, usually slicked to the side and held in place with pomade.

"Close enough," he said. "Now I look like a music bum—like you!" He hit me on the shoulder.

"I'm a few inches shorter, but close enough. Now, comb your hair like mine." He handed me a comb from the counter and I did as he instructed.

"This has got to be quick," he said. "I'm going to go out the door and make sure I'm seen. You come to it a few seconds later and call my name—I mean, your name. That'll get Reilly's attention."

I nodded as he talked, slipping into his jacket.

"I'll take Reilly on a goose chase—I know how to do it, man. I can give you an hour or two maybe, till he figures he's been had."

"You'll get in trouble!"

Sal grinned. "What? For driving my own car around town? Ain't my fault Reilly's a dumpkopf."

Smiling, I shook my head. He handed the money back. He expected me to stick to the original plan, catch a train out of town. I didn't protest, but I put the money on the counter.

"We better get this show on the road," Sal said, heading for the door. As he went to flick the lock, he looked at me. "Good luck, pal. Tell me where you go."

"Thanks, Sal."

❧❧

It worked. For the time being, at least, I was free.

With my own eyes I saw Reilly sprinting after the figure in tails, Sal pretending to be me. I wondered where Sal would drive to, how he'd shake him, if he'd shake him.

Now I was supposed to head to the train station with my stash of money.

But I couldn't do it. I sat in my chair in front of the mirrors, staring at myself, staring at my music, staring at my hands. I heard the stage manager make the call to places. I heard him knock on my door and tell me all was ready.

And still I sat.

Sal was wrong—I knew he was wrong. This thing wouldn't go away. And now I was facing what I'd managed not to face with great effort and copious amounts of alcohol—the possibility that I really was guilty, that I *had* done it and blacked the whole thing out, just the way I'd blacked out so many things in the years since the accident.

Even the accident itself was a mist in my mind.

Maestro, is everything all right?" the stage manager asked from the hall.

"Give me a moment," I said.

I stood. I leaned on the counter and stared into the mirror, searching for an answer.

Did you do it, I asked my reflection.

That night in the studio. Rain on the windows. Ivan and Hans in the stairwell, their voices coming up to me. What else, what else happened that night?

I couldn't remember.

I stood. I ran my fingers through my hair, smiling at my mussed-up "music bum's" look. I turned to the door, carrying my baton and the envelope with me.

"Say, you need another jacket?" the stage manager said, eyeing Sal's suit coat, a half inch too short in the sleeves.

"No." I handed him the envelope of money. "Hold on to this for me, will you? If I forget it, there's a friend it belongs to . . . "

A few minutes later I was in the wings. Deep breath. Head high.

I walked quickly to the platform. I bowed low to the audience, acknowledging their courtesy, and then turned back to the performers, all jammed on to the too-small stage, shoulder-to-shoulder, barely able to move. The violinists were lucky to be able to bow sufficiently.

I smiled at them. I smiled at the soloists, at Renata, at the tenor — God, what was his name — at Liu, Timur, Ping, Pang, and Pong.

Calaf, the baritone singing the Mandarin, the soprano singing Liu, and the bass singing Timur, remained standing while the other soloists sat down. I raised my baton. It did not tremble.

And suddenly, with the opening *andante sostenuto* octaves sharply cutting out the strange first melody with its unpleasant raised fourth — at the so-called "devil's interval," so jarring it was used in the police klaxon calls of Europe — we began.

Chapter Seventeen

IN THE OPENING of *Turandot,* Puccini has sized up the psychology of the mob—ugly, dissonant, sentimental, bloodthirsty, obsequious, deferential, fearful. All of these attitudes and emotions tumble over one another as he sets up the execution of the Prince of Persia, one of Turandot's suitors who failed to answer her three riddles about love.

The crowd loves and fears Turandot. And they love and fear the Prince's execution, relishing the grinding of the executioner's blade, hardly able to wait for the horrible moment of extinction. But this ugly attitude contrasts with their sentimental homage to Turandot, their distraction by the tardy moon. This music is transcendent, glorious.

They love Turandot because they wish they could be her—doling out life and death. They'd like to kill the prince with their own hands. Or spare him, whatever made them feel most powerful.

They cry out for pity and one second later are thanking their *"principessa"* for whatever she deigns to do, whatever tiny mercies she showers on them.

They disgusted me. My face contorted into a mask as I led them through those choruses, the screaming for death, the groveling for pity.

They wished they could kill him with their own hands.

With their own hands—just as I'd wished I could kill Ivan.

Had I?

As soon as the first chords sounded, I knew the orchestra and chorus would triumph. After weeks of rigorous rehearsal, they were filled with confident eagerness to share what they had learned. My direction would be needed merely to rein them in, to cue difficult passages. I was almost superfluous at this point.

No longer nervous, no longer caring about Reilly, only numb and dazed, I found my mind wandering away from the music and its images of China—as seen through Puccini's eyes—and finding other images.

Turandot—she killed men in their prime. I'd killed one, too. My brother in his prime. My brother through my carelessness. Had I killed another through the same carelessness—a lack of attention to my drinking and how it erased memories?

Spittle collected in the corner of my mouth as I sliced that baton through the air, wishing I could stab something else, wishing I could, like Turandot, execute every demon that tortured me!

Sparks and fire. Death, death. That's what they were singing about. The death of my brother.

"Muoja muoja!"

The savage rhythms and octaves rained upon me like sparks.

There he was, not the Prince of Persia, but Michael in a shower of sparks.

"Open the slidegate," Michael had shouted at me that day.

Tired and angry, I complied, pulling the heavy lever that let the warm-glowing steel flood through into a copper mold. Michael was supposed to be working the lever that day, but he had wanted me to take on more responsibility, to learn, to show the foreman I was capable. I'd resented this. I was there for one summer. Did he think I wanted to stay? Damn him! Didn't he know I had to be careful with my hands? I pulled on the heavy lever with all my might.

The steel had moved rapidly, so much more swiftly than I thought possible, and the mold started to groan under the ever-increasing weight.

The music itself was like molten steel, liquid fire cascading into the hall, burning everyone, but especially me. I closed my eyes. I knew the score, I knew the outcome. I didn't need to see it.

But see it I did. My brother in a halo of sparks, hands in gloves, sweat shining face.

"Open the slidegate, Greggie!"

"Muoja! Si, muoja! Noi vogliamo il carnefice! Presto, presto! Muoja! Muoja!"

Damned crowd wanting the executioner quickly! Savages, barbarians! Death will find you all soon enough. I despised them all. All of them. The Reeds. The Ruxtons. The Watts and . . . everyone who had power and money and wouldn't help me.

Michael had grabbed a temperature lance and stuck it into the glowing molten mess, but something was wrong, and I remembered – I remembered! – seeing him grimace and shake his head as sparks flew around us. That frown, so typical of my brother, who was quick to judge, whether it was the temperature of steel or the character of a friend, such a strong young man, with muscles as hard as the steel we forged.

Oh God, Michael, I miss you!

My hands had sweated in the thick gloves as I watched the sickening liquid pouring into the mold, looking as if it would overflow any second. When would Michael give the signal to stop? Finally, Michael looked up at me and waved his arm. I pushed back on the lever.

"Al supplizio! Muoja! Muoja! Presto! Presto!"

Shut up, I wanted to yell at the crowd. Death will find you soon enough! You want to see the execution, you jackasses, you mindless mob? You want to see a man have life ripped out of him? Jesus. I hated them all.

I beat out the rhythm with confident precision.

I had wanted to see Ivan dead. Hadn't I? Hadn't I? Jesus, what had I done that night? Had I killed him?

While I had waited for my brother to check the steel's temperature again, I'd considered going down and switching places with him. I'd wanted to say, "Here, Michael, let me handle that while you take control of the lever." Michael was stronger. He could do it. He didn't need to worry about his hands. I wanted to insist, but Michael would have laughed at me.

So instead, I had held back. I had thought, "If he wants me to make a fool of myself, maybe that will teach him I'm not made for this work. Maybe if I waste a few tons of steel, he and Dad will realize what a mistake it is for me to work here at Sparrow's Point." And I had stayed at the lever.

The sound of that steel—it was like the sound of this music, something awful and beautiful and powerful all at once, something painful.

"Se non appari, noi ti sveglierem! Pu Tin Pao! All reggia! all reggia! Oh! crudeli! Per cielo, fermi!"

The choristers shrieked liked frightened peasants to their queen, their gods. My brow, my hands—sweat covered them.

My hands—that night, I had sat in the studio, my hands on my lap. I had looked out the window. I had listened to Ivan and Hans argue. I had sat in the studio, my hands in my lap.

I had listened.

I had sat in the studio. I had sat there, remembering.

I listened. I waited. Michael had signaled me to open the gate again. But something was wrong. A drain in the bottom of the mold was jammed and the mold was filling up to overflowing. The overpowering smell of hot steel—an odor like that of a dead skunk—had started to make me nauseous. Michael turned and looked angry, making a gesture with both hands indicating I should pull on the stopper lever with all my might to open it. I'd tried. I pulled and pulled and nothing happened. It was jammed. Some cooling metal had obviously clogged the drain hole. I looked at Michael, silhouetted against the flaming sparks, and I knew—

I knew.

I had sat in the studio, remembering. I had seen my brother framed by gold, the gold of melting steel, the fire and brightness of death. I knew—

Oh Michael, I'm sorry, pieta, Michael. Pieta.

I had sat in the studio, my hands in my lap, and I'd remembered.

I had seen my brother, a halo of gold around him, already moving from this life to the next, and I had known—in that instant, in that very second, that Michael was a dead man.

"O madre mia! Non fateci male!" The frightened peasants asked for mercy.

Pieta, Michael. Pieta, Turandot.

The mold was breaking. Its creaks and groans sounded as if it were a sinking ship. Several men nearby came over to help me pull the lever, my father among them. But it had broken free and bounced easily in our hands. My father cursed. I only saw his mouth move. Ugly, like the faces of this mob. Accusing. Had I tried to spare my hands by not pulling hard enough? Had I? I was so careful with my hands back then. Sparks began to fly everywhere as the mold caught fire and started to boil.

And everything seemed to slow, seconds became hours, a wave of an arm took all day, a shout was released in long syllables as death sauntered in and surveyed us.

My brow cooled as the prince and Liu sang their sweet interludes. How good it was to remember. Even these terrible memories — how good it was to have them come back.

I had sat there in the studio, remembering.

"Ungi, arrota, che la lama guizzi, sprizzi fuoco e sangue!" *The chorus returned with their call for blood.*

"Get out of there!" *one of the men shouted to Michael, but he hadn't heard over the hiss and groan and roar of the steel. He'd been too damned stubborn. He'd probably thought he could win against the steel. No one and no thing could beat Michael. While the men had shouted, they'd run backwards, knowing that nothing would stop the steel once the mold broke. Someone triggered the accident siren and its eerie blare began to override all other sounds.*

Flame had burst high up from the mold while bits of hot steel flew around the room, stinging anyone unfortunate enough to be in its way. Men were running for the doors, but I had stood transfixed, watching as my brother tried, to no avail, to pry open the drain hole with a lance. I screamed his name, just as these peasants screamed to Turandot.

MICHAEL!!!

Then, in the blink of an eye, the mass of exploding fire and steel found me, found my hands as I no longer cared to protect them, as I reached forward to try to pull Michael to safety, my eyes locked on Michael's desperate brown irises, which finally looked afraid.

"Fuoco e sangue!"

Fire and blood.

Hands had pulled at my shoulders, voices told me it was too late. A doctor, get a doctor. Jesus, his hands!

My hands — I'd stared at them in the studio. I'd stared out the window. I'd listened to Ivan and Hans argue.

I'd stood. I'd run my fingers through my hair.

I'd cursed.

I'd thought about my brother, about that moment when he'd been lost. Just like now.

I'd seen my brother's face, and I'd wondered again if I had cared too dearly about protecting my hands and not enough about protecting him.

I'd sat in the studio and . . .

I'd wept.

I'd sat at the piano, staring at my hands.

And I'd cried like a baby, sobbing out my guilt. Oh, Michael, forgive me. I hadn't meant to kill you. I hadn't hated you, dear brother. I loved you, just as I loved our father and our mother. Dear Michael, please, forgive me . . .

I'd cried for a long time. And my face and eyes had hurt as much as my hands.

I'd left the building and walked through the city, half hoping some vagabond would assail me and end my life. I wanted peace. I wanted to forget that awful fucking afternoon when I lost my brother!

Sal had picked me up when I'd found a telephone booth and called.

As sure as I was standing there, I knew I'd not killed Ivan.

Then who had — Laura?

The music shifted from savage to heartbreakingly lush and sweet. Heaven after hell. My hands ached, the muscles were contracted and tight from gripping the baton. My face was covered with a patina of sweat, and when I looked at the chorus, the orchestra, or the soloists to cue them — I saw only my brother's eyes when death was about to take him.

Morte. Morte. Ah, ah.

⋘⋙

For three acts, I endured this misery. Reilly didn't find me. Sal must have decoyed him somewhere.

By the time the opera was over, I felt like a wraith, something half-dead and half-alive, a spirit lost in purgatory, waiting for redemption and knowing it would not come.

Drenched in perspiration, I bowed once to the pleased crowd and refused to come out for another acknowledgement, rushing backstage to my room, wanting to shut out everything, especially the music. I locked my door, sat in the chair with my head in my hands, wishing I could cry again, but no tears came.

Chapter Eighteen

A KNOCK AT THE DOOR, and over the noise of the crowd, a man's voice filtering through the thick wood.

"Mister Silensky?"

The detective.

I readied myself. I silently voiced a prayer. I breathed deep and stood, walking to the door to open it. The Prince of Persia on his way to the execution.

And then, another voice, some unknown singer.

"He left right after it was over."

I breathed out. I closed my eyes. I listened as footsteps receded.

I waited until lights went out. I waited. I sat still as death.

How long was I there? I don't know.

At some point, I stood, rubbing my hands on my trousers, then searching for a smoke. I smiled. Sal had left some in his breast pocket. He'd not find such treasure in my tails jacket. I pulled one out and lit it.

And then I marched from the room, walking into the dark night, my footfalls echoing on the pavement.

My feet tapped out the lah-di-dah of my brother's and father's taunts. Lah-di-dah. Lah-di-dah. What made me think I fit into this lah-di-dah crowd? Laura and her family wouldn't give me a second thought if she were safe. I was doomed.

Lah-di-dah.

Jesus Christ, can you get any more stupid? I heard my brother's voice ridiculing me, and I liked hearing it. I agreed with it.

You'll never make enough money with that music of yours, Greggie. Not enough to take care of you, let alone some gal. You are interested in girls, aren't you? Or has that pissy pants music turned your head the other way?

Can you get any more stupid?

No, I don't think I can, Michael. I think I've gotten as stupid as I possibly can be.

I blew smoke into the empty streets.

I was free for the moment, and I'd soak up any accolades I could get. I headed for a post-performance reception, hosted by the conservatory leaders. Originally, Laura and I were to attend this together. She'd shown me the pink frock just a few days ago, a cloud of lace and netting, she'd bought for the event

Shit. I'd looked forward to having her on my arm.

I walked the three blocks to a nearby townhouse feeling as if I were someone else. Someone else accepted with grace the many congratulations and celebratory speeches. Someone else sipped champagne and made timid small talk with Miss Ponselle and the distinguished guests. Someone else engaged in a conversation with the president about future conducting and composition plans.

As if I had a future.

While that "someone else" did all those things, the real me was still and mute, an inner voice intoning "guilty, guilty, guilty." There were moments when this real Gregory came to the surface, and I had to work with all my might to keep myself from flinging a crystal champagne glass on the marble floor and storming out of the glittering crowd so that I could feel the cold air on my skin, so that I could let it penetrate to my heart, wrapping it in ice so it wouldn't throb any longer.

A bejeweled woman spoke to me about the need to sing operas using English translations now that war was on the way.

"I just don't understand," the woman was saying, "how the country that produced Beethoven and Brahms could be so . . . so barbaric!"

I laughed at her. When she stepped back surprised, I sneered.

"Music is not civilized!" I cried, "It's primitive. Drum beats rouse the savages, marches inspire the masses to kill. It appeals to raw emotion, not to intellect. In the wrong hands, it's murderous." And, with a smile on my face, I hummed *Deutchland über Alles.*

"Gregory," the president said, interrupting, "let me introduce you to Demille St. John, our new board chairman . . . " He gestured to an older man standing next to him.

"Ah yes, Amanda Reed told me about you," Demille said, extending his hand. "Are you conducting Miss Ponselle's *Carmen* next week?"

"No, no. That's someone else." I shook the man's hand and watched him recoil as he touched my scars. I laughed again.

While Demille talked, I smiled and nodded, drinking as much champagne as I could get my hands on and trying to drift somewhere else. No one, I noticed, asked any questions about my hands. They were all too damned genteel for that. I was their pet star for the night, and they cooed and fawned over me. Like a rare *objet d'art,* I was passed around from person to person to admire and celebrate. If they could have installed me in their drawing rooms—like Laura's family had done with that Boesendorfer—I was sure they would have done it.

By two in the morning, the crowd had thinned, the champagne was tasting sour, and I was bored. I saw Renata flirting outrageously with the Demille fellow while some other older guy looked on—was that the one in the rehearsal the other day? At least Renata didn't hide who she was. She took what she wanted when she wanted it, and didn't feel a feather of guilt on her shoulders.

❧

They arrested me at my Potomac Street home that night. Sal was coming around the corner, probably to warn me to stay away, and he saw the whole thing. He came up and asked them what they thought they were doing, and he promised to get me a lawyer.

Small, Smythe, and Brumley
Attorneys at Law

Dear Detective Reilly:
Enclosed you will find an affidavit, signed by the chief of psychiatry of Johns Hopkins Hospital, attesting to the ill mental and physical health of our client, Laura Reed Silensky. She is incapable at this time of speaking with authorities, as you will see from the papers. Her life and good health depend on not being disturbed. We will notify you immediately should this situation change, but trust you will be able to gather sufficient material for your investigation from other sources. If you have any further inquiries to make of Mrs. Silensky, please, direct them to our office.
Sincerely,
Thomas N. Small, Esq.

Chapter Nineteen

"HOW LONG were you with the Reed girl that night?" the detective asked me.

I stared at my hands on the table in the tiny interrogation room. My mouth tasted like old cabbage. I wanted something to drink — anything, even water.

"I already told you. I was with her the whole time. From the moment we left the rehearsal with Maestro Roustakoff to the moment she got in her car." I was sticking to that story because it was all I had. And it protected Laura.

A light tap on the door was followed by another man poking his head in. From the way Sean Reilly straightened, I assumed this fellow was a superior.

"We just heard from the girl's lawyer," the man explained. "She doesn't remember anything about that night. He thinks he can get us a statement."

The man left. Reilly looked at me. His gaze said: You've been betrayed, now tell the truth.

But the truth wouldn't save me. Only the lie would, the one that Laura's lawyer was now having her recant.

"I don't need any more," Reilly said at last. "Let's go."

He stood and motioned for me to do the same.

As he handcuffed me to take me to a cell, I said, "She was with me. She'll tell you eventually." But even I didn't believe it.

༺༻

For several nights, I visited hell.

Nothing to drink. No liquor. Just a little water.

Damn, I was cold.

Shivering so much I was sure to rattle a bone.

Sick to my stomach.

Head pounding.

Thoughts — didn't have one. Not one. Blackness is all.

Sometimes a song played, but in some odd out-of-tune way. I screamed for it to stop.

Christ, get me out of here.

Turn up the heat, why don't you? You want me to freeze to death?

Michael — how'd you get in? Where you living now?

Laura, will you tell them the fucking truth, please? The truth we came up with?

You did it, didn't you? You coldhearted bitch — killing one lover and letting the other take the rap. You low-down coldhearted bitch.

Can't I have just one little shot of whisky? It'll do me good. The doc told me I could.

Blackness again. Head hammering. Am I dying? Please, let me be.

Can't talk to nobody. Too sick. Tell 'em no practice today, okay?

Somebody call the Brentwood. Supposed to be there tonight.

Jesus, will you turn on the fucking heat?

≈∽

I heard the clank of the door, the jingle of keys, footsteps — two people coming down the narrow jail hallway. I sniffed the air, smelled vomit. Turned, saw the puke bucket. Oh, god, my head.

Morning sun tentatively lit the cell, but not enough to warm my shoulders or my heart. How long had I been here? Had Laura talked to the police yet? *C'est fumée.* The words of lovers are smoke. The cigarette chorus from *Carmen.* God, I needed a smoke, too.

She'd vouch for me eventually. She'd get it, or her lawyers would. Either she stuck to our story, or I changed mine . . .

"Greggie?" Sal's voice.

"Why not go after that Nazi, huh?" Sal said, appearing in front of my cell. "Why drag you in?" Sal's bombast, I knew, was for the jail keeper to hear, whose keys had jangled at his waist as Sal had made his way to my cell. I smiled and gingerly stood, keeping my hand on the wall to steady myself. "I'm telling ya," Sal said, "they want to wrap this thing up and they don't care whose name is on the sheet. As long as it's not an Irish one."

When I didn't say anything, Sal continued, "My Uncle Giovanni — he's been fingered by the police a dozen times. Just because that damned Mick has been here a couple years longer than our families, he thinks we're all thugs. Huh! He's the thug."

Sal turned to the jail keeper. "We're okay here. Give me a few minutes." The other man left and Sal stepped closer to the cell, placing his hands on the bars so that he appeared to be the caged one, not me.

"Sorry I couldn't come earlier, pal," he whispered. "Thanksgiving."

"What day is it?"

"Monday."

So it had been a whole weekend. That's right. *Turandot* was the night before the holiday. I rubbed fingers through my greasy hair.

"Can I get out?"

He didn't answer that one. "Her family got some lawyer, Greggie, and they're claiming she's crazy or something. They got some doctor looking at her."

Now I grabbed the bars, anger mixing with panic. "But before, she told the police she was with me! She told them already. All she needed to do was . . ."

"Don't matter." Sal scowled, looking into my eyes. "I told you what they wanted. One of you. Don't matter who. That Reilly fellow's really steamed now. His wife lost their baby, my cousin says. Reilly's mad as hell. Thinks this case kept him from being with her. They've already called the Russian's sister to tell her it's wrapped up."

"Jesus Christ!" I stepped back, immediately reaching for the wall to keep from falling over. "But I didn't do it. I know I didn't do it."

"Yeah, yeah. Well, she probably did. And she's letting you take the fall."

"I don't want to believe that."

"Look, I don't have much time. There's something else. They've got your fingerprints on the cola bottle. The one with the poison in it."

"I know! I told them that already!"

"At this point, it don't matter what your explanations are. But you don't worry. I got some cousin who's good in the law. I gave him a call, and he'll be by to get you out. We gotta be thinking about bail now. I'll get my cousin to help out—he owes me a favor."

"Jeez, Sal, I don't have any money."

"You've got your momma's house."

"And the piano."

"Say, you've got everything in that apartment of yours—the new, fancy one."

I nodded. "That should do it."

Sal chuckled. "So the Reeds'll be paying for getting you out, whether their little girl steps up or not."

Chapter Twenty

"THEY HAVE YOU making contact with Laura over a year ago."

Constantine DelMarco, the lawyer Sal had secured for me, placed his pudgy hands palm down on the gray table in his office. He was a doughy man with a big head and thick white hair, small eyes and a quick smile. His voice was sugar-coated gravel, rumbling from his chest in cadences designed to soothe.

I liked him. But maybe that was because he was my life preserver.

I'd been arraigned this morning. And the whole time I'd stood in that courtroom, I'd kept looking over my shoulder. What a sucker I was. I expected her to show up. Or her lawyer or somebody. I was sober, so I figured she'd be, too, her own brand of sober. Something outside that cloud of pretend she lived in, the one where she liked to see singers act out drama on a stage and the one where her mother kept her safe from the rest of the world. I was such a sucker. Of course she didn't show up.

Sal had, though, with the bond to get me out. It was an extraordinarily high amount, but I was lucky they even set bail instead of letting me rot in jail. Sal's cousin talked to somebody who talked to somebody. Sal told me Larry owed him a favor because he'd gotten him a date with Brigitta. How fast she'd moved on.

So here I sat, through the good graces of the Sabataso family, out of a dank prison and in Constantine DelMarco's office, a small suite of rooms above Dinardio's Ristorante. Already the smell of garlic and olive oil wafted into the rooms. The one we sat in was little more than a closet, even though Constantine had ushered me into this "conference room" as if it were a reception hall for royalty. A metal-legged table took up most of the space, forcing me to slide into my chair from the side because its back was already pushed up against the wall. A window in need of a good cleaning let in milky daylight.

"I played at a party for the Reeds' son. That's all." How many times did I have to explain this?

"They'll make it sound like you and Laura struck up a relationship back then, and when you found out what this animal did to her, you were filled with rage. Then you snapped when he fired you and you found out you took second place to his first in that contest." Constantine said it in a cheerful voice, as if he were relating a children's story. *And then the monster ate the little birds. . .*

He grinned at me, revealing a row of perfect white teeth. "But some of this could work in our favor."

"How so?"

"You did the world a public service by getting rid of this guy! He was a rapist, a baby killer. Who knows what else he did, or was capable of doing? Whatever it was, he would have been caught and electrocuted eventually. You saved the state a lot of money by getting to him first."

"You're saying I did it."

"I'm saying I talk to the DA about this and see what we can do."

"I don't understand."

Constantine reached out and lightly tapped my hand in a fatherly way. "The DA might be open to accepting a guilty plea from you on a lesser charge."

I recoiled, the back of my chair smacking the wall as I pulled away.

"Absolutely not! I didn't do it—don't you understand? I did not do it." I was so sure of this truth now that I couldn't let it go. It was a beautiful thing, this truth. It felt so damned good to know it.

Constantine's grin faded to a sardonic smile. He leaned his head to one side and looked at me with equal parts pity and understanding.

"The facts are the facts," he said softly.

"If I could just talk to Laura, I know I can get her to vouch for me. Like I did for her."

Even though I was sober, I still thought I'd be able to win her over, to remind her of how she loved me. She had to love me still.

The lawyer laughed, and my face burned as I realized how foolish I sounded.

"What you have to understand," Constantine said, "is she's not talking to anybody. Her family's seen to that."

I stared at the table, at my hands, seeing them as if for the first time, even admiring the way the scar on the left hand curved and flowed, a graceful rivulet. I half listened to what else the lawyer had to say, nodding or shaking my head when appropriate. Yes, I wanted to go to trial quickly if it came to that, yes, I could find friends who could testify to my good character. It all poured over me while I kept thinking of Laura.

Where was she—what had her mother done? Had she drugged her, ordering more laudanum from the doctor? Was Laura trapped in a cell of her mother's making?

I longed to see her. I ached to see her—and not just because I needed her testimony. I wanted to reassure her that I, unlike her mother, had stayed true. If she'd killed Ivan, I'd forgive her.

Maybe that was the key—letting her know I forgave her. If I could just get to her—

If I could get her to see me. That in itself seemed an impossible task, first storming the barricades of her lawyers, then the moat of her parents.

She was still my wife, dammit! Surely I had some rights.

જ⁀જ

When I walked home a little later, I had a few moments of panic, feeling that cell closing in on me again. Jesus—how many days had I been there—three, four? But I had another cell pushing in from all sides now, this one more complicated. Did I love Laura? Christ, I was afraid I might.

I went home—to the house on Potomac Street, not the apartment near University and the Reeds. I played some music, sweet, sweet music that seemed as fresh to me as if it had just been composed. Mahler. Those *Songs of a Wayfarer*, so true and honest, so heartfelt, back and forth between light and dark, passion and acceptance, the knife to one's chest, the wandering after heartbreak, the realization that both pain and love are good, that life itself was good.

I slept.

I dreamed of Laura on our wedding day. She'd looked at me and blinked, her eyes seeming to say, I entrust you with my heart, don't be careless. Her hands had trembled, the petals of her bouquet shaking. She'd worn a dark blue suit that had made her skin so pale and angelic. She'd kissed me. . . .and later, her glorious hair soft as a cloud on my body, her body entwined with mine. . .

That was memory, not dream. And when I awoke, I ached for her. I needed to talk to her. I needed to explain that yes, I did love her. Or I wanted to find out if I loved her. I just knew I needed to talk to her.

I grabbed my coat. It was late afternoon. I could catch a bus and be there in forty minutes. Surely she'd see me. I'd find a way in. Maybe Gertrude would be kind . . .

. . . .*and I promise you, my beloved, I will not tell anyone your deep secret. I will tell no one your story. I forgive you, my beloved. I will come back and take care of you. You will be safe with me. Together, we can start a new life. . .*
Your only true love,
Hans

Chapter Twenty-One

I STARED AT THEIR HOUSE in the late waning sunshine of a cool afternoon. A few straggler leaves coated their yard. The light on the leaves, on the house, gave it a special glow, as if it were lit for a stage. A couple strolled, arm in arm, two blocks away. I straightened, ran my fingers through my hair, looked at my scuffed shoes . . .

I didn't care. I belonged here. Laura was my wife.

Thus fortified, I strode up the walk and knocked quickly. Gertrude answered.

"I'd like to see my wife," I declared.

She tilted her head to one side, not understanding.

"Laura," I explained. "I want to see Laura."

"Miss Reed is indisposed," she said, her eyes boring through me. What had they told her about me? Whatever it was, it mitigated the effect of any feelings of comradeship between two low-class souls. She clearly felt superior to me.

"Her name is Mrs. Silensky," I corrected. "And I can go to her bedside. It's my duty, as her husband, to see to her care—"

I pushed my way past her and stood in the foyer.

Before I had a chance to head up the stairs searching for her bedroom, Jack Reed appeared from around the corner, newspaper in hand.

"What—what are you doing here?"

"I demand to see my wife!"

His face turned red and his jaw worked. He wouldn't hit me. I knew that. He'd think it below him to physically accost a vagabond like me.

"You should be in jail," he said.

"I'm innocent."

He snorted in disgust.

Amanda Reed appeared from the hall, motioning Gertrude to retreat to the kitchen.

"What's this all about?" Amanda asked. She saw me. "Oh. You."

"She's my wife and I demand to see her," I repeated to Jack Reed. I looked up the stairs. "Laura!" I called, my voice bouncing off the walls.

"Gregory, she's not well," Mrs. Reed said, wringing her hands together, stepping forward and looking from me to her husband.

"And she won't be your wife for long, you murderous bum," Jack Reed said.

"What does that mean?" I asked.

"It means your marriage will be annulled in short order. I don't know what we were thinking to approve such a catastrophic union." Here he glowered at his wife for an instant, before returning his wrath to me. "Laura will certainly not entertain visitors, and you least of all."

Annulled? My heart sank. I remembered her on that bed, her hair on my chest, my fingers running through it. If only I could see her . . .

"Our marriage is valid," I said, trying to sound confident. "And I must talk to her. If you don't let me, I'll have to—"

"What? Call the police?" Jack Reed laughed. "I can't imagine you want more interaction with them, boy."

No, I didn't. But I wouldn't be bullied. "The police might be interested in how you're keeping my wife doped up and imprisoned here."

Mrs. Reed exhaled sharply.

"Please, understand. She's had something of a nervous—"

A flash of white appeared above us, followed by a soft voice.

"Mother?"

She stood at the top of the stairs in a long silky robe, belted tightly. She stood there, an angel, certainly something not of this world. Something slightly off kilter, even leaning a little to one side, and looking very different from the last time I'd seen her. I swallowed hard.

"Oh, my god," Mrs. Reed said at the sight of her.

"Laura?" I whispered.

Ashen and unfocused, she took a step down, steadying herself on the banister. In her free hand, she held an open pair of scissors.

Lucia—that had been the operatic name Ivan had given to her. And now she looked like that ill-fated heroine descending the stairs, knife in hand, after killing her groom on their wedding night. But no blood stained Laura's garb.

She'd killed instead an aspect of her beauty—she'd shorn her hair.

"Laura! What have you done?" Mrs. Reed cried out, rushing up to her daughter.

"Dear Lord!" Mr. Reed said.

She'd cropped those beautiful golden locks that framed her face, that seduced, that beckoned—all gone. Shorn tendrils still stuck to her shoulders. She looked like Joan of Arc, sad, consigned to her fate, otherworldly. She was destroying that which had lured men like Ivan to her. Men like me. My eyes burned and didn't blink.

"I didn't do it, Mother. I didn't."

She meant the murder.

"Oh, child." Mrs. Reed put her arm around her daughter and cried. "Of course, you didn't. No one says you did."

Reilly did. And yes, even I did. Hadn't I come here in part to forgive her for the crime?

I swallowed again and stared. She was as distant, as fragile as a stained glass image.

Still, I had to risk it. Her parents weren't helping her. Not like this.

"Laura," I said, staring into her eyes. "Don't let them drug you. Laura, darling, please let me talk to you. I love you, Laura. I love you."

Did my words penetrate? Her mouth opened just a bit. She looked like she was trying to remember me. Did her mouth move to my name— Gregory?

"Laura. . ."

"Good lord, man, can't you see she's unbalanced?" Mr. Reed glared at me. "Leave her alone!"

Mrs. Reed coaxed Laura to sit on the stair. While her mother stroked her hair, Laura continued to stare at me.

"Please, Laura, let me talk to you."

A tear dropped from Laura's eye.

Mrs. Reed turned to me. "For God's sake, leave her alone now, Gregory. If you love her, you'll leave her alone."

ৼড়৹

I left her alone that afternoon. But I tried again the next day, traveling once again all the way to Roland Park, knocking on the door, being greeted by Gertrude, on and on.

I tried for three days, and we repeated the same act with different variations like a theater troupe looking for just the right way to play the scene.

Only on the last visit did I actually see her again. She appeared once more, at the top of the stairs, and I was gratified to see that this time, she had more color in her cheeks. She actually spoke to me, too. But the words were hardly comforting.

"I'm going away, Gregory," she said. "And I think it best that you leave me alone. I'm very sorry." From her tone, it was clear I was now part of some enemy camp. I imagined she now saw me of the same cloth as Roustakoff. And why shouldn't she?

"Where is she going?" I asked Mrs. Reed, the ever-faithful Roman Guard.

"Someplace restful."

"Where is she going?" I repeated with more insistence. "I demand to know!"

I demanded many things during all those visits. My demands were hollow and treated as such.

Mrs. Reed didn't tell me, but Gertrude did. That day, her departure from the house coincided with my own. I walked with her to her bus stop.

"A sanitarium on the west side," was all she would tell me, before bustling away as if I had the plague.

༺༻

I was so lost in playing the piano that I didn't hear the knocking at first. I had three obsessions that week out of jail—staying sober, playing the Mahler songs, and, of course trying to see Laura. I succeeded at all but the last.

The Mahler drew me again and again because the songs so perfectly captured my mood. The first song talks of seeing one's beloved on her wedding day, marrying someone else. Despite the fact that I had a bride, she might as well be married to another man. Her parents were intent on seeing to that at some point.

Now my fingers found their way through the lilting fourth and final song of the series, with its calm walking tempo, sometimes a trudge, sometimes a stroll.

> *Die zwei blauen Augen von meinem Schatz,*
> *Die haben mich in die weite Welt Geschickt*
> *The two blue eyes of my sweetheart*
> *Have sent me into the wide world.*

"Gregory, open up! It's me, Sal!"

Dramatically pulling my hands off the keyboard, I went to the door where Sal stood, collar turned up against the damp, brown bag in hand. As Sal entered, he shoved the bag at me.

"From Ma. Prosciutto, provolone, some pickled peppers."

"Thanks. You didn't have to."

Looking around the dim, empty living room, Sal took off his coat. "What you been doing all week? Every time I go by, the place is dark. I thought maybe you was even back in jail for a while."

I smiled, sitting on the piano bench, holding the bag between my legs. Sal sat across from me in a chair he pulled up.

"Nothing much to do. I'm supposed to meet with Constantine next week."

"Yeah, I know. I was talking with him. He tells me you don't want any deals."

"That's right."

"With character witnesses and whatnot, you could be out in—"

"Shit, Sal, not you, too!" Whirling around, I threw the bag on top of the piano and stood. Shoving my hands in my pockets, I paced to the window where dusk cast the street in blue shadow.

"Just think about it, okay? Just think about it. My uncle, he did five to ten and got out. Now he's got three kids and a house and is doing just fine."

"Aw, jeez, Sal."

"Please. Just think about it."

I didn't respond.

"Constantine's going to some fancy breakfast tomorrow. Some lawyer's club thing. He'll see the DA there," Sal explained.

"And you think he can talk him up," I said, peering through the living room curtains as if I were a fugitive hiding out. I pulled back. I *was* hiding out, but from the world in general, from life, from reality. As long as I'd been in pursuit of Laura, of seeing her, I had purpose. Now, that goal was gone. She was going away. And from her own mouth I'd heard she didn't want to see me. That had been Laura speaking, not her parents.

"It's the perfect time, man. He asked me to come talk to you once more. To see if you'd change your mind."

I hung my head and stared at the floor.

"She's not going to do it, you know," Sal said. "She's not going to save you, if that's what you've been thinking. If anything, I wouldn't be surprised if she took the stand against you."

"You don't need to rub it in. I've been there every day this week," I growled. I turned to him. "Sometimes I think you believe I did it."

"Look, I don't care if you did it. But, no, I believe you when you said you didn't. I just don't want you getting run over by this thing, Greggie." His voice broke. I was taken aback. "It ain't fair, but lots of life ain't fair. And you've got to grab what you can. I trust Constantine."

"I know. So do I."

"So you think about it."

"I have the weekend," I said.

"It'll be all right, Greggie. Don't worry. No matter what happens, it'll be all right."

Dear Laura,
I'm so sorry you've been hurt by all this madness. If you'd only stay in town.

❧

Dear Laura,
I know we married quickly, but that doesn't change how I feel about you. . .

❧

Dear Laura,
Next week I meet with my lawyer to talk about offering a plea. I didn't kill Ivan. You must believe me. . .

Chapter Twenty-Two

I WANTED A DRINK so bad that Friday evening that I searched my house from top to bottom looking for a bottle. I found some bourbon under the sink, enough for a good tumbler full. I poured the golden liquid into the glass, breathed deep its woody aroma, and brought it to my lips.

But I didn't drink. I entered an epic battle that took place in a few seconds' time. A Goliath of want urged me to take that drink. But, weak as I seemed, I slew him. I threw the glass into the sink, shattering it and my desire.

I sat and penned letter after letter to Laura, crumpling them all and throwing them away. I needed her. I loved her. Yes, I loved her. A discovery.

I walked to a telephone stand and tried calling her. Just one more try. That's all. I'd leave it alone after this. Or so I told myself.

Five rings and I was about to click off, when—she answered! She, herself. Not her mother, not Gertrude. Gertrude was gone by then for the day, her mother occupied, her father reading the paper and drinking his own whiskey?

"Laura . . ." I didn't know what to say.

"Who is this?"

"It's Gregory." I swallowed. "Your husband."

"You shouldn't call."

"Have you stopped taking the drugs, Laura? You sound better, honey."

"I'm not taking anything, no."

"Where are they going to put you? You don't need to go anywhere. You're strong, Laura. You just need—" I wanted to say "me."

"I need some rest," she said, her voice warmer.

"I'm not drinking anymore," I rushed to add. "I'm sober."

"That's good, Gregory."

"I know you didn't do it, Laura—didn't kill Ivan. I thought you did at first, but not anymore."

Silence. Then, "Why did you think I was a murderess?" She sounded like a Reed then, someone unused to being thought of except in the most flattering tones.

"I don't! I don't think you are. I . . .I thought you had just cause to kill him. He was a—"

"I don't like to talk about it." Her voice quivered.

"He was horrible to you—a monster. He didn't love anyone." Not the way I loved her.

"Please, don't talk about him."

"I . . . I want to see you. Before you go. Before I . . ." Before I went to prison?

"I don't think that's wise," she said. "The doctor says I should stay away from anyone who upsets me."

"I won't talk about the case," I assured her, thinking she was referring to the murder charges against me.

"I wish they'd arrest someone for it and be done with it," she said.

She didn't know? They'd kept it from her?

"Laura, they have. They've arrested me."

❧❧

Her parents had told her nothing about my jeopardy. They'd put her under a doctor's care, let that doctor dope her up, and told her a lawyer would see to fixing everything. They told her that I would point the finger at her, and that they would protect her from me. They told her the marriage needed to be annulled, that I'd taken advantage. . .

It tumbled out, in tears and broken sentences, in self-accusations. Just as I had accused myself, she, too, railed against her lack of judgment—how could she have been so childish, she asked.

She wanted to know about my precarious state, she wanted to help. She couldn't stay on the phone. Her mother was coming upstairs. She told me she'd talk to me the next day—Saturday—and she thought she could get away on Sunday. She'd manage to get away somehow. She asked how she could get hold of me. I told her I'd be in our old place. It had a phone.

Now I could breathe again. I showered and shaved. I packed my few belongings, including the Mahler. I went to Sal's and gave him the good news.

"She'll testify for you?"

"We haven't talked about that yet," I said. "I'm meeting her Sunday."

"Sunday?" He scratched his chin. "Why not tonight? Why not tomorrow?"

"I think it's hard for her to get away."

He grimaced, his face conveying what I felt—that she should be racing to my defense.

"So you're going back to the new place?" he said at last.

"Yeah. She can call me there."

"And it's a heck of a lot nicer." He laughed. "I suppose you wouldn't mind a ride."

I grinned. "If you can spare one."

೭♋

I waited for her call. I waited that night, as I smelled the lingering scent of her perfume on the pillows.

I waited all the next day, as I hesitated to leave the apartment for fear I'd miss her.

I had a new cell, a better one, with light and luxuries and pretty pictures on the walls. But it was still a cell.

Was she deliberately torturing me? Had she never intended to call?

Maybe she'd let something slip, and her parents knew about our conversation. Maybe they'd taken her away already, slipping medicine into her tea.

Maybe she'd been cruelly playing with me, avenging herself on me, the second Ivan in her life.

No drink tempted me that day. First thing I'd done upon entering the place was empty all the bottles.

I drank a lot of coffee instead. I finished our meager supply of food—thinking of how poorly she'd cooked. How I longed for her burnt toast and tough roast.

I waited.

I thought I heard the phone ring once and rushed out of a doze on the living room sofa to the kitchen.

But it was a phone next door, its sound carried into our apartment through an open door as its owner raced to capture the caller when returning from an errand.

I thought of going to see her but didn't want to risk ruining her plans by tipping off her parents.

I waited.

That day felt longer than my stay in the jail cell. At least then, I'd been in a stupor, coming out from under the booze. Nothing cushioned this mental torture—no physical ache, no fog of alcohol. I had to suffer it straight up.

By evening's arrival, I was convinced I'd been played the fool again. That's when I wished I hadn't thrown out the liquor. That's when I was glad I had.

Damn you, Laura Reed.

Laura Silensky.

Even I didn't think of her as really married to me. Hah! Even I knew it was a charade, the whole damn thing.

I lit a cigarette and looked at last week's paper, still in the living room. But I couldn't focus. I turned on a record—but it hit a scratch, so I pulled it off. I looked out toward the south at the glimmering lights of the city. Renata would be singing Micaela tonight. If I lived in a normal world, I'd be going to see it, my girl on my arm.

With a sigh, I turned back to the room and turned on some lamps. I sat, my face in my hands, trying to figure out what to do.

Better to turn my thoughts to something productive, to my meeting with Constantine on Monday.

It made me sick to think of pleading guilty. But sicker still to think of being found guilty.

To hell with that. I'd have to take my chances. I wasn't guilty. The system was supposed to protect the innocent. It had to!

I couldn't think about it.

I stood, went to the piano and played.

My fingers found that Mahler again. I'd played it so much that week, I didn't need the music.

The fourth song, the one with the walking rhythm.

Die zwei blauen Augen . . . it began.

Hans. His eyes were crystal blue, so bright they looked like pale sapphires. *Die zwei blauen augen.*

I stopped, my hands hovering over the keys.

The Mahler—something in it was familiar . . .

I stood, racing to the shelves that held our music—my piano pieces and compositions, Laura's vocal scores. I threw one after the other on the floor, looking for it. Staff paper gave hope, then crushed it when I realized it wasn't the right piece. I ran to the bedroom—maybe it was there. I looked through boxes, more shelves. Nothing.

I went back to the living room, which was awash in music. The shelves were bare.

No, it wouldn't be there.

The police would have it—I remembered. Ivan's piece. They'd taken it because it had been inscribed to Laura—or so they assumed in the latest theory of the crime.

I hurried to the piano now, standing, eyes closed, remembering. My right hand found the opening bars of Ivan's song.

In the halls of Fontainebleau . . .

I slid on to the seat, my left hand filling in remembered chords and melodies, slowly at first as I let memory lead me.

I kept playing, trying not to think, just letting the music fill my mind. I was searching, searching for one passage.

There it was! There, hidden in an inner voice. Under the line "those of us who love more boldly"—there it was, the little snippet of Mahler, the dotted sixteenth pattern of *"Die zwei blauen Augen."*

I laughed. An inside joke—just the kind I played on Mrs. Sabataso when I hid tunes in the middle of other pieces, just the way I'd done for Laura when she'd turned her nose up at Tommy Dorsey songs. . .

Ivan had done the same! He'd hidden a message to "his only true love" in the middle of this piece, a little passage that said, "no matter what anyone thinks, you're the one for whom this piece was written."

My only true love. That had been the dedication.

Die zwei blauen Augen.

Hans.

Hans's blue eyes were his most striking feature. He could hide nothing there.

I stopped playing, dropping my hands between my knees, thinking, remembering.

Had Hans killed him after all? He had certainly acted guilty—running away.

But why couldn't I picture him as guilty—his fleeing was an act of fear, not of guilt. Gossip around the conservatory suggested he'd had to flee the police in Germany, that even his father in the *Freikorps* couldn't protect one of his lovers being carted off to a camp. He was deathly afraid of authorities.

Hans's problem was that he was afraid to stay and fight. It was hard to imagine that gentle-voiced soul fighting Ivan, even for the love of Renata.

I remembered what Renata had said, in her argument with Hans:

"Hans, you cry just like a girl. Here, take my handkerchief! *Basta!* I do not tolerate this. Do you think I would not find out? Do you think I do not know you betrayed me? *My only true love*—you disgust me!"

At the time, I'd assumed she was raging at him over the Kliegman, after finding out he'd traveled to New York to sing it for the prize committee.

But could it be another type of betrayal that had infuriated her? A humiliating betrayal, one that such a fiery woman would have trouble tolerating.

Ivan had loved Hans, his only "true" love. She'd sent Hans away, with a coldness I'd not known she'd possessed.

My heart now raced.

Not only had Ivan humiliated her—he'd been prepared to give his finest composition to Hans. She must have overheard—just like me. She'd gone to the rehearsal studios that night, too. How she must have felt listening to Ivan talking about her as if she was something he could bargain away!

She'd killed Ivan because he'd betrayed her, not with another woman, but with a man, a man he professed to love more than any other, a man to whom he would give his life's work, his greatest compositions.

A man who'd brought out of Ivan tenderness and great love—as evidenced by his style change in the winning composition, with its sweeping passages, its melancholy affection. That was the true Ivan, not the mean-spirited, climbing, devious *artiste*. Hans had found the core of him, a better person.

Ivan would have made Hans a star in America, and poor Renata would have been left as the spurned woman—spurned by her lover for another man. Oh, she wouldn't bear that. I knew it.

But she'd told me if she were to kill a man, she'd do it face-to-face. How had she said it—if I were to kill *a man* . . .

A man. She didn't consider Ivan a real man. Besides, she'd say anything to be free, anything.

I stood from the piano, knocking music to the floor. My heart pumped fast. I had to do something—what? Go to the police. I had nothing, nothing but two bars of music and an overheard conversation.

And Renata would be gone soon—tonight she sang Micaela in *Carmen*, and then she'd head to New York to start preparing for the Kliegman.

I had nothing, nothing! I groaned with frustration. No policeman would believe me. I had to prove it. Laudanum—she might still have it with her. Yes, another memory—Hans saying something about her bad back. She'd used it! She might still have it if she still had pain, as Hans had said. If I found it...

I ran to the kitchen phone, this time to place a call, not wait for one.

"Sal!" I said, glad he picked up and not one of his family members.

"She call?" he asked, eager.

"No, it's not that. Look, I hate to ask. Can you come get me? I got a theory . . ." I explained my suppositions. He sounded doubtful but was game to give it a chance.

"Be there in fifteen," he said.

Dear Renata, my darling,
I forgive you. How many times do I need to write it? I will come for you, my love.
And we will escape together. We will go to South America. I have booked passage.
I will take care of you. I do not hate you for what you have done. You know that I
only love you. My love for Ivan was a boy's fancy, nothing more. I thought I loved
him. But I love only you. I know we will be happy together. My heart is free now
that I know I can help you.
Your beloved,
Hans

Chapter Twenty-Three

"YOU GO ON IN, kiddo. I'll park and catch up."

"You know where the stage door is," I said, pointing. "I'll be in the dressing room. Wait for me in the hall."

I rushed in, the music of Bizet's most wonderful opera seeping through the floorboards.

The Fate theme tolled the ominous ending about to take place. I had to hurry.

I ran to the first dressing room, threw open the door, saw only men's clothing. I went to the next and the next, finally seeing her things—the fur she sometimes had worn to rehearsal, the musky scent of her perfume. On the vanity shelf were her purse and ticket. She was to catch an eleven p.m. train. She'd hardly have time to make it. I'd hardly have time to search before she appeared.

I pawed through her purse. Nothing. I opened her small case and rummaged through silks, nylons, jewelry. Nothing!

Wait—my hand grasped a cylindrical vial. I pulled it from the bottom. Disappointment crashed over me. Perfume. I threw it back in the bag, stopped to unlock a suitcase.

Again, I searched, sweat beading on my brow, my eyes desperate to see the bottle of poison. Please, please . . . she had to have it. She couldn't have thrown it away.

Each time my fingers grasped something new, I thought I'd found it—the key to my acquittal. Instead, I had absolutely nothing. I searched again, thinking I'd missed something. Still nothing. I went through pockets and felt linings. I looked for secret compartments in her purses, her jewelry case, her makeup box.

Nothing.

I stood, defeated. Shit—of course she would have thrown it away. Her willpower was fanatical. She'd not let an addiction stop her. She'd have done Ivan in and discarded the evidence as soon as the detective came calling—or as soon as she knew Hans was on to her.

I closed the case, stood up, defeated. Sal would be here soon. We'd go home, and I'd have nothing. I heard footsteps and turned, expecting to see my friend.

Instead, she stood there. Renata, in flaming red dress, a flower in her hair, diamonds at her throat. Despite myself, I laughed. She had been singing Micaela, yet she'd dressed as Carmen, deliberately, to upstage the singer who was the real Carmen in this concert version of the great show.

"Gregory, you came to see me off!"

She hurried in, grabbing a gray dress hanging from a peg.

"They are late—the José, he takes so much time with his aria. And the conductor—not so good as you. The tempos are too slow. I must change and leave. I will miss the bows, but nothing can be done. They already gave me their love—much applause, Gregory, after *Je dis que rien*. A taxi is supposed to come for me."

She stopped, as if realizing for the first time how odd it was that I was there.

"Why did you come to see me, Gregory?" She held the dress in front of her.

I had nothing to lose. "Laudanum—you used it, didn't you?"

She tilted her head to one side. "Why you ask such a question?"

Emboldened, I pressed her. "You had a bad back. From a fall. Isn't that what Hans said?"

"Hans," she whispered. "He says many things. Wrong things."

" I know you used it."

"You know nothing."

"Why did you kill him—because he didn't love you anymore? Because he loved someone else?"

Her lip curled into a sneer. "You know so little," she sneered.

"Because he loved Hans? Is that why? You couldn't stand that, could you? And he was giving the Kliegman piece to him—to a man!"

She said nothing, but her eyes blazed with fury.

"You must go."

I stepped forward, grabbing her by the arms, shaking her, forcing her to drop the dress she'd been holding. "Tell me, Renata! Tell me!"

She just stared at me, her dark eyes now like ice, as if she'd been misused by a man before and knew not to give her attacker satisfaction.

When I stopped, she whispered. "You think you can make me afraid? You? When I was a little girl in *Sicilia*, I hid under a bed while men killed my family. I have never been afraid since then."

"Then tell me, Renata. If you're not afraid, tell me! Tell me what you did with the laudanum."

She said nothing. Her breath brushed my face. She stared. She dared me with that glance to hit her. She dared me to do what she expected all bad men to do. And she wouldn't care. She'd walk away, bruised, but she'd never admit to this crime.

What would unlock her secret?

"Leave her alone!" A low voice came from the doorway, then a hand clamped on my shoulder and pulled me away. I tumbled into the vanity chair.

Hans stood there. Finally, he'd decided to fight for something. He held a gun and waved it at me.

"Leave her alone!" he shouted. He looked at her. "Get your things together. This is over. I will save you."

"She's a killer!" I said. "She'll do it again if she doesn't get what she wants. She has the laudanum somewhere—"

"She does not have the poison," Hans said, staring at Renata. "I have it."

Renata took a step back. But she said nothing to Hans. She stared at him as she'd stared at me—as if seeing what he would do, what he would say, and not caring.

"Do not worry, my love. I left it in my apartment. The police will find it there and think I am the one they seek."

For a second, her hand fluttered to her chest. She was relieved!

"They will not seek. They have their criminal." She gestured toward me, still crumpled on the floor.

Hans shook his head. "I thought about it very much. I thought—when will they come after you, a foreigner, an Italian, the enemy, and me, the enemy also? And I know we must leave. I have left a note, my darling."

"What is the matter with you? They have their murderer!" Two quick strides forward, and she slapped him. "*Stupido! Stupido!*"

But I knew why Hans had done it. By planting the evidence, he was binding Renata to him. And by stating her guilt in front of me, a witness, he was sealing her fate.

He did not shrink from her abuse. If anything, it seemed to stiffen his resolve.

≈୨৯

"We can begin another life. Away from here. Far away. Under a different sky."

"Is that why you left the note? To trap me? To make me so I must go with you?" She shook her head. "*Stupido,*" she repeated.

It was as if I wasn't in the room. Only he and Renata, his precious love. I wondered if I could crawl to safety. But I wanted to hear this, to memorize the confession.

"You ask the impossible," Renata continued. "You know that."

"Renata," Hans begged, his voice sounding wild and intense. "You are all I have."

"I no longer love you*!*" Renata spat at him. "Don't you understand? I no longer love you!"

"*Non, ce coeur n'est plus a toi,*" Carmen sang from the stage above us. "*En vain tu dis: 'Je t'adore!' Tu n'obtiendras rien, non, rien de moi, Ah! c'est en vain.*"

I thought I could slip out unnoticed and started to inch toward the door. In his distress, Hans was waving the gun this way and that as he spoke. It was a treacherous crawl.

"I know what you did," he said. "I know you did not mean to do it. You were angry."

Renata laughed. "Of course I did not mean to do it. You are so idiotic, my dear, so—what is the word—naive."

"We were happy in Fontainebleau," Hans said. "When I met you there—"

"You mean where you and Ivan were together at the music festival?"

The chorus sang of the victories of the bull ring in the distance, their muted celebrations sounding as out of place in the hallway below the stage as Bizet intended them to sound in contrast to the confrontation between José and Carmen.

From the corner of my eye, I saw Sal coming down the hall. I shook my head at him. He stopped and approached quietly.

Then he did something only he would think of, the rascal. He stepped back, and yelled, "That's right, officer, this way—something funny's going on!"

Hans's voice, shaky with fear, shouted to the hall: "Go away! I have a gun!"

"Give *me* the gun, Hans," I said, my hand outstretched. "You don't want nobody getting hurt."

Renata laughed. "He won't give you the gun," she said, not taking her eyes off Hans. "He is too *stupido* for that."

"I know you are afraid, my love," Hans said. "I will protect you."

"It was a mistake," she said, staring at Hans with a mixture of hatred and pity. "You are so blind, you don't understand. It was a mistake! I didn't mean to kill Ivan."

Hans said nothing. I said nothing. Had she meant to kill herself? Someone else. . .

"I meant to kill *you!*" she said to Hans. "Ivan was killed by mistake!" Renata spat the words as if she still wished Hans dead, and it was clear she was happy to have an audience for this humiliation of her former lover.

Hans seemed to shrink before my eyes. Dressed in a rumpled gray suit, his shoulders slumped, his mouth hung open, and his blue eyes filled with unshed tears. I thought he would cry.

Renata moved toward Hans, her hips swaying provocatively, her voice low and sultry. What was she doing? I crouched, ready to strike at the right moment, to grab the gun.

"I put the laudanum in *your* drink! You had the cola, too. You had it in your bag. You did everything like him. You wanted him to love you more, eh? So you drank what he drank. But I put the poison in the wrong drink! Ivan took it by mistake!" she murmured, as if attempting to murder

Hans was a form of seduction. "And if you had told the *poliziotto* I killed Ivan, I would have told them you did it. I will still tell them that. Even with your little note and the poison. You think you are so smart. But who will they believe — the German, the barbarian . . . or the poor woman he has betrayed with another man? I found Ivan's letters to you from Fontainebleau. I will show them to the *poliziotto*."

I made a move forward, but Hans waved the gun at me. "Don't!" he shouted.

"It was so easy," Renata said, as if nothing had interrupted her. "Both of you drinking so much of that cola. The bottle was there, open on the piano. But I was the *stupido,* thinking I was ridding myself of you when it was Ivan who'd left that room!"

Now she laughed at herself.

"Why should I kill *him,* eh? He would give me everything — staying here, singing his works, money. Everything."

Silence, and then her voice softer but still bitter. "And to think I would have given up everything for you. Because I loved you."

She leaned into him, rubbing her hands up and down his arms. I thought she intended to take the gun away from him this way, seducing it from him.

Breathing in her hair, he whispered, "I still love you." But his voice sounded unsure, as if he were convincing himself.

Renata couldn't stop herself. She pulled back and cursed in Italian. "And him — you loved him, too!"

The chorus sang *"Victoire"* above us, masking Hans's soft reply. *Ich liebe dich.*

"Ou vas tu?" José sang.

"Laisse-moi!" Carmen answered. *Let me go.*

"For *you* Ivan wrote that piece," continued Renata. "I heard it all! And I saw you," she said lowly, measuring out every word, "I saw you and Ivan — embracing."

She paused.

"I couldn't watch! I ran upstairs and saw the bottle — it was so easy to pour the laudanum into your drink. So easy. And when you made love to me later, I thought, why does he not die? Why is he still alive, still tormenting me? I only stayed because I thought you knew I'd done it."

Hans said nothing. The music of the opera filtered down. The chorus was singing, *"Viva! viva! la course est belle! Viva! sur le sable sanglant, Le taureau, le taureau s'elance!"* Glorying in the blood of the bullfight, their march-like music was cut short by the ominous Fate theme. *I have lost my soul for you,* José sang.

"I would have let the police believe that I killed him," Hans whimpered more to himself than to her. "I thought you'd killed him because you loved me so much."

"It's over," Renata said, staring into Hans's eyes, "I will be free." Her hands slid up his arms again and toward the hand holding the gun.

Did she intend to take it from him? Or did she intend to have it end here, just as it ended for Carmen outside the bullring when José would not let her go?

Hans stared, pain evident in his wide eyes, shining now with unshed tears. Who had he really loved? Ivan? Renata? Had he latched on to her when his father's troops had carted off another lover—a man, I now imagined—to a camp? Had he resisted his love for Ivan, trying to turn it to Renata? Was he trying to prove that love…to himself?

I didn't know. I only knew that as I stood to help her grab the gun, a loud pop sounded in the room. A sound like a car backfiring, filling the small space, stinging our ears. The smell of gunshot.

And then silence.

"No." My voice.

She shuddered. She stared at him, her eyes holding nothing but contempt. She tried again for the gun. Again he shot. Again she flinched and trembled.

I saw her arm move one more time, as if she would still get the weapon from him. I reached out.

"No, Renata, no," I murmured, in slow motion now. And, yes, he fired again. This time her lip lifted in a sneer, as if this was the outcome she'd desired. To see the dead look of horror in his eyes as he killed her.

She fell back into my arms, a dark stain on her red dress. She lay still. Her eyes continued to stare, dead to the world.

"Goddammit!" Sal cried, entering the room. We both grabbed the gun from Hans, now stunned into motionless shock. Sal pushed him to the floor and held the weapon on him.

"Stay put, you murdering Nazi!" He looked at me. "Go call the police."

The chorus began the familiar refrain from the Toreador song.

Hans sobbed, his right hand touching Renata's hair, stroking it.

Like a tolling bell, the Fate theme sounded.

Dear Mr. Solensky:

The Reed family has asked me to inform you that you should not contact their daughter again. She is under the care of a doctor and must not be disturbed. My firm will handle the annulment of your marriage, which was clearly made under duress and without proper informed consent on her part.

If you do not stay away from Miss Reed, I will be forced to contact the authorities.

Please call or write my office with the name of your legal representative.

Sincerely,

Thomas N. Small, Esq.

Chapter Twenty-Four

MY NIGHTMARES of killing Ivan Roustakoff were over, replaced now by dreams in which I still had a loving wife, and my future with her was as bright as the sun.

I awoke sweating, my hands cramped from clenching them into fists.

I'd only been asleep a few hours. By the time the police had come, taken Sal's and my statements, booked Hans, taken Renata's body away, and let us go, it was nearly four in the morning. Sal made sure Constantine showed up for all this, which meant it probably took longer as he got charges dropped against me. That was a blessing.

Patting me on the back, he'd said, "No more sleepless nights for you, my friend!"

But this was before I'd wandered home—back to the apartment on University Parkway—and before I'd found the letter waiting for me there, hand delivered, from what I could tell while I'd been out, and before I awoke on a Sunday that was to change all my Sundays for four years hence.

When I received the letter from her lawyer—the young man she'd danced with at the Brentwood Club so long ago—I laughed. That was probably why she'd not called. They were tightening their grip. They'd pull her back to childhood with more strength or power than I had to drag her into an adult life with me.

And it probably wouldn't matter to them that I was cleared of murder. If anything, that would make them all the more zealous in the pursuit of their goal. The only reason Amanda Reed had supported and encouraged our union was because she thought her daughter had committed murder and our marriage could protect her!

A mother who thought that—was that love?

So when I awoke at nearly noon, aching in body and spirit, wishing I could get rid of the scent of her perfume, I knew damn well it was over. There had been a slim chance I'd hang on to my wife when the murder case was hanging out there over both of us. Now there was no chance in hell. I wondered if she'd gone to the sanitarium already, the rest home, or whatever it was called.

I brushed my teeth and washed up. I figured I'd start collecting the few things of mine left in this place and get going. I'd give the letter from Lawyer Small to Lawyer Constantine and let them do what was required. I'd not force Laura to stay with me. That was something Ivan would have done—just for the pleasure of seeing her squirm.

Ivan. He'd loved Hans best of all.

It didn't shock me that Ivan loved another man. At the music conservatory, those affairs weren't uncommon.

Had his sister known?

And poor Hans—now without Renata, to whom he'd transferred all his affection after the aborted affair with Ivan.

As I gathered my things, I collected my thoughts. What would I do now?

I was adrift. Hans might be languishing in a cell, but I was still tainted by the scandal, the scars on my hands now emblematic of a deeper mutilation. I was revealed for the imposter I was—someone who thought he could move in these rarified circles, but who belonged, more comfortably, playing popular tunes for the Brentwood crowd, the hired help like Rufus or Gertrude, but nothing more. My father had been right. All of that stuff was nothing but lah-di-dah.

Even the Brentwood job would be hard to retrieve. I placed a call to the club manager and eventually convinced him to put me on the schedule again. I'd change my billing to Greg Stiles.

But it wouldn't be enough to pay my bills, especially the legal ones, which I could hardly begrudge since that lawyer had gotten me out of jail.

I felt dried up. I wanted to stop time and reset the clock. I didn't want to be Gregory Silensky anymore.

Before I left the apartment, I allowed myself two pleasures. I sat down to play the Mahler cycle again, humming the vocal line, occasionally speaking it, or lustily shouting it, going through all four songs now with a sense of victory. Thanks, Gustav, for the clue, I wanted to yell at the end.

The end—it was an apt denouement to my tale. The lover, reconciled to his loss, walks along the street where a Linden tree stands. All is good, he sings. All—*Lieb' und Leid und Welt und Traum* – love and sorrow and the world and dreams.

Was everything good? I wanted to think so. I wanted to think that even pain served a higher purpose.

My second pleasure was turning on the radio—it was a new model with a great tuner and tubes that seemed to heat up faster than most—to listen to the Sunday Philharmonic concert. I sank into a comfortable chair, my bags at the ready to march out after the concert, to find my own street with a Linden tree, and lit a smoke.

I closed my eyes. I listened as the announcer came on. I sank into a happy dream-like stage. I waited.

And then . . .

The whole world changed.

I sat up straight as the announcer interrupted the broadcast.

Pearl Harbor had been bombed.

❧❧

"You hear?"

"Yeah, Ma and the girls are listening right now," Sal said.

I'd called him as soon as I'd had a good sense of what was happening. Pearl Harbor.

Laura's brother—he was there.

"What's gonna happen now?" Sal asked.

"You and me and about a million other guys have a new job, buddy," I said.

He laughed, but it was a low, nervous chuckle. "Yeah. You gonna sign up?"

"I'd rather do that than have 'em come get me." I'd had enough of men of authority taking me away.

"Wait a sec. . ." He listened as another bulletin came on. "Go ahead. What were you saying?"

"I'm saying that you and me—look, I'll call in the morning. We can make plans, okay? We can do it together."

That seemed to reassure him. "Yeah, yeah. Sounds good to me, pal."

We hung up. I listened some more, lighting another cigarette and pacing.

I kept thinking of that spring afternoon when I'd played for Rick Reed's graduation. He'd looked all fresh and eager in his bright white uniform, his parents so proud. He was on a ship out there. God—what was its name? I'd not paid attention. Laura must be worried sick.

I sank back into a chair. She already was worried sick, what with the investigation, her parents' meddling. Crap—this would make it worse.

Dammit. She was still my wife. I wouldn't let her suffer alone. We weren't annulled yet.

I grabbed a jacket, scarf, and hat and strode out into the afternoon, walking north toward their neighborhood. I passed a woman, rushing down the street, clutching her coat closed with gloved hands.

"It's awful, isn't it?" she said as she hurried by. I nodded.

When I reached the Reed household, I thought of going to the back door. Maybe Gertrude would be there and have pity on me.

But I squared my shoulders and knocked at the front. If they wouldn't let me in, at least I'd tell them their daughter was unequivocally in the clear on the Roustakoff murder.

To my amazement, Laura answered. She looked good—clear-eyed and calm.

"I . . . I heard about Pearl Harbor," I began.

"We don't know much yet," Laura said as if there had been no distance between us. "Mother is very upset. Rick is on the *Arizona*."

"Is there anything I can do?" Before she could answer, I gave her my other news. "Ivan's killer has been caught. It was Renata."

She sucked in her breath and shook her head. "Poor woman."

I gave her the briefest summary. She looked down and nodded as I told the tale, saying little, occasionally asking a question.

"Come in," she said when I finished, opening the door all the way. I stepped into the foyer, and she waited for me to hand her my jacket, hat, and scarf.

"Mother!" her voice echoed in the hallway. "Gregory is here. We'll make some sandwiches."

It was as if I were an old friend.

As we passed the living room, I could see Mr. and Mrs. Reed, still as statues, pale as ghosts. Amanda Reed sat in a wing chair by the front window, a handkerchief to her mouth, and her head turned toward the window as if she expected to see her son returning home any second. Jack Reed stood by the fireplace, drink in one hand, arm on the mantelpiece, staring at the silent radio.

"We don't know anything," Amanda said when she saw Laura.

Laura strode to the corner where she turned on the radio. "Why'd you turn it off?"

Jack Reed answered, his voice defeated and tremulous. "It was disturbing Mother."

We listened for a long time to the reports pouring in. Nothing was good.

Jack Reed noticed me.

"What's he doing here?"

Laura answered. "Renata killed Ivan Roustakoff. She was his fiancée."

"Oh . . ." That was a distant story now, replaced by this greater drama.

The phone rang. No one went to get it.

Mrs. Reed started to weep.

I ran to the kitchen to grab the phone.

"Jack?" A man's voice asked.

"Uh, no, this is Gregory." And for explanation, I reached for the title that still applied. "His son-in-law."

"This is Jason Witson. I'm a friend of the family. I was just calling to see if they'd heard anything yet, from Rick."

"Nothing. I guess we better keep the line free," I said.

"Sure, I understand," Jason said. "Would you ask them to call us if they hear anything? We are quite fond of the Reeds."

"Yes, I will."

I went back to Mister Reed and reported on the conversation.

"Thank God," the older man said. "When the phone rang, I thought..."

From now on, any time the phone rang or there was a knock at the door, they'd wonder if it was bad news.

They spent all afternoon like that, hoping for the phone to ring and yet terror-stricken when it did. Several friends called. The minister from the church also rang in. I answered every one while Laura stayed with her parents, listening to the radio. After taking the first call, it had become my job.

As shadows fell, Laura left her mother and went to the kitchen where she prepared sandwiches and coffee. I wasn't sure what to do. I wanted to ask her about the annulment. I'd thought—before the news on the radio—of even asking her to postpone that. I couldn't now.

I watched her, intent on her task, smoothing butter over bread, slicing ham and laying that on lettuce. It was as if I needed to memorize it. Even with her short hair, she was still beautiful, the blue light of oncoming twilight making her skin alabaster, her lips pursed in concentration, her green eyes ablaze with worry.

She said nothing to me, and, in her silence, I felt rebuked.

I had treated her like Ivan had—perhaps a gentler version of the lothario. But a user all the same—taking her because she thought offering herself to me was what she was expected to do, marrying her because of what that marriage gave me. Hell, I'd even come close to betraying our fresh vows with Renata. This she wouldn't know, but she probably guessed. I was no different than the man who'd mistreated her.

"I'm sorry," I said at last.

She paused but said nothing as she put the last piece of bread on top of a sandwich.

Before she took the sandwiches to her parents, I spoke again.

"I'll probably join the Army."

She paused at the door, plates in each hand. Did she blink? Close her eyes? Sigh? I couldn't tell.

"Could you open the door?" she asked.

One more hour. Two. Three. It was dark. Laura gathered the plates and cups and took them back to the kitchen. The Reeds didn't acknowledge me but didn't chase me out.

Now we longed for the phone to ring. It hadn't rung in hours.

And, as if in response to these desperate unvoiced wishes, it did.

I ran to the kitchen.

"Reed residence," I said after lifting the receiver. "Gregory Silensky. Laura's husband."

Time was suspended in that moment, and the line crackled with faraway static.

"It's Rick," I said to Laura as she placed plates in the sink. "From

Hawaii."

From the living room, I heard Amanda Reed cry.

Laura took the phone. She cried, too, tears of joy. "Yes, yes," she said. And "Oh, Rick."

Then Jack came into the kitchen and Amanda, too, and they grabbed the phone in quick succession, repeating Laura's words in variations. "Oh dear. Good lord. Thank God."

"The Arizona was sunk," Jack Reed explained after the call. "But Richard was on leave, so he wasn't onboard."

"What happens now?" asked Amanda Reed, her handkerchief still clutched in her hand.

"He will be reassigned. And await orders," said Mister Reed. "And then..."

Laura stepped forward. "We should call all the others—the people who called."

"I'll help," I offered.

After giving me the family address book to look up the numbers, Laura went to the sink and washed the dishes. I placed the calls, one after another, quick messages of hope—Rick called, he's all right.

Amanda and Jack Reed went to bed. Laura took her father's keys and told me she'd drive me home.

Once on the road, she didn't hesitate. She drove right past our University Place apartment and straight on into town to my Potomac Street home.

I started to tell her I'd left a bag at our apartment but thought better of it. She'd send it to me, or I'd pick it up the next day. It hardly mattered.

At my home, we sat in front of my house waiting for the other to say something. A thousand "if only's" floated between us, creating a river too deep to cross.

If only I'd met you now, sober and staring at the abyss.

But neither of us could speak. I thought she shook her head ever so slightly, as if arguing with herself. But she said nothing. I did lean over and quickly kiss her on the cheek, a chaste farewell, but one filled with tenderness all the same.

1942

Dearest,

If you sign the papers and return them to my lawyer, that is sufficient. In the meantime, I am grateful for your letters, which are a welcome thread to the "outside" world. All I seem to be capable of doing is waiting . . .

There are many injuries of one sort or another here, and I feel the need to hide my hands — they are a mark of carelessness, not heroism. The other men might think I "earned" them in some way.

My sacrifice — a future as a concert pianist — seems small compared to that of others. It seems so silly here, to have a dream of anything except reprieve.

I explain that my hands were injured years ago, and I always say it was my fault. That puts an end to it. I don't want pity.

I'm tired and hungry most of the time. I'm sick of lots of things. But not of hearing from you, my darling. I hope you don't mind if I call you that. Other men have sweethearts outside. Let us pretend you are mine.

Write again soon. Write every day. Every hour. When many letters come at once, it feels like Christmas morning . . .

Yours,

Gregory

Chapter Twenty-Five

SAL AND I ENLISTED the week after Pearl Harbor was bombed. His family went nuts, his sisters weeping and hugging him, his mom just quiet. She gave us both a big send-off dinner with lots of pasta and special dishes her "Sallie" loved. It was something of a somber meal, so I livened things up by playing the piano after, getting the girls to join in singing. Poor Brigitta — she kept her hand on my shoulder.

I was still a married man, of course, but that would end soon enough. I wasn't going to fight Laura on the annulment. I'd begun to see the wisdom of it, especially after the Sunday at her house. She'd been so serene and still, despite the unbearable worry about her brother. She was on the mend, and having me as her husband was a reminder of unhealthier times.

Sal and I thought we'd be in the thick of it right away — Franklin D. made it sound like we'd be fighting the instant we signed up. But we were sent to training camp in Georgia for a long time, then to England, and then to Northern Africa and Italy.

All the time I was gone, she wrote to me. It started out slow, with us taking care of the papers for the annulment. And then it became regular, and I realized a couple things along the way — I was getting to know the real Laura, not that dream I'd married, but a living, breathing individual who had fears and thoughts and goals; and I was still in love with her.

Dear Gregory,
I'm sorry to hear of Sal's injury. Does this mean he will go home?

We had some sad news last week. Tom Small, the young lawyer who handled our annulment, was killed somewhere in the Pacific. Mother says his family is devastated. He was their only child. He was interested in me for a little while. And although I never returned his feelings, I have to say his death has shaken me a great deal. It makes me feel I should have tried harder to like him. I'm taking some food over to them later. Mother made a few things for them. Gertrude's no longer with us. She is now working in a factory. Mother has decided that she and I can make do for the duration. I've learned how to cook at last.

I've also been singing. A small group of Peabody students and I get together to sing choral music — some hymns and religious pieces, as well as a few patriotic numbers and some Mozart. We've sung for a Red Cross fundraiser.

Mother is hardly able to concentrate since the news of Tom's death. We've not heard from Rick in quite a while.
All my best wishes,
Laura

&
Dear Laura,
First, I'm awfully sorry to hear about Tom. Although I didn't know him, losing any friend is hard.

Sal is on his way home now, a hero to his family even though his leg got mashed up in a training accident. To his credit, he actually tried to get them to let him stay. He says he didn't want me to be alone. He has this notion that I'm clumsy and will end up shooting myself before I have a chance to train my gun on someone else.

I'm glad to hear you're singing. You have a beautiful voice. When I get back, I'd be happy to accompany you. Are you still studying with Madame G.?

The food here is just awful. I never thought I'd say it, but I miss your cooking.

Just kidding, hon. I'm sure you're a great cook now. Maybe you can make something for me when I get back. . . .
&
Dear, dear Gregory,
I took some cookies to your friend's house. His mother told me he's due home in another week, so I was too early to see him. But I plan on interrogating him when he is back, to make sure all you enlisted men are being treated well.

Rick called us! He sounded so good. The call was short, and Dad wasn't home, so he was very disappointed to have missed the call. Mother almost missed it, too, but she came in from the store in time to get a few words in to him. Mostly she tells him to take care of himself!

She and I have been helping out at the Red Cross and a church program that sends packages to our men. I will make up a package just for you.

A few more men from our set have been killed or wounded. One, a boy from a *family my mother knows, will never walk again. His mother can't wait to see him, though, so it's a mixed blessing.*

I'll sign off saying what my mother is telling Rick every chance she gets: take care of yourself.

All best wishes,

Laura

PS More sad news – I enclose a newspaper clipping about poor Hans, who hanged himself in his cell last week.

༄

Dearest Laura,

Thank you so much for the cookies which arrived in good shape due to the excellent packaging. They were very tasty! You're right – you have learned to cook! I shared some with a couple pals, who thought you must have been cooking all your life.

All the other things in the box were greatly appreciated, too. Clean socks and writing paper are always needed. I also hope to start reading the book you sent. It seems like we do spend a lot of time waiting for things to happen.

That is sad news about Hans' suicide, but he was a sad case to begin with. I suspected he wouldn't last long after Renata died. He'd lost everything, after all – Ivan, Renata, his future, even his country and family. It stops me in my tracks to think about it. Even over here, with so much danger in the future, I still believe there is one. I see guys who give up and it's a frightening sight. I don't ever want to be that way. . .

༄

Dear Gregory,

Since I haven't heard from you in weeks, I know you must have shipped out. Now I'm the one worrying like crazy, hearing news of fighting here and there and wondering – is he in Africa, is he in Italy?

I'm normally not so good about making church every Sunday, but I've been going each week and saying prayers for you and my brother and all the boys we know. I even say a prayer for a girl from our set who joined up to be a nurse. Can you imagine? She'd already scandalized her family by going to nursing school in the first place. Now she's off to some camp. I have to admit I envy her. I think it would be easier to be in the thick of it than to be waiting. Of course, that's easy for me to say, isn't it? I'm sure you would disagree.

It's just that the waiting to hear is torture. Sometimes I try to reconcile myself to the worst news, until I realize this is a tremendous breach of good faith, that all I'm doing is trying to avoid disappointment. Trouble will find you soon enough, Gertrude used to say.

Sometimes I think it would be nice to work in a factory like she is doing.

But I've doubled my efforts to work at what little I can do. I go to Red Cross and Junior League meetings all the time, and my little chorale is booked into the New Year, performing for all sorts of groups doing good things, mostly for you soldiers.

At one of these events, they had a dance band. They played I'll Be Seeing You and I cried.

151

Please, write, darling, as soon as you can.

ᴄᴇ ᴄᴐ

Dear Laura,

A half dozen letters from you – what a treat that was! I could hardly wait to read them all. We've seen some action, but I've managed to do okay. It's a funny thing, but the first time isn't as bad as all that. Sure, I was scared. But it's the second and third and fourth times that get worse. You have the feeling your luck might be running out.

Some of the boys were hurt terribly. I thought of Sal and how lucky he was just to have the gimpy leg. He's written me some pretty funny letters. He seems to be in good spirits.

I'm so happy to hear you're singing. I can just imagine it. I like to lie back and remember the sound of your voice. You have no idea what comfort that gives me. When I get home, I'll play for all your lessons and practices, if you want.

ᴄᴇ ᴄᴐ

Dear Gregory,

I received two letters from you today! And the last one was dated just a couple weeks ago. So I have been humming to myself all day, absolutely giddy with happiness. I'm happy, too, because Rick is coming home. Like your friend Sal, he was hurt, and it looks like he has a ticket out of everything. It's strange to feel relieved at a loved one's injuries, but that's exactly how we felt when we got the news. He was burned and can't really use his left arm or leg well. He will have to go to a medical center for some therapy of some sort. But I'm looking forward to taking him.

I forgot to tell you that I did, at last, go to see your friend Salvatore. He had me laughing the entire visit. I took him some fruit and felt pretty foolish when I noticed a big basket of fruit on their dining table. I'd forgotten you told me they owned a market. He says to say hello. I hope you are still getting letters from him. He said to tell you that his sister Brigitta married some fellow who got sent off within a month of their wedding and was killed. It sounded just ghastly.

Yes, I would love it if you'd play for me when you return. But I'm not sure I'll go back to school. I'm not sure what I want to do, actually. Mother thinks I should consider teaching, but I don't think I have a gift for that at all. I still think of Alice – she's the girl who became a nurse – and wish I'd followed her path. She's doing well, by the way, and sends her families regular reports that are read out loud at church. I suppose they think a report from a nurse won't be as unsettling as those from actual soldiers.

Do write soon. Write every chance you get so I know you're safe.

ᴄᴇ ᴄᴐ

Dear Laura,

So much has happened by now. I know you've heard the news. Even better news is this – I'm coming home. I have enough points to earn a trip back to the good old U.S.A. Some fellows aren't so lucky and will be shipped to the Pacific.

I'm glad to hear your brother is doing better and is not so down any more.

I'm sure you help lift his spirits. Having suffered a bad burn myself, I'd be happy to do what I can to help him through the pain.

I don't know what my exact schedule will be, but I was wondering if I could let you know when I'm returning, and perhaps we could meet. . . .

❧

Dear Gregory,

Oh, darling – if you didn't tell me when you were getting home, I'd be so angry with you! Of course, I want to know. I want to know every detail. I will be there, come snow, sleet, or rain. I will be there!

Epilogue

AS THE TRAIN approached Baltimore, it slowed. Like the rest of the soldiers and sailors in the car, I didn't wait for the train to stop. Standing, I grabbed my duffel bag and bent forward to peer out the windows, my throat growing dry as I watched the skyline come into view.

Home at last. I saw the back alleys of houses pressed up against the tracks. I smelled the sulfurous air of a summer afternoon. Shit, I felt like I was going to cry. Not now.

Reflexively, I patted my pockets looking for a cigarette. A tall, skinny seaman noticed and offered a smoke. But when I put it to my lips, my damn hands shook too much to light it.

"Here," the seaman said, flicking a match to the cigarette's tip.

Nodding my thanks, I looked through blurred eyes at the hazy sky hanging over the rooftops of Baltimore. I saw the neat rows of homes with their marble steps, a factory spitting out smoke, a baseball field crammed up against a red brick schoolhouse. Smoothing my hair under my cap, I wondered what she'd look like. She'd sent a photo a year ago, but she said her hair was a little longer now. I didn't care.

My problem, I realized in that final push toward war's end, was grasping and keeping. Things just didn't stay in these big scarred hands of mine. I had to learn that skill. I wanted to learn it with her.

Slow, slower, a crawl now, the platform in sight . . . with a final jerk, the train stopped, and the conductors called out, "Bal'mer! Watch your step! Bal'mer!"

But I didn't need to hear. As the train hissed to a stop, I smelled it, the city of my birth—a faint whiff of the harbor's sea salt, the sour smell of a factory, the odor of exhaust and smoke, of people who worked for a living. Of home. Crushing my cigarette out, I hoisted my bag over my shoulder and left. I heard a soldier up ahead laugh, another grouse, "Keep moving, fellows."

≈⁓

Laura!

"Laura, Jesus, Laura..."

She was laughing and crying at the same time. The place was mobbed with people, and more than a few couples were doing just what we were—

hugging and kissing.

"Gregory," she whispered, her eyes closed.

"Let me look at you." I stepped back, still holding her hands.

She was more slender, and she looked taller. No, she just stood straighter. She stared me right in the eyes. She didn't look afraid anymore. What did I look like to her?

"I've planned a meal for you," she said. "At home."

My heart skipped a beat as I remembered our apartment. But, no, of course, she didn't mean that.

"Mother's making dessert. Father's . . ." She looked down.

"Yes?"

"He's gone. He had a heart attack a few weeks ago."

"You should have told me!" I'd talked to her once, when we had arrived in New York.

"No, I didn't want to dampen your happiness," she said. She linked her arm in mine and pointed to my bag. I hoisted it on my shoulder and we started walking to the front doors.

"I'm so, so sorry," I said.

"He lived to see Rick come home and some other boys we know."

"How's your mother taking it?"

"As well as can be expected."

"Is Rick home?"

"He's at a medical center in Western Maryland. I'll take you to see him this weekend."

We stepped out into the sunshine in front of Penn Station. Cars honked, and taxis crammed for spots. I wanted to hug everybody in sight.

"Are you all going to be all right?" I asked, pushing my cap back.

"We'll manage. Mother might sell the house."

"I . . . I can help."

She smiled. "Thanks. But we don't need it. I can handle it with her."

❧❧

Do I need to tell you that I was hopelessly in love with her, that I was perched between passion and fear, hoping she'd love me back, afraid she wouldn't?

As she took me to her house, I felt . . . on top of the world. I was home, alive, safe. I had a great girl to love if she'd love me. I had a lot of pain to forget and to get through still. But I was alive and bathed in the grace of God.

All is good, all is good. Love and sorrow. And the world, and dreams!
Alles! Alles! Lieb' und Leid, Und Welt, und Traum!

Notes from the Author

The title of this book is from a poem by Heinrich Heine — *Der Tod das ist die kühle Nacht*. It has been set to music by Johannes Brahms.

The idea for this novel came to me more than ten years ago, and it has gone through several iterations over the years. First I set it as a contemporary story but quickly realized the characters and circumstances required an older stage. The 1940s immediately came to mind, a time when class distinctions were more acute and when a woman like Laura Reed would have fewer choices about her future. I chose the months immediately preceding the attack on Pearl Harbor figuring this time period would set up a sense of foreboding in readers' minds, who knew what real history would play out by the end of this fictional tale.

I wanted the story to be noir-like and dramatic — like a mystery opera.

All the music pieces mentioned in this novel are ones I love. For those who'd like to listen to them, I can make some specific recommendations. The EMI Classics recording of *Turandot* features Birgit Nilsson, Franco Corelli and Renata Scotto — who could ask for more? Scotto's Liu is heartbreaking. My favorite recording of Mahler's *Songs of a Wayfarer* is another EMI Classics with Janet Baker singing. Even though these songs are from a male point of view, I prefer Dame Baker's warm voice to that of the master of German *Lied*, Dietrich Fischer-Dieskau, maybe because hearing them sung by a woman makes them genderless and more universal. As for *Carmen*, I own the Maria Callas/Nicolai Gedda version (another EMI Classics!), but — I hope this doesn't offend music lovers everywhere — it leaves me lukewarm, if not cold. I'd love reader suggestions on the ultimate *Carmen* recording! For the Schubert songs mentioned in the novel, Fischer-Dieskau is magnificent, of course. And for the Debussy and Fauré, I have yet to come across an artist who interprets them as wonderfully as my late voice teacher at Peabody Conservatory — Flore Wend. French art songs are often over-sung when they require a light, almost ironic touch; her performances will leave you understanding what the composer must have intended. Alas, her recording of Debussy's songs is out of print. If you're ever in the Baltimore area, Peabody Conservatory's library might have a copy. It's worth a listen.

As always, I want to thank my family for supporting my writing habit, especially my husband whose faith in me never falters.

About Libby Sternberg

Libby Sternberg is the author of several young adult mysteries, the first of which (*Uncovering Sadie's Secrets*) was an Edgar finalist. Her first historical women's fiction, *Sloane Hall,* is a Five Star/Gale release, a retelling of *Jane Eyre* praised by Bronte experts. Writing under the name Libby Malin, she is the author of several humorous women's fiction books, one of which has been optioned for film. Before becoming a novelist, she studied voice, earning both bachelor's and master's degrees from Peabody Conservatory of Music.

Visit her website at www.LibbySternberg.com

IF YOU ENJOYED THIS BOOK....please, consider posting a review on Amazon or other book sites.

Follow the story of Detective Sean Reilly in the next book:
LOST TO THE WORLD, by Libby Sternberg

The war is over and Detective Sean Reilly is home but not at peace. In the spring of 1954, he's a widower with two small boys to care for while he tries to solve the case of a Johns Hopkins researcher murdered on the eve of the groundbreaking polio vaccine trials. With the help of new detective Sal Sabataso, he must first discover the victim's true identity and his connection to the polio vaccine work before finding the culprit. He's helped in his quest by a Hopkins secretary, a polio victim herself, who sometimes reminds him of his beloved late wife.

LOST TO THE WORLD

A mystery novel by
Edgar-nominated author

Libby Sternberg

Chapter One

JULIA DELL BIT THE INSIDES OF HER CHEEKS. The smell of a damp wool coat made her gag. She swallowed hard, concentrating on the bland tiles on the floor, the crack in the wall, the soothing voice of the nurse kneeling by her chair, asking if she was all right.

It's March — why is he even wearing it? Wet from rain, warm from the overheated hallways, it smells like —

Pain.

She shook her head. "There's a coat rack down the hall, sir!"

The nurse was asking her if she needed smelling salts.

"No, no thank you. I'm fine."

But the smell of that wool coat — it made her sick to her stomach.

"What did you say about my coat?" The detective stood in front of her.

"It...smells. From the rain."

He sniffed his shoulder and shrugged. "I won't be here long." His voice was sharp, but at least he moved on. And with it, the odor receded.

Hot packs were made of woolen strips soaked to scalding. She'd never forget the smell — and the fear it had come to trigger.

"You've had a shock, dear. Close your eyes and breathe steadily."

She did as she was told, and a happy memory flooded her. A happy memory? Dear God, it was the memory of the moment she'd discovered Dr. Lowenstein's lifeless body!

She had entered the room, let out a yelping scream, and then — she shivered as the sensation returned — she'd quickly *turned* and fallen.

That one sliver of time when she turned, that tiniest moment. Holy mother of God, what a wonderful feeling! She'd turned. She'd turned! She'd moved as if...

She sucked in her lips. *Oh God, it was gone now.*

But in that instant of surprise, she'd felt again surefooted and strong, able to turn away from danger without a second glance. She had forgotten about her withered leg with its smaller shoe. She'd forgotten she couldn't walk without will. One precious moment.

I want it back. I want it back, oh please. . .

Her left hand had brushed Dr. Lowenstein's arm when she fell, while her right had pushed into the broken glass on the floor, scraping and cutting her palm, making an embarrassing mess of things so that she had to explain, when the police and doctors came, that she'd fallen like a clumsy oaf.

There had been the usual mixture of pity and recoil. The detective with the coat, a burly man with reddish hair, had glanced at her with narrowed eyes and tight mouth. You mucked up the scene, that look had said. You mucked it up because you were stupid enough to—and here Julia hadn't been sure what to fill in. She'd been stupid enough to forget about her brace? Or stupid enough to catch the damn disease that led to the brace?

She viewed each possibility with a curious aloofness, a detachment that had plagued her since she had been afflicted with "the summer plague" itself.

Serious illness, Julia had decided when she'd lain in bed with the awful onset of polio ten years earlier, invites the sufferer into the threshold of death. Afterward, you feel as if you are not living so much as writing your obituary. *Julia was such a fine girl, strong in adversity, resilient even when facing catastrophe at work . . .*

Everyone else in her family was healthy as the proverbial horse. Even the usual childhood diseases—the poxes and measles and mumps—had whipped through her parents' house with efficient speed, leaving Julia and her two sisters miserable for a few days and weak for a few more, and then, poof, the suffering was forgotten. There were movies to see, boys to giggle over, songs to croon with, bands to dance to, and the war's end to celebrate.

No more. She'd missed a lot of that.

"Are you feeling better now, Julia?"

Julia opened her eyes. The kind nurse from one of the patient wards beyond the research labs knelt by Julia's chair with ammonia spirits ready. She sat in the hallway, just outside Dr. Lowenstein's Hopkins office, where the detective had allowed them to place a chair for her while she waited for his questions.

Smoothing her gray flannel skirt, Julia shook her head. "Yes, thank you." It was a plain skirt, not at all like the softly feminine and extravagantly full skirts so fashionable now. She didn't like to draw attention to her legs.

"It must have been the shock of it." The crisp nurse straightened and placed the ammonia bottle in her pocket.

"Yes," Julia murmured as the nurse wrapped a bandage on her bleeding hand. Yes, it was the shock. A miracle, that shock had been.

She shook her head. No self-pity. She was one of the lucky ones. The late president had spent most of his adulthood in a wheelchair. And others she'd known at the rehabilitation center had spent their last days in the torture chamber of the iron lung. *Yes, count your blessings.* Why was it she only remembered to do that after first being tortured by her losses?

"May I have a few words with you now?" a tired, low voice said. "I'm Detective Sean Reilly." He loomed over her, his hands dug into the pockets of that blasted coat. When he saw her wrinkle her nose, he heaved a sigh and took it off, looking around for a place to put it. The nurse offered to hold it for him and whisked it away.

"You won't be tying up the lab for long, will you?" she said in that bright tone of voice she'd learned to use to get people to leave her alone. Cheerful Julia, the model patient, the model daughter, the model secretary. The rehabilitation crowd had even talked of putting her name in for the March of Dimes posters until she'd spoiled the possibility with an angry fit in the lunch room one day, all because her wheelchair had been too far from the table. She'd apologized afterward, telling the nurses she'd "try harder," but it had been too late.

"What?"

"Dr. Lowenstein. . ." She waved her hand toward the lab where the doctor's body lay. "He wasn't involved in the research. But others are. It's almost polio season." She sat up straighter. It was important work and her boss was part of it, if only in a small way. She wouldn't let these detectives delay it.

The detective stooped to talk to her as if she were a little girl, and she found herself mentally pulling back. Did he feel the need to affect this pose for her because she was a cripple, akin in his eyes to a child or mental defective?

"Could you describe to me what happened when you found your boss?" he said, ignoring her question. He pulled out a notebook and pencil, preparing to write with grubby fingers whose nails were ragged from chewing.

"Not my boss," she said. "Dr. *Jansen* is my boss. Dr. Lowenstein's secretary isn't in."

He sighed. "What time did you discover Dr. Lowenstein?"

"I came in early—before eight—and I was the only one here," she said. She'd already told another detective the story. And Mrs. Wilcox. And the nurse. And . . . others she couldn't remember now. "Dr. Lowenstein was in his lab with the door shut. He sometimes comes in early. I heard voices. Someone was with him, a man I think—"

"Do you know who it was?"

"No. I just heard them talking—"

"Arguing?"

"Maybe. I don't know. Their voices were muffled but...strong." Dr.

Lowenstein was a quiet man, so any rise in tone, even to what most would consider normal, stood out as unusual.

"Did you hear any of it, make out anything?"

She looked down, thought. She'd been rushing to her office to finish typing Dr. Jansen's paper. It didn't matter that it was for a small journal. She always felt that any kernel of information about polio could be the one piece of the puzzle that solved it all, that led to discoveries and cure. Her mind had been on that. To her right, behind the pebbled glass window on Dr. Lowenstein's door, she'd heard them. Two men. She'd thought at first it was another doctor. They could be quite passionate about their various theories, and she'd assumed they were arguing over the amount of CCs to be used in an experiment or how to attenuate a strain of the virus or how to get the best tissue from the monkeys they used. But Dr. Lowenstein didn't do polio research, so she'd discarded that theory, or rather, filed it away to be pondered later after she'd finished her work for Dr. Jansen.

"Dr. Lowenstein said something like 'I've had enough, Buck' at one point. That's all I remember."

"Buck?"

"I think that was it."

"Anyone by that name here?"

"Not that I know of."

"The other man — was he another doctor?" He shifted his weight.

"I know all the doctors on our floor and then some. I didn't recognize the voice."

"You didn't hear anything else?"

"Like I said, I heard them when I passed the office. Once I went into mine, I didn't hear any more. I was typing."

"So when did you go into the lab again?"

Time had passed quickly after she'd gone to her office that morning. She'd been consumed with finishing her typing before Dr. Jansen came in for the day, which was usually at nine-thirty. But a little before nine, the phone had rung.

". . . it was a man, asking to talk to Dr. Lowenstein," she said. An odd, raspy voice, faintly familiar, so low she'd almost asked the caller to repeat his request. "Dr. Lowenstein doesn't always answer the phone in his lab, and his secretary wasn't coming in today, so I got up to go tell him he had a call."

"And that's when you…"

"Found him dead on the floor. Yes." She raised her eyebrows, daring the detective to think she was soft.

"You knew immediately he was dead?"

She straightened her shoulders. "No, I just saw him on the floor, bleeding, not moving." She'd thought he'd passed out, maybe had a heart attack. "It wasn't until I fell that I determined he wasn't breathing." She looked around. She wanted to talk with Mrs. Wilcox, to make sure things would move forward despite this calamity. Perhaps she should help move them along.

"How much longer will you be here?" She tilted her head toward the hallway. "The doctors have work to do."

He ignored her question, flipping a page after writing some notes. "So you came in, saw him on the floor, fell, and then determined he was dead."

"Yes!" She cleared her throat as her face flamed with irritation. If she'd been able-bodied, she would have bent over, shook the doctor's shoulders and tried to rouse him. But, no, she'd fallen because of her brace. What did the detective think he was proving by eking out this detail from her?

He looked up at her eyes, as if probing for something. "Just needed to have the sequence right," he said as if reading her earlier thoughts. "My boss would ask me." He shrugged his shoulders as if to apologize, then stood.

Not liking him towering over her, she pushed herself up as well, but without her cane she wavered. When he saw her reach back to balance herself against the wall, he lightly grabbed her right arm.

"Steady," he said, his eyes narrowing in concern, "you've had a big shock."

"My cane—it's still in the lab." He had a strong, kind grip. She regretted her quick judgment of him. She was always doing that—seeing people's reactions through the filter of her affliction. A thousand times she told herself to stop.

"I'll fetch it for you," he offered. But she shook her head.

"I can do it!" She pulled away, nearly tumbling with the effort.

"I don't want you in the crime scene," he said, irritation now coloring his voice. "Stay here. I'll get it for you." He walked past her without a second glance and disappeared into the room. She heard him talking to others—another detective, a coroner—and in a few seconds, he returned holding her cane out to her. She took it with a quiet "thanks" and slipped the metal band around her forearm while grabbing the handle grip.

"What happened to the caller—the one who asked for Dr. Lowenstein?"

"I don't know. I assume he hung up eventually."

"You were the only one around this morning?"

"I didn't see anyone else. I was in early, before the offices usually open."

"This whole lab is involved in the polio research?" He swung his pencil around indicating the quiet hallways. This part of the hospital wasn't a hospital at all. It felt more like a library with hushed voices in labs and offices. The researchers could work for hours without saying anything to colleagues. Sometimes Julia had been surprised to come upon a doctor in a lab so silent it could have been a tomb.

"A part of it. Most of it is in Pittsburgh where Dr. Salk is working. But the doctors all have different theories, different methods, different tasks." She felt weak, as if a weight were on her pressing her down. But she squared her shoulders. "Dr. Lowenstein wasn't involved in all that, though. He did other research. His secretary would know."

"She's not in, you said."

She looked around, blinked in the bright light of the halls. She really wanted to move on, to get back to normal, her normal. That would steady her.

"Do you need me for anything else?" she asked him.

"I'm not sure." His eyes narrowed as he sized her up. "Not right now."

"Then I'll get back to work." They all had to get back to work. She'd find Mrs. Wilcox and have her move these people along.

"Where do you live?"

"What?" She leaned on her cane and stared at him. Was he being fresh?

"In case you go home early, I'd like to know where I can reach you if I have more questions." He had his notebook open again with pencil poised to write.

"I won't go home early."

He sighed heavily, and his jaw muscle worked. He flipped the notebook closed with a clap.

"Fine. I can get it from your office anyway." He turned away from her and walked back to the lab.

৵৵৵

Two hours later, she found herself with a bad case of the shakes, sitting at her desk trembling as if it were twenty below zero.

"You should go home," her office mate, Linda, said, looking up from her typing.

Maybe she would…but the phone rang, pulling her out of her anxiety.

"Are you the crip?" a man's voice said as soon as she answered. "The one talking to that policeman?"

She sucked in her breath. "Who is this?" Her voice trembled. Linda noticed.

"You okay?" Linda got up from her desk and came over.

"Who is this?" Julia repeated, but the man just snickered and hung up, the dial tone replacing his ugly voice.

"Julia?" Linda asked, reaching out for Julia's arm.

"It was…nothing. A prankster." But her hand shook so much that she didn't settle the receiver into its cradle, and it fell on to her desk. "I think I will go…I don't have anything important now."

"I'll tell Mrs. Wilcox." Linda scurried to pick up her own phone and dial their office manager. While Linda talked to Mrs. Wilcox, Julia called home to arrange a ride.

"Mrs. W. said that's fine," Linda said, hanging up. "She said Dr. Jansen called to say he's under the weather, too."

Julia frowned. The man hadn't had the courage to call Julia after he'd berated her about finishing the paper he was not present to pick up, nor to offer condolences over the shock she'd experienced. Typical. She swallowed her irritation. It wasn't for her to question these things. The doctors worked like artists, listening to their inner muses. They had important things to do. Poor Mrs. Wilcox—having to deal with such a temperamental crew. But she'd already handled worse. Her husband was gone five years now, and her only child, a son, had died at Normandy.

"You've been a trouper. I wouldn't have stayed," Linda said, watching her get ready to go.

Julia noticed her staring at her collar. There was a little drop of blood there, on the neckline of her sweater set. It was from her fall. One more reason to go home early—to properly wash the stain before it settled in. It was a new set, too, soft white cashmere, as light as air, with a beaded flower embroidered near the shoulder of the cardigan. Julia spent an inordinate amount of time choosing clothing that drew the eyes upward. White set off her curly, chin-length chestnut hair, another of her good features.

"I hate the idea of the investigation stopping things," Julia said as she limped to the coat rack. Linda beat her to it, pulling down her soft gray cloth coat and helping her into it.

"Don't worry about that. Things are already kinda stopped."

Julia froze and looked into Linda's eyes.

"What?"

"Oh. I thought you'd heard." Linda looked at the doorway as if checking to make sure no one would overhear. She was a monumental office gossip, often getting the news about hospital goings-on before anyone else. Most of the time, her stories were accurate.

"Dr. Bodian had to go down to Bethesda," Linda whispered. "To the National Institutes of Health. They're trying to figure out if the polio trials should go forward."

Julia felt as if touched by an electric wire. "Because of Dr. Lowenstein's death already?"

"No, no. Something else. There's some trouble at the Parke, Davis lab in Detroit. The chimps they got there—some of them—came down with it. With polio, I mean. Well, with what they think is polio. I was going to tell you this morning. I just heard it."

Oh, no. Julia slumped. The monkeys were used to test the vaccines that were being produced in the labs for the upcoming vaccine trials. Everything had seemed so hopeful. And now...

"That's awful." Despite her effort not to show her grief, she felt tears well in her eyes. It was this morning's terrible events, that was it, a delayed reaction.

"Oh, honey, don't get upset." Linda put her arm around Julia. "It don't mean things will be put off. Dr. Bodian just needs to check things out, straighten 'em all up."

It could mean far worse things than the trials being "put off." It could mean outright cancelation. No vaccine. No cure. Thousands upon thousands of children and young adults facing what she'd faced. For a second, she held her breath, remembering.

"But it's getting late," Julia murmured. She herself had caught polio in early summer. Epidemics could start as early as March, and it was now almost April.

"They'll fix it," Linda said, but Julia knew she was only saying that to make Julia feel better. Linda didn't have the same sense of urgency as Julia did about the trials.

As was her habit, Julia forced a smile and straightened, shrugging out of Linda's embrace.

"Do you need me or Susan to do any of your stuff for you?" Linda asked as Julia pulled on her gloves.

Julia thought of Linda alone in the office without Susan. She wouldn't burden the girl with her assignments when Dr. Kenneth Morton was loading her up with so much. She knew that some other labs around the country thought it extravagant that the doctors at Hopkins each had his own secretary, but there was more than enough work to go around, and if one of the girls was ever out, the others often had to work overtime to make up for the absence. They didn't just work for these doctors anyway. They served as a general typing pool for other researchers who didn't have secretaries.

"No, I'm caught up," Julia lied.

"You have a ride? I could call a cab for you."

"I'm fine. Thanks."

Julia turned to leave the small room she shared with Linda Marie Boldari and Susan Schlager, the other secretaries on this research unit. Susan, Dr. Lowenstein's secretary, was out spending a few days visiting her aunt in Easton on the Eastern Shore. Julia wondered if anyone would think to try to contact her.

Julia paused at the door. "Do you think you could call Susan tonight—and tell her the news?"

Linda nodded, frowning. "I guess I oughta. Poor Suse. Dr. Mike was a dream boss." She sighed and went back to her desk.

Even though Linda was two years younger, Julia always felt as if the secretary were an older sister. She was certainly more experienced with men. Linda had had a string of beaux before and during the war, according to her stories. Now she was engaged to a day shift manager at Continental Can. Julia felt closer to Linda than to Susan, whose lack of experience and education seemed a willful rejection of the unknown.

In fact, Julia had to admit she disliked Susan. Once, Susan had refused an offer of fudge from Julia, and Julia was sure it was because Susan thought she could get the disease from her.

Julie tried to be nice to her, though. Why, just the other day Julia had taken care of something for her when a smudged envelope from Susan to Dr. Lowenstein had been returned to the office because of insufficient postage. Figuring it had been something personal, Julia had put it in another envelope and sent it to Susan's home. She'd felt very good about herself for that act of charity.

No, not always so good. Sometimes it made her feel uneasy. She'd suspected what was in that note to Dr. Lowenstein...

Can't think about it.

Julia quietly slipped out, pausing in the hallway to tie a blue silk scarf around her head, a Christmas gift from her sister Helen. *It matches your eyes,* Helen had said when Julia'd opened it, and Julia had felt the need to be effusively thankful. Helen was so easily upset if things didn't go according to her expectations. She'd been engaged at the end of the war to Tommy Radcliffe. He'd written he was on his way home and then....

And then catastrophe. His parents had notified Helen to tell her Tommy was missing and presumed dead. Some foolish parachuting exercise near Berlin that had gone awry. His body wasn't recovered. Helen hadn't recovered either. And the world marched on.

Sometimes Julia resented that, too — the way people like Helen and Mrs. Wilcox were expected to get over their sorrow, and the way their pain was never adequately acknowledged. The world was cruel.

Julia walked from the research section into the main hospital, through hallways filled with nurses and lab-coated doctors, the busy hum creating a background noise that comforted her with its sense of urgency and importance. She nodded to some workers, said hello to others. One, a short man in frayed shirt, gave her a gentle smile as he passed. He, too, walked with a cane, but he always seemed to be hurrying, as if to prove he could outpace any able-bodied man. He stopped when he came to her.

"Did you hear about Dr. Mike?" he whispered, as if they shouldn't talk about it. This was Earl, the poor soul who tended the research monkeys. His past experience with polio made him especially suited to the job. Like Julia, being afflicted with the disease meant he was in no danger being around it. Julia always felt a bit uncomfortable around him, though, because he assumed a familiarity with her that she didn't think appropriate. Just because they were both polios didn't mean they shared anything else.

Yet even as his friendliness irritated her, it also made her feel guilty.

Did she shy away from the man because he was a polio, because she, like everyone else, only wanted to associate with people who were whole?

"I found him," she said. "His body."

His eyes widened. "Lord almighty!"

She looked at her watch as if in a hurry.

Earl noticed her impatience. "Guess you need to get back to your boss." He spoke so softly she barely heard him among the hubbub of the hospital.

"Um-hmm," she lied and walked away.

Everyone knew Dr. Jansen was demanding, even Earl, the monkey-tender. She'd worked here for five years, only the last one for Dr. Jansen, and she'd been grateful to land the job.

Because Dr. Jansen was viewed as something of a tyrant, few envied Julia her position. He demanded long hours when he had reports to write and unreasonably accused her of forgetting things he'd never told her about in the first place. But she treated him with a patronizing detachment, always ready to offer the soothing word that calmed his storms. Everyone thought she was a saint, but she was really just immensely relieved. Relieved to have this job "out in the world" and grateful for her parents' agreement to let her take it. It was her father, after all, who often came to pick her up when she had to work late, or when she was just too damned tired to take the bus.

Before this job, she'd worked in a small legal office near her home. Just two lawyers in a wood-paneled second-floor suite on Belair Road, an office as smoky and claustrophobic as her own life. The steep stairway to their office had been daunting at first, but she'd met that challenge daily, strengthening her resolve for further challenges. The work, mostly wills and real estate transactions, had tired her faster than the stairs.

She'd caught a terrible cold her last winter with the lawyers that brought her to the edge of pneumonia, and she'd shamelessly used her illness to convince her parents she needed to find another job. "The smoke bothers my lungs," she'd said. They'd acquiesced to her new arrangement with frowns and whispered conferring, resulting in her father's insistence on picking her up from work some days so she wouldn't have to depend on buses.

Today was one of those days. When she'd called her mother to say she'd be coming home early, Mutti had insisted—*your* Vater *can pick you up, don't be silly now, really, Julia*—and now Julia had to wait for him on Broadway, feeling guilty for pulling him away from his job at Glen L. Martin all the way over in Middle River. He was a supervisor there, having risen through the ranks quickly during the war when the big plant was draped in camouflage and buzzing with activity.

She hurried outside, past the hushed offices of hospital administrators and the nervous rooms of patients, into the lobby where the statue of

Christ the Healer ignited both awe and self-examination (she always felt He was looking into her heart and finding her lacking), out into the misty, raw rain.

There was nowhere to sit. Oh well, she'd stay put. She'd much rather be out here than in the stuffy building. Already, the air was reviving her, making her feel alive. She stared at the rooftops of houses and the traffic beside the hospital. It made her feel important, all this bustle around this place, as if she herself were involved in the healing that went on here.

After a while, a familiar voice called out behind her.

"Julia!"

She turned and forced a smile, leaning on her cane. "Will!" Suddenly, she was so tired. Fatigue worried her. It was how the polio had started—with a soul-crushing tiredness.

William Beschmann came toward her through the doors. Tall and awkward, with a prematurely receding hairline, Will wasn't what most women would call "a catch," but he was the man who'd caught her. With a sunny disposition and carefree attitude, he seemed to be just what she'd needed when she first met him. His war had consisted of playing poker and doing the books for an Army unit stationed in the Philippines after the bombs were dropped, giving him the status if not the history of a veteran.

Will now worked in the Hopkins accounting office, which was where she'd met him when she'd gone there over two years ago to straighten out an accounting mix-up with a grant from the National Foundation for Infantile Paralysis. They'd been seeing each other for two years and had been engaged for only a month. Her left hand was still ringless, however, because Will, to her disappointment, had not proposed with ring in hand. He'd left that purchase for a time when they could shop together so he'd be sure to get what she wanted.

What she wanted was her fiancé to know what she wanted, to sweep her off her feet with romantic gestures. She sometimes wondered, to her shame, if she would have said yes so quickly had she known he didn't have a ring. But Will was a good man. She shouldn't be choosy.

"I heard about the murder," he said in a stage whisper, his eyes darting to and fro to make sure no one had heard. Like Earl, he seemed to enjoy the drama of the incident.

"I'm not sure why everyone assumes it's a murder," Julia said. She looked toward the road, trying to spy her father's Buick. "He could have just fallen on his own."

Will quickly shook his head. "It must have been awful for you, hon. Are you headed home? You should have called me. I would have driven you."

Yes, she should have called him. But she craved solitude. She'd discovered a dead body. She deserved...something.

"My father's in the area," she lied, "so he's stopping by." She gave him a mock frown of concern. "It's cold. You should go in." He was only in his shirt and tie. Will didn't always wear a jacket to work, and this annoyed Julia. She didn't see how he expected to get ahead if he didn't dress like someone capable of being in charge of things.

"Lowenstein was kind of a cold fish, wasn't he?" Will pressed, ignoring her concern.

Her mouth opened in surprise. Yes, Dr. Lowenstein had kept to himself. But he'd been nice enough. Susan, his secretary, liked him. Of course, one of the reasons she liked him was because he was so undemanding. And he always got her a gift for Christmas—that was a kindness, especially considering that he was Jewish. Whatever anyone knew about him, this wasn't a time to review the man's faults. This was the time to mourn. Or at least to be silent.

Here was something else that annoyed her about Will—his social clumsiness. Ever since the engagement, it seemed as if she couldn't talk to him without noticing some fault. What was wrong with her? She was physically clumsy, and he tolerated that. She should be able to look past his flaws as well—shouldn't she?

"I...I guess. I don't know." She didn't want to say too much. She kept thinking of that detective asking her questions.

She saw a dark blue Buick with a scuffed right fender pull up to the curb below. Her father.

"I have to go, Will. He's here!" She moved her cane in the direction of the curb.

"I'll call you this evening—after the news!" He squeezed her lightly on the arm before she left. "Don't worry about anything."

As she made her way down the shallow steps, she had to shake off another pang of irritation. Will didn't need to tell her not to worry. She had done nothing wrong. But even as she brushed aside worry, it pushed back in. She was the person to come across the body, after all. My God—maybe she'd be a suspect.

Chapter Two

SEAN CAUGHT UP with his partner at the Lowenstein house in Homeland a little after noon. He wasn't a moment too soon. Poor Sal was politely but desperately trying to turn down an invitation to tea by a lonely neighbor, the woman who'd let Sal in.

She was a tiny woman, nearly a foot and a half shorter than Sean. Even Sal, who was no giant, seemed large in comparison. Her pewter-colored hair was streaked with white, and she didn't wear it long and pulled into a bun like so many older women. No, it was short and curly, a younger style. Her face was covered with makeup as well, but it couldn't hide her extensive map of wrinkles. Her age was therefore accented by these choices, rather than masked.

"I was just telling Mr. Sabataso here that he could join me for some tea and biscuits in my sunroom. I live just next door. I'd be happy to answer any questions you have about our dear doctor."

Sean raised his eyebrows at Sal, whose eyes widened in a quick negative response.

"I'm afraid we'll have to be getting on to the station house, Miss....."

"Mrs. Wellstone." She held out her hand, and he carefully shook it. It felt like a bird skeleton, full of fragile bones. "The poor doctor. I was only a neighbor, of course, but it was a shock to hear he was gone. And in so frightful a manner."

Sean acknowledged her sympathy with a nod and looked at Sal. "Have you had a chance to look around?"

"As best I could."

Sean imagined it had been difficult with Mrs. Wellstone hovering.

"I'll take a quick look myself, if you don't mind." Sean glanced over at the old lady. "You go ahead and keep Sal company while I finish up." Sal shot him a grimace.

Sean heard the woman continue to chatter while he made his way through the clean, neat house, trying to focus on the task at hand while his thoughts wandered elsewhere.

That polio research lab — he was scared enough of his twin boys coming down with it, had even considered not sending them to kindergarten because of it. He followed all the warnings. "Don't mix with new groups, don't get chilled, don't get overtired, but do keep clean." Christ, he had that damned poster memorized. Any fever could be the beginning of...no, he couldn't think like that.

Robby had felt warm this morning, too, and had been more quiet than usual. Was he coming down with something? Or was he just going through a bad stretch again?

Robby and his twin brother, Daniel, had been quick to slip into night terrors and groundless fears if they didn't feel safe. And they hadn't felt safe for nearly a year—ever since their mother, Mary, had died. Died in the very hospital he'd been at today. Another ward. Another floor. The one where they treated patients with cancer, a disease that branded you as bad as leprosy. No one uttered the word.

That snobbish secretary with her aversion to the smell of his coat— God almighty, he'd had enough of hospital odors himself and had barely restrained himself from saying a thing or two about that.

Nothing to be done about it. He gave himself a mental shake and focused his attention on looking through the house. Sal had probably had enough of Mrs. Wellstone by now.

Although Sean was no expert on antiques, he guessed that many of the finely carved chairs, bedsteads and tables came with names like Louis this or Queen Anne that. There were three bedrooms upstairs, but only two were set up as such. Nothing but clothes and toiletries and the like were in the bedrooms.

But the third upstairs room was set up as an office of some sort with a large kneehole desk and wooden filing cabinets filled with scientific magazines. He took some time going through those, but all he found were the usual personal papers that told him little. Copies of the house deed. Bank statements. A ledger with financial transactions. Sean scooped up these and took them with him. He opened another desk drawer, a larger lower right one built to accommodate files. It was empty. Had Lowenstein not had enough to fill it? Sean looked around. No, that wasn't the case. There were some piles of magazines and scholarly papers on his desk. Maybe he'd not had time to put them away. Or maybe—

He hurried downstairs and bypassed the living room where Mrs. Wellstone was explaining to Sal how difficult it is to grow roses when the summer's too damp.

If Dr. Lowenstein had come into contact with the polio germs, did they linger on clothes and furniture? Maybe he should ask to be off this case. He couldn't take any chances with his boys, now that Mary was gone.

Into the dining room, kitchen, closets. Nothing out of the ordinary. Nothing in pockets. No hidden boxes or safes. A room to the left of the foyer was set up as a music studio and library with piano and books and music stand. Down in the basement, it was even barer. The old furnace and oil tank sat on one side, a washing machine on the other, indoor clothesline for the maid to use in bad weather. A few shelves with gardening items and tools for the occasional repair. If anything, Lowenstein's house was unusually clear of any nostalgic mementoes or reminders of his past. Not even any photographs of relatives, Sean thought. Odd.

The phone buzzed, cutting his thoughts and momentarily silencing Mrs. Wellstone. When it buzzed again, she called out, "I could answer that, if you'd like."

"No, no, I'll take care of it," Sean heard Sal say.

Sean smiled and made his way back up into the kitchen, just in time for Sal to hand the receiver to him.

"Dick Weyman," Sal said, raising his eyebrows.

Weyman was a fellow detective.

"Hello," he mumbled, while plopping the papers he'd gathered on a nearby table.

"I been calling all over for you," Weyman said. "Tried the hospital, and they said you'd left. Figured you were at the vic's house. Your housekeeper called here a half dozen times looking for you. Says to call home. Something about one of your boys."

He closed his eyes. *Oh God.* His neck and face warmed.

"Uh-huh. Thanks, Dick."

He dialed his home number as soon as the line came free again. *Jesus, not Robby. Don't let Robby...*

"Mrs. Buchanan, is there a problem with the boys?"

Her voice squawked over the line, irritating and reassuring Sean at the same time. "Robert came home from kindergarten with the sniffles and now seems to have a bad fever, Mr. Reilly. I took his temperature an hour ago, and it was a hundred and one. I was thinking of calling Dr. Spencer but thought perhaps you would want to know...."

He should have told her to keep him home this morning. But he didn't like to baby them, to make them even more fearful. Sean sighed and looked at his watch. It was nearly one. He'd wanted to type up his notes from the morning's interviews. It wouldn't take him long, and it was a point of pride that he knew how to type. And then there were Lowenstein's papers to go through. But if Robby had a fever—Jesus, he didn't want to fool with that. He could hear the boy crying in the background.

"Is he...does he complain of anything else? Any aches or stiffness?"

"His head hurts, but you know how he is. Silent as stone."

"Definitely call Dr. Spencer, and I'll be there as soon as I can," he said into the phone, feeling his gut pull him toward home. Robert would want him there, and he needed to see the boy with his own eyes, to make sure he wasn't coming down with this plague. Was this case a warning to him—to keep his boys safe from the disease? He was always looking for signs now, feeling he'd missed other important ones in the past.

Sal appeared in the doorway, overhearing his conversation. It would be the fifth week in a row Sean had had to take off early for something related to the kids. Daniel had fallen the week before, and Mrs. Buchanan had been afraid he'd broken his wrist—he'd only sprained it. And the week before that, Sean had had to speak to Sister Angela, their kindergarten teacher, about a fight they'd gotten into. And the week before that—he couldn't remember.

He didn't need to go home for all those things. But he always felt if he didn't do it, he might be missing some turning point, some imperceptible moment that would mean the difference between happiness and disaster.

Mary had complained of being tired a year before she'd fallen ill. So tired she'd asked Sean if he could leave early one day and help with the boys. And he hadn't. If he had—would he have seen the disease creeping into their lives as she'd stood bathed in light from their front door, looking as frail and unreal as an angel?

She had been an angel, too, a slip of a girl with the sweetest hint of Ireland in her voice. Patient, kind, a loving wife—and never a complaint from her. Not even when they'd lost their first babe in a miscarriage. My god, she'd comforted him, then. Only later had he heard from a nurse how she'd cried.

For a little while after Mary had died, he'd actually felt immunized against other griefs. It would have been too cruel for the God he believed in to strike his family with any other tragedy after such a wrenching loss. But time marched on, and with it his sense of safety faded. Now he saw trouble lurking around every doorway, floating through every window. He wouldn't be caught unawares.

"Everything okay?" Sal asked, patting his pocket for a cigarette. Finding one, he lit it and blew a plume of smoke.

"Robby's sick."

"He couldn't have caught anything from this..." Sal gestured to the house. So he'd thought of it, too, the possibility of taking germs home with him. "It's probably just a cold or something."

Sal was a good soul and an unlikely friend. Right before the war, Sean had worked on a case that had nearly put Sal's best friend, innocent of a murder, in prison or worse. But once he'd come on the force after the war, Sal had learned quickly that Sean was a man he could trust. He'd let bygones be bygones. The war did that—made the years before it recede into mist.

"I was going to type up my notes and then head home."

"Look, I can do it," Sal said softly so Mrs. Wellstone wouldn't hear them.

But she was too curious to be deterred by low voices. She showed up at Sal's elbow.

"Who was that on the phone?" she asked, as if she were part of the detective force.

"Nothing we can talk about, ma'am. Top secret," Sal said with a wink toward Sean. Then Sal ushered the woman to the living room, toward the front door. "Thank you for all your help. We can let ourselves out. My partner has the key. We'll be talking to you again soon. Keep your doors and windows locked, now. Don't let any strangers in..." He kept up a constant flow of talk as he walked her to the door, not giving her time to respond, or to protest being forced out of Lowenstein's home.

Clutching Lowenstein's papers by his side, Sean caught up with him in the living room as Sal closed the door on the old lady.

"Hand 'em over, pardner," Sal said with a smile. "Your notes."

Sean just shrugged. Sal had covered for him a few times, saying he was out on a case, but Sean wouldn't ask him to do it again. He'd used up all his vacation days when Mary had been sick, and as understanding as his boss had been in the past, there were limits. Sean was discovering them now.

"I'll manage," Sean said.

"O'Brien won't miss you. Probably doesn't even know when we're there." Sal held out his hand. "Besides, I have a favor to ask."

Sean smiled. Sal was just a pup on the job and yet already jaded. Maybe that happened to all of them after serving in the war. Sal had been wounded in a training accident and mustered out early, not seeing action. He was sensitive about it, though, especially since a lot of his buddies were gone. Sean didn't press. He knew men who didn't like to talk about their experiences, especially those who'd served in the South Pacific. He'd heard stories of that fighting that curdled his stomach and made him glad his war had ended in Europe.

"These are papers I found upstairs. Just take them back to the office and drop them on my desk." Sean handed the bunch to Sal, glad to be rid of them. "I'll look at them in the morning." He took out his notebook and motioned to the sofa where they both sat down. "You don't need to type these, but let's go over them, in case I missed something." He flipped through the pages, talking his notes out loud as Sal puffed on a smoke:

"Preliminary findings — Dr. Lowenstein died from several blows to the head, struck above and around the man's left eye and ear. Lowenstein's hands were clean. It was likely the first blow knocked him down and out, and the murderer kept punching to make sure the man was gone."

Had Robby complained of a stiff neck in the last day or so? He couldn't remember.

"The only witness was Julia Dell, secretary for another doctor — Jansen — who wasn't yet in. No one else was on the floor. She heard arguing. Thought she heard the name 'Buck.'"

It was too early for polio. Probably just a cold. He'd ask the doctor about the risks.

"The office manager, Adelaide Wilcox, has a list of doctors who knew the victim. I talked with some, but they don't know of anyone who had a beef with the vic. Still to interview — Jansen and some docs who are in Bethesda now. Something to do with a snafu with the polio vaccine. Monkeys infected or something. Something that might derail the vaccine work. Wilcox emphasized that — maybe she thought it was sabotage, related to the murder? Wilcox doesn't have much else on the vic."

Sean looked up at Sal, who was finishing the cigarette, looking for an ashtray. "What did you get from the Wellstone lady?" Sean asked.

"An earful, let me tell you." Sal read from his own notes. "She let someone in this morning. Some doc — in lab coat and everything. Said he was a fellow doctor who needed some papers Lowenstein had left for him, something related to 'important research.'"

"She give you a description?"

Sal grimaced. "Brown hair, medium height, thin, long face."

"Could be you."

"Or half the city."

"What about Lowenstein's cleaning lady?"

"Didn't know who he used."

Sean looked at his notes. He wanted to leave now.

"I can tell O'Brien you're doing some more questioning," Sal said.

Sean's mouth twisted into a lopsided smile. "You don't have to—"

Sal held up a hand. "No, I have a favor to ask, remember?" He flipped closed his notebook and launched into it. "You know my sister Brigitta, her husband was killed in It'ly."

"Yeah, I remember you telling me about her." And about a thousand other relatives who Sean never kept straight.

"Well, I kind of promised my mother that I'd ask if you would like to meet Brigitta, maybe take her out for coffee or something. She's a nice gal. You might like her."

Sean barked out a good-natured laugh. "That's hardly much of a favor, Sal. It's not like it would be a hardship."

Sal grinned, relieved. "She is a looker. Even if she is my sister."

"I'll call her tonight," Sean said. "I've got your number." Sal still lived at home, although he complained daily about his need to find a place of his own.

"No, she lives near the harbor. Little It'ly. Here, I'll write it down for you." Sal scribbled fast, as if afraid Sean would change his mind.

Sean placed the paper in his jacket pocket. "You still don't need to cover for me," he said. "I'll tell O'Brien myself I'm leaving early, and he can dock my pay."

Sal shook his head.

"Look, you know you're going to be thinking about this case, figuring it out from now till Sunday and back again. And that will all be on your time, off the clock. Just do what you have to do. O'Brien's supposed to be at a meeting. Might be gone the rest of the day anyway."

Sean smiled as he stood. "Are you liking anybody yet?"

Sal flattened his mouth into two thin lines. "I talked to a couple docs, too. Got what you got. Lowenstein wasn't a very sociable fellow. Nobody knew much about his personal life."

"No next of kin in his file at the hospital either," Sean added.

"You know, did it strike you odd, where he lives—Homeland?" Sal asked, nodding his head toward the outside. They were in a well-to-do, exclusive neighborhood not far from the Hopkins university campus. Although the medical school and hospital were located on Broadway, the university was farther in town to the west. Homeland was slightly north of it, a neighborhood of social scions, bluebloods, trust fund folks.

Sean nodded. "Yeah. Not the sort of place for a Lowenstein."

Sean mentioned the empty drawer, the strange lack of photos.

"Not even a birth certificate," Sean said. "I just grabbed those." He pointed to the stack of financial papers he'd handed over to Sal.

"Whoever Wellstone let in—you think he cleaned the place out?" Sal asked.

"Don't know. I'm hoping the papers tell us something." And as Sean looked at them, he wondered again if they were a death trap, capturing the unseen germs that spread the disease.

Chapter Three

THE RAIN STOPPED as Sean drove home, and the city smelled like just-turned earth, the odor of springtime. It gave him no joy.

When Sean had returned from the war, he'd felt as if he were coming home to an eternal spring, a time when everything was warm and soft. No more hell. He'd set about having a family right away, but Mary'd had "female troubles" that delayed their parenthood, scars or something from the previous miscarriage. When the boys had finally come, he remembered thinking, "this is heaven." He'd gone to the hospital chapel, wordless thanks in his heart. He was so... Damned. Happy. To be alive.

He'd bought the house right after that, and they'd started hoping for more children, even praying the Rosary together some evenings, pleading their cause.

Mary had thought she was pregnant. But she hadn't been. She'd been sick.

He let out a long sigh and pulled the car up to the curb in front of his house.

Inside his home, he rubbed his boys' heads when they came out to greet him, half listening to Mrs. Buchanan as she told him when the doc was expected and how she needed to take off a week from Friday because her sister was coming into town and they were going to Hutzler's Tea Room together.

This last bit of news jostled his thoughts to the present, away from the scene of Lowenstein lying on the floor with blood pooled around his head, away from that blasted smell of antiseptic and something rotten that lingered in the air at a hospital. God, he needed to forget that smell.

"Do you know of someone else?" he asked her as she pulled on her coat and hat.

"Now, Mr. Reilly—" She always called him Mr. Reilly even though he was fifteen years younger than she was and more than once had told her to call him Sean. "I've told you I don't know anyone willing to take on an all-day job. Did you talk to the Sisters like I suggested?"

No, he hadn't. When did he have time to do that? He couldn't do it during the day—they were all teaching. And at night they abided by Grand Silence and wouldn't answer calls.

"I'll find someone," he murmured, holding open the door. "Are you sure you want to walk?" He pointed to the still-wet sidewalk, glistening with puddles. If the weather was bad or it was dark, as it often was in winter when he returned home, Mrs. Buchanan's husband would pick her up. Otherwise she walked the three blocks out toward Old Philadelphia Road, then down it a block and into her street below his toward the city.

She waggled her gloved hand in the air. "You certainly can't take me home, not with Robby being sick!" Her sturdy shoes clomped out her departure, and he turned back into the house.

Robby now dozed, curled up on the sofa with his thumb in his mouth. He wore pajamas, the blue ones with the sailboat pattern on them that Mary had picked out her last Christmas. The boy's feet and ankles poked out a good two inches from the hem, and for an awful second Sean imagined the boy in a hospital emergency room with nurses looking disapprovingly at the child's apparel. He'd have to get them new pajamas — new clothes in general — this weekend. But how would he do it if Robby were still sick?

Daniel hung on to his leg and asked for some candy. When Mary had been in the hospital, Sean had taken to bringing them home a Hershey bar or other treat.

"Will you read me a story?" Daniel pleaded, looking up at him with eager eyes. Sometimes the treat was a Golden Book from the drugstore, a fairy tale or adventure story.

Sean rubbed Daniel's blond head. "Nope, son. I hurried home because of your brother." Disappointed, Daniel let go of his father's leg and slid to the floor where he crawled under a barrel-backed chair near the door. "I'm hungry," he said.

Sean ignored him and went to the sofa, sitting at the edge of Robby's feet while he leaned over him to stroke his head. The boy felt hot, but he couldn't tell how hot. He'd meant to ask Mrs. Buchanan if she'd taken his temperature again.

"Does your neck hurt?" he whispered to the boy. Sean wondered if Robby would guess the reason for that question. Kids picked up things, and the boys were more susceptible than most to fears. Robby shook his head. A tear curled out of the corner of his eye and made its way down his cheek toward his nose. Sean pulled a handkerchief from his pocket and wiped his son's face.

"Raise your arm for me, son." Robby dutifully complied, and Sean lightly tickled the boy's feet, causing him to flinch while a slight smile floated across his face. No paralysis.

Sean wished Robby would complain more. He was often a silent sufferer, tears appearing out of nowhere, leaving Sean puzzling over what series of events had led to the outburst. Was he crying now because he ached or because he'd wanted Sean home earlier?

"The doctor will be here soon. You'll be fine. He'll fix you up!" he said with false cheer.

"He won't have to go to the hoppital, will he?" Daniel asked from his hiding place across the room.

Sean snapped out a reply. "No. The doctor will give him some medicine, and he'll be right as rain!" Danny's mouth turned down. Sean had sounded too angry. Maybe he was. Maybe he was daring God to prove him wrong. He patted Robby's feet and stood. "Let me make some tea. Tea with honey." That's what Mary had always made when they had sore throats.

"I want a soda pop," Daniel said, coming out and following him into the kitchen on the back of the house. "I want to watch telebision. But Robby says it hurts his eyes."

"We don't have any soda, Danny. Why don't you go in the bedroom and get a blanket for your brother? That's a good boy. We'll watch something later." The television had been an extravagant purchase last year, something he'd bought on credit to cheer up Mary. He was still making payments. He gave Danny an encouraging nudge toward the hallway and watched him clatter away, glad to be useful.

In the kitchen, Sean set the tea kettle on and made the sad discovery that his cupboard was bare. He had meant to stop at the store on the way home. Damn. Peanut butter, crackers, a can of beans, and a tin of sardines, which the boys wouldn't eat, sat on the shelves. Maybe the doctor could stay a minute longer while he ran out? No. And the little store up the street would close at four and stopped deliveries at two because they were looking for an afternoon delivery boy. He reached for the phone on the kitchen wall to call Mrs. Buchanan.

"...no, that wasn't Ava Gardner, honey, it was Rita Hayworth...." A familiar woman's voice came across the party line. Sean would have to wait.

He looked at his watch. If he hurried, he could be back in less than ten minutes. Two minutes up the street, five at the store, another two back. He turned off the tea kettle and walked back to the living room.

"Danny, I'm going to go outside for a few minutes. Just a few minutes. To that store up the corner. Won't take me long at all." Danny was at his brother's side, glad to be of help, tucking the blanket around Robby's feet and legs.

"Can I come?" Danny asked.

"No, you have to be a big boy and watch after your brother." Sean grabbed his coat and pulled out his keys. Ten minutes. Less than that. He knew exactly what he'd buy and where on the shelves it was located. "You stay here with Robby. Don't you leave the house." He took off his watch and handed it to Danny.

"See that big hand? When it moves from the two to the four, I'll be back."

Danny took the watch and stared at it, his mouth hanging open. He looked up at his dad with a mixture of fear and surprise. He was happy to have the watch, but unsure of its price.

"Danny, I'll be back by the time it reaches the four!" Sean sprinted out the door, trying to give the impression it was a race against time, a game they'd both enjoy.

ﾇﾍﾌ

Sean made it back in seven minutes, laden with canned soup, a loaf of bread, butter, milk, soda pop, and two Hershey bars.

When he came in the door, Dr. Spencer was kneeling by Robby's side, stethoscope at his ears, listening to the boy's chest. Danny was nowhere to be seen, and for one panicked moment, Sean feared the boy had run off.

"Daddy!" Daniel careened around the corner from the hallway toward Sean. "I was hiding, Daddy!" Sean nodded to the doctor, patted Daniel's head and took the groceries into the kitchen.

"Take these out of the bag for me, all right, son?" Sean chucked Danny under the chin and noticed his face was red. He had been crying. "What's the matter?" he asked, bending down to the boy's level.

"Nuthin'." Danny sniffled. "I forgot what you told me about the watch, that's all."

Sean hugged him, imagining the boy's fright when Dr. Spencer came to the door. "There's a treat in the bag for you. See if you can find it."

In the living room a second later, Sean stood near the sofa and waited for Dr. Spencer's verdict. He had a question he wanted to ask, but he didn't want to interrupt the man's examination.

"Looks like he might have a touch of strep," the doctor said, putting his instruments away. "I don't like the looks of those tonsils, though. You might want to consider having them out."

"Is that necessary?"

The doctor stared over the tops of thick glasses. Dr. Spencer was in his fifties with thin graying hair, each strand of which seemed glued in place on his head. He wore a suit the color of his hair, and a rumpled raincoat was draped over the chair by the front door.

"It would avoid these sore throats." He bent over his bag, pulled out a medicine bottle. "Two tablespoons a day—one in the morning, one at night." He handed the bottle to Sean. "I don't imagine you have time to run to the pharmacy."

"You're sure it's nothing worse?"

"I'm positive. Seen it a hundred times before." Dr. Spencer straightened. Sean waited for him to offer a scolding about leaving the boys alone, but Dr. Spencer remained mute on that topic.

"Doctor, I have a question before you go." Sean handed the doctor his coat and helped him into it. "I'm working on a new case. And it's down at the Hopkins lab that is doing some of the work on the polio cure—"

"Not a cure. A vaccine," Dr. Spencer corrected him.

"There wouldn't be any risk of me bringing home any...any polio..."

"Germs?" Dr. Spencer finished for him. "Only if you came into contact with the actual virus and even then..." He rubbed his chin with his hand. "To tell you the truth, I don't know." He laughed softly at his own lack of confidence. "Every time I turn around seems they have a new theory as to how it spreads. In the water. In the air. Years ago they even thought cats were carriers." He shook his head. "Thousands of 'em were thrown into rivers by angry parents."

He looked at Sean's worried face and changed his tone. "I'm sure it's safe. It's Hopkins, after all. They don't do shoddy work. But if it worries you, why don't you ask one of the researchers or their assistants?" He patted Sean on the arm. "You're a good father to worry about that." Sean knew he was telling him he didn't hold it against him that he hadn't been there earlier.

Sean saw him to the door, but the doctor stopped and asked him a question.

"What's the case, if I might ask?"

"One of the doctors. Suspicious death."

"Oh my. Who was the victim?"

Sean saw no harm in telling him. It was probably already in the evening paper. "A Dr. Myron Lowenstein."

Dr. Spencer's eyes widened. "My goodness, I knew him in New York! A wonderful professor—so kind and generous. Everyone loved him. An amazing teacher—there wasn't a thing he didn't know. Brilliant, and he was young—at the time!" He tsk-tsked and shook his head. "I hadn't realized he was in Baltimore. What a tragedy. I'm sorry to hear of it."'

کیجی

Later that evening, after the boys were tucked in bed, Sean made two phone calls.

The first was to Sal's sister, to take care of the favor he'd promised his partner.

Sean dug through his pocket, found the paper with her info on it and quickly dialed the number before his party line phoner had a chance to get on the wire. It barely rang once before a mellow woman's voice came over the line.

"Is this Brigitta?" He struggled to read his handwriting and the last name he'd scribbled in a hurry.

"Yes," she said, sounding wary.

"This is Detective Sean Reilly. I work with your brother, Sal." Now that he had her on the line, he realized he wasn't sure how this should go. Oh hell. Just be direct. "I was wondering if you'd like to have a cup of coffee or something some time."

He heard the smile in her voice when she answered. "My brother is playing matchmaker, is he?"

Sean chuckled, relieved to have her state the obvious. "I guess he is."

"Did he force you to call?" She didn't sound annoyed. Just amused.

"No. No, he didn't. I was quite happy to ring you up." He liked the way she sounded. Comfortable and undemanding.

"All right. Then I'll let you buy me a cup of coffee, officer. And we can tell Sal he did good."

They set a time and place—noon the next day at a lunchroom downtown—but Sean didn't make much conversation because he was eager to move on to his next call. Brigitta didn't seem disappointed when he told her he had to go.

The next number he dialed was Susan Schlager's, Lowenstein's secretary.

She answered, sniffling, after five rings. He introduced himself, and before he had a chance to ask any questions, she started sobbing.

"I—I just heard the news." She gulped in air. In the background, Sean heard a radio and a man's voice, like someone talking to a neighbor.

"Did you work for Dr. Lowenstein long?" he asked.

"Just three years," she said, her voice low and scared. The man in the background called to her, and she must have put her hand over the receiver to answer, but Sean could still hear her say, "It's about my boss. I have to take it." The man's response was unintelligible but rancorous. When Susan came back on the line, she was almost whispering. "Before that, he used whoever was available to type his stuff and all."

"Did he have any enemies?"

"I don't think so. He was a quiet man."

Sean thought of what Dr. Spencer had said about him. "Was he well-liked?"

She laughed, but it was nervous, as if she were putting on a show for the man in the background. "I—I don't really know. He was very private," she said. "I didn't know much about him. Beyond his work."

"How about his friends?"

"He didn't have any that I knew of—or that he let on. Like I said, he was—"

"Private," he filled in. Was she really this ignorant of the man's personal life or was she hiding something? He tried a different tack.

"Did anything happen in the past few weeks that left you uneasy? Troubled?"

She paused, and he heard the man in the background clearly now, telling her he was hungry and he didn't want to wait.

"I can't remember anything." But she said it so quickly that Sean wondered if she just wanted to get off the phone.

"Thank you, Miss Schlager," Sean said.

"Mrs..." He heard her telling someone she'd be right there, and the man yelling something back at her. "It's *Mrs.* Schlager," she said to Sean in a rushed voice. "And I have to go—"

Before she had a chance to say goodbye, the phone went dead.

Chapter Four

"LET YOUR *VATER* TAKE YOU in to work. You've had the terrible shock." Elise Marie Dell's watery eyes stared at Julia from behind round spectacles. Julia's mother sat at the kitchen table, light glinting on her reddish hair, now darkened by age, secured by pins into a tidy bun on the back of her head. She spoke with a slight German accent, one that had rendered her all but mute during the war years. Now that that terrible time was over, she still acted and spoke in small increments, as if being too bold would draw unwanted attention.

Julia poured herself a cup of coffee from the electric percolator on the table while her sister Helen concentrated on making some breakfast specialty she'd read about in a magazine the day before. Helen was a thinner version of Julia with lighter hair that in brilliant sun sparkled with reddish highlights. Like Julia, she kept it short and curled in a style that looked carefree but required sleepless nights in hard curlers preceded by chemical permanent wave sets administered in the family kitchen by their mother.

Today Helen wore a belted robin's egg blue dress with bolero sleeves in shantung silk, its collar turned up to frame her perfectly made-up face. Julia knew Helen had just finished sewing the dress using a special "high fashion" pattern she'd bought on sale at Woolworth's. She might work in a dress shop, but Helen aspired to a higher sense of couture. To protect her creation, Helen had tied a starched white apron with two-inch ruffled hem around her waist. She had whipped eggs and other things in a bowl and was heating a cast iron skillet. Now she dashed a droplet of water on to the hot surface, its hiss indicating it was ready.

"I'm not that hungry," Julia said as she hobbled to the chair across from her mother.

Helen didn't look at her. "They're French crepes. Sort of like pancakes, except more elegant." Helen shot her a quick smile, and Julia felt like hugging her. Helen was so...delicate...ever since the end of the war. Even though she was four years older than Julia, Helen seemed as if she'd stopped growing in 1945, the year she'd turned twenty, the year the war ended. What a celebration that had been—when victory was declared in Europe. Her father had even bought a bottle of champagne. Her mother had been equally happy—now she'd find out the fate of her sisters and brothers—and they'd all shared a giddy evening drinking together and laughing, her mother telling stories about her family she'd not felt free to share again until they were no longer her adopted country's enemies. They'd gone to church together that evening, talked with neighbors and friends, huddled around the radio, laughing, planning. Helen had talked about how she wanted to use the silk from her fiance's parachute to make a wedding veil.

Then, just three weeks later, Helen had received the phone call from her fiance's mother, giving her the bad news.

Helen had stopped at that moment. She seemed to be stuck preparing for things. Preparing for her own life as a wife. Preparing for her own household. Preparing for—

"Here, try this." Helen brandished a plate in front of Julia. Two delicately-rolled pancakes dusted with powdered sugar nestled near a dollop of strawberry jam.

Julia smiled at her sister. "Mmm...smells great!" She wasn't pretending. Now that food was in front of her, she was hungry. She grabbed a fork and started eating, thinking for the hundredth time that Helen's culinary adventures were going to add ten pounds to her figure in no time if she wasn't careful. She complimented her sister on the new dish as her father entered the room.

"How's my girls?" he asked, kissing Helen on the cheek while she worked.

Howard Louis Dell was a stocky man no taller than his daughters. His thick salt-and-pepper hair stood up in a short bristle-brush style around a face carved with deep wrinkles from the smiles he beamed on the world. As was his custom, he sat at the table and opened the paper while patting his shirt pocket for his Camels. Elise recognized her cue and stood to fetch his coffee as he lit a smoke with a slim silvery lighter, a Christmas present from Helen and Julia, who'd pooled their money this past holiday. Their oldest sister, Beth, had embroidered him some handkerchiefs. With three children and a fourth on the way, Beth didn't have a lot of money to spare, so Julia and Helen hadn't even asked her to go in on the gift, something Beth had resented, to the younger girls' dismay.

After Elise put the coffee in front of her husband, she touched him on the shoulder and kissed him on the forehead before sitting down herself. Helen served her father, then went back to cooking, this time for her mother.

"I'm going to make a cake this morning, Jules," Helen said without turning from the skillet. "Red velvet it's called." She looked at Julia and winked. "With frosting."

Julia responded with a close-mouthed smile to the private joke—their mother, whose culinary skills were slight, only made one kind of cake, yellow, with no frosting. All three girls had giggled over this as they'd grown older, recounting to each other the moment they'd discovered — usually at a friend's house for a meal — that other mothers made cakes with creamy icings or other fancy toppings.

"Don't you have to work this morning, Helen?" Julia asked.

"Mr. Montague said I should come in at noon and work until seven. He's keeping the store open one night a week now." Helen worked at Montague Fashions, a ladies wear shop on Belair Road.

"You will be walking home at dark," Elise said, pronouncing her "w's" like "v's."

"I'll pick her up," Howie said, putting his paper down, stubbing out his cigarette and diving into his breakfast.

The walk home would be perfectly safe, but the Dell household now seemed to operate on the principle that disaster waited around the next corner. Their mother went to Mass every morning, Julia knew, as part of a deal she'd made with God when Julia had first fallen ill. And her father left nothing to chance as far as his girls were concerned.

Julia believed the polio had changed them. They hadn't paid much attention to the threat, hadn't taken some of the zealous precautions of other families, using antiseptic on hands, avoiding crowds, and especially swimming pools. But no one knew really where it came from. A thousand hypotheses circulated. Contaminated milk, insects, exhaust from cars, sewers — one fantastic theory from years ago had it that poisonous gases from the first war in Europe carried the germs, which were breathed in by sharks, who then breathed them out again on America's shores.

Neither Julia nor her family knew how she'd contracted the disease. One day she'd been happy and healthy, kissed by summer's joy, and the next she'd been knocked down to humiliating dependence by "the summer plague." If they'd paid more attention, would they have been able to prevent it? The question haunted her parents, she knew. And she felt guilty about knowing.

Julia scraped back her chair, using the opportunity to escape. "I'll take the bus. You shouldn't have to chauffeur us all over the place, Dad." She grabbed her plate and took it to the sink. Helen, who had just finished cooking her own plate of crepes, sat at the table in Julia's spot. Helen didn't protest their father's offer to pick her up even though the store was only a mere five blocks away. Oh, Helen, thought Julia, worry lines creasing her forehead.

For months now, both Julia and her sister Beth had been nudging Helen to learn to drive. For Julia, it was out of the question. But Beth had learned and enjoyed its liberating effect tremendously. Both sisters thought that if Helen drove, it might unstick something and push her out of herself. Helen, however, resisted.

Elise looked from daughter to daughter and then to her husband, trying to decide whether to prompt him to drive both girls. Before Elise could speak, Julia hurried down the front hall to the coat closet. If she rushed she could just make the eight o'clock bus into town. As she pulled her cloth coat and scarf from the hanger, her mother appeared behind her, wiping her hands on her floral cotton apron.

"Your father can take you. Helen can walk. Maybe I walk to meet her." Elise tilted her head to one side, studying her daughter. "You look pale. And it's cold today."

"Mother, I'll be fine." Julia leaned her cane against the wall and buttoned her coat.

"Maybe you shouldn't go in at all."

"Really, Ma, I'm not sick."

"You came home early yesterday." She spoke quietly as if she didn't want Howie to hear.

"I was shaken up, that's all. It's understandable." Julia tied the scarf on her head and began to pull on her gloves.

"But, Julia, the murder. You shouldn't work where there was a murder!" Her mother crossed her arms over her chest.

Julia opened her mouth to protest but stopped herself as she stared at her mother's vulnerable eyes. Only as tall as her daughters, Elise Dell always gave the impression of towering over them. In a quiet, persistent way, she dominated their lives, never out of thought. She had a frail build, pale complexion, and blue eyes that compelled affection. She enjoyed dressing up for special occasions and prided herself in looking ten years younger than her age. She followed the lives of movie stars with childlike pleasure, listened to radio soap operas in the afternoon while having a cup of strong coffee and would become teary-eyed over a gift of perfume or inexpensive paste jewelry. What she lacked in household skills over the years she'd made up for in — in what, wondered Julia as she slowly smiled at her mother. In something irresistibly likable, a natural charm that made them all want to revolve around her and take care of her despite her faults. Julia could think of no one in the world like her mother. Now she looked afraid, an emotion Julia was seeing more and more in her mother's eyes as time wore on, and the inevitable but ordinary tragedies of life chipped at her cushioned heart.

"It might not have been a murder," Julia said, taking her mother's hands in hers. "It might have been an accident and everyone is going crazy over it."

Her mother shook her head. "It was in the paper this morning. Didn't you see it? They said murder."

Julia had seen it, but still she reassured her mother. "If it was...someone who killed Dr. Lowenstein...it was probably something personal. A feud of some kind." Balancing her weight on her good leg, she leaned forward and hugged her mother. "Don't worry about me. I'll call you from the office today."

She turned, grabbed her cane and left, closing the heavy oaken door with a quick whoosh. The Dell house, an old pre-war Victorian, sat in a quiet tree-shaded neighborhood in the Shrine of the Little Flower parish, a church just built. Sometimes Julia dreamed of owning her own home — a sleek new "rancher" style like the ones she'd seen in Helen's magazines. No stairs.

The brisk air and bright sunshine felt good on her cheeks as she walked to the bus stop three blocks away. She liked being on her own; she liked breathing deep and feeling as if each step were a new beginning.

As she walked, Julia remembered something she could have told her mother to comfort her. The detective hadn't called her yesterday afternoon. He'd wanted her number in case he had more questions. He would have called with more questions — maybe they'd solved the case already, or maybe they'd determined it was an accident, after all.

❧

Sal Sabataso pulled his Chevy up to the curb in the well-to-do neighborhood of Homeland in the city's northern section. When he'd arrived here yesterday, he'd thought at first he'd written the address down wrong, and had pushed his new gray fedora back to scratch his head as he'd reread the slip of paper. Nine-oh-six Willow Lane. It wasn't the kind of place a Lowenstein would fit in.

Big brick houses with well-tended yards lined the street of the swank and exclusive neighborhood. Now Sal walked casually down the road, studying the homes, noting the new and expensive cars along the curb, in contrast to the old but well-kept colonials with freshly-painted shutters and gleaming doors. Everything felt clean and polished here. And the quiet — in his neighborhood, quiet always felt like a prelude to something happening, something noisy and alive. Here the lack of sound felt disapproving, as if unseen eyes were waiting for him to speak too loudly or say the wrong thing.

Sean would have shrugged it off and done his job, talking comfortably with friends of the deceased, getting what he needed and moving on. It was one of the things Sal was trying to learn from his partner — how to get people to open up to you and how to pretend, at least, that you fit in anywhere. Sal had a knack for sticking his foot in it. On more than one occasion, he'd managed to rile up a witness to the point of clamming up entirely. Or he'd go to the opposite extreme — as he had with Mrs. Wellstone yesterday — and be so damned chummy he got their life story complete with footnotes.

But Sean had been late this morning, so Sal had popped into their boss's office — Mark O'Brien was the fellow's name — and told him they'd be out on the Lowenstein case that day, being careful to say "*we'll* be out," so O'Brien would think Sean was meeting him somewhere. The poor fellow needed a break after what he'd been through with his wife.

Up ahead, a woman hugged her coat to herself as she walked two scampering Boston terriers. Sal picked up his pace as if he belonged here but muffed it by stumbling over a tree root and cursing under his breath. He recovered his sensibility and approached her, touching his hat and smiling as he came nearer.

"Morning, ma'am," he said, trying to imitate the gentle and confident voice of his partner. The woman merely nodded her head as she strode toward him.

"I was wondering," he said, stopping in front of her, "if you know of Dr. Lowenstein."

The woman's smile left her. "No one I know by that name lives around here." She stood in front of him now, and her coat was open just enough for him to see the gray uniform of a domestic servant.

Just yesterday, old Mrs. Wellstone had been quite talkative about her neighbor. Maybe this maid had embraced the snobbishness of her employers and didn't want to admit that a Jew resided in the neighborhood.

"Who lives here?" he asked, pointing to Lowenstein's house.

She looked at the white shingled home with an arched trellis by the front door and fat boxwoods below the windows.

"That would be Dr. Mike's house," she said. "Poor Dr. Michael Lowe." She pronounced the name loudly and carefully so that he understood this man was entitled to be here.

"Oh, I'm sorry. Don't know why I got the name wrong." He tried to remember yesterday's talk with Wellstone. The woman had been a bit hard of hearing. And how many times had he said "Lowenstein" anyway? Just once, at the outset of their conversation. The rest of the time, it was "the doctor," or "your neighbor." Jeez, how'd he miss that? And what about the papers Sean had scooped up—any of them have the name Lowe on them?

"Were you a friend of his?" she asked archly. The dogs pulled at the leashes, and she strained to hold them back.

"Yeah...uh, I worked with him," he said, not wanting to give away his police identification. It could scare her off. She must not have seen the papers, the stories about "Lowenstein's" murder. She sounded like she only knew "Dr. Mike" was dead. Maybe Wellstone had blabbed to her maid, and word had gotten around.

She looked at him, as if she had better things to do. He wished he had a biscuit or cracker to feed the dogs, but his pockets were empty. He wondered if Sean carried such things for circumstances like this. "I was supposed to stop by this morning."

"You're a friend and you didn't know he'd passed away?" She shook her head as the dogs tugged at the leash. "I really don't feel comfortable talking about it." She let the dogs lead her away.

"Damn," he muttered. As soon as she was out of sight, he walked up to Lowenstein's door. It was locked, of course, and he didn't have the key. Sean had pocketed it yesterday from among the deceased's belongings at the lab.

He opened the mail slot on the door and peered at some unreachable envelopes and a flyer on the floor. He could make out a gas bill and a church notice about the Lent and Holy Week schedule that year. Both addressed to Dr. Michael Lowe. Yesterday's mail, delivered after they'd left the house.

He heard a car rumble to life down the street, so he pulled away from the door and walked to another neighbor's house. There he was able to talk to another maid at the door, this time a plump Negro woman with a white lace cap to match her apron. The mistress of the house, a new bride, was already out for the day. Yes, the maid knew of Dr. Lowe, but she was miserly with information until Sal told her he was with the police, investigating Dr. Lowe's unexpected death. After a shocked silence and a murmured "Lord have mercy," the maid was more forthcoming.

"Did he have many friends?" Sal swept the neighborhood with his arm.

"He was a quiet man. Didn't join in much. Except at church," the maid said. She didn't move an inch from the front door. "Mrs. Wellstone's a member, the house on the other side of him, and sometimes he'd give her a ride on Sunday."

"That would be the Cathedral of the Incarnation?" he asked, remembering the envelope.

"Yes, sir. The Episcopal cathedral."

"He ever talk about where he came from—like the west side?" Sal asked. The west side of town was a Jewish section.

She shook her head vigorously. "Far as I know he's always been here." She nodded her head toward Lowenstein's home. She lowered her voice. "Mrs. Wellstone has a key to his house. Every year he went away, and she'd have her maid pick up his mail and such."

Sal knew about that.

"He have someone like you to help out?"

She smiled. "Angie Hamilton. Comes by every Friday."

He spoke with her for a few more minutes, during which time she told him how "Dr. Mike" had seen to a bad bee sting of hers last year that had "swelled up her arm" so bad she could barely move her fingers. "He was real nice to me, too," she confided, "tended to me in his living room, not the kitchen, even though I was afraid of him spilling medicine on his things."

"He was nice to Angie too?"

"Mmm-hmm. A real gentleman. Always gave her a gift at Christmas and time off at Easter."

He handed her his card. "I'll stop by later, but if you think of anything, give me a call."

She went back to her chores, and he went back to his car, slipping behind the big wheel quickly, unsure whether to be proud of his detective work or disappointed with its meager results. As his fingers touched the keys to start the ignition, movement in his rear view mirror caught his gaze. An old Ford lumbered into view, its driver peering at street addresses. The car looked out of place here. It was dusty and noisy, its right front fender dented in. Sal slumped down in the seat and watched.

The driver pulled up to the curb by Dr. Lowenstein's house, digging the front passenger side tire into the curb. *Guess I know who dented that fender,* Sal thought, peering out from under the brim of his hat.

A woman in a gray suit got out of the car, looking up and down the street before approaching Dr. Lowenstein's door. She raised her gloved hand to knock but stopped before fist hit wood. Her hand then flew to her mouth, as if realizing the occupant was no longer among the living. She pulled a handkerchief from her purse and blew her nose, shaking her head in sorrow. She then tried the knob of the door. When it didn't give, she tried lifting the sash of a nearby window, but it wouldn't give either. She looked over her shoulder after this effort as if afraid someone had seen her. She raised her hand to her brow, as if distraught, and looked up at the house, assessing other avenues of entry. After a few seconds, she hung her head in defeat, obviously giving up. She turned and walked back toward her car, still looking down.

By this time, Sal had exited his vehicle and met her at her own. She looked up, startled, brown eyes watery from crying. Her features were small but her cheeks well rounded, giving the impression that she was a bit overweight when in fact she was slender as a reed, her thin suit hanging on her frame. Her lipstick was too red, and her dark hair unfashionably long, curls crushed at her neck by a metallic clip. She wore rhinestone earrings and a matching necklace that looked like children's jewelry.

"Could I have a word with you, ma'am?" Sal asked.

"No!" She rushed to the driver's side, but Sal followed her there and placed his hand on the door so she couldn't open it.

"What's your name? What you doing here?"

She visibly cringed at his sharp words and looked about to cry.

"None of your business."

"I'm with the police," he pressed. "How'd you know Dr. Lowenstein?"

"Oh God. I..." She looked back at the doctor's house as if he could help her. "I worked for him. I'm—I was—his secretary. Susan Schlager." She gathered her wits, sniffling back her fears. "I just wanted to see if I could get in and get some of his research papers—before they were lost forever. In the investigation."

Sal didn't believe her, but a quarter hour more of questioning got him no other explanations, and she broke down sobbing so hard about her boss that Sal gave up, once again thinking how he'd done something wrong, something Sean would have handled better. After taking down her phone number and address, he let her go, following her all the way into town where she parked and went into her office.

Chapter Five

"MAIL'S HERE."

Linda stood in front of Julia's desk, sorting envelopes. "Is he in?" Linda nodded toward the hallway with the labs and doctors offices.

"Yes, but his door is closed," Julia said, picking up envelopes Linda tossed on her desk. Dr. Jansen hadn't said much before disappearing into his office an hour ago. A quick comment on "how awful" the news was about Dr. Lowenstein, a question about the course of the investigation. When Julia had little information to offer him, he'd seemed annoyed. Then again, he often seemed irritated to her. She was used to it. She had notes to type, several meetings to arrange, supplies to order and now the mail to sort. She'd left his paper on his desk, finished and free of errors.

Although Dr. Jansen's role in the polio research was only peripheral, mail had increased dramatically as word had leaked out about the possibility of a vaccine. Heartbreaking, pitiful letters had begun arriving by the dozens—mothers pleading for cures, wives and husbands offering money for a chance to try the "new medicine." What must the mail have been like in Pittsburgh, at Dr. Salk's lab, if they were inundated here?

The first time she'd read one of the letters, Julia had been overcome with both pity and embarrassment as she'd recognized her own family in each plea. Her mother had urged her, when she'd begun work at Hopkins, to "talk with the doctors" about her case. Even now, Mutti thought a cure was possible. It made Julia feel as if she'd let her mother down.

If it were left to Dr. Jansen, the letters would have all been thrown away. But Julia typed responses to each one, a simple message she'd had Mrs. Wilcox approve, thanking the correspondent for the letter but making no promises. Now, as Linda dropped letter after letter on to her desk, Julia couldn't help heaving a long sigh. Since she'd lost half a day yesterday, she had no time to spare to respond to all these.

Behind her, Susan Schlager spoke up. "I can answer some of those for you if you need help, Julia." Linda shot Julia a knowing glance. Susan was afraid of losing her job now that her boss was dead. Julia looked at Susan with sympathy. The poor gal had been so shaken when she'd arrived late for work that she'd hardly been able to talk. She'd sat, gloved hands in her lap, for a good ten minutes gathering her wits just from walking past the lab where her boss had worked. When Julia had offered her condolences, though, Susan had tried to brush them aside. "I'm all right. He was just my boss, that's all. I'm worried about my job. Steve bought a new car so's I could drive the old one, you see, and we can't afford for me to be out of work."

Julia turned and smiled at her now, trying to ease her mind. "Thanks, Sue. That would be helpful. I'll open the letters and show you what to send them. I have a file."

"Do you think you'll keep working once you're married?" Susan asked as Julia turned back to her desk. At first Julia thought the question was directed at Linda, whose wedding plans were far advanced. But then she realized Susan was talking to *her*, fishing for possible openings on a new job for herself now that Dr. Lowenstein had passed away.

"I guess so. I hope so," Julia said, suddenly imagining a life with nothing to occupy her time except tidying a little home. As much as she wanted a place of her own, that vision filled her with the same sense of claustrophobia she'd experienced working in the law firm on Belair Road. She'd miss working, she decided, and would have to let Will know she intended to keep her job. Maybe he wouldn't like that.

"I think that's it," Linda said, dropping the last envelope on to Julia's blotter and taking a similar collection to her desk. She also handed a few items to Susan, addressed to Dr. Lowenstein.

"If you're worried about a job, Sue, you could always clean the cages," Linda teased. The scientists used chimpanzees for the polio research, and the girls disliked the animals intensely. They were smelly and noisy and, Julia thought, pitiful in a way that elicited anger, not mercy, in her heart. The secretaries had jointly agreed that they'd stick together in rebuffing any attempts to have secretarial staff do anything related to the chimps' care. Julia was particularly vulnerable in this regard because she'd had polio and therefore wouldn't be at risk of catching anything from infected animals. Last year when the lab was short-staffed, she'd been afraid — maybe unreasonably so — of being asked. When she'd confessed her fear to Linda, the girl had marched into Mrs. Wilcox's office, informing her that none of them would tolerate such a request. Mrs. Wilcox had found a new animal tender that very week, Earl Dagley.

Susan just snorted, and Julia smiled as she slit envelopes with a marble-edged opener, quickly skimming the notes and placing them in a neat pile.

"I wonder if Dr. Mike left a will," Susan said.

My god the girl is shallow. Has she always been like this?

"Any news from Bethesda — did Dr. Bodian find anything?" Julia asked.

"Don't know," Linda said. "It would be awful if things had to stop." At Susan's quizzical look, Linda gave the girl the explanation. Susan's mouth dropped open, and she reddened. "Dr. Mike didn't have nothing to do with the polio," she said indignantly, as if the killer had made an outrageous mistake.

Julia picked up an envelope with strange, boxy lettering on the front. Sometimes children wrote the letters themselves, either pleading their own cases or those of their siblings. Julia frowned, prepared to read a sweet if poorly spelled cry for help.

Instead, her eyes widened as she looked at the note. She took in a quick breath.

"Oh my God!"

"What?" Linda said.

"This is...vile," Julia said, putting the letter down as if it were something rotten and moldy. "I can't believe someone would—"

"Julia, what in the world is it?" This from Susan.

"Listen—'Soon the whole world will know that the Jew doctors are once again trying to infect our children. This Jew plan has been going on for far too long and must be stopped. I have friends in important positions who will aid in the fight against the...'" Julia's voice petered out, and she turned to her office mates. "It's really too much. I can't believe someone would send something like this."

Susan's face paled, and she sat straight and still. "Dr. Mike got them all the time." She pursed her lips, her eyes darkening with the rage of the falsely accused. "He wasn't involved in the polio research!" she repeated.

Julia's head shot up. Was Susan upset because of the anti-Semitism in the notes or because it was directed at the wrong man when Dr. Lowenstein received such letters?

Linda came back over to Julia's desk and stood reading over her shoulder. "Dr. Jansen's not Jewish, is he?"

"What does it matter?" Julia asked, indignation crawling up her throat. "This is despicable! A Jewish conspiracy? It's just the sort of thing that happened—"

"You should give it to the police." Linda put her hands on Julia's shoulders. "That letter." She turned toward Susan. "And any you received."

"I didn't keep them," Susan said in a small, whiny voice, as if being accused of incompetence and feeling the need to defend herself. "Dr. Lowenstein wasn't involved."

"Give what to the police?" a strong male voice asked. Sean Reilly stood in the doorway, his hat in one hand at his side. He wasn't wearing his wool coat, and his face was ruddy from the cool air.

A blush coursed over Julia's own face as she looked up at him.

"Letters," she explained, handing over the one she'd just received. Julia studied him while he read. His eyes were shadowed by half-circle smudges, and his thick, wiry hair looked as if he'd forgotten to comb it.

In a tumble of overlapping conversation, the three women shared with Sean what they'd just discussed, with Susan annoyingly repeating in grave tones how Dr. Lowenstein was not involved in the polio research. To Julia it sounded as if she were really saying, "Dr. Lowenstein was not involved in *this* Jewish conspiracy." An inarticulate worry smoldered to life in Julia's mind, something she couldn't define, a thought she put away for consideration later. Dr. Lowenstein was dead. A Jewish doctor. The letters. The mishap at the Parke, Davis lab...

"Do you know if any of the other doctors received these?" Sean asked, pocketing the letter.

"Mrs. Wilcox would know," Julia said. "The office manager." She reached for her cane and stood. "Here, I'll show you to her office."

⋙⋘

Sean knew where the office was, but he followed Julia all the same. Maybe he'd grab the opportunity to talk with her. He'd come to the hospital that morning with the intention of interviewing Susan Schlager and Dr. Jansen, both of whom had been out the previous day. He'd especially wanted to get there early to try to talk to the Schlager woman alone. He'd gotten the impression from the telephone conversation that she wasn't a woman who talked freely when others were present. He wanted to go over this with Sal, but his partner had been out by the time he'd gotten started on the day.

Sean had been delayed, as usual, by tending to his boys. Robby was still not rallying, which troubled Sean more than usual because of all this polio business. But this morning, Mrs. Buchanan had caused the problem, showing up late, complaining of "biliousness" in accusatory tones. She'd repeated an often-uttered threat about "only agreeing to help him out for a little while," urging him to talk to the Sisters again for names of ladies who could care for the boys.

He'd tried teasing her out of her ill humor by saying he'd never find anyone as skillful or as lovely. She'd risen to the bait—somewhat—by patting her tightly curled hair and saying that maybe what he needed was a new wife and not a hired hand.

Yes, well, wouldn't that be fine—if the good Sisters of St. Benedict's could find him a woman willing to jump into his bed as well as his children's lives. He'd like that. He'd not had a woman in that way since— since long before Mary had died, since illness had stolen her as a lover before death robbed her as a companion.

While he followed Julia Dell through the Hopkins labs, images returned. He'd paced hallways like this too many times, stepping outside Mary's room to get some air. A lie, that was. The hallways weren't the place to get fresh air. They were a place to stop aching, to breathe naturally, and then to brace himself to go back in again and hold her hand, pretending she would be coming home soon to see her boys. They both had known she wouldn't, yet they'd both kept up the pretense.

It troubled him now how hard that had been for her. They'd have been better off sobbing in each other's arms and cursing the heavens together. Instead, she'd lain quiet, afraid to look at him for too long. Oh, he'd caught her on occasion. When he'd fallen asleep in the chair, he'd awakened to see her staring at him. And in that brief moment, only truth had spoken, and it had been hard and empty. The truth had been she knew she was leaving him, and he'd known it as well, but to say it would have been to give up on God. And they couldn't betray God in front of each other, no matter what went on in their hearts, because they'd both hoped the other had enough faith for the two of them.

Those memories were more vivid to him now than all his war years, and they stung him more deeply. You expect death in battle after a while. Coming home from the war, he'd expected what every other GI thought he was entitled to—peace.

He should have asked Sal to do this interviewing. He could have gone to Homeland to look into the deceased's background. But Sal had already left for Homeland when he'd arrived at the office, leaving a discreet note tucked just under his telephone saying he'd told O'Brien, their boss, that they were working the case together.

Julia and Sean's pace was slow—not because of Julia's bad leg so much as because of the slim skirt she wore. It restricted movement, a problem for her more than most. Poor gal. Her good leg was shapely enough, and she had a pretty cupid-like face and sweet figure. She dressed well. Her creamy blouse with full sleeves reminded Sean of something from older times, something distinctly soft and feminine. She would have looked like a real sophisticate in fancy shoes with little heels. But instead, she had to wear heavier footwear, something akin to what the nuns, or Mrs. Buchanan, wore.

"How long have you worked here?" he asked as they walked.

"Five years."

"For Dr. Jansen all that time?"

"No, I started for a Dr. MacIntyre. He retired last year."

"So you've only been working for Dr. Jansen for a year?"

"That's right."

He'd already determined that Jansen was a difficult man. A lab assistant of some sort had given that up yesterday.

"Do you like it?"

She turned and smiled. "Yes, I do. He's a challenge, but Dr. MacIntyre was, too, in his own way."

"How so?"

"He would hardly say a word if I made a mistake, and I made quite a few when I first came here. I'd only find out he was displeased later—when I asked for a day off or something like that."

"You prefer a man to just yell at you outright."

She laughed but didn't look at him. "I prefer directness. Dr. Jansen is direct." She pushed through double doors, and they entered another long hallway.

"How about Dr. Lowenstein?"

She looked at him curiously. "He wasn't my boss, but I occasionally did things for him when Susan was out. He was a nice man."

"The call he got yesterday—was it someone you recognized?" He'd been over this somewhat, but now that she was calmer, maybe she'd remember something.

"I could barely hear him, to tell the truth."

"Did Lowenstein get many calls?"

"I don't know. I never counted them. Maybe less than what Dr. Jansen or Dr. Morton received." Soon they were outside a closed door and she stopped.

"You felt sorry for him?"

"I guess I did. Thought he was lonely."

"Did he seem unhappy?"

She paused, thinking. "Maybe. Like someone who's got a big cloud over him all the time because something happened to him..."

Like you, he thought. The cloud was there, despite her cheeriness. It was her eagerness, he decided, that gave it away, as if every new face, every new encounter would be the one that solved something for her, or returned something lost.

"But he impressed me more as a man who'd come to peace with a problem in his life."

"Is that so?"

She straightened, aware that he might be mocking her. He saw her pretty face redden. It was so pale that blush easily painted her feelings there. Poor girl.

"Dr. Lowenstein was a talented doctor," she said.

"Did it bother you then that he didn't use that talent on polio?"

Her blush deepened, but he had to pursue every lead. How did she react when she was angry—did she lash out? Would she have lashed out at Lowenstein?

"They all have different talents," she said, turning and walking the few steps left to Wilcox's office where she stopped. Her eyes moved away from his scouring gaze, and she stared at his chest.

He preferred directness, too. "Is something wrong?" He looked down. His blue-green tie sported a dark stain the size of a dime. Another thing he didn't do well without a wife—take care of laundry. One of the boys had rubbed a greasy finger there the last time he'd worn it. Damn. He liked to present a good face to the public. He pulled out a handkerchief and started rubbing it for show. Then, to make sure she knew he wasn't the slob, he offered an excuse. "My son, he isn't the most careful."

When he looked up at her, he noticed her smile freeze for a second before relaxing into a more natural line. "You have a boy? How nice."

"Two boys. Twins."

"You and your wife must be very proud."

"My wife's — I'm a widower."

"I'm sorry," she said. "Really sorry." She did sound sorry, he thought, but in an odd way, as if she were convincing herself she had compassion.

❧

At the end of the morning, Sean had a stack of the threatening letters in a big file folder and the only contact information Mrs. Wilcox had for Lowenstein — his lawyer at the firm of Patelson and Moore, a tidbit she'd pressed the payroll department for, knowing the police would want to contact somebody. Mrs. Wilcox had saved and catalogued all the letters, complete with envelopes, what mail shipment they'd arrived in, and any other notable features.

Organized and meticulous, she answered his new questions with care. She seemed surprised, in fact, by how little she had to tell him about Dr. Lowenstein, and he sensed this embarrassed her, that she felt she should have tried to know him better. She'd pored through files, she said, looking for next of kin, and found no one to contact. Dr. Lowenstein wasn't especially close to anyone at the lab. He worked on muscular reactions unrelated to the polio research, had specifically said he didn't want to be involved in it when he was interviewed. As far as she knew, he took all his vacations at a lake house in New York. She knew he lived somewhere near her, she told Sean, but wasn't familiar with the neighborhood or "what type of people" lived there. From that, Sean assumed she, too, was surprised to find a Jewish man in insulated Homeland.

While visiting with Wilcox, Sean was set upon by a gruff doctor in lab coat and thick spectacles. Dr. Morton, the other researcher on Lowenstein's floor. First he'd gone after Wilcox, in a soft but insistent voice, pressing her for information on a "Dr. Bodian" and admonishing her for not letting him know when Bodian had left. Then Wilcox had introduced Morton to Sean.

"Do you need to talk with me?" the doctor had asked quickly. "We can do it right now. Mike was a decent sort but kept to himself. I didn't know him well. He was doing interesting work on muscles that might help people like Jansen's gal. So it would be good if you could open up his office. Maybe somebody else can pick up where he left off, and that upstart in Pittsburgh won't get all the glory."

The upstart in Pittsburgh? Dr. Salk, Mrs. Wilcox explained after Dr. Morton had rushed away. And then she'd repeated Morton's question about allowing people into Lowenstein's office.

"As soon as I can," Sean had said.

"Everyone's racing against time now," she said.

"I'm doing the best I can, ma'am," he said, not hiding his irritation. Christ, it'd only been a day.

She stiffened. "Do you know how many children were struck with polio last year, Mr. Reilly?" When he didn't respond, she answered. "Nearly 36,000. And that wasn't a bad year compared to the one before. In '52, it was nearly 60,000." She stood, walking to a filing cabinet to put away papers from her desk. "The season keeps getting longer, too. It used to be we didn't see cases until summer. Now they crop up in the spring and continue sometimes as late as November." From another drawer, she pulled a file and opened it on her desk, splaying out several black and white photographs.

"This is what you could be delaying—something to prevent this sorrow." She pointed to the pictures, each filled with images of children and young adults working with therapists or in the living coffin of iron lungs. These weren't the smiling posters of the March of Dimes campaign, filled with sunny optimistic children whose upbeat attitude shamed you into parting with your coins. In these pictures, faces were grim and gaunt, some even pained as muscles were stretched or time crept by while motion ceased.

He looked at them quickly, only long enough to let her know he'd gotten the message. Dammit to hell. Now he had to solve a murder in time for polio research to go forward. He wouldn't be shouldered with that burden.

"I thought this lab wasn't as involved..."

She cut him off with a shake of her head. "Maybe not as much as Pittsburgh, but it's all important work. Dr. Bodian, for example, is one of the country's preeminent experts."

He gritted his teeth and kept his thoughts to himself. "We'll open up the scene soon."

After leaving her, Sean tried to talk to Dr. Jansen but once more was thwarted. The man had gone to a meeting at the university campus by the time Sean checked in again with Julia, probably off to that important work saving babies from infantile paralysis. He did manage to speak with Susan Schlager, though. She was still as high-strung as a scared kitten, so he suggested a stroll for a breath of fresh air.

But it was more of what Adelaide Wilcox had offered up, slim details filled out just a wee bit with some color that painted a clearer portrait of Susan than of Dr. Lowenstein. Susan had liked her boss—but it was in spite of the man's creed. He was the best of the three of them—the bosses of the secretaries who shared an office—and this was a point of pride with her. She was never distressed by the anti-Jewish letters, she told him, because "Dr. Lowenstein wasn't in with that kind." When pressed, she observed that he didn't take off for the holidays the way the other Jewish doctors did. And she'd seen him eating bacon in the cafeteria. She nodded her head in approval at this. Once, he'd driven her home when Steve, her husband, couldn't pick her up when they only had the one car, and he was "the perfect gentleman," walking her to her door and making sure she was in safely before returning to his car and driving away. Sean got the impression that was more than Susan's husband would do under similar circumstances. She ended their talk by assuring Sean in conspiratorial tones that Dr. Lowenstein wasn't pushy at all, "like *them.*"

When he stopped back at the station before heading out to meet Sal's sister for coffee, Sean learned just how "unlike them" Dr. Myron Lowenstein really was. He checked in with the coroner's office for their report. They confirmed the first findings—a blow to the man's head had killed him. But there was other news—if Myron Lowenstein was a Jewish male, he'd left the world uncircumcised. Maybe they'd put too much assumption on his name. A Lowenstein didn't have to be Jewish, right? Sean didn't know.

A few seconds after hanging up the phone, Sean saw Sal return.

"Our fine old Doc—" Sal began.

"—isn't Jewish," Sean finished for him.

Sal threw his hat and notebook on his desk while Sean gave him the coroner's report.

Sal nodded. "He might be Myron Lowenstein at the lab. But he's Mike Lowe to his upstanding Homeland neighbors."

"I wondered how Lowenstein would get in that neighborhood," Sean said. "I think others did, too," he added, thinking of Mrs. Wilcox.

"He wouldn't," Sal said, sitting in his chair. "It's some sort of protected neighborhood, some covenant or something controls who can buy in. But Mike Lowe fit in just fine. Went to church at the Cathedral of the Incarnation."

"Episcopal?"

"You got it." Sal leaned back, his hands behind his head. "Didn't join in much beyond that. Folks knew he was a doctor in research at Hopkins, but that's about all. It's a private kind of place to begin with, so he seemed like everybody else. They're all in for a surprise when this all comes out. Only bits and pieces in the paper so far."

"How come Wellstone didn't offer this up?"

Sal grimaced. "I don't think she heard me right when I first approached her. She's a little deaf. But I talked with a maid this morning—walking some dogs—and she didn't know no Lowenstein, only Lowe. She told me how Wellstone's maid looked after his house when he went away every year and gave me his cleaning lady's name."

Sean filled him in on his other talks and his need to reach Jansen and the law firm that handled Lowenstein's private affairs.

"I'll give them a call," Sean said. "Patelson and Moore."

"That's an old Baltimore firm."

"Exactly. Not the kind that deals with a Lowenstein, if you know what I mean."

"Anything else?"

"Why the two names? I mean, I can figure the Lowe part out, but why go by Lowenstein at work if he ain't. . . a real Lowenstein? I'd also like to know who tried to talk to him yesterday morning, who called him." Sean stood and brushed off his jacket. "But I'll get on that after lunch."

"I can join you."

"Don't think so." Sean said. "I'm meeting your sister."

Sal smiled, then sat up, remembering something. "I ran into that Susan secretary at the victim's house," he said, telling Sean about the encounter. "She mention it to you?"

"Nope," said Sean. "That's fishy."

"She's hiding something." Sal frowned. "Maybe we should talk to her husband."

"Maybe we should just *tell* her we're going to talk to her husband." Sean smiled. "My guess is that would open her up a bit more."

"I'll get on it. You shouldn't keep Brigitta waiting, or I'll hear about it, partner."

Chapter Six

BRIGITTA LORENZO SAT in a booth of the Old Towne Diner off of St. Paul Street near Lombard deciding how long she'd wait before heading out. Fifteen minutes, she decided — a polite enough interval should he be legitimately delayed, but a short enough period to provide her with time to run errands before her lunch hour was over.

She wore a navy blue suit with a cropped jacket, one of her favorite outfits. It and the silky, draping polka-dot blouse accented her good figure and set off her umber complexion. She eschewed the shorter hairstyles of the day and kept her full, dark hair brushed in heavy waves just below her shoulders. Men liked long hair and so did she. She'd recently discovered she could achieve a neat look by wetting her hairbrush in the morning and running it through her thick locks for at least fifty strokes, then lightly combing her fingers through it using men's brilliantine. She tempered its masculine odor with a spritz of lavender perfume. It was a relief not to have to deal with metal curlers that kept her awake half the night just to make sure her hair wasn't too curly. She wished she'd thought of it earlier.

Although Brigitta was a widow, she'd packed away her sorrow with her lacy wedding gown the year after hearing of her husband's death. She'd only been eighteen at her wedding, nothing more than a child, really. She'd thought at the time that her wedding night had initiated her into the full bloom of womanhood, but as days and years went on she realized that even that much-anticipated act — one she'd come to enjoy — had not completed the task.

No, she marked her transformation from girl to woman the day she refused to move back in with her family despite many tearful entreaties on the part of her mother and muttered curses on the part of her brother Sal. That had been the day she'd decided to stay in the little apartment she'd shared oh so briefly with Ernie, her husband, and to learn to provide for herself. That had been the day she'd packed her wedding dress in fine blue paper, and placed the box on a top shelf in her closet along with her regrets and her girlish dreams. The next day she'd enrolled in a typing class, paying for it with the last of Ernie's army life insurance, and six weeks later she'd landed her first job as a clerk for Carroll Shipping at the harbor.

She'd left them five years later and now worked as a full-fledged secretary for Ryan, Dennis, and Smathers, a law firm on St. Paul Street.

Until a month ago, she'd been the mistress of Gavin Smathers, the attractive—and married—junior partner in the firm. But Brigitta was ultimately no fool, and when it had become clear that Gavin had no intention of leaving his wife, she'd neatly and simply ended their affair, thanking him for his gifts and his time but making it absolutely clear she was no longer available for his bed.

She'd realized after breaking with Gavin that she'd given up on him months before. She'd been surprised and pleased to feel a sense of relief that she didn't need to keep hoping things would change. It had tired her out, all that baseless hope. She was much better at facing the world as it was, not wishing it were better. Now she had her eye on the office manager position, which was opening up because Diane Rivers was expecting her first child. Diane liked Brigitta and was going to put in a word for her. Once Brigitta received that promotion and the resulting raise in pay, she might even think of moving. She'd saved her money wisely over the past ten years—not just her salary but the extra cash Gavin had slipped her on occasion. She thought she had enough for a down payment on a house—if she could get a mortgage as a single woman. She'd use her "Mrs." title for that task, and call in Sal to co-sign if she had to.

But she didn't like to think about that too much—hope too dearly and you put dreams at risk. No more wishful thinking. She'd keep her joy locked away until that plan was closer to fruition.

Brigitta pulled the hem of her white glove back and looked at her watch. Five more minutes. And then she could tell her brother Sallie—he'd always be Sallie to her even though he used Sal at work—she'd tried to meet this latest fellow.

"Excuse me, are you Brigitta Lorenza?" A muscular man stood near her booth.

"Lorenzo," she said, smiling up at him. "That's me. You must be Sean." She gestured to the seat across from her and looked him over as he slid in. Tan face, tough look about him, a little on the disheveled side, sad eyes. Sal had told her about his wife.

"I'm sorry I'm late," he began.

"I only just arrived myself." She pulled off her gloves and picked up the menu, even though she'd already studied it and knew what she would order. Chicken salad and coffee.

He followed suit and pulled out a menu, too. Brigitta had been on enough of these set-up dates to feel some pity for the poor guys involved. They always looked so awkward and uncomfortable. Try as she might, she couldn't get her brother to understand that he really didn't need to introduce her to men. Even when she'd been with Gavin, she'd met her fair share of eligible men willing to give her more than a second glance—and a depressingly large number of ineligible men willing to do the same.

"Sal tells me you're working on an interesting case," she began. "Can you tell me about it?" She set her menu aside, signaling she was ready to order.

Grateful for the opening, he looked up and shared some information—really only what she'd already read in the paper. But this seemed to relax him, and by the time the waitress took their orders, he was talking quite easily about his children and his house. At this last bit, she perked up, asking him questions about its style and how long it had taken him to buy it.

All in all, it was an enjoyable lunch, and when he suggested going out for a movie "sometime soon," she didn't offer her pat excuse—I'm afraid I'm heading out of town for a short while—that she used for the candidates her brother sent her way. She looked him in the eye, smiled, and said, "I'll look forward to your call."

مہمہ

Sal decided not to confront Susan Schlager directly but to watch her for a while first. It seemed like something Sean, with his longer experience as a detective, would do.

He sat in his car, keeping an eye on the door to the Hopkins labs, the door that a friendly nurse had told him was the one used by everybody because it was close to the parking lot down the street. If Susan Schlager had been unsuccessful in her attempt to retrieve something from her boss's house that morning, maybe she'd try again at lunch. Sal was going to give her fifteen more minutes before going in to pry more out of her.

Just as the sand drifted through the hourglass of his self-imposed time limit, she appeared, walking with speed and determination toward the lot at the corner. He slid into an upright position and turned on the motor. Within a few moments, she was heading out of town, and he was following her.

Sure enough, she made her way north to Lowenstein's neighborhood. Because it was a quiet place with little traffic, Sal hung back, parking his car way up the block from the victim's home, behind a couple of thick-trunked trees. He eased out of his car and slunk into the shadows of one of the trees, watching.

She didn't disappoint. Once again, she went up to Lowenstein's door. But unlike in the morning when she seemed unsure and overwrought, she now walked with confidence. From her purse, she pulled a key.

Sal straightened. Of course. Lowenstein had probably left a key at the office, maybe even left it with her for those times when he needed something from home or needed...her. Had the two been a couple? Nosy Mrs. Wellstone surely would have picked up on that bit of slanderous gossip. Maybe they'd been discreet...

After Susan let herself into the house, Sal followed, mentally debating whether to surprise her inside or to wait. Wait, he decided, and see what she brings out. He walked slowly, hands in pockets, toward the home as if he were on a meditative stroll. When he passed Susan's car, he decided to take a side trip and investigate there first. After quickly glancing up and down the street, he opened the passenger side door.

She'd foolishly left her purse on the floor. He didn't move it, but opened it with a flick of his fingers. It, like the car, was neat as a pin, holding a change purse with a few bills and more coins, a lace-edged handkerchief, a lipstick and compact, and a slip of paper on which were written "bread, eggs." The glove compartment was equally tidy, with car registration and a few maps in rows. The only item carelessly strewn in the car, in fact, was a map of the city open on the passenger seat. Its crease ran through the Hopkins campus, so that the only square visible was of the very neighborhood they were now in.

With a quiet click, he closed the door and ambled down the street toward the Lowenstein home, eventually leaning against the wall by the door, out of sight should Susan glance out the window, and hidden from neighboring houses' view, safe from the smiles and jabber of Wellstone.

৵৶

Something troubled Julia.

Dr. Jansen had returned from his meeting at the university almost immediately after Detective Reilly had left. He'd glided into her office so quietly, looking over his shoulder as if he'd been waiting for the detective to leave. In fact, it occurred to Julia that it was awfully odd how quickly he'd returned. She'd mentally calculated how long it would have taken to travel to and fro, and that had hardly left time for any meeting at all. It was as if he'd just made up the meeting—she certainly hadn't had it on her copy of his calendar—to avoid the detective.

And when he had turned up in her office, things were odder still. Linda and Susan were out—Linda to an early lunch and Susan to speak with Mrs. Wilcox about "her situation" before heading to lunch herself—leaving Julia all alone. Standing in front of her desk, Dr. Jansen had talked to Julia quite a bit about Dr. Lowenstein's death. Dr. Jansen wasn't usually a talkative man, certainly not to the secretaries. And while the occasion of Dr. Lowenstein's death was extraordinary enough to lead to unusual behavior, it was the questions that Dr. Jansen had asked, the comments he'd made, that had unsettled her the most.

"Did the police check his calendar?" he'd asked, nodding toward Susan's desk.

"Why, yes, I think so."

"Not that that would necessarily show anything out of the ordinary," Dr. Jansen had quickly added.

But when she'd agreed with him, he'd come back to it again, even suggesting that he take a look at it in case the police missed anything. And he'd walked over to Susan's desk, asked Julia where he might find the calendar, and quickly skimmed it when she'd pulled it from Susan's upper left drawer. After satisfying himself with this piece of detection, he'd seemed unusually nervous, even laughing a little at how "this business has us all on edge."

He'd left the room after that, only to buzz her a few minutes later, asking her to come in to see him. He'd been sitting at his desk still in his overcoat, a fact which he'd seemed to notice only when she'd entered. While he'd removed it and hung it up, he'd asked, in what had sounded to her like an artificially aloof tone, if she knew where Dr. Lowenstein kept his notes on his latest experiments. "You've done a few jobs for him now and then, haven't you?" he'd said in a high, cheery voice. She'd told him she knew nothing about his research and suspected Mrs. Wilcox was the one to talk to about that. She probably arranged with the other doctors involved to decide how to handle his papers.

"But what if they're important to the police?" Dr. Jansen had asked her. His false cheer dropped, replaced by his usual sharp tone.

"Then I'm sure she'll turn them over."

"But perhaps she won't know if they're important!" He'd sounded frustrated and upset and dismissed her soon after. She swore she saw him enter the lab where Dr. Lowenstein had been killed.

It was this that triggered her desire to call Detective Reilly. Dr. Jansen shouldn't be rummaging around in there. No one realized how terribly competitive some of the doctors were, almost more interested in beating each other to a discovery than in the discovery itself. She sometimes thought of them as opera divas. Certainly Dr. Jansen fit that bill. She'd typed some letters for him to colleagues that could only be described as petty fits of jealousy disguised as "advice." Early on, she'd gently suggested he rethink sending such messages, but he'd sharply informed her that she was to type the letters, not analyze them.

She pulled out a telephone book and began flipping through pages looking for the number of the police. Shouldn't it be easier to find? *My god, what if it were an emergency?*

She removed her hand from the receiver. *Calm down, Julia, don't be stupid.*

She took a deep breath. She'd investigate this on her own.

She reached for her cane and went into the hallway. If Dr. Jansen was in Dr. Lowenstein's lab, the commonsense thing to do was to go there and tell him he should leave the room alone.

She also wanted to ask him if he knew what had happened to the vaccine trials. Mrs. Wilcox hadn't said yet what Dr. Bodian had discovered on his trip to the National Institutes of Health.

As she approached the room, she heard her boss muttering to himself, not unusual. He occasionally talked a problem out loud.

She thought she heard him saying, "where is it, what did you do with it," over and over again in a voice that bordered on frantic. This was not his usual tone with himself—he might be sharp with others, but he used a good-natured voice when talking to himself.

She shook her head and limped forward, catching Dr. Jansen by surprise when she entered the lab.

"Dr. Jansen," she said, firmly and quietly, "you really shouldn't be in here."

Startled, he turned quickly to face her. In his hand was a gun.

Chapter Seven

WHILE SAL WAITED for Susan Schlager to leave the Lowenstein house, he listened. It was quiet outside, only the chirping of birds and occasional barking of a dog breaking the silence. But inside, he heard her footsteps up the stairs and down again, cabinet doors being opened, drawers pulled out and shut, and then, the muffled sound of weeping. He thought he heard her say something to herself, too, something like, "What now? What now?"

After a few minutes of this, Sal's attention was pulled elsewhere as the postman made his way down the street. The detective retreated to the side of the house before the mailman saw him, reappearing when the man had slipped the day's mail through the door slot and moved on to the next house, gaze fixed on the addressed envelopes in his hand.

It was barely a minute before the door opened, and Susan Schlager appeared, eyes red from crying, her attention on the stack of envelopes in her hand as she walked down the front steps. She quickly leafed through each one, scanning the addresses.

"Mrs. Schlager," Sal said, coming from the shadows.

She jumped, the envelopes falling to the ground. Looking over at Sal, she opened her mouth in surprise, and he could tell her first impulse was to run, but she stopped herself from pursuing that guilty-looking path.

"You followed me!" She tried to sound indignant.

He stooped to pick up the envelopes. "What are you doing here again, ma'am?"

"I told you before. I—I was looking for some research papers of Dr. Lowenstein's. He was working on some important...things...and was writing a paper. I thought maybe the paper could be published posthumously." She pronounced it post-humously, a mistake Sal himself had made once, only to be corrected by a college-educated girlfriend. Former girlfriend.

"Did you find them?" he asked, looking through the mail himself.

"No, I didn't!" Again she tried to act indignant, but she wasn't a good actress, and even if she were, she was too nervous to give a decent performance.

"So you decided to take the mail instead?" He held up the day's pile.

"I handle his mail at the office," she said after a pause.

He looked at her. She didn't have her purse, and her suit was too thin to hide a file or other papers. The only thing she'd come out of the house with was the mail. Had she been waiting for it?

"Mrs. Schlager, you're looking for something, and we know it. Maybe we'll have to come to your home and talk to you there, look around a bit…"

The reaction wasn't instantaneous. Her face went still as ice at first, then her lower lip began to tremble. Silent tears poured from her eyes, and her grief and fear were so profound that Sal felt like a ham-handed brute for his innocent-sounding suggestion. He reached out to touch her arm.

"Was there something going on between you and…" He nodded toward Lowenstein's house.

She stepped back away from his comforting hand and took a deep breath, gaining control.

"No! Absolutely nothing," she said with the vehemence of the wrongly accused. "And I've told you everything I know. Why won't you believe me? You don't need to come to my home to talk to me. I'll just say the same thing. I'll come to your office if you like. I'll answer your questions for hours. Nothing will change." The words tumbled fast as she tried to persuade him.

He wasn't sure what to think, so he asked her a few more questions about Lowenstein and his habits, wishing Sean were with him to fill in the gaps he was surely leaving. From her answers, it was clear she only knew Lowenstein's office routine and, in fact, had never been to his home until that morning. The map in the car had told that tale even before she said it out loud. After asking her to turn over the key to the house to him, he let her go, still hinting he might pursue this at her home, but that only got him more promises to talk to the police as much as they wanted. Sal watched her get in the car and drive off before heading back himself, feeling like a failure.

☙❧

Julia would never be able to run away from a gun. She was more vulnerable than most. When she'd first been paralyzed, her greatest fear had been fire. Once she'd mastered walking with a cane, that fear had receded. And now this—a new fear.

Her body chilled as she stared at Dr. Jansen, stared at the gun in his hand as if it occupied an equal space to the man who held it.

She should have called the police, should have followed her instincts.

She should scream. But her tongue seemed paralyzed now, as well.

Dr. Jansen stood at the far end of the room, the gun in his right hand pointing toward her and the door, his mouth hanging open in shock and surprise. His receding hair was disheveled, as if he'd been running his fingers through it in frustration. Behind him, on the black-topped lab counter, were several files, their papers spread out in untidy angles. One had fallen to the floor.

Julia swallowed. "Dr. Jansen," she said softly in the most reasonable tone she could muster. "I'm not going to—"

"Good lord, girl, you gave me a fright!" The hand with the gun dropped to his side. Julia breathed more easily. But still her heart pounded.

"Why do you have—that?" She pointed with her cane to the weapon, and he stared at it as if someone had placed it in his hand unawares.

"I—I—well, you've seen the letters. You know that there are people—out there—who want to do us harm, who want to stop the vaccine trials!" He scowled at her as if she was the reason he had to carry a gun. "I felt the need to protect myself. God knows Dr. Lowenstein could have benefited from such foresight."

As the shock of having Julia startle him wore off, so did his lack of inhibition. He looked at her pale face, as if seeing for the first time the effect a pointed gun would have on her.

"I'm sorry if I scared you," he murmured, pocketing the piece in his lab jacket. His lab jacket—did he always carry a gun in that pocket?

"You should talk to the police about those threatening letters, Dr. Jansen." Julia tried to sound reassuring, to let him know she was on his side. "I'd be scared, too, if I got things like that."

"They can't help. No use involving them."

"They're already involved," she reminded him.

He gave out a little snort of disgusted laughter. "A bit too late, wouldn't you say?"

"I still think—"

"I'm all right!" he snapped. "I'll take care of it."

He'd just held a gun on her, and he was the one acting insulted? She was used to his peevishness, but this was too much. She turned to leave before he became even more irritated, but stopped at the door when she remembered why she'd come into the lab in the first place. She squared her shoulders. To hell with his irritation.

"I don't think you should be in here," Julia said. "The detectives might want to look through the lab again." She stared at the papers, and he followed her gaze. Quickly, he turned and began shuffling papers back into file folders.

"I just needed to look up something—some tests Dr. Lowenstein was running," he said over his shoulder. "That's all."

"Let me help you," she said, coming closer, but he turned back and issued a sharp "No!" followed by a question unrelated to the matters they'd just discussed. "Did you finish typing that paper I'm submitting to the Infectious Diseases Journal?"

Another long article with a long list of footnotes. The paper filled more than a dozen legal pages and would take several days to finish, with corrections and revisions, as was his habit. "Why, no, I—"

"I'd like that as soon as possible, Miss Dell. By this afternoon."

She knew it didn't need to be into the journal for at least another week. And she also knew that he might not even submit it, that this might just be a piece of work to keep her busy and out of his hair. "Yes, sir."

Angry but impotent to lash out, she reached for anything that would sting. "I understand the vaccine trials might be delayed," she said, as if any delay could be laid directly at his feet.

He looked up as if she'd slapped him. "Who told you that?"

"I—I just heard it around the office. Dr. Bodian went to Bethesda...."

"Yes, he did. They're rushing things in Pittsburgh, that's the problem."

A curious comment from a doctor just as eager to solve the polio problem as Salk.

"But thousands could be affected if they don't hurry," she said. "The polio season—"

"The polio season will come and go and hardly a child could be affected. It's bad one year, not so bad the next. Who's to say we need to hurry this time?"

The very tips of her ears burned with his heartlessness. How many children had been afflicted the year she was paralyzed? If it were only one child...it mattered.

She waited for him to leave the lab, but he just stared at her. "Is there anything else?" he asked.

He wasn't going to leave, and she couldn't force him. She shook her head and exited the room. As she walked back to her desk, she chewed on her lower lip, wondering again if she should contact Detective Reilly, or if she would just seem like a tattletale. She frowned, remembering another action she'd taken that could be construed as such. No, she thought. I was just handling things in a businesslike way.

✿✿

Sal Sabataso looked up at Sean's smiling face as he entered the office. "What I tell ya—she's no wallflower, right?"

"No, Sallie, a wallflower she is not!" Sean enjoyed watching his partner redden at the use of his nickname. "We might go out again."

"Praise Jesus. I can tell my mother I did my duty."

Sean shifted from good-natured banter to business. He didn't bother to take off his coat. "I was going to see if I could talk to that Dr. Jansen this afternoon. You want to come?"

"Sure. Just let me finish this report." When Sean lifted his eyebrows, Sal explained. "That burglary we wrapped up last week."

Sean didn't say anything. Sal hated the paperwork and often did it late. Sean had already covered for him on this latest bit of procrastination.

They made a good team, watching out for each other.

As Sal worked, he told Sean about his encounter with Susan Schlager and his elimination of the theory that she had been the victim's lover.

"Just because she needed a map to find his place doesn't disprove that theory," Sean said, sitting at his desk. He would call Lowenstein's attorney at Patelson and Moore while he waited for Sal. "They could have met at hotels."

"A man lives alone and he springs for a hotel room?"

"Maybe he was afraid of nosy neighbors."

Sal shrugged and went back to his paperwork.

Sean found the number for Patelson and Moore, then dialed through. In an authoritative voice, he asked to speak with Mr. Patelson himself, giving his police identification when asked and acting as if this were news of pressing importance. After several minutes of silence, he was put through.

"May I help you?" Soft and confident, Patelson's tone made it clear he would be the one deciding whether help would be given, no matter what Sean's request.

"I understand that Dr. Myron Lowenstein had his legal matters handled by you," Sean said after identifying himself. "As you know, the doctor just passed away." Sean waited, but Patelson remained mute. "Did anyone in particular benefit from his estate?"

He heard Patelson breathe out but couldn't tell if it was a sigh of relief or irritation. "He had a will with us," the lawyer said, now very businesslike and clipped. "But no one person benefits from his modest estate. He left everything to charity."

"No relatives?" Sean asked, fumbling for more time. He sensed Patelson wanted to get off the phone.

"None that I am aware of."

"Any friends of the deceased — people inquiring about his estate?"

"No one has contacted me in that regard."

"Any interest at all — from anyone?"

"As I said, no." The lawyer sounded increasingly annoyed.

"How long have you handled Dr. Lowenstein's affairs?"

There was a pause — Sean figured the lawyer was deciding whether it was worth it to withhold the information — and then Patelson responded. "Since about 1947, I believe."

"How'd he come to you?"

"Really, Detective Reilly, I have no idea."

"But your office — it doesn't handle many people like Lowenstein," Sean said, carefully enunciating the doctor's last name so his meaning would be clear.

"The man is dead," Patelson said in a tight angry voice. "And should rest in peace. Now, I really must go. Contact my secretary with any further questions, and I'll be happy to answer them when I can."

Sean didn't think Patelson sounded happy to answer any more questions at all. He hung up the phone and looked over at Sal, but his seat was now empty. He was about to go find him when he saw him leaving the office of their boss, Mark O'Brien. O'Brien, a tall heavy man with bushy eyebrows and thick dark hair, didn't look pleased. He stood with his hands on his hips at the doorway, and Sean picked up the last of what he was saying.

"....you'll be in the soup, too, if I catch you covering for each other again."

Shit. Now what?

"Everything all right?" Sean asked. Sal returned to the desk.

Sal shrugged but didn't look at him. "Yeah. He's just pissed 'cause I was late with the report."

Sean stood. "Let's go," he said. As they left the office a few minutes later, Sean vowed never again to let Sal cover for him when he was late.

⋘⋙

"Tell them it's true, honey."

"Don't be silly. We'd have read it in the papers."

"Or heard it on the radio."

Will Beschmann sat on the edge of Julia's desk, teasing the other secretaries. He winked at Julia as he continued his tale of Gene Kelly running off with Doris Day to get married in Las Vegas.

"It's very hush-hush," Will said, winking again. Julia shot him a smile but quickly dropped it as she resumed typing. She didn't have time to chitchat if she was going to finish the article Dr. Jansen wanted typed by the end of the day. Already she'd had to redo two pages because she knew he wouldn't accept too many erasures and type-overs. He was a perfectionist. Will's conversation kept distracting her.

She'd told Will she didn't have time for lunch or even a break when he came by, but he'd run to the cafeteria for her, bringing her back a tuna sandwich and chocolate milkshake. She'd been grateful and touched at first. She was hungry, after all, and it was thoughtful of him to bring her something. But she'd only been able to eat half the sandwich because she wanted to start typing right away. She didn't want to ask her father to come get her again today if she stayed late. Will had lingered to "pass the time," saying it wasn't nearly as "pretty" in his office.

"Well, where do you get your information if it's so hush-hush?" Susan asked. She sat at her desk, obsessively straightening things to give the impression she was busy. After she'd come back from her lunch, she had offered to help Julia with the typing, but there was no good way to divide the project.

Linda laughed. "Next you're going to tell us you know somebody who works in Hollywood." She sat at her desk proofreading the work she'd typed the day before.

"As a matter of fact, I do. Isn't that right, Jules?"

"Huh?" Damn. She made another mistake. She rolled the paper up three lines and deftly erased the type, then repositioned the paper to type the correction. She peered at the type-over through slitted eyes. It was good enough. "Shouldn't you be getting back to work?"

Will wasn't much of a go-getter, which Julia had learned to accept. But now she worried he was actually turning into a slacker. She knew he took his time at lunch and never seemed in any hurry to get back to his job. Sometimes she felt this was her fault, and she needed to encourage him more to be punctual and attentive to his duties.

"Just a minute, I have some time," he answered with no acrimony. He smiled at Linda. "Look, it should have been clear they had something going on when they did that movie together."

"Doris Day and Gene Kelly?" Linda asked, incredulous.

"Yeah, they were in that one last year. *Singin' in the Rain*," Susan added, proud of her film knowledge.

Will concurred. "That's what I'm talking about."

Linda snorted out a laugh. "Some know-it-all you are. That wasn't Doris Day in that movie. It was Debbie Reynolds."

Julia's fingers flew over the keyboard as she half listened to the conversation. She was only on page five. She estimated she had another dozen to go at least. And then Dr. Jansen would review it, make changes. And, depending on how extensive they were, she might end up completely retyping the article. She finished the page and pulled it out of the roller with such force that it ripped at the bottom.

"Dammit!" she cried. And immediately flamed with blush. She never cursed. At least not out loud.

Linda turned toward her. "Can you tape it, hon? It's just the first draft, right?"

"I wish I could help you with it," Susan said weakly.

"Dr. Jansen requires first drafts as clean as the final copy," Julia said in an angry monotone that she immediately regretted. Without looking up, she pulled another sheet of paper from her stationery drawer and began the page again.

Will stood, finally taking the cue that he should leave. "I better get going before they discover I'm missing," he said with a cheer that now fell flat. "I'll call you later, Jules."

She just nodded without turning from her job. He would call and they would talk and she would go to bed and get up and start everything again. Dr. Jansen would be mad, she would still wonder about him, and nothing would be different. A weight settled over her, one she'd not felt in a long time. She blinked fast and took a deep breath, then sat up straighter in her chair. She'd type five more pages, then throw away the rest of the sandwich and get a glass of water for a quick break.

As she settled into a new rhythm, the office resumed its usual afternoon cadences. The phone rang at Susan's desk, and she answered in appropriately mournful tones, explaining to the caller that Dr. Lowenstein was deceased and providing an explanation that both Julia and Linda had helped her devise for just such moments. "The police are investigating, but we don't know anything beyond what's in the papers. There will be a memorial at the hospital, but a time hasn't yet been set."

Linda slowly flipped pages, often scratching at one with a pencil. Those were the ones she'd have to retype. Linda wasn't nearly as good a typist as Julia and spent half her time redoing work. It was one of the reasons she was always behind. Julia often helped her out.

Just as she had reached the quasi-hypnotic state that allowed her to type with greatest accuracy and speed, Julia heard footsteps in the hallway. Will again? He really had to stop this. It wasn't good for his job —

"What now?" She turned in her seat toward the door. But Will wasn't standing there. It was Detective Reilly with another man, one of the detectives who'd been there the day of the murder. As her face warmed, he smiled.

"Just checking to see if your boss is in," Sean said.

She stood, figuring it best to take them directly to Dr. Jansen, instead of ringing him first.

"No need to get up," he said, wincing slightly at her effort. But this only made her stand straighter and walk around the desk with more purpose.

"I'll show you his office." She walked by them, wrinkling her nose now at the faint odor of her half-eaten sandwich. She'd throw it away in a trash can outside the office so it wouldn't stink up the room.

"You remember my partner — Sal Sabataso."

She didn't but nodded her head at the introduction. As she reached the doorway, her phone rang. She quickly grabbed it, racing through her usual greeting only to be met with...nothing.

"Hello?" Silence greeted her. She shrugged and started to hang up when a voice, a man's voice, came over the line.

"Are you talking to the detective again?"

She didn't answer. The voice, so soft it sounded as if the caller was standing a foot away from the phone and whispering, continued, hard and low: "Do you think he believes a crip like you?"

She felt herself tremble. "What do you want?"

"Leave it alone. Just leave it alone." Click.

"Julia, you all right?" Linda asked. "You're white as milk."

"Just tired, I bet," Susan chimed in. "You've been doing a lot of walking today."

Julia shook her head and didn't answer. Instead, she moved past

Detective Reilly and his partner into the hallway. She wanted to be out of that office. She wanted to look, to observe—who knew what she was doing? The hallway was empty.

"Do you mind telling me who that was?" Sean asked as she led them forward.

"No one I know." She felt embarrassed by the call, as if the detectives had heard her called a "crip." She peered into offices and labs as they walked, searching for the person who would have seen the detective enter her office.

"Someone who upset you."

"Just a prank caller." That was a lie. The caller had scared her. What foolishness was she pursuing by not telling them? First she couldn't wait to tell him about Dr. Jansen. Now she avoided telling him about the calls. Enough. She stopped and faced Sean.

"Someone asking me if I was talking to the detective again."

"Again?" Sal asked.

"He called before."

"Threatening calls?" Sean reached out and touched her arm, his face a mixture of concern and annoyance. "You've received others?"

"Just one. I thought it was a reporter wondering what was up."

He expelled a quick breath and gritted his teeth. "When did it happen? Tell me everything."

So she did, giving him information on this call and the last one, watching him take notes, feeling lighter and safer with every scrawl across the page. She should have told him about the first call when she'd received it. She was too used to soldiering on.

"You should tell us if you get another call—as soon as you get one," Sal said to her, irritated.

"They're probably nothing," she said, "don't you think?" She looked at Sean, but he didn't smile.

"Do you have any enemies here? Anybody you argue with, don't get along with?"

Maybe her boss, she thought, but she couldn't imagine anyone else disliking her enough to want to frighten her.

"No one I can think of."

"Maybe we should get someone watching her, tap the phone," Sal offered.

She flashed them her bravest smile, an automatic reaction to any pain. "Really—that seems a bit dramatic."

Sean shrugged. "It's not a bad idea. After all, you were here when it happened. If the killer knows that..."

It could be nothing more than a prank, she thought. Sometimes people stared at her. Older boys had taunted her at a bus stop, calling her crip and gimp, her first week on the job. Once she'd overheard a woman telling her child to stay away from her so he wouldn't "catch that disease." She sometimes told people she'd hurt her leg in an accident to avoid letting them know she'd had polio.

She wasn't in the mood to recount these sorry stories, so she led the detectives down the corridor, past two labs where quiet scientists looked through microscopes and recorded observations, past a row of windows that let in dusty sun, past closed supply closets and lavatory doors, each step a journey toward normalcy until at last, she felt comfortable again, secure in her world.

They were nearing her boss's office, so she grabbed the opportunity to mention, at last, in the most casual of tones, Dr. Jansen's excursion into Dr. Lowenstein's files.

"Other doctors might need to access his material, after all," she said and was proud of how she made it sound, as if Dr. Jansen was just one among several who had tried to get at the files. She wasn't "telling" on him that way.

"I thought you said Dr. Lowenstein wasn't involved in the polio research," Sean said as she stopped in front of a half-closed door.

"He's not." And immediately got the implication. Why would Dr. Jansen need to access his files? But Sean's attention was diverted to the office just beyond the door. Dr. Jansen had heard them approaching and was standing—to greet them or fend them off wasn't clear.

"I was wondering if we could have a few words with you," Sean asked, and before the doctor could answer, he had pushed the door open and let himself and his partner in.

࿊

"Susan, not you, too!" Julia stood in the doorway to Lowenstein's lab staring at her colleague who, like Dr. Jansen earlier, was looking through drawers and papers. Julia had heard movement in the lab on her way back to her office and, despite her scare there, forced herself to investigate.

"He was my boss," Susan said defensively, tapping a stack of papers on the lab counter, as if she had every right to make things right. "Besides, he was doing important work that needs to be preserved."

Julia's patience was at an end. "It can wait! He was doing work on muscle reactions. It hardly falls into the same category as that of the polio doctors!" And the more the investigation was bollixed up with people rummaging through Lowenstein's things, the longer the labs were disrupted, delaying that important work.

Susan cocked her head, returning anger with anger. "Dr. Mike wasn't working on your precious polio," she whined, "but he was a good doctor doing things that would help people— people who could be helped!"

This was too much for Julia, whose hand shook on the cane as she leaned to the side. "Dr. Mike could have helped people like me if he'd deigned to put his mind and talent to it instead of wasting it on endless busy work that looked good in journals but had no practical value!"

She turned and left the lab, hurrying back to her office. As she crossed the threshold, her gaze caught sight of a short figure in the hall. Earl Dagley, the animal tender, stood sheepishly in the corridor near the stairwell, a sheaf of supply request forms in his free hand. When he saw her, he smiled a quick scared grin of acknowledgement and continued on his way. Damn again. He'd heard her "speech" and probably thought she was a bitter survivor lashing out at the world— speaking ill of the dead, to boot!

✖✖

Sean and Sal learned two things in their afternoon interviewing.

Dr. Jansen was either an extremely nervous man, or he, like Susan Schlager, was hiding something. And he fit the description of the "colleague" who'd gained access to Lowenstein's house the morning of the murder. Thin, medium height, long face, brown hair. Throughout his talk with Sean, he kept looking at his watch and answering every question with a question of his own— *why do you need to know that, who else have you talked with, have you contacted any of Dr. Lowenstein's friends?*

They asked where he was on the fateful morning, and he was quick with a reply. At home. His housemaid could verify it. He gave them her name and number. After the Jansen interview, they'd split up, knocking on lab doors and chatting up anyone they came across, doing a far more thorough sweep of the lab and its nearby offices than either man had been able to accomplish earlier. They talked to nearly a dozen folks, from high-ranking researchers to lab technicians. Nobody was close to Lowenstein or Lowe or whoever he was. But they all thought he was a swell guy. Kind. Thoughtful. And generous— he'd given the cleaning lady fur-lined gloves at Christmas when she'd complained of the cold stiffening her hands. She'd not been around the morning of the murder, she told them with regret. She'd taken the day off because she was going to work the weekend.

"He was a swell guy all right," Sal said cynically at the end of the day. "Seems like only one person in the world hated him. Hated him enough to kill him."

✖✖

Tired but satisfied, Sean pulled into his street later than usual that night. Mrs. Buchanan had agreed to stay so he could do a proper grocery shopping, and now he was loaded up with enough supplies to last through an atomic bomb disaster. He'd even bought a small box of chocolates to sweeten Mrs. Buchanan's disposition. Although she'd agreed to the extra hours, she always acted as if it was an imposition once he came home.

His domestic problems in hand, his thoughts turned back to the case. It was moving slowly. That nervous Dr. Jansen had begun to look good to them, but Sal had checked out his alibi, and it was right as rain as far as they could tell. Jansen's housekeeper had been at his home, and she'd vouched for him. The doc had been home during the morning hours—the time that the coroner had estimated the death had occurred. He hadn't left the house until after the folks at Hopkins had called in the death. Still, they should keep an eye on him. Housekeepers could be bought. Jansen'd given out her name and number awfully quickly.

Sean wanted to solve this case as soon as possible. That would impress O'Brien and maybe get both him and Sal back on the right foot. He loosened his collar as he pulled up to his house, easing in behind an old black Ford.

With a dry throat, he recognized the car. Dr. Spencer.

Chapter Eight

JULIA'S BEDROOM STILL FELT as if it belonged to a little girl. Its cheery pink ruffled bedspread and matching curtains, the dresser with embroidered doilies and velveteen jewelry box, her tattered copies of *Jane Eyre* and *Pride and Prejudice* on a shelf near the window stopped time to a period of her life when she didn't have to worry about the weight on her leg.

She'd begged off after-dinner socializing with her family—her sister Beth was visiting with her children—and retreated to her room so she could think about her tumultuous afternoon and why she'd been so filled with anger for most of it.

It wasn't just Dr. Jansen. Or even Will. She'd been shocked at the things she'd said about kind Dr. Mike. Where had that come from—that well of resentment? She hadn't been aware she'd harbored those feelings until they'd spilled out of her mouth at poor Susan. She caught a glimpse of herself in the mirror above the dresser at the end of her bed. Who was she? What was she capable of?

She perched primly on the edge of the bed, flipping the pages of the copy of *Life* she'd taken from the table downstairs.

Saying she was tired had been no lie. She was drained, feeling as hollow as her cane. She wished she could curl her legs under her and read like she had when she was younger, but it would have taken more effort than it was worth. *It's amazing how many muscles it takes to keep oneself upright without effort.* Her bad leg's calf muscles were useless, and her thigh muscles were weak. Bending that leg under her torso meant thinking about using her other good leg's muscles, along with those that threaded up her lower back, to balance herself so she wouldn't topple over.

And she hadn't even realized how much she enjoyed sitting that way until it had required concentration to do it. Her mind roamed to the brink of this thought before retreating from its implications.

What comfort do I now take for granted that could be snatched away in the blink of an eye?

Dead tired from a long day, she closed her eyes. She'd stayed at the office until six-thirty typing that stupid article for Dr. Jansen, only to find he'd left for the day when she'd dropped the finished draft on his desk.

She'd had to admit she was partly relieved he wasn't there. After Detective Reilly had left that afternoon, Dr. Jansen had come into the office and acted like an interrogator himself, barking out questions to each of the secretaries—which of you girls is telling the detective foolish stories? And then he'd lectured them all—when he'd known darn well it was she alone he should be talking to—about the importance of the researchers' work, how they all needed access to important material and that included material in Dr. Lowenstein's office. And how he himself would never violate a police directive if he'd known about it in the first place.

Julia hadn't mentioned Susan's foray into the closed-off lab. She was tired of being reprimanded for doing what was right and proper.

Her thoughts were interrupted by a soft knock at her door and the entrance of her sister Beth. Beth had been at the house when Julia had returned with her father and Helen, whom they'd picked up on the way home. Julia could hear the raucous cries of Beth's three boys in the living room below. The television set was on, and the muffled sounds of a variety show carried upstairs.

"Can we talk?" Beth asked, brushing a stray hair from her cheek with one hand and rubbing her distended stomach with the other. Beth was seven months along with her fourth child.

After Julia nodded yes, Beth plopped on to the bed next to her sister, laughing as she nearly fell over to the side, adjusting for her extra weight.

Julia had a hard time remembering when her sister hadn't looked harried. Her long, straight brown hair was always in an untidy bun, her clothes were often stained, and her stockings holey or nicked with runs. Beth's husband, Stuart Ridgeman, an ex-Marine, worked at Bethlehem Steel, and they lived in Dundalk on the eastern side of the city in a new bungalow. Stu was a rugged, silent man, and Julia would have wondered if Beth had a hard time with him if it weren't for the fact that Beth was perpetually cheerful. When Julia had gone to work at the labs five years ago, Beth had been a little standoffish, afraid she'd catch something from her sister that would endanger her pregnancies and children. But gradually that fear had worn off, replaced by Beth's usual sunny nature. Of the three girls, Julia reflected, Beth was most like their father in personality—open, happy, always ready to find the silver lining in even the darkest clouds.

"You look beat," Beth said, leaning forward to scrutinize Julia's face.

"Had to work late," Julia said. And then she'd come home to hear Will had already called, and she'd had to call him back or look terribly rude to her family, but all she'd wanted to do was eat and rest.

"I have to pack up the rascals soon, but I wanted to ask you something," Beth continued. "Dad worries me."

Julia shifted her weight and sat up straighter. Oh, no, something else to fret over. "Why?"

"He looked awfully tired tonight."

"You think everybody looks tired!" Julia lightly punched her sister in the arm. "You just told me I did."

"Well, you do." Beth grinned at her sister, then turned serious. "But Dad looked a little worse for wear to me at dinner tonight. He didn't eat a lot."

Julia rolled her eyes and spoke in a conspiratorial whisper. "Macaroni with canned gravy and Esskay hamburgers isn't exactly gourmet, Beth. We all love Mutti, but she's not the best cook."

Beth relaxed and smiled again. "I know, I know. But he usually eats more. At least a full helping. He didn't finish tonight. And last Sunday, he looked — oh, haggard."

"Some people might say you look haggard."

"And they'd be right," Beth quickly agreed, laughing. "But I'm young and strong and can take it." She turned more serious again. "Dad actually complained to me about his back hurting."

This caught Julia's attention. She never remembered her father complaining about any physical problem, ever. Even when he had a cold, he never mentioned it, just sneezed and coughed and blew his nose and didn't say a word. He'd broken a bone in his foot three years ago and hadn't even gone to the doctor until they'd forced him to after watching him limp around for two days.

"I think we need to get Helen driving," Beth continued.

"What does that have to do with Dad?"

"If Helen drove, she could pick you up when you have to work late."

"I don't work late that often...."

Beth looked at her from the tops of her eyes. "At least once a week. Sometimes more. And sometimes Dad just comes and gets you at the regular time."

Suddenly Julia felt guilty. Life would have been easier for her family if she'd continued working at the law firm down the road. But that would have meant not meeting Will, not getting engaged, and her parents had been overjoyed at that news. When they married, Will would be responsible for taking her home from work, and that would relieve her father of the job. She was lucky. Will was a good man.

"I can try to talk to her, too," Julia said. "Do you want to do it together?"

Beth tilted her head to one side. "It might help. Might make it seem more serious."

"We'd have to do it when Mom and Dad weren't around," Julia said.

"Or maybe—" Beth snapped her fingers and sat forward. "Maybe we don't tell them. Maybe we don't even tell Helen."

"What?"

"I drive," Beth continued. "I could teach Helen. I could just take her out in the car one day, to an empty lot, and start teaching her."

Julia laughed. "You mean kidnap her to teach her to drive?"

"Well, yes, I guess so!"

They spent another quarter hour talking about Beth's plan and about Julia's job. Beth managed to get the story of Julia's bad day out of her, even down to the details that were still bothering her.

"...and then he buzzed me on the phone and asked me to make reservations for him to a conference in California, some small researchers group he's never been interested in before."

"So what?" Beth stood, her hand on her own aching back. One of the boys was crying, and it was clear she was anxious to leave now that they'd solved the problem she'd come in to talk about.

"A few minutes later he buzzed me to—"

Their mother's voice carried up the stairs. "Andrew bumped his knee, Beth. He is wanting his mother to give it a kiss." She pronounced "kiss" as "*küss.*"

"Be there in a sec!"

"Anyway," Julia continued, easing herself to a standing position, "he buzzed me a few minutes later to say I should just book the passage to California, and he'd handle the return trip."

Beth was moving toward the door. "Maybe he has friends out there he wants to visit. I don't understand why that's a big deal."

Julia could see her sister's impatience. "You better get going," she told Beth. She waved her toward the door. "And let me know how I can help with the kidnapping scheme."

❧

The house was quiet, the living room dark. Where was Mrs. Buchanan?

"Danny?" Sean called as he rushed to the right, down the short hall to the two bedrooms. Blood pounded at his temples, his hands turned cold. Had there been an emergency? Had Mr. Buchanan come by to drive them all to the hospital? *Oh Jesus, not this...*

"Daddy!" The boy came scampering out to him, clad in his pajamas. His face still carried a smear of jelly, and his eyes were red and watery. When Sean tousled the boy's head as he hugged his father's leg, Sean noticed Danny was hot.

Dr. Spencer came from around the corner, too, black bag in hand, followed by a dour-looking Mrs. Buchanan.

"I called him when Danny was ailing late today," Mrs. Buchanan explained as she rushed by. "But I really must go, now that you're home." She said it as if there'd been no agreement for the longer day. As she retrieved her coat and hat and left, Sean lifted Danny up and stroked his head.

"Just have to share everything your brother has, do you?" He kissed his son on the cheek.

"Afraid so," Dr. Spencer told him. He heaved his bag on to a table and handed Sean a bottle. "Here. You won't need to run to the pharmacy."

Sean smiled his gratitude. "You'll send me a bill?"

Dr. Spencer nodded. "Of course." He reached for his heavy dark coat, draped over the back of the sofa. Sean helped the older man as he struggled with the sleeves.

"A secretary at Hopkins gave me the hardest time about my coat yesterday. Said she couldn't stand the smell." Sean chuckled. "She's a polio herself."

"A wool coat like mine? It probably reminds her of the hot packs from rehabilitation, poor soul."

When Sean looked perplexed, Dr. Spencer continued. "After the polio patient recovers from the fever, they use hot packs—hot, wet wool—to loosen up the muscles for stretching exercises. They place them on the muscles—on the back, the legs—and let them rest there until they lose the heat. At first, they're burning hot, but eventually they become clammy. It can be quite uncomfortable, even painful. And then the exercises themselves—as they try to determine which muscles will recover—hurt as well. One of my patients told me. I'm sure it's not a pleasant memory for any polio."

So she hadn't been snobby, thought Sean. He was too quick to judge.

Dr. Spencer buttoned his coat.

"I saw the photograph of Dr. Lowenstein in the paper," he commented, putting his hat on and grabbing his case. "Didn't recognize him—I must be getting old." He laughed and headed toward the door.

Sean followed him there, hugging Danny close. The boy was sucking his thumb and falling asleep on Sean's shoulder, creating a warm spot that radiated peace.

"What was different about him?" Sean asked.

Dr. Spencer stopped at the door and looked out at the street as if seeing his past there. "I remembered him as a tall, thin man."

"People pick up weight over the years," Sean said. Lowenstein, in death, had been stocky.

Dr. Spencer turned and smiled at him. "I know. But they don't grow back hair. For the life of me, I remembered Dr. Lowenstein as balding."

The doctor left. Sean put Danny to bed in the small twin opposite his sleeping brother, after first determining that they'd eaten supper. He then went into the kitchen and pulled out the morning's paper. There was Lowenstein's photo all right. A stocky, nondescript man with even features and a full, bushy head of hair.

Dr. Lowenstein wasn't Jewish. He wasn't even...Lowenstein. Who was he? Why'd he take Lowenstein's name?

Sean reheated some coffee from the morning—Mrs. Buchanan never cleaned that pot, knowing he liked a cup some evenings — and read the rest of the paper while in the back of his mind he tried to figure how to determine who the victim really was.

An hour later, Sean remembered his groceries and ran to the car to retrieve them. The ice cream he'd bought for the boys was ruined, but he managed to salvage the rest.

Chapter Nine

"SUSAN DIDN'T CALL YOU at home to say she'd be late, did she?" Linda looked up as Julia entered the room.

"No, she didn't." And it was unlikely she would have, considering their encounter yesterday, Julia thought as she stowed her purse in her lower right desk drawer. "Why?"

"Dr. Morton has some meeting this morning, and he asked me to pick up some pastries for it yesterday. Susan said she'd do it." Linda looked at her watch. "The meeting starts in a half hour. I thought she'd be here early."

Given how anxious Susan was about maintaining employment, it was odd she'd be late. Julia sank uneasily into her chair.

"She's probably just delayed by the errand," Julia said unconvincingly.

While Julia readied herself for the work day, Linda continued to talk. "My aunt called last night all upset. Their little boy's in the hospital."

"Oh, no! The one in Virginia?" Julia searched for and found a memory of Linda talking about her family.

"Went fishing with some friends and it was warm so they peeled off their clothes..."

Linda didn't need to say more. Julia knew the rest of the tale. He'd come home feeling tired, and by morning he couldn't walk across the room to go to the bathroom.

"It might not be polio," Julia said, and the obvious falsehood of her statement embarrassed her. She turned back toward work, became businesslike. "It's early."

"If those doctors don't figure this out soon, somebody will have to pay," Linda said with unusual bitterness.

She walked to the door and looked down the hall. "I might run down to the cafeteria and get a few things, just to be on the safe side." She looked back at Julia. "If Sue brings in stuff, we'll have ourselves a treat."

            ❧

"But if I have enough capital. Why shouldn't I be able to get a mortgage?" Brigitta Lorenzo sat comfortably in a sleek light chair in front of her boss's desk. Unlike the other partners, Gavin eschewed the heavy cherrywood desks and chairs that made their offices feel like anterooms to funeral parlors. Gavin had had an interior decorator do his in light woods and yellow- and rust-striped chairs, all clean, straight lines with no ornamental carving. If it was new, he wanted it. Which, Brigitta often thought, was one of the reasons he'd probably wanted her when she came to work for him. He was the first in the office to use an intercom for his secretary and to regularly use one of the newer Dictaphone machines instead of asking her to take dictation by shorthand.

Morning light streamed through the windows behind Gavin's desk, causing her to squint. She changed position, crossing her legs under her cream-and-blue tweed dirndl skirt, showing off her shapely ankles clad in delicate blue pumps. With the end of the war had come softer, more feminine clothing, and Brigitta enjoyed every new fashion that appeared on the scene. No more military-like shoulder pads and suits, no more heavy shoes. Fuller skirts and softer curves were the trend now, and Brigitta had plenty of curves to show off. She especially liked the way this suit emphasized her small waist, not thickened by pregnancies like those of her sisters.

Gavin Smathers leaned back and smoothed his thick blond hair with his hand. "You're a single woman," he said as if she were dense. "A bad risk."

Brigitta silently fumed. Not just at the unfairness of banks arbitrarily deciding she'd be a bad risk for a home loan because they assumed all women would marry, leave employment, and have babies. No, she was angry at Gavin. They had managed to maintain a reasonably comfortable professional relationship since she'd ended the affair, but occasionally Gavin said or did something that indicated he believed she thought too highly of herself. His pride had been wounded. People didn't reject Gavin. He rejected them.

She'd only sought his counsel this morning on such a personal matter because of her uninhibited excitement about an immediate prospect. A friend, Maria Brody, had called her last night to tell her about a house about to go on the market in her neighborhood because the owner, a widow, was moving in with her daughter who lived in New York. It was just north of downtown and beyond the very exclusive areas that no one in Brigitta's family could ever afford. But it was a good neighborhood, a respectable one that would probably make for a wise investment. Maria's home was a small, shingled cape cod on a tree-lined street in Cedarcroft. Just off of York Road, it was near bus lines and a market. It was precisely the kind of place Brigitta dreamed about—far enough outside the heart of the city to feel "away," yet close enough to keep her from having to buy a car immediately. That was another dream.

Brigitta yearned for her own house the way some women lusted after diamonds and furs. She'd witnessed how her family's investment in a row home in Little Italy had provided not only shelter but a barrier against bad times. No matter what happened to them, they had their home. They could sell it, stay in it, rent it—it was to them what stocks and bonds were to people like Gavin.

If Brigitta wanted true independence, she had to have her own place. It was yet another immunization against the ills of the future. Her whole life since Ernie had died seemed to be a journey toward this purchase.

"It's hard for me to believe that every single bank in the city of Baltimore would deny me a loan when I am capable of such a hefty down payment." She uncrossed her legs and put her hands on the arms of the chair, ready to stand. She'd ask someone else for advice, she thought, or go directly to bankers on her own.

"A lot of people are buying houses." Gavin leaned forward, his elbows on his desk and his hands in front of his face steeple-style. "Banks don't need to lend you the money as much as you need it from them."

She stood. "I'll make some calls myself," she said, regretting how snappy it sounded.

Gavin, ever the gentleman, stood as well. "Don't get angry at me just because I'm telling you the truth."

She didn't want to start the day with an argument. She'd learned the hard way that that would lead to peevish assignments and unnecessary overtime.

"I'm not angry—" She heard the phone ring at her desk outside the door. Smiling, she used that as an opportunity to leave.

"Gavin Smathers office," she said in her perfect mellow greeting voice when she stood at her desk, receiver at her ear.

The voice of Valerie Glickman, a former secretary at the firm, zinged across the line. Valerie had left a month ago to work for Patelson and Moore. They'd promised her more money and the possibility of more responsibility, but Valerie wasn't happy. Of course, it would take a lot to make the ever-complaining Valerie happy. Valerie would have had a shot at the office manager job had she stayed, and Brigitta immediately felt cautious as she cheerfully said hello to her friend.

"You free for lunch?" Valerie asked in her nasal twang.

"What do you have in mind?" Because she'd gone out to lunch with Detective Reilly the day before, Brigitta had hoped to go shopping on her lunch hour today.

"I've got some important stuff to tell you," Valerie whispered.

Brigitta smiled. Valerie always acted as if she were a spy among enemies. She relished office gossip but wouldn't dare divulge a word of it over the telephone.

"I can meet for a quick bite at noon."

Valerie breathlessly designated an eatery—Hutzler's Tea Room—and when Brigitta hung up the phone, she grimaced. Now she'd be spending money on lunch *and* be tempted by the latest spring clothes on the way to the restaurant. She resolved to eat frugally.

ళ్ళ

Sean looked over at Sal's empty desk and frowned. His partner had said nothing about coming in late. Sean craned his head to see if O'Brien was in, but the chief's door was closed and blinds were drawn. If he was lucky...

He wasn't lucky. O'Brien's door swung open, and the man himself appeared, scanning the room, his gaze lighting on Sean. He waved his hand to Sean to come see him, before disappearing again into his office.

As Sean approached, he mentally reviewed the case. This new angle — figuring out who Lowenstein really was — would be a good thing to talk about. It would show O'Brien the case was more complicated than a usual homicide, and it would give Sean a chance to expound on the various approaches he'd take to determining the victim's true identity. And if O'Brien was getting heat from the docs, Sean was prepared to release the crime scene. It was only one lab anyway. Surely those fellows had work to do elsewhere. Even so, Sean was uneasy as he paused at the door to make sure O'Brien wasn't on the phone.

When Sean had been promoted to detective years ago, he'd forged a careful relationship with his boss. His first case, a homicide, had been complicated by the wealthy sister of the deceased leaning on everyone in City Hall to solve it before the victim was in the ground. Not a comfortable way to start, and O'Brien had cut him little slack. O'Brien had been understanding during Mary's illness, though. But eventually understanding wears out, and even the most patient man — which O'Brien was not — decides that it's time for the world to march on.

"Sit down," O'Brien said, waving him to a cracked leather chair. He jabbed a cigarette out in a tin ashtray. "I got a letter from Averill Patelson this morning. Messengered over." He handed the heavy linen paper to Sean.

It was nothing new. Simply what the lawyer had told Sean when he'd called. Lowenstein had left his money to charity. It was an odd letter, though. Odd, too, that Patelson would feel compelled to send it.

"One of your detectives, whose name I'm afraid was not recorded by my secretary, called asking about the death of Dr. Myron Lowenstein. I would like to assure you that I would be happy to cooperate as much as possible in this unfortunate tragedy. But I'm afraid I have no more information to share than what I've already provided your detective. My client left his money to charity and has no living relatives of whom I am aware."

Sean peered at O'Brien over the letter. "My client?" Sean repeated from the letter.

"Why's that strike you as queer?"

"Seems like he's trying to avoid saying 'Lowenstein.'"

O'Brien shrugged. "Is he impeding the investigation?" O'Brien had little patience for lawyers.

"No. What he says here is what he told me." Sean tapped the letter. "Nothing more. Nothing less."

"What else you got?"

So Sean spent a few minutes going over his work so far, telling O'Brien that the first step was determining who Lowenstein really was.

"He wasn't a Hebe trying to pass, you mean," O'Brien said.

"Don't think so. My kid's doctor didn't recognize his photo as the Lowenstein he knew. So it wasn't just a matter of trying to fit in. I think he's not Mike Lowe either. If he was, why not use that name at the lab? He's someone else entirely. I have a call into New York University where Lowenstein used to teach."

"All right." O'Brien patted his shirt pocket and pulled out a pack of Pall Malls. He offered one to Sean who shook his head. He'd stopped smoking when Mary was sick. She'd not been able to tolerate the smell after a while. The smell of anything, good or bad.

"You think he was trying to be this Lowenstein to do big work? You know, be famous?"

Sean shook his head. "He wasn't involved in the 'big work' on polio, if that's what you're getting at."

O'Brien nodded. Sean stood to leave, but O'Brien stopped him.

"Where's that partner of yours?" O'Brien lit his cigarette and took a deep drag.

Sean looked quickly over his shoulder to see if Sal was in yet. "Doing some follow-up at the hospital."

O'Brien blew a concentrated burst of smoke into the air. "Bull shit." He crossed his arms and glared at Sean. "He called. He has car trouble. You two try to scam me one more time, and your pay gets docked—both of you."

❧

An hour later, Sal straggled in, apologizing for the delay. Sean brought him up to speed with the case and told him about his confrontation with O'Brien.

"He's just talking big," Sal said, standing behind his chair.

Sean shook his head. "He's mad at me." He looked up at Sal. "Don't you get sucked into it. I don't want you covering for me anymore."

Sal gave a mock salute. "I was going to try finding Lowenstein's cleaning lady. Wanna come?"

"I'm waiting on a call from somebody at NYU. Where Lowenstein taught."

"I'll see you later then." Sal sauntered toward the door, first ducking into O'Brien's office. "I'm going out on the case, chief. And I let Sean know."

Sean laughed and shook his head.

As his partner rounded the corner toward the stair, Sean's phone rang.

"Is this Detective Reilly? This is Maureen O'Donnell. I understand you called."

At the sound of her voice, pain pinched Sean's heart. Mary'd had a voice like that, with a muted brogue, soft, sweet, still colored by the land of her birth.

"Thanks for calling me back." He cleared his throat and sat up straight. "I'm trying to find out what I can about a Dr. Myron Lowenstein, and I understood he taught at the university some years ago. I was told you knew him."

She laughed a little, and here again Sean's heart was pierced. She had the same gentle chuckle of his Mary, too, a laugh that told the world she knew she was loved and loved dearly, the way a child is loved, with no fear of ever losing it.

"I didn't know him. I work in the university archives, Detective. So I know how to get information about him. Spell his name for me, and I'll see what I can find."

In the space of a quarter hour, she determined for him that he'd worked at NYU from 1930 to 1938, a fact Sean already knew from the files Mrs. Wilcox had on him at the Hopkins lab. Maureen also had a list of papers he'd authored, but nothing in their titles pointed Sean in any particular direction. Finally, he asked if there was a photograph of him.

"We have some yearbooks. I could look for his picture."

"Would you mind letting me know—and sending it to me if you find it?"

"Certainly, Detective."

He hung up the phone feeling like...going home. Going home and crawling into bed. Just the way he'd felt the weeks after Mary's doctor had talked to him, really talked to him, about what was in store. Just a moment was all it took to pull him under. Sometimes he thought he still saw her in a crowd. He'd not noticed before how many women had the same shade of red-blond hair.

Get on your feet, Sean. One in front of the other. That's what got him through before.

He needed to ask Mrs. Wilcox some more questions but decided to forgo a call and do it in person. Getting out would help him shake the blues.

❧

"No, she didn't say she'd be late," Adelaide Wilcox said to Julia, standing in the doorway of the girls' office. She'd stopped by to let them both know that there was no news from Bethesda, nor from the detectives on opening up Dr. Lowenstein's lab. Julia had burst out with the question about Susan, immediately regretting it. Now if Susan came in and had wanted them to cover for her tardiness, Julia would be the one who'd tattled.

But the girl might just be moping at home for the day, denying Julia the opportunity to make things better between them.

"I tried calling her a little while ago," Linda volunteered. Yes, right after Dr. Morton had stopped in after his meeting to comment on the stale donuts Linda had purchased in the cafeteria.

"Well, I suppose if she's ill she might not be answering," Mrs. Wilcox mused, not convincing herself or them. "I'll try her myself. Let me know if she shows up."

She left the room.

☙☙

"They had an argument. I...I heard them." Earl Dagley shifted his weight from his cane to his good foot as Sean listened. The detective had run into the little man on his way in to see Mrs. Wilcox and decided to ask him a few questions about the lab. Dagley knew little of the goings-on outside his monkey rooms, but he had been upstairs—to ask for time off around Easter—when Susan Schlager and Julia Dell had quarreled in Dr. Lowenstein's lab. Reluctantly, he'd spilled what he knew.

"She seemed real mad at Dr. Mike," Earl said of Julia, "seeing as how he didn't do anything with the polio stuff. And the other one got all hot under the collar about that."

Sean frowned. Julia had found the body, was the first person on the scene. Did she harbor enough resentment to harm a man just because he wasn't using his skill to find something that would fix her problem? There was something simmering beneath the surface with her.

"What about you—did it bother you that 'Dr. Mike' wasn't working on the polio?" Sean peered at Earl who grinned and looked down.

"I didn't have no idea what any of 'em was working on. I figured he was working on it, too, until I heard otherwise."

Sean asked him a few more questions about his own whereabouts the morning of the death—Earl had been delayed because of a late bus that day—and went off to find Wilcox, figuring he'd stop back in the secretaries' office on his way out.

Mrs. Wilcox confirmed Earl's alibi but seemed oddly distracted. The Schlager girl hadn't shown up that day. It put Sean on edge, but he continued his questions about Dr. Lowenstein, probing the woman about the victim's summer house.

"I had to contact him once when he was on vacation—to tell him he need not return early." Adelaide Wilcox looked at Sean over the tops of her glasses. Her hands were folded on her desk in front of her, the portrait of a prim, knowledgeable librarian. "You see, when he went on his summer holiday three years ago, he was working on an experiment with Dr. Rollins about the effect of repeated electric shocks on muscle reaction times. Dr. Rollins was computing the data but wasn't finished when Dr. Lowenstein left. Dr. Lowenstein even thought of delaying his departure."

"It was that important?" Sean asked.

Her lips lifted in a faint smile. "It was to them. Dr. Rollins was eager to publish the results, and Dr. Lowenstein wanted to be here to help prepare the paper." She opened a desk drawer and pulled out a thick address book. "Although heaven knows why — Dr. Lowenstein always let his coworkers take the credit. He rarely — if ever — agreed to have his name put on a paper. Always said it was important to give the younger doctors a chance at fame."

Didn't want his name out there, Sean thought. People who knew the real Lowenstein might contact him.

Mrs. Wilcox flipped through pages and stopped. "Here it is — the rental agent for the cabin he always took in upstate New York." She wrote the name and number on a small piece of scrap paper, a neat pile of which she kept by her desk lamp. "I had to call him to tell him Dr. Rollins wouldn't be ready with the data until he returned, so there was no need to rush back." She handed Sean the paper. "There's no phone in the cabin, apparently. I had to leave a message for him."

He thanked her for the information and asked where Dr. Rollins's office might be. When she gave him that, he then asked for Susan Schlager's home address, and she gave that to him, too, somewhat eagerly.

"I hope she's all right," she said to him as he left.

Chapter Ten

VALERIE LOOKED AROUND the quiet restaurant and sighed. Even when she was doing something she liked, she always gave the impression of yearning for something more, and now Brigitta imagined Valerie was thinking how she wished she could eat here more often if not for—well, there were infinite possibilities. If not for Valerie's miserly husband who insisted they sock away every penny for their children (whenever they came along). If not for the less-than-expected pay Valerie was making at Patelson and Moore. If not for Valerie's busy schedule at said employer.

She was a petite woman with jet-black hair styled into a limp pageboy with sausage curl bangs. Her wide eyes and tiny mouth made her look mouselike, and she added to that image by dressing in muted colors and plain skirts—things that you forgot as soon as she walked out of the room. Today she wore a gray wool skirt that looked at least five years out of date with a pale blue blouse and gray cardigan.

Maybe, thought Brigitta, that was part of Valerie's problem. After years of looking like a timid creature, she'd become one. She'd only taken the job at Patelson and Moore at her husband's urging. He himself was a clerk at Baltimore Gas and Electric. Saving money—first for a house, now for children—seemed an obsession with him, according to Valerie's tales.

A black-uniformed waitress came over and took their orders. Chef's salads for both of them and hot tea. Brigitta opened a cigarette case and offered Valerie one. After a quick look around—her husband didn't like her smoking—she accepted, and they both lit up from Brigitta's lighter.

"So what is it that's so important?" Brigitta asked. Comfortably resting her elbow on the table, she smiled at Valerie, expecting to hear juicy stories of a secretary changing jobs or getting pregnant or married (or both) or even news of the lawyers themselves, their personal troubles or legal missteps. Valerie knew it all.

"Diane Rivers's job," Valerie said, blowing smoke away from the table. "Oh honey, you're not going to get it."

This was not what Brigitta had expected to hear at all. Her smile dropped, and she sat up straight.

"Did Diane tell you? She doesn't really know who is going to get the job, you know. It's not up to her ultimately."

Valerie held up her hand to stop Brigitta's speculation. She leaned into the table. "It's not Diane."

Cool relief settled Brigitta's stomach. She'd hate to think Diane had betrayed her in some way.

"Diane really likes you," Valerie continued, "and apparently had a big argument with the partners over the whole thing. Burst out crying and all."

Brigitta did recall a day last week when Diane had looked sullen, her face red and her eyes watery. She'd chalked it up to pregnancy.

Her throat dry, Brigitta asked, "Then why—and who told you anyway?"

Looking to and fro first, Valerie continued. "Well, you know Schuyler Moore's secretary, Betty Matthewson? She goes to church at St. Brigit's and she just joined the Sodality there. Diane Rivers's mother is the head of the Sodality. Betty said this weekend she was talking to Mrs. Mulescovich—that's Diane's mother—and she—Mrs. Mulescovich, that is—was worried because Diane had been so upset that weekend. She—Diane's mother, that is—was afraid it was bad for the baby. Who knows what's bad for a baby? My sister hardly ate a thing her first five months, and you couldn't even tell she was expecting until she had a healthy eight pound baby boy!"

God, Valerie exasperated her with her tales of Sodality meetings and mothers. Just say it and be done with it. Brigitta pasted a smile on her face. "Why was Diane so upset?"

Valerie took another puff on her cigarette and coughed. The waitress came by at that moment with their tea, and they both waited until she left before continuing.

"Well, honey," Valerie said, stirring sugar into her cup, "Diane likes you. Respects you. Everyone respects you." She gave Brigitta the kind of smile one flashes to a terminal patient to keep them hoping for a cure. "You're the smartest legal secretary in all of Baltimore, if you ask me. Ask anyone! You probably could be a lawyer yourself the way you've helped your boss research past rulings and the like. Which is why I'm sure you'll be fine when this is all over and done with. Someone will snatch you up in an instant!" Valerie tried to snap her other fingers to emphasize her point, but the result was an impotent brush of flesh on flesh.

Brigitta put her cigarette out so Valerie couldn't see her hand shaking. Someone would snatch her up in an instant? That couldn't mean—no, no, Valerie probably just assumed she'd leave Smathers's office if she didn't get the promotion. After all, she couldn't stay there knowing they'd pass her over. They'd assume she was a weakling, willing to take whatever crumbs they dished out. Yes, that was it. Even Valerie had figured that one out.

"You know Gavin's wife is Charles Ryan's daughter," Valerie said.

"Yes." Charles Ryan's daughter and Stanford Dennis's goddaughter. Ryan, Dennis and Smathers was one big happy family. Brigitta swallowed.

"She heard some rumors, I guess." Valerie didn't look at Brigitta. "You know how people talk, how they read into things. Things like how Mr. Smathers gave you that diamond bracelet for Christmas. How he asked you to go on that business trip to Philadelphia with him." Now Valerie looked up at her. "Some people just have dirty minds, Brigitta. Really dirty minds."

So Merle Smathers knew about the affair. So what? Surely it wasn't Gavin's first. Why, Brigitta had heard similar gossip about his previous secretary. That had been the reason she'd left, Brigitta had heard.

And then the enormity of her stupidity hit her as if she had dumped the entire teapot on her lap. She became enflamed with anger—not at Gavin, not at Valerie, but at herself. Of course. The previous secretary had had an affair with Gavin. And she'd gone—not of her own volition as Brigitta had been told, but because she'd been asked to leave.

What had the story been? Oh, yes, she remembered now—Rosa had decided to go to night school, and she'd wanted a job that required less of her. Rosa. She'd been Italian like Brigitta. Probably dark-haired and voluptuous. My god. Gavin had a "type," and she'd stepped neatly into the space left by the previous occupant.

Valerie continued to talk, but Brigitta barely heard. Instead, she catalogued the mistakes she'd made with Gavin. She'd been too cocky when she took this job, that was it. She'd been so proud of herself, taking the business classes, excelling, landing a job with Carroll Shipping and then having the nerve—even against her family's wishes (they were always so cautious)—to apply for another, better position. In Brigitta's family, you found something and held on to it like a dog with a bone. You held on to it before someone tried to take it away from you.

She realized now that she'd grown so used to discounting her family's cautions that she had ceased to listen to them even when they had value. Her mother had told her not to go to Philadelphia with Gavin. She'd tsk-tsked, shaken her head and then her finger at Brigitta as they'd washed dishes after a Sunday supper.

"What will they say of you, all the workers in the office? What will his wife say?"

A good and sensible question. But by then Brigitta had been convinced she was the one setting the boundaries of her affair with Gavin, and she was careful and discreet. No one would know. Her mother was always telling her the sky was falling.

"...and so Gavin's father-in-law told him he had to let you go by the end of the week. Plain and simple...."

Had to let her go? She wondered when Gavin was going to drop the axe. Maybe that's why he'd been churlish this morning. He'd known he had an unpleasant task to perform, and he'd been dreading it. Perhaps he'd been prepared to go from crushing her dreams of owning a home to crushing her livelihood, but then the phone had rung, taking her to her desk. He'd had a meeting with a client after that, and she'd taken off for lunch when that meeting was through.

"....but I heard Mr. Smathers kicked up a fuss. Said it wasn't fair..."

Where did Valerie get all these details? Brigitta let her smile drop. Valerie didn't have the details. She probably added those herself, creating the drama that was missing from her own life.

Their lunches arrived, but Brigitta now had no appetite whatsoever. She made a valiant effort, however, placing food in mouth, chewing, swallowing. It tasted like paper to her and had the same texture. She felt utterly humiliated, done in by her own hard-won self-confidence. But she would feel even worse if Valerie suspected anything. Then Brigitta would feel...like Valerie herself, small, inconsequential, incapable of making bold moves without messing up.

So she pretended instead that she'd heard the rumors, too, and that's precisely why she had been intending to hand in her notice.

Valerie's face went froglike in surprise, her eyes bulging and her mouth open. Oh, yes, Brigitta told her, nodding seriously. I was typing up my resignation this morning when you called. I've just been struggling with how to break it to Mr. Smathers.

"But you don't have another job, do you?" Valerie asked, awestruck at Brigitta's daring.

"I have some savings." She drank the last of her tea and pushed her half-eaten plate to the side. "Would you be able to stay under the circumstances?"

Valerie said nothing. Brigitta knew the answer. Valerie would lap up any humiliation as long as it paid, and her husband said it was okay.

As a display of her supreme confidence in the future, Brigitta insisted on paying the bill.

Outside the big department store building a few moments later, both women blinked in the sunshine. "Oh, Brigitta, I'm so glad you're not getting fired. Let me know how it goes when you tell that dirty-minded boss of yours you're quitting."

"Sure thing, Val."

"Oh — and one other thing. If Diane Rivers is looking for other names to, you know, put in for her job — would you mind mentioning I wouldn't mind coming back to Ryan, Dennis and Smathers?"

Brigitta forced a grim smile. "Of course not, Val. I'll tell her before I leave."

They parted ways, and when Brigitta arrived back at her office, she didn't even take off her gloves before marching into Gavin Smathers's office and announcing in icy tones that she had found a better job and was leaving the law firm.

Weeks ago, she said, when he asked when she'd secured her new position.

Then why did you wait to tell me?

I was afraid you'd be disappointed, and I knew you were involved in some important cases. I didn't want to throw you.

She'd smiled, daring him to challenge her unselfishness.

When will you be leaving?

I'd like to go as soon as possible. This afternoon, in fact...

Where will you be working?

Oh, you don't know them. It's a small firm north of the city in the county seat. I really couldn't turn it down. They're offering me better pay, a larger office – in the countryside, a lovely building – and have even hinted at helping me with legal studies should I decide to pursue the law. Maybe we'll meet again in a courtroom... He'd smiled at that.

"You'd make a damned good lawyer, Bridgie," he said with no rancor.

She packed up her desk, left a note for Diane – mentioning Valerie's interest in the position as well as her gratitude for her friendship – and went home where she cried for an hour before drinking a half bottle of wine by herself.

⋘⋙

Susan Schlager lived in a small brick row house in a new development just east of the city near the county line. Sean approached the house carefully, looking for shadows passing windows, but it was as still and dark as an office after hours. He could smell lunches cooking and children laughing in nearby homes, but the Schlager place was locked tight, curtains drawn against the day's sun. He'd come here after leaving Hopkins – he'd not been able to find that Dr. Rollins Adelaide Wilcox had mentioned. He'd try him later.

He went to the door and just listened. Was that a phonograph playing? He leaned forward, straining to hear. Then he knocked. No answer.

"Can I help you?" A woman in a floral housedress, with hair in curlers under a fine net, opened the door one house up.

"I'm looking for Sue," Sean said with his most charming smile. "She's my cousin. Thought I'd surprise her."

The woman didn't lose her frown but didn't retreat. "They keep to themselves," she told Sean. "Couldn't say where they were."

"Probably at work," Sean said, pushing his hands in his coat pocket. "Should've called them last night, I guess."

She huffed out a long breath. "Probably wouldn't have heard the phone anyway. They had one heck of a...well...discussion last night. Went on for some time." She looked as if she had better things to do but wanted to say more. A little girl, about the same age as Danny and Robby, came up to her, tugging at her dress. She asked her mother for some more of something, and the woman patted her head.

"Yeah, Sue and Steve can sure go at it sometimes," Sean said, trying to keep the conversation flowing.

"If you're Sue's cousin you might want to talk to that husband of hers," the woman said, not hiding her indignation. "He sounds like he 'goes at it' a little too much, if you ask me." The little girl tugged at her again, and she retreated after a quick goodbye.

So the Schlagers had argued the night before, loudly enough to annoy their neighbors, probably disturbing that little girl's sleep. And now Susan Schlager was missing. Maybe Susan and her boss had been lovers. Her husband finds out and goes after the boss, then his wife?

Sean looked at the lonely little house, wondering what secrets it held. He'd come back in the afternoon, when Steve Schlager was home. Maybe even Susan would turn up by then.

Now it was back to Hopkins to catch up with that Dr. Rollins, maybe poke around to learn more about Susan Schlager.

Chapter Eleven

IT OCCURRED TO SEAN on his drive back into the city that waiting for Steve Schlager to show up that afternoon could pose a problem. Sean needed to be home on time or risk Mrs. Buchanan's wrath again. He couldn't be lingering after hours should Steve Schlager's shift end beyond five o'clock. Sal would have to pick up that slack.

Sean stopped at a pay phone at Hopkins to call his partner, but Sal didn't pick up. He didn't let it ring long enough for another detective to catch the call. He didn't want a message sitting on Sal's desk if O'Brien should start nosing around.

He hung up the phone feeling like a slacker. Maybe if he called Mrs. Buchanan...no, he discarded that idea. The woman was so prickly lately she might lecture him once again about finding other help. He'd have to try to catch up with Sal later.

He made his way upstairs to the research labs, thinking how he had to get his thoughts together better on everything. Here he was on his third or fourth trip back to Hopkins, scrambling to pick up scraps of info. And here he was still trying to think of ways to rejigger his schedule so he could do some after-hours work if need be. There was a girl in the neighborhood who looked like she was in high school. Maybe she'd be good enough to use for a couple hours here and there. He'd find out this weekend...

He exited the stairwell and nearly collided with the polio secretary. Julia.

Her face looked tired. Shadows circled her eyes, and she leaned heavily on her cane. He remembered what Dr. Spencer had told him about the smell of hot wool and how a polio never forgot that odor. He was about to apologize for his lack of sensitivity the other day when she snapped at him.

"Did you have to tell Dr. Jansen that I was the one who let you know he was in Dr. Lowenstein's lab? I didn't think you'd tell him I tattled on him! I wasn't doing that when I asked about the lab being opened up. . ." It was as if she had been stewing over this, just waiting for him to arrive. Her free hand flew to her face as if to stop the outburst from reaching his ears.

Her hand wasn't really free, though. She'd been carrying a sheaf of papers which now dropped to the floor. Mrs. Wilcox heard the commotion and came into the hallway. Both she and Sean bent to pick up the papers for Julia, typed sheets filled with scientific verbiage, an article of some sort.

"Is there a problem, Julia?" Mrs. Wilcox asked her.

"No. I'm sorry. I'm so clumsy," she murmured.

"Maybe you can show me to Dr. Rollins's office," Sean said, trying to make her feel at ease, useful. He looked over at Mrs. Wilcox. "I didn't catch him earlier."

Julia looked at Mrs. Wilcox, too, as if asking permission.

"You go ahead," Mrs. Wilcox told Julia. "Show him the office."

"All right. But—but I did need to ask you something." She said it as if she didn't want Sean to hear. Mrs. Wilcox looked at her watch and handed her the papers she'd retrieved.

"Go ahead."

"It's just some travel arrangements for Dr. Jansen. I'll stop by later."

Sean handed her the papers he'd collected as well. After thanking him, she nodded her head down the hallway. Even though he now knew where Dr. Rollins's office was, he wanted to talk more to Julia.

"This way," she said and led him past Mrs. Wilcox's office into a different part of the labs. Hopkins was really an amalgam of buildings, wings added on to the original medical school and hospital, adjacent buildings purchased and refitted. The one they entered now was a completely different building joined to the other one by a slightly sloping hallway.

"Is Dr. Jansen going somewhere?" he asked her as nonchalantly as possible.

"To a conference," she said. "Now, please, don't go telling him I told you."

"I could get that information from a number of sources," he lied. "Where's he headed?"

"California." She tried to pick up her pace, but her fatigue got the best of her and she had to stay at his side. "He goes to them all the time."

"Is he presenting that paper?" He pointed to the papers she now firmly grasped in her free hand.

"No, that's for another publication entirely."

"It must be interesting working for a researcher." He'd get no information out of her if she was nursing a grudge against him.

"It's all right."

"But being around all these discoveries—" He swept his hand in a half circle in front of him. "And you get to read it first. In those papers you type."

"This paper," she said, holding up the article, "is a meticulous account of how Dr Jansen used chimpanzees to weaken the polio virus. It's very thorough—but not an exciting document to type."

"But it's a step toward a cure?"

"Not a cure. That would be something completely separate." Her voice softened. He was beginning to get her good graces back. "A vaccine."

She stopped to talk to him. "It's a tedious process. The doctors pass the virus through the monkeys, keeping track of which strain they're using and which monkeys they infect—chimps don't naturally contract polio, you see, they have to be infected with it—and as the one virus moves through monkey after monkey, it should weaken until it's so weak it won't hurt you, but it would still be able to provide the antibodies to make you immune from infection in the future."

He nodded, interested in the information and glad she was warming to him once again. He offered to carry the article for her, apologizing for taking her away from her work, and was gratified when she handed it over. It wasn't that it weighted her down. It just made her "off balance," he noted, to carry anything.

They continued down the hall and around a corner, now walking past older labs, their counters filled with huge glass jars and tubing and the smell of formaldehyde.

"But Dr. Salk, in Pittsburgh, isn't taking that approach," she said, clearly proud of her grasp of the work. "He's inactivating the virus—killing it—and trying to come up with an effective vaccine with a dead virus."

"It would still work?"

She nodded but didn't look at him. He noticed that when she walked she was careful to keep her eyes on her path. "Yes. And it would be less risky. A live virus always carries the risk of infection, you see. And in polio work, that risk is not one that some people want to take any longer."

"Because of the kids?"

"There was a vaccine trial many years ago, apparently, that ended up infecting a lot of kids. Dr. MacIntyre, my old boss, told me about it. It's bad enough when things go wrong, and it's adults getting treated. But when it's children..."

"So that's why they're focusing on the killed virus approach...."

She laughed a little. "Some doctors think the live virus is the only sure way to guarantee immunity. Dr. Albert Sabin leads that charge. They all argue as much as politicians!"

When she laughed, her face lost its musty sense of fatigue. Her eyes shone and her pert nose wrinkled. He noticed she had a faint smattering of freckles on her cheeks, covered over with a brush of powder.

"Hopkins could have been at the forefront of the vaccine work," she said, "when Isabel Morgan was here."

"She was a superior secretary, I take it?"

She laughed again, this time throwing him an amused glance. "She's a doctor—like the men! She actually devised a killed-virus vaccine. She grew the polio virus in monkey brains and then inactivated it with formaldehyde—formalin, it's called. Then she immunized other monkeys, and they didn't catch the disease!"

"Why isn't it being used?"

"You don't just run out and try something like that on people," she said with a touch of condescension. "There are lots of questions you need to answer first. Like what if the immunity in the monkeys didn't come from the dead virus but from a small part of the virus that survived the inactivation? And how much formalin is just enough to kill it so that it still triggers antibodies when injected into folks? Doctors can argue for days over stuff like that— how many cc's of something to put into a syringe."

"You sound like you could be one of them with all you know."

"When you type their papers over and over you pick up stuff." She turned another corner where they stood in front of a stairwell. He didn't want her to have to go down it with him. But he wanted to keep talking to her.

"What happened to Dr. Morgan—did she die?" He stopped at the stairwell.

Julia shook her head. "Might as well have. She left Hopkins to get married."

He looked at her, studying her face. "I take it you don't intend to do the same."

She blushed deeply but didn't answer. "Dr. Rollins's office is down a flight. I could introduce you."

"No, that's all right. You can go back to your office. I've troubled you enough." And then he remembered what Dr. Spencer had told him about the hot packs and how he'd wanted to apologize to her.

"I'm sorry for the other day, about my coat," he said, feeling uncomfortable. "I had no idea what that smell would mean to you. Someone explained it to me."

Two bursts of red flamed her cheeks, and she looked at the floor, brows coming together.

"For goodness' sake, don't be ridiculous. You couldn't help it. I was—" And here she glanced at him briefly, panic flitting across her bright eyes. "I was upset. That's all. Really. It had nothing to do with—" She lifted her cane and put it down again. "With this."

It had everything to do with that. And her embarrassed response to his apology did as well. He couldn't seem to strike the right note with her.

"Susan Schlager still hasn't called in?" he asked, changing the subject.

"Not that I know of."

"She do this sort of thing before—not tell anybody where she is?"

"No. She's usually a good worker."

"Know anything about her husband?"

He saw her pause, evaluating whether to say something. "Nothing except that whatever he says, Sue does." Perhaps realizing how gossipy that sounded, she hastened to add in a softer tone, "Sue is a good wife."

He nodded.

"About your boss, Dr. Jansen. One more thing—this conference in California he's attending. Could you give me the information on that?"

She frowned.

"I won't say anything to him about you giving me the info, I swear. I'll say I heard it from another doctor," he said. "I just want to see if it matches up with other information we have," he lied.

"All right. But it's at my desk. I'll have to phone you."

"Here's my card." He reached in his jacket pocket and pulled out a card with his phone number on it. "Thanks for all you've told me. Learned something. I'll tell my boys about it."

Her face relaxed again. "It's no trouble really. I—I enjoyed talking with you." And, as if to prolong their time together, she added, "It *is* exciting work. To be part of it, that is. It will help millions of people."

She turned and left him.

His interview with Dr. Rollins a few minutes later was short. Nothing new to discover. The man had only collaborated with Lowenstein on the one article. And he'd been touched by how Myron insisted Rollins take all the credit. Lowenstein's name hadn't even been on the final published paper.

৵৵

Late afternoon when the sun's rays cut across the west like a knife to Sal's eyes, the young detective sat hunched in his car again waiting outside the Schlager house. After a frustrating morning exploring the world of cleaning ladies and housemaids who worked for the research doctors at Hopkins—and finding few at home to talk to—Sal had returned to the office to talk briefly with his partner. Sean had offered him a kingdom if he'd work late by staking out the Schlager household.

Sal didn't need a kingdom, but he could do with a cold beer. It was warm in the car, and he wouldn't mind a foamy Natty Bo' to take the edge off the day.

Sal sized up the neighborhood while he waited. He couldn't help compare every place to his own family's locale in the eastern section of the city where working class folks lived—tall, narrow row homes with marble steps, populated with people whose first language wasn't English and who still shopped in markets where they could speak in their native tongues.

The Schlagers' neighborhood was the next step up and out from that, still row houses but with a little more square footage on their small plots of land, land that grew grass, not concrete, and closer to the county line and to green parks with open spaces.

He'd taken a slow drive through the alley out back before knocking on the door and then setting up his watch. Yards were tiny but big enough for patches of green and long clothes lines where the day's wash had been dried and folded in late afternoon before the man of the house returned. The Schlager household's line, however, held a man's shirt and work pants, stiffly flapping in the breeze, left out too long.

At a little before six-thirty, a big blue Chevy pulled up and parked. A tall burly man with reddish hair unloaded a couple bags of groceries and let himself into the Schlager home, using his key. Susan obviously wasn't around to greet him.

How would Sean play this? For the past hour, Sal had been turning that over in his head. Reveal he was a detective at first or merely start asking questions, leading up to the revelation of his association with the police? Which would get more information from the guy?

Aw hell, he'd let instincts guide him. Sal got out of his car, pushing his hat back on his head and rubbing his tired brow. He twisted his stiff neck this way and that and, thus loosened up, approached the door. After a few knocks, it opened in a rush, and Steve Schlager, cold beer in hand, stood before him, not saying a word.

"I'm looking for Susan," Sal said simply, watching for a reaction from the man's ice-blue eyes.

"She's not here." His voice was lightly accented, his high right cheekbone marred by a thin scar. His eyes told Sal nothing. Sal glanced behind the man. A television flickered in the shadowed living room. Furniture looked new, but there were few pieces of it—a small sofa and one chair plus the TV.

"Where is she?" Sal countered.

Schlager narrowed his eyes and put his beer on an unseen table. He stepped forward. "What's your business with her?" He looked ready to fight.

"Police business," Sal said, not giving way. "It's about her boss."

At this, Schlager visibly relaxed, but he didn't move back. "She's not here," he repeated. "She's visiting her aunt."

"The one on the Eastern Shore?" Sal asked, remembering her whereabouts before the murder.

"Yeah, that's the one."

"Do you have her telephone number?"

"She doesn't have one."

"What about her name?"

"I don't know it."

"No Aunt Rita or Mabel or Henrietta?"

"She always says she's going to see her aunt. No more."

"And you don't wonder? What if she had car trouble?"

The man shrugged as if he hadn't thought of that.

Sal tried a different tack. "How you know it's her aunt she's going to see and not somebody else?" he asked in a soft, insinuating voice.

Schlager got the meaning. His face reddened and his jaw tightened. "I would know," he said. "Believe me, I would know."

"When'd she leave?"

"Last night."

"When she expected back?"

"She didn't say."

Sal pressed him on a few more details, but there was no more information to be had. Either the man really didn't know or was damn good at pretending he didn't know. The most he learned was that Susan's maiden name was "Dugan."

He looked at his watch and sighed. He'd grab a beer at the corner tavern near his place, then head home. Tomorrow, he'd try to find any Dugans he could on the Eastern Shore, hoping this aunt Susan was visiting was a spinster from her mother's side of the family.

✍✍

As it turned out, Mrs. Buchanan wasn't angry with Sean that night. She was asleep in the chair by the door, the radio playing accordion waltzes.

For this he'd hurried home. He'd left the office in such a rush, he'd not had time to go through all of Lowenstein's papers, so he'd brought some home with him. He'd have a photo of Lowenstein from NYU soon. Maureen O'Donnell had called while he was out, telling him she was putting a yearbook in the mail to him.

He walked past Mrs. Buchanan into the kitchen where the loaf of bread he'd bought the day before was on the table with an untidy slice cut from it. His heart gave a leap at that sight. Danny had obviously cut it himself. The boy came padding out of the bedroom to Sean and hugged his leg.

"I fixed dinner for Robby," Danny whispered.

"You did now, did you?" He hoisted Danny up and kissed his cheek. His face was cool. No fever. "What did you make?"

"Sam'iches." Danny nodded his head seriously. "Butter and lettuce and jelly. But he wouldn't eat it." This too was accentuated with a grave shaking of his head. His lower lip stuck out in a pout.

"Are you hungry?"

A silent nod.

Sean set him on a chair. "You stay right there, and I'll be back in a second to fix you something." He picked up the knife and deposited it in the sink before heading into the living room where he gently nudged Mrs. Buchanan awake.

Flustered, she blinked her eyes and patted her hair but offered no apologies. "Henry can't pick me up tonight so I'm walking," she said after she'd stood and retrieved her coat. Sean helped her into it.

"I'm sorry I can't take you."

"No problem, Mr. Reilly. The fresh air will do me good."

He couldn't have agreed more.

After she left, he fixed Danny a bowl of soup, tried to coax a few spoonfuls down Robby's throat by pretending they were airplanes coming into a hangar, and changed the sheets on Danny's bed. He gave Danny a sponge bath in the bathroom, not wanting to risk chilling the boy when he was still recovering. He bundled sheets, pajamas and other dirty clothes together and took them to the basement washing machine where he threw them in with some Borax detergent. When he turned the machine on, however, silence. He tinkered with the old equipment for a few minutes, but nothing would get it running again. Shit. He hauled the wet clothes upstairs to the bathtub where he soaked and cleaned them as best he could, hanging them over the shower rod, towel racks and in the kitchen to dry.

He read a bedtime story to the boys about a father who steals money for his daughter only to have her perish from a fall when she tries to prevent his misdeeds, and then had to answer frightened questions about whether he'd ever do anything like that. Finally, he kissed them good night and retreated to the living room.

After opening a beer, he sat on the sofa with Lowenstein's papers spread before him.

But he couldn't bear to pick up a page, let alone read it. Everything blurred together. He was too damned tired. He just wanted to rest.

No, not rest. Be...companionable. Talk with someone. Someone who'd make him smile, cheer him up. The lack of that—that was what kept his mind a muddle.

On the table by his side was the slip of paper with Brigitta's number on it. She'd said to call again. He got up and went to the kitchen where he dialed her number. Sitting in a chair at the table, he cradled the phone and his chin in one hand while the other stroked the beer bottle. On the fourth ring she answered, sounding bleary as if he'd awakened her.

"Brigitta, I'm sorry....this is Sean. I can call back another time if you're busy...."

"No, no. It's a good time. Really. I was just thinking of you."

They talked, and it felt good. Just small stuff—about the weather, a little local politics, places they knew around town. She asked where he lived and seemed interested in his house when he started bragging on it. She said she wouldn't mind seeing it.

He made plans to pick her up the next day.

His phone rang almost as soon as he put it down.

"She's gone missing and it smells funny to me," Sal said over the line. No need to explain. Sean knew he was talking about the Schlager woman. He listened while his partner described the interview with Susan's husband.

"I might follow him tomorrow," Sal offered. "If she doesn't turn up."

A heavy sigh escaped Sean's lips. "I'll start checking morgues then, too."

Chapter Twelve

SEAN DREAMT MARY WAS ALIVE. Just a soft ordinary dream, maybe more memory than dream itself, where he saw her laughing in the kitchen after burning his toast, sitting on his lap and kissing his face. And then, warm, joyous lovemaking.

It wasn't the first time he'd had that dream. He always awakened from it feeling light and happy. A few seconds later – despair. He'd rather not have the dreams when all they did was lead to a raw pit of longing.

Maybe it was the dream. Maybe it was just the light of day. But as he fixed the boys' breakfasts and shaved for work, Sean became vaguely uneasy about having asked Brigitta Lorenzo to his house that night. First, the boys were still recovering. Not a good time for a guest to arrive. Second, what in hell would he do with her once she was here? He hadn't thought of cooking dinner for her or entertaining her in any way. And how would she get back home if he had the boys to watch? Not only that, but it was Friday, and on Fridays he liked to treat the boys to an ice cream, or a game, or even just a ride.

Not a good plan, Reilly. He peered at his face in the fogged mirror, stretching his neck to see if he'd wiped off all the lather. Not a plan at all, in fact. He'd only asked her because he was lonely. He stood up straight and stared at himself. *From now on, Reilly, no decisions when you're bushed and feeling blue.*

It wasn't that he didn't like Brigitta. He'd enjoyed talking with her last night. She'd lifted him from his low mood. And she certainly was one good-looking broad. He just felt she was in a different league than he was. A little more sure of herself. A little more...whole.

He swiped his face one more time with a towel and walked to his bedroom.

"You boys finishing your cereal?" he called out to Danny and Robby.

"Yes, Daddy," they said together and then giggled.

He grabbed a shirt from his closet, making a mental note to take the rest of his shirts to the cleaners that day. He scooped them out of the basket by his bed and put them in a pile on the edge of his dresser.

Brigitta has had time to adjust to losing her husband. He knotted a green striped tie, hoping it went with his brown suit. *I haven't adjusted yet.* That caused a twinge of panic, that there might be a time when he would be just like Brigitta—over it. He needed this longing for Mary to remember her. When it went away, it would be another death.

He tugged at the tie, pulling the long ends free so he could try it again, more neatly this time.

Brigitta seemed to have done okay after her husband's death, maybe even better. If not for his death... she'd not have found her job, her life.

There was no "other side" to his loss. If not for her death, he'd be a happy husband and father today. He was defined by what he used to be.

Like the secretary, Julia. He remembered her irritation yesterday.

He and Julia were both missing something. He had no call to pity Julia. He was just as bad. His life without Mary had left him severed from part of life, distant, unable to feel everything—except the fear that things could get worse. He fooled himself if he thought it would get better, that eventually it wouldn't hurt so much, this missing Mary, wanting her, thinking it had been a nightmare from which he'd awaken. Just as Julia was made "whole" with her crutch, so, too, would he cobble together some kind of completeness. But in the end, it would be just a crutch—another woman, drink, work, or just the goddamn march of time. It would prop him up, but it wouldn't make him who he was before. Never could be that again.

"Daddy, can we play outside today?" Danny stood at the door, dragging his worn stuffed teddy bear. Robby came up behind him, looking pale and sweaty.

Sean quickly slid into his suit jacket and rubbed both their heads. Robby was still warm.

"Not today. Too cool outside for you two invalids." He heard a soft knock at the front door. Mrs. Buchanan was there. "I'll move the chairs out of the way in the living room and you can play racing cars there."

❧

Two hours later, Sean rubbed his eyes. He and Sal had been poring through Lowenstein's papers for half the morning, and he was already tired and bored. Nothing had popped out at them. Nothing had indicated anything out of the ordinary.

He'd started the day on a grimmer task, calling local hospitals looking for someone who fit Susan Schlager's description after determining she once again hadn't shown up at work. Sal had started even earlier, camping out at the Schlager house after dawn, tailing Stephen Schlager to Bethlehem Steel for the seven to three shift.

"Seems odd," Sean said at last, thinking back to what Wellstone had told them of a fellow going into the victim's house. It hadn't been the Schlager man—he didn't fit the description. Jansen was the match there. "If Jansen had killed Lowenstein, he'd be a little more careful about showing up to loot the guy's house, don't you think? Probably would have broken in somehow instead of letting a neighbor know he was there."

Sal shrugged. "Look—all these doctors think their shit don't stink. Jansen might figure we're too stupid to put two and two together."

"It might help to know what Jansen was looking for—or what he took," Sean said, remembering the empty file drawer and Julia's account of Jansen rummaging through Lowenstein's papers at the lab. It would be nice to know what Susan Schlager had been looking for as well, but she was nowhere to be found herself. "Let's talk to him again."

Sal looked at his watch and stood. "I'm going to see Lowenstein's cleaning lady. I've tracked her down through another maid." He picked up a sheaf of bank statements and dropped them on Sean's desk. "Here— payment for leaving me with Mrs. Wellstone the other day."

Cleaning lady. Damn. Sean had forgotten to bring his shirts to the drycleaner. At least he could call about a repair to his washing machine.

As Sal left the stationhouse, Sean found a repairman's number and put in a request for the fix. He then phoned Mrs. Buchanan to let her know the man would be by. His phoning put him in mind of another task he needed to perform—calling the real estate agent who'd handled the cabin rental for Dr. Lowenstein. He pawed through his notebook and found the number Adelaide Wilcox had given him, then quickly had the operator get the line for him.

A man with a distinct upstate New York twang answered. "Ethan Pendleton here." After Sean introduced himself, Pendleton quickly offered assistance.

"I'm investigating something for Dr. Lowenstein and need some information," Sean began. "Could you tell me a little about any friends, visitors, family he had come to the cabin?"

"He was a loner, that one," Pendleton said. "Never saw a soul come with him or visit him neither. Came every year at the same time. Said he liked the solitude. Far as I could tell he spent the week reading and listening to music. You can hear a gramophone for miles in this neck of the woods. Nice music, too. Symphonies and such."

"He never had any visitors?"

"None that I ever saw. I live at the crossroads to his place and I'd have known if folks were traipsing down that way."

"Did you talk to him much yourself, Mr. Pendleton?"

"Off and on. I'd chat a bit when he picked up the key. And then I'd make sure he had firewood—no central heating in those cabins, you see, and he used the fire for burning up old papers and such he didn't need any more. And once I had to see to a repair on the back porch when some boards rotted through."

"What did he talk about?"

"Oh, the usual. The weather. The woods. He was a real nature lover.

Knew this area real well, it seemed. Knew about lots of plants and animals. Why, he even fixed up a neighbor's dog once. That's right—I remember it now. A collie it was, beautiful thing with a dark coat. Twisted its leg somehow every which way. Dr. Lowenstein put a splint on it so it wouldn't hurt the creature. Vet's a good fifty miles away, you see."

Sean noticed that Pendleton called him Lowenstein.

"Anyone ever call him Mike Lowe?"

Pendleton laughed. "No, sir."

So Lowenstein didn't bother to change his name at the cabin.

"He always said coming up here was like coming home," Pendleton added. "Was not too pleased to hear I was selling the place."

Sean sat up straight.

"When did you do that?"

"Told him last summer a year ago I was putting it on the market. I'm getting too old to keep it up. He wanted to buy it, of course. But I already had a fellow who'd put down ready cash. But that ended up falling through."

"Did you let Dr. Lowenstein know?"

"Oh yes. I wrote to him. Told him it was available as always. Hadn't heard."

Sean asked a few more questions of the man before getting off the line.

Nothing. Sean sighed heavily. He had nothing more about Lowenstein than what he already knew. The man was a loner. The man loved solitude. That went with being a loner. Okay, he did learn the fellow loved all God's creatures, great and small. Had a soft spot for something that was hurting. Well, he was a doctor, wasn't he?

He looked back at the papers in front of him and ruffled through them. There was Pendleton's letter to Lowenstein, still in the envelope, the top neatly slit. Sean put it aside and picked up the bank statements instead. All right, he'd finish this bit of reading and go through his notes again.

Nothing in the pile of papers had yet yielded a spark, so Sean almost didn't notice the pattern at first. But it was so regular, so neat and constant, only a fool would miss it. Sean might be tired and pulled in a dozen different directions, but he was no fool.

Over the past year, Lowenstein had been withdrawing regular sums of money every month. Five thousand dollars each time.

Sean's breath quickened At last, something. He thumbed through past statements until he found when the withdrawals had begun. September. So Lowenstein'd taken out a total of thirty-thousand dollars since the fall. All around the middle of the month.

He'd been murdered around the middle of the month. Sean got on the phone and called the bank, explaining who he was and what he wanted. No, Dr. Lowenstein's account didn't show a withdrawal for five thousand dollars this month.

Someone had been blackmailing Lowenstein. And the good doctor had decided to make it stop.

❧

Sal's interview of Angie Hamilton was long and sad. A young Negro girl who still lived with her parents in a dilapidated row house near the Orleans Street Bridge, Angie didn't even know about her employer's death until Sal told her. She didn't read the paper much, she tearfully told Sal when she heard the news, and the radio had broken a month ago. She hadn't been due to clean the doctor's house until that very afternoon.

She'd invited him into her home, and he sat with her on a nubbly green sofa, the only piece of furniture in the living room. Net curtains let in milky sunlight from the front bay window. He heard a baby crying upstairs.

"I was just going to ask him if he needed me more than once a week," she said, rocking bath and forth. "I was headed there this afternoon for my regular hours." She blew her nose into a neatly folded handkerchief, and the tears rolled again. "He was such a nice man. I don't have any other bosses like him. I mostly work for women. Dr. Mike, he even let me bring Kenny to work with me sometimes."

Another wave of grief overcame her, and Sal found himself patting her gently on the back.

"He even took a look at Kenny one time for me. You know, like a real doctor. Said he looked real healthy. A strong boy." At this memory, she smiled with pride.

"Did Dr. Mike ever have any visitors?"

"No. Not while I was there."

Sal described Jansen and asked if she'd ever seen him. No, not once. She knew what work Dr. Mike was involved in because he told her about it. That was one of the things she liked about him, how he treated her like they were the same. Not servant and boss, but equals. She recounted for Sal all she could remember of the conversations they'd had over the five years she'd worked for him. He wasn't always home when she cleaned (Mrs. Wellstone provided a key to the house), but when he was there, he played records for her sometimes and talked about the music—he liked German composers, she said seriously as if she herself were a music lover. When she was done her cleaning for the day, he'd ask her to put on a cup of tea, and he'd sit in the kitchen drinking it and talking to her while she washed dishes or finished some other chore.

"Sometimes I made up things to do while he sat there just so's I could listen to him talking." He encouraged her to go to night school—she was enrolled now—to get her high school diploma, and insisted she even think about college, giving her some materials about Morgan, the city's Negro college. From her account of his kindness, Sal wouldn't have been surprised if the doctor had planned to help pay for her schooling.

She was bereft at the news of his passing and not just because it meant the end of some economic security for her. She'd genuinely liked the man, maybe even hopelessly loved him a little.

When Sal left her, he felt shaken for the first time by the victim's death. Here at last was one person who would miss him in all the world.

⤳⤳

This is what happens when you allow yourself to be carried away, Brigitta Lorenzo thought.

She sat in a lavender kimono at the skirted vanity in her tiny apartment bedroom, smoothing on Revlon Rosy Pink lipstick with the confidence and skill of a master painter. The radio played the soft sounds of a Perry Como hit, and she occasionally joined in the words. *And yet they say it's not unusual/For people to feel this way./The way I do....*

It was midday, and she'd only awakened an hour ago. Her head throbbed from a mild hangover. Too much wine, too late in the evening. She was glad Sean had awakened her from an early doze last night. After their phone conversation, she'd taken some aspirin and gone to bed. She'd have felt much worse had it not been for that preventative action.

She picked up the cigarette—her second that morning—and inhaled a long drag. Then she walked to her closet and pulled out several outfits. The navy blue suit and polka-dot blouse—it accented her looks and was still very professional. A cream-colored straight-skirt dress with wide belt and turned-up collar—could be considered provocative because of its open neck. A full-skirted bottle-green suit with short cropped jacket. Hmm...that was fashionable but subdued. The color wasn't the best for her, though. It made her skin look a little sallow.

Nonetheless, she put the others away, leaving the green outfit on her bed. Female office managers wouldn't feel threatened if they found something obscure to criticize about her appearance. Men, on the other hand, didn't notice things like color and hue as much. They'd only see her small waist and the way the jacket hugged her chest. Perfect.

She checked her makeup and hair and slipped on stockings, hooking the garters quickly and smoothing her legs. She buttoned the demure white silk blouse, stepped into the skirt, and pulled on the jacket. She took one last puff of the cigarette and grabbed her purse and gloves.

She might not have had a plan when she handed in her resignation, but she had one now. She'd already put in a call to her friend Diane Rivers who was both relieved and horrified to hear what she'd done. Diane would happily provide a letter or call of recommendation. And Diane wouldn't volunteer the information about Brigitta no longer working at Ryan, Dennis and Smathers. Prospective employers who talked to the office manager would assume Brigitta was still there, and Diane wouldn't see the need to set them straight.

It had been foolish to quit before she had another job. But she was fixing that as best she could now.

Yes, I work for Ryan, Dennis and Smathers, she heard herself say, *but I've been wanting to leave for some time to work in a firm that* — and here she'd say whatever it took to make them believe she'd had her eye on that particular office for some time. She was counting on her poise and self-confidence to convey just how level-headed, capable, and eager she really was.

Brigitta bent to take one last look at herself in the mirror. She'd get a job. As fast as possible. She'd calculated her savings, and she knew she could last for six months or more without a position. But she didn't want to chip too far into that pile of hard-earned cash. She still cherished the dream of owning her home. She'd find something. She knew precisely what law firms she wanted to visit, and she had the cab fare in her purse to get her downtown. She planned to be finished by five at which time Sean had said he'd stop by her office to pick her up. She'd be waiting out front as if nothing had happened. No use telling him the sordid tale.

܀

"German music?"

"That's what she said." Sal draped his jacket on his chair and sat down, throwing a couple of bologna sandwiches at Sean that he'd picked up on the way back to the office. "Why — what you thinking?"

"Well, he's not Jewish. But he hides under cover as one. And someone's blackmailing him, but he decides to make it stop. You said Schlager had an accent — he could be German, too. Maybe we should talk to his neighbors. Could be Lowenstein was running from something he did during the war and decided to stop running. Only whatever he's running from is something Schlager is involved in, too...." Sean flipped a pencil over, then opened one of the sandwiches. "Hiding out as a Jew is a pretty good cover."

Sal shook his head. "By all accounts, this guy was a saint. You said the rental agent said he was good to animals. Angie Hamilton said he was more than a good boss to her and even tended to her kid. Everybody else says he was generous to a fault. Gave all his money to charity, according to his lawyer..." He shrugged and began eating as well.

"Guilt. He could be atoning for what he did during the war." Sean wiped a crumb from his mouth. It was the only theory he had so far, but it still seemed awfully far-fetched. "Besides, some of those characters they hanged probably loved children and small animals. They just hated Jews."

"Lowenstein was good to Angie and she's colored. Those Nazis weren't too fond of Negroes, if I recall," Sal said.

"Susan Schlager wasn't too fond of Jews," Sean said, remembering how she'd made a point of saying Dr. Lowenstein was different from "them." A theory danced in his head. Her husband — had he been blackmailing Lowenstein? Had Steve Schlager sent his wife to get the latest payment the morning after the death? No, if Lowenstein was a money machine for them, Schlager wouldn't have wanted him dead. He'd have wanted him doling out the goods every month. Susan had been looking for something else.

"Is there some agency or something we could contact to find out who's still on the loose?" Sal looked over his shoulder to make sure O'Brien was nowhere to be seen and then propped his feet up on his desk.

"You mean like a gallery of Wanted Posters?" Sean smiled. "Don't know, Sallie."

"C'mon, don't call me that." But Sal smiled, too. "You seeing my sister again?"

"Tonight, as a matter of fact."

Sal just nodded. "Back to your idea—how's Jansen figure into this?"

"He's a 'fellow traveler,' in the soup with Dr. X. Afraid Dr. X is going to expose them both—maybe because of the blackmail? So he's trying to get the goods, but it's too late...."

"He offed Dr. X to keep him from divulging the secrets?"

"Maybe..."

"Now that Dr. X is dead, though, it seems like Jansen'd more likely be on the run—if he did it, that is."

"That's my thought. He's hanging around too long." And so was Schlager, if he was guilty of something. Sean sat up straight. "Wait a minute—Jansen's headed out of town. To California for some conference."

"He coming back?"

"I don't know." Sean crumbled up the sandwich paper and threw it in the wastebasket by his desk. "We need to talk to him again."

"I can do it."

Sean started to protest—he wouldn't mind going back to the hospital and talking to Julia Dell—but thought better of it. Sal could handle the doctor. Sean wanted to look at the house again. Lowenstein had to have kept some family mementoes—unless he really was a cold-hearted prick. Sean had gone through the house too quickly the other day because of Mrs. Wellstone hovering about waiting. And then once he'd discovered the personal papers and the empty file drawer, he'd not pursued it further.

Sal finished his sandwich and threw his paper away as well. "Only thing is, if Jansen was a fugitive Nazi, like you think Dr. X was, Jansen either ain't German or learned English pretty good. No accent."

"Did Lowenstein have one?"

"Nobody's mentioned it."

"Find out, Sal." Sean stood, reaching for his jacket.

"You know, we also gotta find the blackmailer—if there is one." Sal stood, too. "You think maybe that was Jansen? Maybe he was the one doing the threatening, but things got too hot..." His voice petered out as his theory ran into a brick wall.

"Don't think so." Sean smiled. "At least we're getting closer. We're zeroing in on Lowenstein."

As they made their way to the door, Sal offered another angle. "You know, we shouldn't be neglecting that crip secretary. She found the body. Sometimes the one who did it makes the call to the police..."

∾∾

Julia was angry. She'd heard from Mrs. Wilcox that a polio outbreak was suspected on the Eastern Shore. They weren't positive yet, but it would mean the season was beginning early, and the vaccine work wasn't yet done. It would mean more children hurt as bad as she and worse. And all because...

Because everything was too slow. The doctors arguing with each other. Their plodding. And the obstacles in the way. She wondered if the murder investigation distracted them, slowed them down.

She'd had to miss lunch because Dr. Jansen insisted she retype his article—all because he'd remembered a paragraph he wanted to insert on the second page. Even she could see it added nothing to the paper and was merely a bit of excess verbiage where he waxed poetic—or at least thought he did—about his calculations. All it did was create extra work for her. If this was how they worked in the labs...no wonder it was all too slow.

When she'd read the paragraph, she'd silently fumed, her good foot tapping nervously under her desk in the empty office. Linda was meeting her fiancé for lunch because he had the day off, and Susan was out again.

The thought of Susan made Julia's skin prickle with irritation. Susan was one of the reasons Julia felt she couldn't afford to look anything but dedicated to her job now. Not only was Dr. Jansen still acting colder than usual after his interview with Detective Reilly. Julia'd also learned that Susan—a girl she'd thought was at least friendly if not an outright friend—had gone behind her back to try to make the case for why *she* should have Julia's position. And on the very day after Dr. Mike's murder! Susan had gone into Mrs. Wilcox and told her—

Julia took a sharp breath and stared straight ahead at the wall above her typewriter, biting her lower lip, willing tears to stay put. She would not cry. Dammit, she would not cry.

Linda had told her before leaving for lunch. Linda had grabbed her hat and gloves to head out, stopping by Julia's desk and leaning in so no passersby could hear.

"Listen, I didn't know if I should say anything but it's eating me up not to." She'd looked quickly at the open door. "Susan asked Mrs. Wilcox to tell Dr. Jansen she was interested in your position."

At first, Julia had been merely amused—and maybe a little filled with pity for poor, desperate Susan. Then Linda had buried those feelings with her next revelation.

"She told Mrs. Wilcox it would be safer for you if you were working somewhere on the first floor." Linda had tried to laugh to make it sound silly. She had then tried to reassure Julia. "Don't worry about it, hon. Everybody knows Sue's slow as molasses — in more ways than one!"

But all Julia could think about was how slow she herself was, weighted down with the brace, the cane. She reached down to push the metal away from her leg. It was irritating the skin, rubbing a red spot on her calf. Some people thought that the paralysis meant you had no sensation in the affected limbs. That wasn't the case. She had sensation, just no control. She remembered when she lay in the hospital the first week during the acute phase of the disease, her body useless to her from the neck down. Trapped, she'd watched in horror when a wasp had flown in the window and landed on her arm. When she'd called out for the nurse, the insect had stung her. She'd felt that all right. But been unable to shoo the pest away.

As upset as she was, she had to finish the paper. Dr. Jansen would be back by two-thirty at the latest. Finish the paper, make the hotel reservations, work so hard and cheerfully he'd want no other secretary but Julia...

She typed and typed, her thoughts wandering. With bitter satisfaction, she thought of the bad impression Susan was making being out two days in a row with no excuse. That certainly wouldn't look good to Mrs. Wilcox.

But would Dr. Jansen even notice Susan was away? Maybe he was already considering her as a replacement for slow, clumsy Julia.

Her fingers froze as anger cascaded from head to toe, warming her with a deep glowing blush. She was a good secretary to Dr. Jansen, staying late when he needed her, putting up with his moods, remaining silent when he misremembered his instructions to her and berated her for doing the wrong thing.

And all for what? He never noticed. He never complimented her. He'd snatch up a new secretary, one who was whole, in an instant.

Why did she try so hard to please him when he probably saw her as little more than a charity case? He was a cripple himself, she thought. Cut off from the world, never happy, always brooding about something. She wondered if the detectives knew that Dr. Jansen hadn't been in on the morning of the murders, if they'd pursued that angle at all.

Her palms sweaty, she rubbed them on a handkerchief tucked under her wristwatch. She looked at the time. Mrs. Wilcox would be out to lunch now. The detectives had looked at Dr. Lowenstein's file, but probably not Dr. Jansen's. At least not yet.

Julia pushed her chair back and reached for her cane. She'd only be gone a few minutes. Just long enough to get that file.

৵৩

Sean took his time going through the old house. He made sure he parked down the block so Mrs. Wellstone wouldn't be tempted to "visit" with him.

Sean always felt his strong suit was thoroughness—when he had the time, that is. Rushed, he could make snap judgments and overlook important details. But he had the patience to work a scene inch by inch if given the time and opportunity. He had it now.

The house retained the damp chill of the previous days, and Sean left his coat on. He started in the bedroom, looking in bedside tables, dresser drawers, closets, even under the mattress and behind pictures on the walls. He noted that the pictures were either European prints or landscapes—mostly forests and mountains, American scenes that reminded him of schoolbook pictures of the land the settlers had found.

He approached each room with similar method, starting in one corner and working outward, pulling up rugs and looking for false bottoms or backs to drawers and cabinets. Several hours later, he'd finished the upstairs.

He had nothing in hand but it wasn't wasted work. Immersing himself in the dead man's possessions began to give him a sense of who the fellow was. He was tidy and organized—his shirts and ties were arranged by color. He was not from around here—the pictures he chose spoke of a yearning for someplace in his past. He was a religious man—the books by his bedside were spiritual in nature, a well-thumbed Bible (New Testament included), meditations on the book of Job and a thin collection of essays on the subject of the Prodigal Son.

Well, you knew some of this already, he reminded himself as he went downstairs. His record at Hopkins said he was from upstate New York.

Downstairs, he started in the kitchen but found nothing there but meticulously organized dishes. Then on to the living room. Here a large oil painting hung over the mantelpiece, something in dark rusts and greens, an Indian, small in comparison to the landscape around him, standing on the edge of a precipice looking into a lush valley below with blue-shadowed mountains in the distance. New York, thought Sean. Something out of *Last of the Mohicans*, a book he remembered from his boyhood days. He should get it for Robby and Daniel.

A cobalt blue bottle sat on a table by the sofa. Sean picked it up and fingered it. It was ordinary, not at all like the expensive and delicate pieces that decorated other tables in the room—porcelain cigarette boxes, German figurines, silver vases and crystal decanters. This was heavy and empty. He sniffed it but smelled only dust. An old medicine bottle. The kind you'd have found decades ago before the war. Was it a memento from the victim's early years in medical school? It seemed out of place. Sean pocketed it and kept looking.

At last he landed in the music room. He'd put it off because he knew it would require the most comprehensive look. All those books on shelves along one wall. All that music. He leafed through what rested on the piano—all German music, Beethoven, Mahler, even some Wagner. He took a few seconds to read some titles of books. Again, religious themes— contemplations on the psalms, commentaries on the gospels, a few books by well-known preachers and even a hymnal. Other than that, there were some novels by acclaimed authors, some old classics, and tattered, well-used medical books.

Sean began with these, pulling them down looking for nameplates or even a handwritten name. Nothing. Someone had taken the trouble to rip these out. The doctor had left nothing to lead to his past identity.

As he replaced the last of these, Sean's gaze fell on an old copy of the book he'd just been thinking about. *Last of the Mohicans.* He smiled—he'd been right to assume the doctor's yearning for that stretch of the country.

He reached up to grab the book, thinking again how much Danny and Robby would enjoy it. Maybe he'd read it aloud, chapter by chapter for them, in the evenings. It would be better than the story he read last night— that was from a book the nuns had let the boys have. He flipped through the pages, thinking of how his sons would like this story of adventure and heroism.

As the yellowed pages flew by, a half dozen photographs drifted to the floor.

Splayed about his feet were old pictures, some black-and-white, some in brownish tones, the kind of photos professional photographers take.

Sean shook the book to see if there were more and bent to gather those that had dropped around his feet. Something—something from the victim's past, something personal, something besides the blue bottle and the professional resume.

Family photos. An unsmiling man with bushy hair and moustache—a slightly thinner version of the deceased—stood beside a seated white-dressed beauty with a waspish waist and Gibson girl hair. She held a baby on her lap. Another child—a boy in sailor suit, looking to be about two or three—stood by her knees. The other photographs were similar formal poses, several of the children as they grew older, staring into the camera with serious, wide eyes. The only un-posed shot was of the man, sleeves held up with garters, white apron on, standing beside a shorter man with similar features and identical moustache, in front of a storefront of some sort. Sean could make out only two letters painted on its surface—LL. But there was the source of the bottle—Sean could see a neatly arranged display in the window. Six bottles in three tiers sat in the corner by the door. A pharmacy of some sort?

He turned it over. Of all the photographs, this was the only one with any writing on the back. "Father with Uncle Heinrich. 1929."

Sean spent another hour meticulously shaking out each book in the room, but nothing yielded the same kind of treasure he now held in his pocket.

✑✑

"No, Dr. Lowenstein didn't have a German accent," Linda said, smiling. She looked at Sal as if he had two heads.

Sal sighed and wondered if he should have put it differently. He was such a bumbler. He'd already gotten on the wrong side of the Wilcox woman. He'd asked her what kind of checking the labs did on who they hired — he'd wanted to know how they'd verified if Lowenstein was who he said he was. But it had come out sounding like he thought Wilcox herself did a shoddy job, and she'd been cool, almost huffy, at his implication.

"What about Dr. Jansen?" Sal looked at the secretary, wondering if she knew more than she'd told him about Susan Schlager. He'd already asked her if she'd heard anything, and Linda hadn't a clue. Where was the one with the bum leg? She hadn't been in when he'd arrived. "I mean, was he from Germany — his parents maybe?"

Linda smiled as if about to laugh. "Why all this focus on Germany?"

Before he had a chance to answer, she volunteered, "Dr. Jansen's parents live in Detroit," she said. "He just got back from visiting them not too long ago. Julia told me."

"Where they from — you know, originally?"

"Sweden," Linda said quickly. "I mean, I think that's where they're from."

"What about Susan Schlager's husband, where he from?"

"Not sure. Sue doesn't say much about him. Why?" she pressed.

Sal ignored the question. "You ever talk to him on the phone?"

"No."

So she wouldn't have heard Schlager's accent. Had Susan deliberately hidden the guy's background — and, if so, was it significant or just a natural desire to shield her husband and herself from lingering anti-German feelings after the war?

"Do you want to know where I'm from, too?" Linda teased.

Sal gritted his teeth. "No. Just Jansen and Lowenstein. And anybody else they worked closely with."

Linda stood, a folder in her hand. "Then I suggest you go downstairs." She walked to the filing cabinet near the door and, without looking at him, added, "Leon and Grace both work extremely closely with Dr. Jansen. And I know they're from overseas."

Christ — no one had mentioned their names before. Sal wrote them quickly on his notepad. "Where are their offices, and what do they do?"

"They're very involved with the polio research," Linda said as if he should have already known this. "Offices are in the basement, down the long hallway to the right of the stairs. Just ask someone when you get down there." She smiled at him.

He thanked her and left.

ᏬᏉ

The basement hallway was quiet and empty. At regular intervals overhead lamps cast brash light against the shiny white-painted walls. Sal narrowed his eyes. It felt more like a ward from a lunatic asylum down here with heavy locked doors and a sense of danger. Where was this "someone" he could ask about where to find folks? He passed several closed doors with "storage," "linen," and "boiler room" stenciled on their pebble-glass windows. These folks might be involved in polio research, but it was probably no more than cleaning offices and labs. Okay, he could take a joke. But even so, he'd talk to this Leon and Grace. Sometimes you got your best information from people who stayed silent and watched while they did their jobs.

Up ahead, a door opened, and a short, ginger-haired man stepped out. He had a cane, like the secretary upstairs, and started to walk in the other direction.

"Hey, sir! Could you help me out here?"

The man turned and looked at Sal. He was small-featured as well as short. His face was round with fleshy cheeks and tiny eyes like gleaming marbles.

"Yes, sir?"

"I'm looking for a Leon and Grace. I need to talk to them."

The man tilted his head as if he didn't understand, then without a word, went back to the door to the room he'd just left. Pulling a key ring from his pocket, he unlocked the door and waited for Sal.

As Sal approached the room, he heard odd murmurings and rustlings. His throat went dry. Jesus, maybe there *were* mental defectives down here. Did the doctors experiment on them? The smell was foul, too, like piss and worse. He wrinkled his nose as he walked through the door.

And stared at two tiers of cages, wrapping around the room, each filled with a chimpanzee. There must have been two dozen of them, or more.

"That's Edsel." The man pointed to a listless chimp in the farthest cage from the door. "And over there is Fran and Gracie." He turned to point out two chimps on the opposite wall who were grooming themselves. "But I'm afraid you're too late for Leon. He passed on this morning, poor fellow."

Sal's neck warmed with anger. Damn it to hell. He certainly was an easy mark, wasn't he?

He cleared his throat and stood up straight, then asked the man—Earl Dagley was his name, the animal tender—about the monkeys, acting as if he'd come down specifically to question him on their care and treatment.

Dagley was all too eager to oblige. Sal had the impression he had few opportunities to talk, at least to people. He seemed to have a real affection for each of the animals in his care, speaking of them by name, relating their special eccentricities. At the very end of the conversation, Sal asked him about Lowenstein, Jansen, and Susan.

"A great man," Dagley said, shaking his head sadly. "Dr. Mike was a real gentleman. A great boss." About Dr. Jansen, he was less effusive but still complimentary—probably, thought Sal, because that doctor was still alive and able to affect Dagley's employment. "Dr. Jansen is sometimes sharp, that's true. But these doctors, you have to understand, are under a lot of stress these days. They can't afford to suffer fools, if you know what I mean. They're doing God's work."

At the mention of Susan, Dagley's face clouded. He knew who she was, and, by his posture and expressions, it was clear he didn't like her.

"She didn't have much to say to folks like me," Dagley offered when Sal pressed him.

"You mean to people in your kind of work?" Sal gestured to the hallways, indicating those who worked in the hospital's ancillary services, the cleaning staff and the like.

Dagley's mouth twisted into a half smile. "No, people like this." He held up his cane and shook it. "I think she was afraid she'd catch it from me."

Sal's eyes closed to slits. "But she worked with a crip—a polio victim—every day."

"That don't mean she likes it."

Sal questioned him more on what he meant, but Dagley's observations weren't based on any specific event, merely fleeting moments where Susan looked away when he came into view, or said hello to other workers in the hall while avoiding him. It was small stuff, but Sal didn't doubt that Earl was on the mark. After years as a polio victim, his senses were probably acutely attuned to snubs.

Sal thanked him and left, wondering if Julia was attuned to those snubs as well and if they'd bothered her enough to do something about it.

❧

Things always go wrong when you want them too much. Brigitta consoled herself with that thought as she sipped coffee at the lunch counter in Hutzlers. It wasn't as nice as their tea room, but you could get a good, cheap hot dog and coffee here, and nobody would bother you. Because it was well past the lunch hour—nearly closing time, in fact—she had the counter to herself.

She'd broken a well-manicured nail when opening the lobby door to the first law firm she'd visited. And the office manager there had been less than welcoming. Rude was more like it. Lectured Brigitta on how hard it was for some of the fellows who'd been in the war finding jobs even now ten years later. *Too many women are hanging on to jobs they have no business holding.* Brigitta had sat, gloved hands in her lap, smile frozen on her face, and just nodded. Secretarial work is a woman's job, she'd offered. But the office manager had rebutted that as well. She knew of a good man who'd be a great secretary, she'd scolded Brigitta, but didn't want to try for the jobs now that that field was such a "henhouse." Brigitta suspected her application would collect dust for some time there.

At the second law firm, she'd snagged her stocking on a dented trash bin. Luckily, the run had stayed under her skirt, but she'd been constantly aware of how she arranged herself when sitting after that, and she worried that it had made her appear distracted. At least at that firm there was the possibility of an opening—one of the girls was getting married in June. She hadn't yet put in her notice, but the secretary who'd interviewed Brigitta was sure the young bride wouldn't stay for too much longer. Brigitta would have to check back.

And finally, at the third firm she'd stopped by, an inky typewriter ribbon left carelessly on the side of a desk had fallen, leaving a black streak near the hem of her jacket. Oh, the secretary at the desk had been profoundly apologetic, offering to get some water to dab out the stain. *No, thank you, I'll just take it to the cleaner — and thinking, another bill I can't afford.* Brigitta had thought the entire office had looked careless and ill-tended and the secretaries unhappy to be there. Even if they'd had an opening, she'd have been reluctant to jump at it.

"Anything else, hon?" The waitress poured her some more coffee.

"No, thanks. Just the check." She opened her purse and removed a cigarette case. She had time for a relaxing smoke before she had to head down to her old office where she'd agreed to meet Sean. She had that all planned out, at least. She'd told him to pick her up a half hour after everyone else usually left. So she wouldn't have to run into any of her former colleagues. Grimacing, she looked at her stained jacket. She could take it off and drape it over her arm when they were together. He wouldn't see the smudge.

She was looking forward to their evening more than she'd anticipated. It seemed a lifetime ago that he'd said he'd call her, a time when his call would have meant little more than an opportunity for a friendly smile. But when he'd telephoned her last night in the midst of her depression, she'd grabbed his offer like a lifeline

Just because Gavin had been a cad didn't mean she should rule out all men. She sipped some coffee, studying her chipped nail. Sean was solid and dependable. Maybe she'd unnecessarily limited herself by focusing so obsessively on establishing her own financial independence. With two incomes—well, she'd stopped thinking about that when Ernie had died, but maybe it was time to resurrect that dream. Two incomes would mean not just a home but a fashionable home. Someplace in Cedarcroft where her friend lived but a better home than what she could afford on her own. Marriage didn't have to mean giving up...things. It could mean enriching one's life, not in the financial sense alone, of course. No, there were other advantages to marriage. Sean looked like a good, strong man. A man capable of providing a woman with satisfaction, with passion.

She shook her head. *Listen to yourself, Brigitta. The man asks you out and you're already thinking of marriage. Take your time. Don't rush into things. This is how you landed in this current mess. No plan.*

࿏

Sean strode into the office with the blue bottle and photographs, being careful to stop in to see Mark O'Brien first. He was on a mission now to make sure O'Brien noticed everything he was doing to advance the case. O'Brien looked busy, but that didn't stop Sean from spending a good half hour filling him in on everything he'd learned — in minute detail, in fact. In detail so excruciating that it would have qualified as a good bedtime story. By the time he was finished, Sean knew O'Brien was glad to be rid of him.

With a smile, Sean went to his desk where he found a note from Sal. No German accents, nothing to indicate Dr. X or Dr. Jansen were from that country. Nothing more on Susan Schlager. He'd tried calling around for her aunt on the Eastern Shore with no luck. He'd talked to some of the Schlager neighbors and found the couple kept to themselves. One neighbor thought he was from Austria, another thought he was a German POW, another that he was Polish.

It was just five o'clock. Sal had left for the day.

Folding the note, Sean's smile turned to worried frown. Sal hadn't indicated he'd actually talked to Jansen. But if Jansen found out they were nosing around again, he might skip before they had a chance to zero in.

He grabbed his keys, tidied his desk and made for the stairs. If he hurried, he could stop by Hopkins before picking up Brigitta at six. Just a quick check-in with Jansen.

Chapter Thirteen

"THESE NEED TO BE REDONE." He handed her the stack with the marked pages on the top. With a sinking heart, she saw that those pages were at the beginning of the article. Perhaps the corrections were minor things, things she could accomplish with an ink eraser and carefully inserted letters.

No. Dammit. He was adding new words. Unnecessary words. She looked at him from the tops of her eyes as she banged the papers on her desk to straighten them. She'd be there for hours if he expected this tonight. Surely he didn't...

"I'll be stopping back this evening to finish up some things, so if you put it on my desk, I'll be able to reread it before the morning." He looked at her as if daring her to protest. And she couldn't afford to do that. Maybe he was deliberately provoking her so he could tell Mrs. Wilcox how unwilling she was to perform. Julia was sure Susan would have promised to work late as often as needed. She could even hear her simpering to Dr. Jansen: "Poor Julia, she can't help it. That leg tires her out something awful."

"Yes, Dr. Jansen." She turned toward her typewriter but knocked over a pencil holder in the process, spilling pencils, pens and erasers on her desk and the floor. With a red face, she bent to retrieve them as Dr. Jansen left the office.

He didn't get far. In the hallway, she heard the detective, Sean, greeting him, asking if he had a few minutes. Dr. Jansen wouldn't like being questioned. Good. So he would be delayed this evening, too.

"I'm in something of a hurry."

"This won't take long."

"Really, I can't stay. Can we do this tomorrow?"

Julia smiled, listening to his discomfort. But that reminded her. She needed to slip his personnel file back into Mrs. Wilcox's office. She shouldn't have taken it in the first place. It had been a petty thing to do.

But there was something in it the detectives might want to know. A couple things actually, one of which she'd known already. That other detective had asked Linda—the secretary had told her—about it this afternoon—where Dr. Jansen was from. Detroit. Detroit was where the Parke, Davis lab was, the one with the infected monkeys.

She pulled out fresh papers and put them in her typewriter, half listening to the conversation in the hall.

"....she identified you as the man who came to Dr. Lowenstein's house. What did you take?"

"How dare you accuse me of taking anything!"

"A file is missing. From his upstairs den. Lower left desk drawer. What did you take?"

Dr. Jansen was silent.

"I can get your fingerprints..."

"Really! It's not like I've never been in Mike's house. He...he did have me over, you know. I am a colleague..."

"Dates and times."

"What?"

"Give me the dates and times you were at his house."

"I don't think I can remember. For god's sake, it was a long time ago...."

"You've only been here a year. Should I check with your secretary?"

Julia heard Detective Reilly take a step, then stop abruptly as if being pulled back.

"No, no, that won't be necessary. I don't remember the times. But I do remember now what I was looking for when I...I went to his home. I..." He sounded nervous, as if he was struggling to get a story straight. "Dr. Lowenstein was involved in some research related to muscle reactions. Poliomyelitis affects nerves that control muscles. He'd told me I could...stop by and get the papers. I was in a hurry and when he didn't answer, his neighbor came by asking me if I needed help. I should have come in and asked him myself, of course. I realize that now. But then again, he had perished by then so.... Those papers were what I was looking for in his lab, too."

"Where are they?"

"I didn't find them. They were gone!" Dr. Jansen's voice rang with anger, and Julia wanted to rush out and tell the detective that when Dr. Jansen was his angriest it was usually because he'd made a mistake or was caught in an inconsistency. She rolled a blank page into her typewriter and busied herself preparing the corrected papers on the stand to her right.

"Why did you lie to me?"

"I didn't lie. You accused me of taking something. I didn't take anything. Yes, I went to his house...."

"Did you know Dr. Lowenstein before you came to Hopkins?"

A pause. Then, "No." Soft, not at all like the strong responses earlier. The liar, thought Julia.

"Don't leave town."

273

"I hadn't planned on it."

"Aren't you going to a conference in California?"

Oh, no. Why did he have to mention that now? It would get Julia in trouble. Sure enough, Jansen's angry voice confirmed her fears.

"Did my secretary tell you that? She had no business...."

"No, she didn't tell me, Doc. One of the other girls mentioned it."

Julia breathed out and smiled. Sean Reilly had no idea how much he'd helped her with that lie. Dr. Jansen might now wonder if it was Linda or Susan who'd spilled the beans.

"Well, yes, I am going to a conference. But not for a few weeks."

"What is it and where?"

"The National Society of Immunology. San Francisco."

Not the National Society. Its western chapter was meeting there. Strange that Dr. Jansen was going to a regional meeting. One more thing to tell Sean. Julia started typing. In a few seconds she heard the men parting. If she worked quickly, she might get out of the office in a couple hours. Words on the page became meaningless symbols as her fingers responded automatically to what she read, leaving her thoughts free to wander. She'd have to call her father for a ride. She didn't relish taking the bus late at night. But maybe she should. Beth had said their father had been looking tired lately. He did way too much for them. Helen really needed to learn how to drive. And maybe Julia should, too. Maybe there were levers she could have attached to a car....

"Miss Dell..."

Startled, she jumped in her chair. Detective Reilly stood in front of her desk.

"You can call me Julia."

"Do you mind if I ask you a few more questions?" When he noticed her gaze dart toward the hall, he reassured her. "He's left and he thinks I have, too."

She breathed out a long, relaxed sigh. "You can ask me. Go ahead."

"I need to know how much you know about your boss."

A laugh burst from her. "That's hardly 'a few more questions.'"

He grinned, a lopsided smile that made him look boyish. "Then a lot more questions."

She opened a drawer and pulled Dr. Jansen's file out. "Well, funny you should ask. I had to look up something today. From this." She handed it to him, feeling guilty as she did so. But really, if Dr. Jansen were involved, the police should know. She was doing a public service. He raised his eyebrows as he took it.

"I'm not sure if this is useful," she added, "but the conference Dr. Jansen is attending is a western chapter, not the national meeting of the Society."

"He usually go to chapter meetings?"

"Not that far away."

Sean nodded.

"And..."

"What? I'll probably find it anyway." He tapped the folder she'd given him. "In here."

"You will. Dr. Jansen is from Detroit."

"So?"

"He visited his family there not too long ago." When Sean's face remained blank, she explained. "Detroit is the location of the Parke, Davis lab that just had problems with its monkeys. They looked like they were infected with polio, from the vaccine."

"So you're thinking sabotage?"

"I don't know. It's probably nothing." It seemed like nothing as soon as she'd said it. It seemed like a little girl playing detective. Or a secretary trying to get back at her boss. Why was she doing this? "Like I said, you'd have found it on your own anyway."

"Do you mind," he asked, "if I just take a few moments?" Without waiting for an answer, he sat in the metal-backed chair in front of her desk, flipping open the folder and scanning the pages. Would he notice, she wondered, what else she had seen? She chewed on her bottom lip, debating whether to tell him. She'd probably already said too much. And now that she'd said it, she felt very low about it.

She knew why she'd shared it—because Dr. Jansen had been unkind to her, because Susan had been unkind, because the world was unkind in general. She sighed.

He was a detective. Surely he'd see it. Especially after having just questioned Jansen. Why would her boss tell such an obvious lie? He had to know he could be caught in it.

While he scanned the file, he asked her if she'd heard from Susan today and if it was a habit of Susan's not to show up like this.

"She's visited her aunt before. But she always calls in." Julia thought for a moment. "We all assumed she's upset about Dr. Mike."

He looked up, his face creased with concern, but before she had a chance to say more, her phone rang. His expression immediately changed, and he reached over to grab it before she did.

"Let me," he said, lifting it from its cradle. He remembered the "crank calls."

"Hopkins lab," he said in a serious voice. Julia blushed. She never answered the phone that way. She saw his face soften as the caller said something, then he handed the phone to Julia.

"It's your sister, Helen."

✦✦✦

"Get your coat. I'll drive you home."

"Don't be silly. I—I..." She turned and looked at her desk, the half-typed page in the typewriter, the pencils and pens still in disarray by the pencil holder, paper clips by the side of her blotter. She started to neaten it, but he stepped over to her and touched her on the arm.

"Julia?" He studied her face. Her eyes were wide and scared, watering with unshed tears, her face drained of color. Her arm trembled under his hand.

The phone call had done this. As soon as she'd said hello, her face had gone ashen, and she'd nervously twisted the cord as she'd asked a quick series of questions.

When did this happen....is Mutti with him....is he conscious....did he say anything....

Her father had collapsed on the kitchen floor after dinner. Her sister Helen thought it was "just pneumonia" — *he coughed a great deal, you see* — but Julia had offered that explanation as a question, too, wanting Sean to confirm that such collapses were always due to something once dreaded, now curable.

"I can't find my purse." But as soon as she said it, she opened the bottom drawer of her desk to retrieve it. She bent over, placing her right hand on the back of her desk chair. But as she leaned forward, the chair rolled backward, and her balance shifted, causing her to take a little hop on her good leg to retrieve her equilibrium. He could see the shame this caused her as the tips of her ears reddened and a lone tear fell from her eye. He reached both arms out to steady her, one on each shoulder.

"You've had a shock. Tell me where things are, and I'll get them."

She crumpled into the chair and pointed. "My coat."

He fetched it for her and helped her to her feet, then gently guided her hands into the sleeves. She still trembled, and he worried about her walking.

"Let's get going. Where are they taking him?"

Her mouth fell open, and she looked at her coat as if seeing it for the first time. "Oh dear. I don't need this." She fingered the lapel. "They're bringing him here. To Hopkins. The emergency room."

He knew that terrain all too well.

"Come on, then. I'll show you where it is." He folded the Jansen file and stuffed it in his pocket, then looped his arm under hers. She didn't resist. He helped her lock up the office, and they set off down the hall. He'd get her settled and be on his way.

They didn't speak while he led her through quiet hallways and down elevators. And what could he say anyway — that everything would be all right? The lie would be apparent before the breath left his lips. *It's not good for her to have someone like me standing by her. I have no more faith in "cures."*

And no more faith in the insincere platitudes uttered by nurses and doctors as impersonal as talk about the weather. *Oh, yes, Mr. Reilly, she's doing much better this morning. Radiation, Mr. Reilly, has shown some very promising results in patients in your wife's situation. The fatigue is a normal part of this illness, Mr. Reilly.*

It hadn't just been an illness. It had been cancer. He'd only told his uncle the truth. Everyone at work knew his Mary had been sick and died. Maybe they guessed what had felled her. Don't say it and it won't darken your own door.

He'd had to ask — and even then he'd asked only obliquely — how much time. He hadn't put it like that, though. He'd sat at her bedside staring at her blue-veined eyelids closed in drug-induced sleep, holding her translucent hand. He still remembered how warm it had felt to him, how utterly alive. He'd looked up at the nurse and asked, "Should I be calling the priest now?" The nurse had merely nodded.

His Mary had received the Sacrament that night, unable to swallow Communion, unaware of the oil anointing her brow, the Latin prayers chanted over her body, the body she'd left so quietly in the wee hours of the next day that he couldn't pinpoint exactly when she'd gone....

They were there. He pushed through large double doors, leading Julia to the waiting room, helping her to the registration desk where she learned her father had not yet arrived. He seated her on a bench and realized he couldn't leave her alone. Excusing himself, he found a phone booth and called and left a message at Brigitta's office that he'd have to miss their "appointment."

Then he called Mrs. Buchanan and told her he'd be late, explaining he was at the hospital with a friend whose father had taken ill. This strangled Mrs. Buchanan's protests before she had a chance to utter a word. Memories crackled across the phone line. So many times when Mary had been ill he'd had to call Mrs. Buchanan to say he'd be staying at the hospital. So many times she'd silently understood, offering to stay overnight with the boys. In those days she'd not complained. She'd not even charged him extra. She'd cooked and cleaned and even left him homemade bread. Now she murmured a soft, "oh, I see," before asking him when she should expect him. He didn't know. He'd be home as soon as he could.

When he returned to the waiting room, he saw Julia hugging a very pregnant woman who looked like an older version of her. A man stood to the side holding a boy. Two other boys stood next to their father. One sucked his thumb and looked mournfully around. Just like Daniel had looked when he'd come to visit his mother in the hospital for the last time. Uncomprehending.

Sean swallowed. Maybe he could go now. But as he thought this, he saw Julia reaching behind her, her hand searching for the cane which had fallen to the floor. He rushed forward to retrieve it, handing it to her as she turned. When she saw him, her eyes softened with gratitude.

"Detective Reilly…"

"Sean," he said. "Call me Sean."

" —this is my sister Beth and her husband, Stu." She gestured to them both. "Beth said they should be here any minute."

And at that moment a crisp nurse came through the doorway asking for the family of Howard Dell. In a rush she was gone.

He sank into a chair, his hands fingering his hat between his legs. Dammit, he couldn't go now. He pictured her coming back to the waiting room, expecting to see a friendly face, wondering where he'd gone. That Stu fellow would be wise to take the little ones home to bed if things dragged on. And then Julia and her sister would be left in the lurch.

He settled back in the hard wooden chair. As he did so, he felt the Jansen file bend in his pocket. All right, he could at least get some work done. He took it out and began leafing through the pages once again.

It didn't take him long to find it. Dr. Jansen had been at NYU at the same time as Dr. Lowenstein. He'd lied about not knowing the victim before he'd come to Hopkins.

≈✥≈

"Brigitta! Thank goodness I saw you!" Diane Rivers stood before her friend on Lombard Street, one gloved hand holding her hat on her head as a gust of wind threatened to dislodge it. Diane wasn't "showing" yet, but her long face looked puffy and haggard, and her ankles were swollen in her smart black pumps. "I had a call for you."

Brigitta smiled. Maybe it was one of the law offices she'd interviewed at that afternoon. Her luck was turning!

"A Sean Reilly phoned to say he was sorry, but he couldn't meet you. An emergency of some sort."

Brigitta's smile stayed in place, but her heart sank. "Thanks, Diane."

"I hope you weren't waiting here long."

"Not long. No. Just arrived." In truth, she'd been there twenty minutes, stepping behind a portico every time she saw one of her former office mates leave the building. She was hungry and tired and had been looking forward to seeing Sean. She had been prepared to suggest they ditch the trip to his house and go out to eat instead. She'd even chosen the restaurant—a dark, comfortable steak house just two blocks away that made excellent martinis and served perfect sirloins. At home she'd be opening a can of tuna.

"I can't say enough how sorry I am about all this," Diane said.

"It's not your fault." *No, it was mine. I'll never make that mistake again, trusting the wrong sort of man to be fair.* She broadened her smile. "I'll be on my feet again before you know it. I had several great interviews today and have more lined up for tomorrow."

Diane grinned, too, a smile of relief. "I'm so glad. I didn't want to worry you, but I might be leaving sooner than I thought. My doctor told me I should be off my feet more."

Brigitta couldn't help it. Her smile dropped, replaced by grim acceptance. She hoped Diane would interpret it as concern for the baby.

"So I won't be around to cover for you too much longer," Diane continued.

"Oh, dear. I'm sorry to hear that—that you're doing poorly, that is."

Diane waved the air nervously. "I think it will be fine. My doctor's a very cautious man. But Bill, he would like me home. I think I'll probably be doing more at home than in the office!" She laughed.

"How much longer will you be here?" Brigitta gestured to their building.

"Just a month. If that." Diane looked down, her fingers clasping the handle of her smart red leather purse. "I told them today that I'd like to leave in two weeks. They asked if I could stretch it."

Brigitta made a few more minutes' small talk, asking the polite questions about her friend's health and future, catching up on the day's office gossip. But all the while Diane talked, Brigitta thought of one thing. She had to find a job, any job, within two weeks, or getting a reference from her former employer would be impossible.

৵৽

When she first appeared in the doorway, she looked as if gravity was pulling her to the ground, pulling all of her there so hard she had to fight to keep herself upright. And then when she caught sight of him, everything lifted, almost imperceptibly, her mouth relaxing, her eyes opening from a worried frown.

He saw these things because he had been there, too, in that entryway by the registration desk, with a soul as weary as his body. He'd stood in that exact spot, rubbing his hand over his face as if that would wipe every vestige of fatigue and hurt away. If he'd seen a friendly soul waiting for him, it would have lifted fifty pounds off his shoulders.

He stood and greeted her. "Well?"

"A heart attack," she said. She touched his arm when she spoke. He knew about that, too, the need for contact. "They're taking him to a room. My mother and Beth will stay. Stu's got the kids in the cafeteria, but I was going to get a ride with him. Helen's home and I have to call her. She stayed home to tell me when I came home from work—in case she didn't get me at the office."

"I'll take you home."

She studied his eyes, looking for an answer. She didn't know him. Why should she accept a ride from a virtual stranger? Something flickered across her face. Determination maybe. Or maybe resignation.

"All right. Let me tell them."

৵৽

She should have called Will.

That's what had flickered through her mind as she sat in Sean's car, headed toward home. Not once during this crisis had she thought of calling her fiancé. *But it happened so quickly and Sean was there. It could have been Linda who stayed and then offered a ride and I would have been just as blank, just as thoughtless about Will....*

No, if Linda had stayed with her, Julia would have remembered to call Will at the first opportunity. Linda would have been a reminder, the good fiancée, the woman who knew her place in life. Was that it? Dammit, she didn't know. And she was too tired to reason it out.

"You didn't have to stay," she told him, staring out the window of his car later at the darkening streets. "Who's watching your boys?"

"A neighborhood woman. I called her."

With a flash of insight she realized he'd been through this before. He hadn't hesitated or asked directions when guiding her to the emergency room. He'd known exactly where it was. She turned to him, but his eyes were on the road, gleaming in the light of passing lampposts.

"I'm really sorry," she said. And when he asked her why, she looked straight ahead and told him what she suspected, that his wife had been there, that he'd sat through his own vigils.

He remained silent for a few seconds, then asked her if he was headed in the right direction. She couldn't tell from his voice if she'd offended him or touched him or neither.

"Is he going to be okay?" he asked at last.

"The doctors said..." Now it was her turn to pause. What had they said? Nothing definite. Just as when she had polio. She sighed. "The doctors have a hundred different ways of saying maybe."

She heard him chuckle softly and turned to see him nodding his head.

"It was the same when I was sick," she continued, now surer of his mood. "When I starting feeling bad, really bad, my mother asked the doctor if it was polio. Specifically asked him. And he said 'we can't be sure. It could be the flu.' My god, he knew. He just didn't want to tell them, didn't want to say it in front of me. At least he told them to get me to the hospital right away."

"What happened then?"

"A nurse took one look at me and said 'she has polio.' They verified it with tests, of course. But she knew and wasn't afraid to say."

"Sometimes you find a nurse like that."

"They're with you the most, so they are either compassionate or tyrants," she said, now warming to her subject. "The tyrants can't stand the wailing and whining and crying. Maybe it's because they can't do anything about it. So they decide it's the patient who's at fault. The patient should act better."

"Is that what happened to you?"

"You mean after the fever broke?"

He shot her a quick worried look. "I really don't know much about polio."

"The fever lasted a week, I think. I don't know. I lost track of time. I was delirious. Couldn't move anything below my neck, had trouble breathing, but I had enough sense not to complain of that. Any time they asked me, I said I could breathe all right. I pretended. I perfected a technique of taking shallow breaths when they were around and willing myself to look happy. I was terrified of being put in an iron lung. I dreamt I was in one. I kept forcing myself to stay awake so I could protest if they tried. I decided I'd rather die than live that way." Her voice shook with conviction as she remembered lying there, helpless, her parents unable to visit except once a day, and then when they came in, they were unfamiliar creatures garbed in masks and gowns because she was in isolation. Her mother, pulling the mask off to kiss her on the forehead and murmuring prayers in German. Her father, trying to be cheerful but eager to leave, unable to see her like that. It angered her as she thought about it. Unfair — she'd felt that way then, and she still felt that way today. She'd gone swimming and been struck down. Unfair.

"What happened after that?"

"The exercises and hot packs."

"My boys' doctor told me about those."

She didn't say more. She was afraid of how she'd sound, angry and weepy by turn. Angry at how cruel it felt to have scalding strips of hot wool burning into her flesh, then turning clammy and cool because the nurse dawdled on her way to remove them. Angry at having her legs bent and her neck pushed down and everyone knowing it would hurt like hell but not saying anything, not once saying "there, there, we know it's painful."

The goddamned silence about it all was what had bothered her the most after a while. The refusal to admit that the whole process of physical therapy was a nightmare. They were expected to be cheerful, like the March of Dimes children featured in movie reels and on posters, smiling as they hobbled forward, grateful to be alive, thankful to regain the smallest crumbs of movement.

And that, too, had been another torture. Wondering what the limit would be, where the muscles would stop coming back. Some polios stayed in wheelchairs. Some, like Julia, graduated to canes and braces. She remembered how surprised and hurt she'd felt when she was discharged eight months later. She'd expected to stay until she was rid of the brace and cane entirely. *No, Julia, dear, you go home when you've accomplished the most you can.* They'd given up on her. And they were the ones constantly goading the polios to strive, to struggle, telling them they could do it, they could get it back! Dammit, they didn't even come to pick you up if you fell in the hallway. You have to learn, they said, smiling, how to get up on your own.

"Is this your house?"

She looked up, her memories fading into a fog of resentment. "Yes, yes, it is. Thank you so much. I don't know what I would have done if you hadn't been there." It came so naturally, the mask of pleasantness.

"It was nothing, really." He exited the car and came around to open her door. She swung her legs out and placed the cane on the curb, but she was so tired that it was hard to push herself up. He noticed and grabbed her elbows, hoisting her forward toward him until she was practically in his arms.

And then she was in his arms, smelling his suit jacket, drinking in its scent because it smelt like a man. And he put his hand at the base of her head, and leaned forward, his lips poised over hers, so close she could smell his breath, the scent of life itself.

It was spring, the season of longing, and it was dusk when the sky's royal blue faded to the edge of black, and every hope she'd ever had seemed scattered on the cool, soft evening breeze. She had to grab it or ache with longing the rest of her life.

She wanted — everything. She wanted the world back. She wanted this kiss especially, her hands clinging to his coat sleeves like a child, her face scratched by the late day stubble on his chin.

But he stopped, pulling away from her lips, brushing the top of her head with a tender kiss, a sigh escaping his lips. He offered to walk her to her door. She declined, thanked him again, and was on her way.

Chapter Fourteen

NOT ALL THE LETTERS were anti-Semitic. Some of them merely urged the doctors to stop experimenting, to stop working against "God's will." They referred to the polio as a "plague sent by God to teach us a lesson, to lead us away from sin."

Why had he felt guilty when he'd driven, boys in tow, into his office this Saturday morning to pick up the Lowenstein file? He'd looked over at Sal's desk and been stabbed by remorse. Yet he'd not made any commitments to Sal's sister. He'd even phoned her when he'd gotten home last night, just to make sure she'd received his message about missing their date.

Brigitta had been real nice about that call, so nice, in fact, that she'd suggested making him dinner. Tonight. How could he have refused? He'd owed it to her. Christ Almighty, Sean. What the hell are you doing?

He'd arranged the letters into two piles, both chronologically, on his kitchen table. The largest pile contained the anti-Semitic ravings. A smaller pile contained the general anti-vaccination research messages. He was looking for a pattern. He'd gone into the office that Saturday morning to retrieve his notes because he was restless, about the case, about last night. He knew they had to corner Jansen again — that had gone out the window for the time being when he'd helped Julia with her father.

What had it felt like when he'd fallen for his Mary? He hardly remembered anymore. He'd been introduced to her at church by a friend of his uncle's. He'd gone over to her house — she'd been living with a maiden aunt who then passed away a year after their marriage. The aunt had looked him up and down, had asked him a dozen questions. He'd just joined the police force, was still a beat cop then, and she'd admired him in his uniform. He remembered the thrill of getting Mary alone, taking her to the movies, putting his arm around her shoulder and smelling her hair as she leaned into him.

Was that what he'd felt last night when he'd wanted to kiss Julia Dell? Or was he just hungry for a woman, any woman?

Not any woman. He'd not tried to make a move on Brigitta. But that was different, wasn't it? He'd only seen her once, in the bright light of day.

She was a good-looking woman. It's possible he would have acted the same under the same circumstances.

Oh, hell. He looked up. Danny stood in the doorway, newspaper in tow.

"What you want, son?"

"Jerry Soloski's Dad made a kite for him."

Sean smiled. "Out of newspaper?"

"Dunno."

"Come here."

Danny shuffled into the bright kitchen and climbed on to his father's lap when Sean patted his leg. He felt his son's brow. It was cool. Outside, sunshine lit the cloudless sky, and a soft breeze blew. He'd even opened the back door to let some fresh air in, to blow out all the musty germs.

"It might do you good to get outside for a little while," he told Danny seriously. He rubbed Danny's hair. "But you have to wear your jacket and cap. C'mon now. Go tell your brother to get ready. I'll take you both to the park."

❧❦

"There's no debating this. You'll learn. Period." Beth tapped her finger forcefully on the kitchen table, locking gazes with her sister Helen, whose porcelain cheeks flushed a rose pink at the thought of learning to drive.

"Maybe *I* can learn," Julia added. "They can outfit the car in a special way or something. Roosevelt drove."

Beth looked at her with a skeptical grimace. "Don't be silly. You can do other things." She turned her attention back to Helen, reaching for her sister's fragile hand. "You'll enjoy it, Hel, you really will. I was scared, too, when I learned. Now I love it. Stu's even talked about getting me a little used car, something I can have to take the kids to school, go to the store and whatnot when he's working."

A shriek came from the other room. Beth's sons were arguing over crayons. With an irritated moan, she pushed her heavy body up and went into the living room where her strong disciplinary tones reverberated.

Julia cringed. "Mutti's supposed to be sleeping in."

Helen smiled. "No more."

"Beth's right, you know. About you learning how to drive."

"I know." Helen sighed. "Part of me wants to learn. I just wanted to take my time."

"Sometimes it's easier when we have to do things quickly. Dragging them out makes it worse."

Helen just looked at her hands, nervously turning the charm bracelet on her wrist. One of its charms was her engagement ring. Julia wished she wouldn't wear it, even on the bracelet.

"I bet you really will enjoy it, Hel. I bet you'll like it so much you'll wonder why you didn't learn earlier."

"I know!" Helen stood and walked to the stove where she pulled a whistling kettle off and began brewing a pot of tea. "I'll learn to drive, and you can cook for Mutti. So she can take care of Father."

"That's a good idea." An excellent idea, in fact. An idea that nicely overlapped another one she'd thought of last night after Sean Reilly had brought her home and nearly kissed her. "In fact, I've made a decision. I'm going to break my engagement with Will. I'm needed here."

Helen turned around, teapot lid in one hand, tea bags in the other. "What?"

Beth appeared at that moment, holding the hand of three-year-old Andrew, his eyes red and his cheeks glistening with tears. "What did you just say?"

Julia took a deep breath. She hadn't planned on doing it this way, but sometimes, as she'd just explained to Helen, quicker was better. "I said I am going to break my engagement. I'm needed here. Helen will be doing the chauffeuring. Mutti will be taking care of Father. I'll take care of cooking and cleaning. And I'll contribute money from my job. If Father's going to be out of work, we'll all need to chip in."

Beth let out a disgusted snort of laughter. "One way to improve their financial picture is if they have one less mouth to feed. You getting married and out of the house would do that."

Julia's mouth dropped in astonishment. Sometimes Beth infuriated her. "I don't eat that much, for goodness' sake!" She stood, slipped her arm into her cane, and went to the cabinet where she retrieved saucers and teacups. Balancing them against her chest, she took them to the table, carefully setting them at each place.

"Really, Jules, you don't need to prove you're capable of doing things," Beth continued, going over to her and grabbing cups from her. "The best thing would be for you to go ahead with your plans. Mutti will be very disappointed if she found out you were thinking of not marrying Will. Right, Helen?" They both turned to Helen whose back was to them as she fixed the tea. She didn't answer immediately. In fact, she waited until she had put the teapot on the table before saying a word.

"I think you could tell her you're running off with the postman and she'd nod and say '*gut, gut,*' right now." Helen poured the tea. "She's too upset about Dad to take in much of anything else."

"All the more reason not to add to her worries," Beth persisted.

At that instant, their mother appeared. Her usual neatly-combed hair sported an off-center bun. Her face was pale as wax, and her eyes rimmed with dark circles. A smile of greeting flickered on her lips as she went to the table.

"I must get to the hospital to see your *Vater*," she said. She looked at the teacups and a frown creased her brow. "No coffee?"

"I'm sorry, Mother," Helen said, pouring her some tea. "We were out. I'm going to go get some with Beth. She's going to teach me how to drive."

Both Julia and Beth looked at each other, their eyes wide with pleasant surprise. Elise Dell, however, looked afraid. "But who will take me to see your *Vater*?"

Beth let Andrew scamper back to the living room and moved forward to put her arm around her mother. "I'm taking you. Don't worry. We'll all stop in and then leave you to stay with him. We'll take care of the rest."

They fussed over their mother for another quarter hour. Beth redid her hair. Julia kept at her to eat something. Finally she ended up snapping at them to leave her alone and get going. Beth whispered instructions as their mother went into the hallway for her coat and hat.

"We'll visit him for a half hour—just a half hour—and then let her talk to him for the rest of the time. I'll take you to the store after that, Helen, and then we'll go driving."

"What about your kids?" Helen pointed to the living room.

"They'll sit in the back seat."

"I could watch them," Julia volunteered.

"They run me ragged, and I have two good legs, sis." Beth smiled at Julia. "No, you can go with us or come back here and tidy up."

"I most certainly am capable of watching those children," Julia snapped.

"Oh, for goodness' sake, Jules. Let's not argue."

"Girls! Girls!" Their mother's voice came from the hall. "I vill meet you in the car."

⨳⨳

She couldn't let go of the idea. She even began mentally rehearsing how she'd tell Will. *I just can't begin to think about marriage at this time. The doctors say my father will have to stop working. They have a little money saved but not much. He'll get a pension of some sort, of course, but it won't be what he would have received had he worked longer. I can't in good conscience abandon them at this time.*

In her imagination he was disappointed but accepting, even admiring her for her sacrifice. And Sean Reilly would admire her, too, when he found out.

That was the only problem with this idea. If Sean Reilly found out, he might have to go through some other opinions of her first before he got to admiration. He might think poorly of her for getting close to him when she was promised to another man, for example. And he might even think she wasn't worth wasting time on if she was renouncing men in favor of sacrifice for her family.

She didn't have much time to worry through too many of those thoughts that day, though. Beth had been right. The boys did run her ragged, almost running away entirely after she'd forced them to take afternoon naps. And she was only watching two of them. Andy had gone with Beth and Helen. How did Beth do it, she wondered with a sense of unease. Surely it was just as hard for her.

≈•≈

Brigitta fixed her makeup and opened the cabinet in her tiny apartment kitchen. Two cans of tomatoes, a garlic clove, some herbs. She threw a cardigan over her shoulders and grabbed her purse. She'd walk to the nearby market and buy fresh pasta, not the boxed dried kind, some crusty bread, salad greens, a few cannoli, and pick up a bottle of Chianti on the way back home. She would make a feast for Sean Reilly.

He'd sounded so contrite last night when he'd called to apologize for standing her up that her own self-pity had been quickly replaced with sympathy for him. So she'd suggested a rain check tonight. He'd protested at first, saying he couldn't find a babysitter for the boys so quickly, and she'd had a brainstorm. She'd go to his place and fix dinner for him.

She wasn't used to being rejected. She didn't like it. It rattled her. And now she felt the need to grab for acceptance wherever she could find it before she spiraled down into the dark place she'd found herself in after Ernie's death, with no prospects, no future, with the possibility of moving back home.

God, it made her want to gag to think of that. She couldn't do that. Not now, not after she'd learned to be an independent woman, someone of whom her Italian family would never approve. She hid a lot from them.

She had to reconfigure her dreams. She need not give up on them entirely. She merely had to plot out a new plan.

Her thoughts turned to Sean. What a decent, stable man he was. He had potential. She'd been wrong, she lectured herself, to think she could go it entirely alone as a single woman. And she'd been detoured, she thought with disgust, by the affair with Gavin. It had taken her out of the game for too long. There could be a man out there worth compromising for. A man like Sean, for example.

She quickly walked to the market, greeted the owner in Italian, smelled the fresh basil leaves, tapped the bread, scrutinized the fresh pasta. Yes, she could certainly enjoy this, this leisurely preparation of meals, this savoring of the ordinary. There was independence in it, too. She didn't have to conquer the world. Being a good man's woman was a mountain worth conquering, one she could put her considerable skills and organizational powers to. It certainly beat moving back home.

Humming to herself, she paid for her purchases and strolled back to her apartment. She'd wear the blue plaid skirt and white blouse with its voluminous sleeves and plunging open-collar neckline. When she leaned over, she knew her finest feature would be shown off to advantage.

Chapter Fifteen

"THIS IS MRS. LORENZO, BOYS. She's going to fix us dinner."

They stared at her with silent eyes. The blonder of the two—was he Danny or was it the other one—sucked his thumb. Both wore dirty-looking pajamas. Sean had explained they had been sick but were better now. Good lord, she hoped they still weren't contagious. What should she say to them? Yes, her sisters had children. But she never watched them and barely tolerated their noisy shenanigans at family dinners. What did one do with children who weren't one's relations?

She held out her hand. "How do you do?" Her face flamed when they cowered behind their father's legs. Obviously, one didn't do that.

Sean rubbed their heads and smiled. "I hope you're hungry. You go play while I talk with Mrs. Lorenzo."

They remained in place. Sean bent to them and whispered some coaxing words. Eventually, they ran down the hall into their rooms.

And so the evening began.

With the children out of the way, Brigitta breezed into the kitchen. Here her organizational skills came to the fore as she quickly identified the pots and pans she'd need and found a large towel to tuck into her skirt as apron. Oh, she was smart enough to know she shouldn't reach for any of the aprons still hanging on the pantry door. She knew those had belonged to *her.*

It wasn't that Brigitta was manipulative. She was intuitive. She herself would flinch if someone waltzed into her apartment and cavalierly grabbed one of Ernie's hats to wear, even after all these years. She wasn't sentimental. She was polite.

She found some whiskey and improvised a cocktail for Sean, telling him to put his feet up in the living room, "turn on the television, read the paper," and she went to work with the determination and intelligence that marked all her endeavors. In a half hour's time, she had set the table—with two candles burning romantically in the center—made the meal, and dished up two children's portions to be served on special trays in the boys' room. This last task, she decided, was a stroke of genius. They were cute little tykes. But this was an adult dinner.

Sean seemed to appreciate her attention to detail. He wasn't the least bit reluctant to get his children eating in their separate room. And when he sat down with her, his attention was solely on her accomplishments. He complimented her cooking. He praised her "way with the children" (in truth, she'd hardly said more than a few words to them), and he lavished admiration on her appearance. By then he'd had another whiskey and was making good progress on the bottle of wine. She opened another.

Not that she thought it was the liquor speaking when he commented on her looks. She knew in the dusky shadows of early spring evening, her eyes glowed in the candlelight. She knew that her skin's olive hue shone through the transparent silky sleeves of her soft blouse. And she knew that its low neck showed off her well-proportioned breasts to greatest advantage. She saw Sean glimpse that way several times throughout the evening.

He talked about his kids mostly, about how hard it was for them to be without their mother. And she nodded and sympathized. It was real sympathy — she had experienced loss herself. She needed him to like her. Even to love her.

Because the instant she'd stepped over his threshold and taken a quick tour, she'd fallen in love with his house. Its open living and dining area. The neat, small bedrooms off the hall to the right of the kitchen. The shaded front yard and open back one. The smell of greenery bursting with life outside the kitchen screen door. This was what she dreamed of when she thought of owning her own home. This sense of belonging, of being rooted to a spot, and no one could take you out except with the utmost force. It might not be the fashionable neighborhood she'd dreamed of, but it would do.

While he put his children to bed, she washed up and enjoyed the last of the wine. By then even she was tipsy. Happy and bright, she felt sure that whatever her past troubles, good news waited around the corner.

So when she sat on his sofa with him that evening, she let him "put the moves on" her, even encouraging him to touch and caress, to kiss with the yearning she, too, felt. She responded with equal vigor. And before both of them knew what was happening, they were making love on the sofa, being careful to be quiet so as not to wake up the boys. It was quick and satisfying, both of them still half-dressed. She could tell Sean was hungry for a woman. That fed her own excitement.

Afterward, he was blissful but apologetic. "I didn't mean to...be so forward." And she was appropriately modest, pulling on her brassiere and slip, quickly buttoning her blouse and skirt.

He piled the children, still sleeping, into the back seat and took her home shortly afterward, walking her to her door and kissing her, less passionately, at the door.

"Call me, Sean. I'd be happy to make dinner for you again."

"Yes, yes, I'll do that."

❧❧

When Sean took the boys to Mass the next day, he skipped Communion. He'd have to go to Confession first. He voiced silent prayers of regret and penance throughout the service, not hearing a word of the sermon, letting the boys scramble beneath the pew until an old woman tapped Robby on the head and told him to shush.

❧❧

On Sunday evening, Helen gently knocked on Julia's bedroom door and entered before waiting for permission. Julia was already in bed, her leg brace leaning against a chintz-covered chair, her cane by the side of the bed. She was propped up on lacy pillows reading a movie magazine with Elizabeth Taylor on the cover.

"She's so beautiful," Helen began, pointing at the photo. "Sort of exotic looking."

"It's her eyes." Julia admired the picture as well. "They're hypnotic."

Helen sat on the edge of the bed. "Whereas mine are merely sleep-inducing."

Julia smiled and tapped her sister's arm with the edge of the magazine. "You have lovely eyes. And hair. And skin."

Helen rolled her lovely eyes and smoothed her skirt. She still wore the straight gray skirt and pink shirt she'd had on earlier when they'd gone to Mass together before visiting their father. The blouse set off her skin, giving her a rosy glow.

"I wanted to tell you that you were right," she said to Julia. "About driving. I absolutely love it." She smiled.

"I knew you would, and it's only been two days." Beth had taken Helen out again that afternoon.

"Beth says she thinks I'll be able to get a license in record time. She's going to find out how and when I can do it."

Julia pushed herself up farther. "I'm proud of you." She patted her sister's hand on the coverlet. She sensed Helen had more to say, that the bit about driving was merely a prelude to her real reason for coming in the room, so she smiled even more broadly, silently trying to coax from her what had prompted this visit. They used to jabber like starlings, giggling to each other before they fell asleep. A wall had descended with the polio, and then hardened with Tom's death. They had never regained the easy intimacy of the two younger sisters aligned against their "elders," Beth included.

"I'm not sure how to put this." Helen twisted an edge of the coverlet in her fingers. "But I wanted to offer you the same kind of encouragement you offered me. About the driving, that is."

"You think I should learn?"

Helen looked up. "I meant that you encouraged me to do something I wanted to do but was afraid to do."

"All right. What is it I want to do but am afraid to do?" Julia continued to smile.

Helen's smile faded. "Break your engagement."

Before Julia had a chance to respond, Helen continued: "You mentioned it yesterday. You said maybe you should break with Will to help out more at home. That's why I bring it up. I'm not trying to be nosey."

Julia had prayed about this at Mass, asked for guidance. And as she'd looked at the strong back of her mother, at Helen's now-serene face, she'd backslid. She'd chastised herself for being ungrateful. Will was a good man. It would disappoint their mother to discover yet another daughter who didn't appear to be headed down the church aisle any time soon.

Helen misinterpreted her silence. "I'm sorry. I *am* being a busybody." She stood, but Julia reached out and pulled her arm so that she sat back down again.

"No, you're not." Julia sucked in her lips. She shouldn't cry. It was so silly. But she was so....

"I'm confused, Hel. I don't know what to do, what to think!" She stared at the ceiling, and the tears did fall, sloppy and wet, on to her bedspread. Helen immediately went to her dresser and pulled a freshly pressed hanky from a top drawer.

"You're so neat, Jules," Helen said, referring to the dresser.

Julia laughed. "What a catch!"

Helen smiled and patted her good leg. "When you made the offer to let go of Will because of Dad, I thought you seemed...relieved. To have an excuse to break the engagement."

Julia nodded and blew her nose.

"If you're not sure about Will, maybe you shouldn't get married."

"That's the problem. I'm not sure. What if I make a mistake and regret it? Break the engagement and wish I hadn't?"

Helen thought for a second. "Do you really see that happening?"

Julia shook her head slowly. "Beth would say I was foolish to give up Will." She stared in Helen's eyes. "After all, he likes me in spite of..."

Helen tapped Julia's bad leg. "This?" She pursed her lips and sighed. "Really, Jules, that shouldn't be a consideration. You should be loved because of everything you are. Not what you...aren't. You're a wonderful person."

"But I do have this one not so wonderful thing."

"It's nothing." Helen waved her hand. "Nothing. And if Will makes you feel like he's giving you a gift by loving you in spite of your leg, he's no gentleman."

Despite her sadness, Julia smiled. "You're rather sure of yourself. When did this happen?"

"Today. When I discovered how I'd held myself back because I was afraid."

Helen stood and kissed her sister on the forehead. "Just think about it. You don't need to make a decision right away. I wanted you to know that I'll take up for you if you do decide to break the engagement."

"Geez, Helen, you make it sound like you never really liked Will." Julia meant it as a lighthearted barb and expected a protest. But Helen didn't respond. She merely smiled and left the room.

Chapter Sixteen

WHEN SEAN ARRIVED AT WORK on Monday, Sal was already there, on the phone, trying to reach Jansen's cleaning lady again. She was out of town, it seemed. Odd that she would be unavailable all of a sudden when she'd been around to talk to them last week—after Jansen had given out her number. When Sal hung up the phone, Sean pointed out the obvious, how suspicious it looked to have Jansen's housekeeper disappear. That made two people missing now, the housekeeper and Susan Schlager.

Sal's hand still rested on the receiver. "I'm thinking we're giving him too much time."

"He has an alibi. We can't arrest him just because he's acting nervous."

"Maybe his nerves'll make him slip up if we keep the pressure on. It's possible he has the two women somewhere. We need to pressure him."

Sean nodded. "He lied about knowing the victim."

Sean told him about the file on Jansen showing he'd been at NYU at the same time as Lowenstein.

"But our Lowenstein isn't necessarily their Lowenstein."

"It still has an odor. We just don't have enough to haul him in."

Both men thought silently. Silence was bad for Sean, though, around Sal. He didn't want his partner asking how things were going with Brigitta. Seeing Sal that morning had made it all the clearer that he had to straighten up and fly right with her. He wasn't the kind of man to take a roll in the hay with a broad and move on. He shouldn't have treated her like she was that kind of woman.

Sean stood.

"Come on. Let's try to get the info on the housekeeper." He headed to the coat rack and retrieved his hat and coat. Sal followed, doing the same. "Maybe Jansen's cleaning girl has a husband, a sister, a mother. Where she live?"

"With her mother."

Sean smiled. "All right. Let's get going."

❧❧

After a brief visit with her father, Julia went to her office and spent

Monday morning filing, typing, and listening to Linda prattle on about her wedding plans.

After being so busy last week, Julia found herself at loose ends as the lunch hour approached. Dr. Jansen wasn't in yet, and it appeared he'd not shown up Friday night as he'd said he would to look over the paper she'd not finished typing because of her father's heart attack. He would have surely left her an angry note about that. It had taken her no time to finish it, and she'd already placed it on his desk. She looked over at Linda, now absorbed in a task.

"I think I'll grab a bite to eat and then go see my dad," she said. "Could you pick up my phone for me?"

"Sure thing, hon. Take all the time you need."

Julia had thought a lot about what to do about Susan and her job. She needed to show an over-eagerness, she'd decided, to do more, to be the best possible secretary a doctor could have. She needed to be positive and cheerful, just as she'd been at the rehab center.

She didn't head to the cafeteria or her father's room. Instead, a few moments later, she sat in Mrs. Wilcox's office, telling the office manager how she was more than willing to put in extra hours if the other doctors needed help that their secretaries or typists couldn't provide.

"I don't want you to think I can't handle the work," she said, sitting up straight, her hands in her lap.

"I thought you'd be asking me for time off under the circumstances." Mrs. Wilcox smiled at her across her desk. "How is your father doing?"

"He's doing well," she said. "I was going to visit him on my lunch break." She sucked in her lips. "For just a little while," she added, not wanting to sound as if she'd be taking extra time.

Mrs. Wilcox studied her. "Julia, you don't need to prove—" She stopped herself, then said, "I'll be sure to note your willingness to do more. You're a fine secretary and would be an asset to any of the doctors."

Julia blushed. She knew Mrs. Wilcox was telling her that her job with Dr. Jansen was safe if she had anything to do with it.

"Thank you."

"In fact, if you are serious about taking on extra hours, the labs might be in the position soon to hire more workers, and I'll certainly put your name on the list for extra assignments if need be."

Julia tilted her head to one side, wondering how to ask for more information without appearing too nosey.

Mrs. Wilcox smiled again. "I don't mind telling you—news seems to travel fast around here anyway. We just found out we are to be the recipients of a very generous gift. It's through the Foundation, but the donor specifically requested it be targeted at the Hopkins polio work."

"Who is it?"

Mrs. Wilcox shook her head. "An anonymous donor. This generous soul is handling it all through a lawyer." She sounded very happy to share the good news and gave Julia more details on how the donation was being handled.

A little while later, Julia left Mrs. Wilcox's office a happy woman. She knew the office manager was on her side, and she now knew the labs were receiving a small windfall of cash that should provide secure employment for Susan, should she deign to return to work, as well as Julia. Susan would be no threat if she felt her own work was safe.

After a quick, cheery visit with her father, Julia headed to the cafeteria.

౭৩౨

"How's your father?"

She looked up as if awakening from a dream. Sean saw her turn crimson. Confirmation that he hadn't imagined their embrace last week. But damn...he'd embarrassed her with that clumsy move. Now she was on edge around him. Maybe he should apologize...

"Resting. But better."

An awkward pause. Then, she relaxed and gestured to an empty chair opposite her. "Please, join me."

"I only have a few minutes." But he sat down anyway. He wanted to sit with her. When he'd seen her in the cafeteria, he'd immediately decided to seek her out instead of going back upstairs to look for Jansen again. He hadn't thought of Brigitta, about two-timing, about anything except wanting to talk to her.

The morning had been moving slowly, and that had put him in a low mood. The chat with Jansen's housekeeper's mother looked like a dead end. The woman had told them her daughter was in Georgia, had gone off to tend to a sickly aunt. She'd shown them the telegram that had carried the message. Sal had thought Jansen could have sent it himself to get the housekeeper out of town, but Sean had been skeptical. The mother had given them a telephone number to call. The housekeeper wasn't out of reach, just out of state. After that discovery, they'd come back to the hospital, and Sal and he had split up, trying to cover every place the doc might be. Linda, the other secretary, had suggested the cafeteria.

"How's the case going?"

"Slow." He didn't know what else to say. But he didn't want to leave. He felt like asking her what to do. What to do about Brigitta even. Christ, what a mess he was, thinking of stuff like that. Making the moves on one woman and wanting to ask another about it.

Julia's eyes were blue, almost gray, and the curls of hair at her temples were slightly damp, like his boys' hair when they got so involved in something they didn't notice the effort they were putting into it. He wanted to just stare at her face. Something about it soothed him, the way her lips lifted at the edges as if she were on the verge of a smile, the long line of her graceful neck, the pert nose. He imagined she was called "cute" a lot, and he wouldn't be surprised if it bothered her. But he liked her cute. It let the sweet Julia shine through. Not the edgy cheerfulness she ordinarily let everyone see. Sean didn't like phony cheer. He'd had enough of it.

"Zeroing in on a few things." No point in telling her that her boss was one of them. "Say, thanks for the file. I will have to keep it for a while. Is that a problem?"

"If Mrs. Wilcox notices it's missing..."

"I'll tell her I asked for it when she wasn't around."

This appeased her, and she lost the worried look. But it flickered back when she asked if he'd heard anything about Susan, the other secretary. He shook his head.

"You get any more of those phone calls?"

"No." She smiled at his concern.

"I'm very sorry about your father."

"Yes. Well. He's recovering." She twisted her hands together. She was nervous again. "He won't be able to work for a while," she said at last.

"That's hard." He remembered the strain his missing work due to Mary's illness had caused on his finances. "Will your family be all right?"

She nodded. "My sisters and I will chip in. I might pick up some extra work." She smiled broadly now and leaned into the table. "The labs apparently are about to get a big gift and might hire some new staff." She laughed. "It will mean they can afford to pay me to do more."

"A big gift, huh? Where do they get their cash anyway?"

"Mostly grants from the National Infantile Paralysis Foundation. That's the March of Dimes to most folks. They're very generous." She leaned farther into the table, and he could see a patch of pillowy breast beneath the buttoned collar of her silky blouse. "The Foundation not only provides money for the research but for extra costs the hospitals incur to take on the research. They thought up this system. Otherwise, hospitals and medical schools didn't want to take the grants."

She leaned back now, an old pro lecturing him on how major research institutions were run. It charmed him, her desire to show off her knowledge. "Ever since the end of the war — and the use of penicillin and the like — hospitals have lots of empty space. So the research has spilled over into that empty space. That's why our labs seem so higgledy-piggledy."

He smiled as she talked. He wanted her to keep talking. "So where's the gift from?"

"Oh, the Foundation. But they got it from someone who insisted the money be spent here at Hopkins, on our polio research." She sounded proud, as if she herself had snagged the prize.

"That's quite generous. Who's the moneybags?"

"Nobody knows. It's an anonymous gift! Mrs. Wilcox only knows it was handled through this donor's lawyer. Averill Patelson."

అౄఞ

As soon as she'd uttered Averill Patelson's name, he had to get back. Lowenstein had left everything to "charity," according to his lawyer, Patelson. This had to be the gift. To polio research at Hopkins, from a man who didn't want to be involved in the polio research, who insisted on working on other things, other areas of scientific investigation.

Sensing his urgency, Julia had added some of her own. "There might be an outbreak on the Eastern Shore," she'd said. He'd reassured her that nothing he was doing would slow any doctors' progress. If anything, he thought after excusing himself and leaving, Lowenstein's death and subsequent gift might now be responsible for aiding the vaccine effort.

As luck would have it, Sal was looking for Sean anyway and came into the cafeteria as Sean was leaving it. They met at the door.

"Jansen was in but didn't stay. Apparently, he left in a hurry. Not even his secretary knew he was in." Sal gestured with his head back toward the cafeteria where Julia still sat. They hurried down hallways toward the door. "I tell ya, Sean, he's getting ready to fly."

Sean nodded. "I've got another lead. I think our victim left all his money to the Hopkins lab."

"That's not surprising."

"To the *polio* research."

"But he didn't want nothing to do with that."

They pushed through heavy doors to the street. Sun glinted off cars, and the air smelled of sulfur from factories and car exhaust. Spring was coming. Cool weather could tease them yet, but the relentless march to warmth and sunshine was on. It tugged at Sean for more than one reason. Mary wouldn't be with him to enjoy it, to see the boys laughing as he took them fishing. And it meant polio season was beginning, adding to his now-relentless worry about the health of those he loved. He hoped that outbreak Julia mentioned was contained. He'd meant to ask her about the vaccine trials and the problems in Detroit—the city where Jansen hailed from—but that would be another conversation.

As they walked to the car, Sean remained so silent that Sal asked if everything was all right. Yeah, buddy, he wanted to say, except I'm screwing a broad I have no intention of tangling with, and she happens to be your sister. Instead, he said he was fighting a headache.

Sal started to make a joke about drinking too much beer on a Sunday night when both of them caught sight of a familiar face up ahead on the busy street.

Their prey at last—Jansen! He still wore his lab coat and was rushing down the sidewalk like a champion walker in a warm-up race. His elbows stood out and his white coat flapped in the breeze. Both Sean and Sal took off after the man.

"Jansen!" Sal called when they were within a few feet.

The doc didn't turn around, but Sean saw him twitch as if his name had physically struck him on the nape of the neck. Without a glance backwards, Jansen increased his pace, taking longer strides and breaking into a trot. They ran after him, making their way through visitors to the hospital, nurses on their way into work, a few doctors talking so earnestly they didn't move out of the way when the detectives approached. They were about to grab Jansen on the shoulder when he ducked into a doorway a janitor was leaving on the side of one of the Hopkins' buildings.

The door slammed shut, and Sal reached for its knob. Locked from the inside.

"Dammit!" Sean knocked on the door, but he knew it was no good. Sal went after the janitor, returning a few seconds later.

"Only way in is through the door we just left," Sal said. "I shouldn't have called to him."

"Yeah, well." Sean shrugged and turned. They knew Jansen was in the hospital now. "You stay here, cover the doors on this side. I'll go back in to get him."

"What about the other exits? This place is a castle!"

Sean smiled, struck him lightly on the shoulder to let him know everything was okay. "We do what we can. I'll meet you here in a half hour. Watch the doors."

Chapter Seventeen

SEAN QUICKLY MADE HIS WAY through other doors to the building Jansen had disappeared into. The doctor had made a poor choice. The ground floor of that building was a tight maze of narrow hallways, supply closets and, from the noise behind various doors, the monkey cages. He wouldn't have had time to make his way up and out another exit. So, he'd take the coward's approach and hide.

Sean rushed down hallways without making a sound, pushing open doors, listening, breathing low. No one was about in this part of the hospital right now. Cleaning workers must have been upstairs mopping hallways, and the monkeys were all right on their own.

At the end of the hall, Sean came to the door Jansen had ducked in.

A lavatory door faced him. Of course...

"Dr. Jansen, I presume?" Sean quietly pushed open the door. Yup, there he was.

Jansen jumped from his position leaning against a far wall and went to the sinks, pretending that had been his intent all along.

"Are you hounding me?" He soaped his hands several times, rinsed them, soaped them again as if preparing for surgery.

Sean pushed his hat back on his forehead. "Are you avoiding me?"

After turning off the spigots, Jansen looked around. No clean towels. He scowled and shook his hands several times, the wrists flicking daintily. "What do you want?"

"Who do you know in Georgia?"

"Nobody!"

"Isn't that where the March of Dimes got started?"

"You mean Warm Springs? I have nothing to do with it. Couldn't even locate it on a map." Jansen crossed his arms over his chest and literally looked down his nose at Sean. "That's a different arm entirely. The huckster arm, if you ask me, of the research. The world will rue the day we let public relations charlatans get involved with pure science."

"Your housekeeper's in Georgia."

"So?"

"You send her there?"

"Absolutely not!" Jansen's voice rang with righteous indignation. "If it will get you off my back, I'd pay to have her brought back."

Sean took another tack, going back to the subject Jansen had just mentioned, one he seemed willing to talk about. "Why are you so angry with the folks in Georgia, the March of Dimes, Dr. Jansen?"

Jansen put his hand on his cheek, staring at Sean as if he were no brighter than one of the monkeys in the rooms nearby. "They're rushing things, pushing too hard. They promised the world a vaccine, gave everything a sense of urgency. My god, they make people feel like they're guilty as sin if they don't contribute to the March of Dimes. Those poster children—it's the height of exploitation!" He laughed. "Of course, Jonas doesn't mind being exploited."

"Jonas?"

"Salk." He spat out the word. "On the cover of *Time*, on the radio. Surely you've seen it, heard him."

"You thinking you deserve it, maybe?"

Jansen narrowed his eyes and spoke with venomous contempt. "Really, detective. One can believe a colleague is wrong and not be jealous." He sighed with exasperation. "Jonas is working on a killed virus vaccine. It's a quick and dirty way to get things going. But a live virus vaccine is the only kind that offers any kind of permanent immunity. Albert Sabin has it right, but the whole crew at the Foundation—Basil O'Connor and his minions—want something now to show the poor folks in Ohio and Kansas and Idaho that their dimes amounted to something."

When Sean looked blank, Jansen continued, his voice getting stronger and more sneering. "So they've made Salk into a celebrity! My god, they'll be making a movie about him soon."

Sean remembered Julia's explanations of the different types of research and her comments on how temperamental the researchers could be. Could this be a strong enough motivation to kill? But Lowenstein wasn't involved in the polio research. It didn't fit.

"And you think your work, this Dr. Sabin's work, is more important? It's not getting the money?" he pursued.

"It's not getting the attention or the...the..." He stopped. A smile curled up his lips, and he laughed. "Oh, no. You're completely wrong. You think that Dr. Lowenstein's death had something to do with this scientific debate?"

"What were Dr. Lowenstein's views on the subject?"

"He wasn't involved in the polio research at all, man! Haven't you learned anything in all your skulking around?" Jansen moved forward as if to leave, but Sean spread his legs out and stood firm. Jansen wouldn't get past him until he was ready to let him go.

"I asked you what Dr. Lowenstein's opinions were."

Jansen stopped, stared Sean in the eyes. Jansen's own eyes were small and watery. He looked afraid. "Dr. Lowenstein scrupulously avoided the subject."

"Why was that? The man worked in polio in New York. Why'd he abandon it?"

Jansen gritted his teeth and stared at the floor. "He probably saw where it was going and wanted to avoid the circus." He looked up at Sean, and when he spoke his voice was low and bitter. "And he was right. It has become a circus."

"Why didn't you tell me you knew Dr. Lowenstein in New York?"

Jansen's face went white, his mouth dropped open and then closed again before he answered. "I did not know Dr. Lowenstein in New York," he said slowly, enunciating the doctor's name with particular care. "It's a large state, and the university was a large institution."

"So you admit you were there?"

"Of course I admit that. Is it a now crime to have attended New York University?"

Sean studied him. He was hiding something, all right, but what?

"I had nothing to do with Dr. Lowenstein's death," Jansen said. "Absolutely nothing. I wish the man were still alive! I had questions for him...about his research. I wanted answers. Now he's gone."

Yes, Jansen wanted answers to something. That's why he'd gone to Lowenstein's house and pawed around his lab.

"Look," Jansen said, "I need to get back to my lab. If you continue to harass me, I'll have the president of Hopkins complain to your superiors. Now get out of my way."

Sean didn't move. "Not until you tell me where Susan Schlager is."

His eyes widened, but fear didn't make them glow. Instead, it was bemusement, as if Sean were an idiot who'd made a mistake in front of a crowd.

"Probably nursing the wounds inflicted by that brutish husband of hers."

"You know him?"

"I know that Susan Schlager never exhibited any clumsiness at the office yet had an amazing affinity for running into doors some weekends and sustaining black eyes."

Sean swallowed, embarrassed not to have pursued this angle more forcefully. "Her coworkers didn't say anything..."

"Her coworkers are girls who believe in fairy tale endings."

Not Julia, Sean thought. Had she known? Damn. Why hadn't he asked her?

Jansen stepped forward, and this time, Sean moved aside.

❧

"Brigitta would know somebody." Sal sat on the edge of Sean's desk. "She knows people at a dozen different lawyers' offices. She could find out."

They had come back to the office and recapped what they'd learned. Before returning, Sean had run upstairs to ask Julia and Linda a few more questions about Susan and any bruises the girl might have exhibited. Both women had become sullen and unresponsive. Yes, they'd noticed Susan sometimes had a bruise or two, once even a shiner. But she'd told them she'd fallen or run into something. They had believed her.

No, it was more accurate to say they wanted to believe her. Even Julia. Like Jansen said, they were girls with fairy tales.

Sal and Sean had talked through the possibilities on the way back to the station. If Stephen Schlager was a wife beater, maybe Susan was holed up at home, too embarrassed about the latest round of bumps and scratches to come in. Naw, they ruled that out. She would have called in sick. Of course, if her injuries were too devastating, she wouldn't be telephoning anyone. But wouldn't Schlager himself have done the calling then, to make sure his wife's job wasn't endangered? Instead, the man hadn't seemed to care one way or the other.

They had calls into several Eastern Shore police departments, trying to find Susan's mysterious "aunt," but so far, no leads. Those were small towns over there, too, where everybody knew everyone else's business. It was looking more and more like Susan Schlager didn't have any aunt on the shore and had used that as a ruse to get away. But had she been running from something or to someone? Sal still favored the latter theory, thinking she and her boss might have been more than friends and met at hotels and the like for their two-timing.

"There's no lover to meet now, though," Sean had pointed out. "So where'd she go?"

One more thing to puzzle out. Sean wasn't hopeful about Susan's fate and felt a gnawing sense of guilt over it. He should have tried harder to find her. He'd been too distracted by the boys, by his thoughts of Mary, by Brigitta, and now...Julia. He had to get hold of himself. He was falling to pieces inside.

"I should call Patelson and Moore," he told Sal, tapping a pencil on his desk. "My hunch is Lowenstein is the fellow who left all his money to the March of Dimes."

"From what you've told me about him, Averill Patelson won't be giving up that information," Sal said. He leaned back and ran his hand over his face. "Brigitta might know someone in that office."

Sean waited for Sal to say he'd call her, and when he didn't, Sean realized Sal expected him to do the telephoning. He pushed his chair back as if about to run an errand.

"Go ahead and call your sister," Sean said, pointing to the phone on Sal's desk.

Sal smiled. "No, buddy. I'm sure she'd prefer to hear from you."

Dammit. No way out. Sean scooted back in and picked up the phone, dialing Brigitta's office as Sal went downstairs to retrieve the day's mail. When Sean asked for Brigitta Lorenzo's desk, though, he was greeted by an awkward silence. "I'm sorry," the receptionist said, "but she's not here. I could let you speak to our office manager, Diane Rivers, but she's out sick." That was all right, Sean said, thanking her. Hmm, maybe Brigitta took the day off? Funny she didn't mention it the other night. She'd even said she had a busy day on Monday. He looked for her home number and dialed that. On the third ring, she picked up, sounding drowsy.

"Brigitta? Are you all right? I tried you at your office."

She cleared her throat. "Yes. Yes, I'm fine. Just took the day off. I have some vacation coming to me, you see, and decided to enjoy the weather."

He explained what he needed, and without hesitation, she offered to help. "I was just talking with a secretary over there the other day," she said. "I'd be happy to give her a call and see what I can find out. She's quite the gossip, so I'm sure she'll know something."

"Thanks, Brigitta." An awkward silence. She was waiting for the intimate small talk, to be followed by a request to see her again. Crap. He should see her again, if for no other reason than to set things straight. "Uh, maybe when you call back we can make some plans. Or something."

"That would be nice, Sean." He heard the smile in her voice. "You could come over here for dinner. I'll make you another good Italian meal."

"Gee, that would be fine, but the boys — they'd be a handful at a stranger's place." He didn't want to take the boys with him on this mission. He didn't want another meal. He just wanted out.

"Can't you get a sitter?" Her voice sounded strained. *Aw, shit.*

"I'll...I'll see what I can do."

"Why not stop by tonight, Sean?" She was tentative, afraid of being disappointed.

Dammit to hell.

"We'll see."

He got off the phone just as Sal came back up carrying some envelopes and a brown package.

"Special delivery." He plopped it on Sean's desk. It was from NYU — the yearbook the secretary there had promised. Sean ripped open the paper, revealing a brown leather-bound book with the year 1934 embossed in silvery letters. One page was bookmarked by a slip of paper. Sean flipped to it. There was a photograph of Myron Lowenstein, M.D., Ph.D., professor of pediatrics. Squarish face, so little hair he looked completely bald, drooping mouth, slim figure. Not the "Mike Lowe" they'd found on the Hopkins lab floor. He took out the slip of paper and read it.

"Dear Detective Reilly: Enclosed is the yearbook for 1934 which features a photograph of Dr. Myron Lowenstein. I asked several secretaries and doctors who

were here during Dr. Lowenstein's tenure if they knew what became of him. Several of them informed me that he traveled to Germany shortly after this photograph was taken with the intention of bringing some relatives back to the United States with him. He never returned and is believed to have perished in the war. He was officially declared dead in the state of New York in 1946. I hope this information is helpful. Please, return this yearbook at your earliest convenience. We don't have many from this year left and need the copies for our archives...."

Sal, who was reading over his shoulder, softly whistled. "So our doctor really is dead after all."

Sean looked up at him. "Both of them."

∼ల∾

Several hours later, Sean got ready to leave. He'd spent the rest of the afternoon tracking people down by phone. He'd managed to get hold of Jansen's housekeeper in Georgia, and if she'd been paid to leave town, she was an awfully good liar about it. Her story about a sick aunt rang true to him. He'd even heard a woman coughing up a storm in the background. He'd also confirmed that Jansen was registered for the conference Julia mentioned in California. If the guy was skipping town because of the murder, he was making a good show of it.

Both Sal and he made more calls about Susan, broadening their search to include beach towns in Delaware. Sal left early to talk with her neighbors some more and try to catch her husband again. Here was another case of a suspect not acting guilty. If Schlager had done something to his wife, he was awful casual about it. It was as if he really did believe she was off with some aunt. After Sal left, Sean had made some calls to hospitals again, describing Susan, asking if anyone had seen someone like her. No luck with those he reached.

About four o'clock, Brigitta had called him back but only to say she hoped to hear from her friend at Patelson's office before the end of the day, and she'd be happy to share the information with him over a glass of wine and a good dinner at her place.

Her voice had sounded so hopeful, he couldn't say no. He'd told her he could stop by for a short visit and then he had to get on the road to the boys.

He'd set things straight, make a clean break, and hang his head in shame as he drove home. He'd be offering up novenas for this mess for a long time before any priest would grant absolution.

∼ల∾

Brigitta looked at herself in the mirror and patted perfume behind her ears. Her head hurt, once again from too much wine consumed the evening before as panic had overcome her. That's why she'd been dozing when Sean had called her the first time. Something else hurt, too, something that whimpered deep inside, sorry for herself for again being stupid. Sleeping with a man on the second date. And the first date had been a set-up by her brother. *Really, Briggie. What were you thinking?*

Sighing, she leaned into her vanity, propping her head up with her hands. She'd not even bothered to look for a job today. She'd felt weighted to her bed, overcome with paralyzing grief, just as she'd felt when the telegram had come about Ernie. This time, though, she was mourning the death of her dreams. She felt foolish for believing they'd come true. Independence, a home of her own, her future in her hands alone—they were gone.

Diane Rivers had called her that morning, shortly after Sean's call, in fact. Her voice had been shaky, and she'd sounded as if she'd been crying. Something to do with the baby and having to stay completely off her feet or risk losing it. So she couldn't help Brigitta out anymore, couldn't promise to come through because she was home for good now. She was awfully sorry....

Yes, that's okay, take care of yourself now, I'll be fine.

"Maybe I will be fine," she said to her reflection. "I liked him. Really liked him. He's kind, a gentleman, dependable." And how he'd wanted her. It made her shiver remembering his eagerness, almost like a boy doing it for the first time, and his solicitude after the act was over. *Did I hurt you... I'm really sorry for being so forward. I shouldn't have...here, let me help you get your blouse on....*

He might have regretted how it made him look to be so eager. But she was damned sure he didn't regret how it had made him feel overall.

"I love you, Sean," she practiced in the mirror. Yes, it was easy to say. No pricks of unease or revulsion. What were his children's names? Danny and Bobbie? *I love you, Sean.* Just thinking it made her begin to feel it. She could love him. Women did it all the time. Why had Brigitta thought she could be different? It was better to just accept the way things were supposed to happen, instead of swimming against the tide. Part of her was relieved to lay down that struggle.

❧

"She looked at Mr. Patelson's files," she told Sean hours later, uncorking some Chianti. "And couldn't find a Lowenstein or a Lowe."

"But I know he was a client."

Brigitta shrugged and poured him a glass of wine, setting it on the table in front of the sofa. The room was in shadows already, even though evening wasn't yet upon them. This side of the building faced north and lost the day's light early.

"She said that there *was* a big will recently. A client of Patelson's, that is." She poured her own glass of wine and sat next to him. "But it was a man by the name of Hill. Richard Hill, she said. Left everything he had, down to the last penny, to the March of Dimes."

He sat up straight and patted her knee. He'd looked downcast and bedraggled when he'd arrived, as if he was afraid. She hadn't liked that look. It meant he was uncomfortable with her, with their intimacy. Some men were like that. They wanted a woman but didn't want to settle with the one they wanted. Gavin certainly had been that way, and she wouldn't make that mistake again. When she'd seen that look on Sean's face, she'd determined their talk would include a modest plea not to think poorly of her for the other night, complete with promises for a more chaste future. If that's what he expected...

His hand stayed on her knee. Perhaps it wasn't what he expected after all....

≈◊≈

"I love you, Sean."

Sean sat on Brigitta's small, hard Victorian sofa, his arm around her shoulders, her head on his chest. He might have come to her apartment to break off their relationship, honorably telling her he didn't want to lead her on, but he'd ended up doing just the opposite. Oh, he hadn't *said* anything that would lead her to believe he was interested in a commitment. No, instead, he'd done it.

After she'd given him the info on Lowenstein's real name, he'd felt lit with excitement. This was it, the first good break in the case. He now knew who the victim really was. Sure, it was a common name, but it was a name, a real one, when all they'd had before was the phony-baloney Myron Lowenstein or Mike Lowe to go with. So how had his gratitude and excitement over this piece of news shift into other forms of excitement?

He'd kissed her. She'd been so close, dammit, and she'd leaned into him, and he'd said "thanks so much for this, Brigitta," and then...

And then she'd been in his arms, and it was a whole different story. She'd started crying—for Christ's sake, what do you do about a crying woman—telling him she'd lied about work, that she'd lost her job because of some son of a bitch boss thinking she was too smart for her own good, and then...

And then he'd kissed her to wipe away the tears. And then he'd— Christ, he couldn't believe how little self-control he had—he'd made love to her again. Right there on the couch like a couple of nervous youngsters. It must have been his missing Mary. That had to be it. Because this second time had just proven what he'd learned after the first. He didn't love Brigitta. When the sex was over, he just wanted to go home and fast. But now...

She twisted her finger around a button on his shirt. He really had to go. He'd told Mrs. Buchanan he'd only be a half hour late. It was past that time now. Dammit, he'd even left work a little early so he wouldn't be late going home, risking O'Brien's wrath by loudly proclaiming he was "chasing down a lead" as he'd headed for the stationhouse door.

Heaving a sigh, he pulled away, first kissing Brigitta on the top of her head.

"I have to get going or I'll lose my sitter," he said with fake cheerfulness.

"Oh..."

He stood, straightened his shirt, buckled his belt, grabbed his jacket and hat. "I know I said it before but I don't usually..."

Brigitta stood, too, and placed a finger on his lips before kissing him. "I know. I don't usually either. Maybe it's best if we try not to...in the future."

Good idea, he thought. And then he paused, searching for the right words, wanting to say they shouldn't do anything, even see each other, in the future. But when he mentally heard himself saying those things, the words sounded like something from a person he didn't know. He was a weak man. He'd changed this past year, he'd given up on being strong.

She saw him to the door, and he promised to call her — what else could he say — before putting on his hat and leaving.

"If your sitter gives you a hard time, don't forget, I'm available now!" she called to him as he hurried down the steps.

❧

His sitter, it turned out, gave him more than a hard time. She handed in her notice. When Sean showed up nearly an hour later, delayed even further by a flat tire on Pulaski Highway, Mrs. Buchanan was weepy with rage. She'd been in her hat and coat for over an hour, she told him, fury barely contained in her clipped voice. Her Albert was going to take her to the movies that night. But now they'd missed the opening for sure. And Albert wasn't one to reschedule things like this, so Mr. Reilly could just consider this her last day watching those beautiful, sweet motherless children. He'd taken advantage of her good nature long enough. She'd warned him to speak with the Sisters about finding someone else. She'd told him on more than one occasion. But he hadn't listened, and now it was too late. She would stop by to see the boys from time to time, but she was going to live her own life now, thank you very much.

Sean had the impression this was a speech she'd rehearsed in her mind many times before.

After she left, Sean sank into his living room chair with his coat still on. Danny crawled up on his lap, his thumb in his mouth, while Robby turned on the television and asked if they could have hot dogs for dinner.

"Hot dogs sounds terrific, boys." Sean put Danny on the floor next to his brother and went into the kitchen. After he draped his coat over a chair and placed his hat on the table, he closed his eyes for a moment, wishing he had prayers left to offer up, prayers for forgiveness. And then he dialed Brigitta's number.

"Look, I know you probably didn't expect me to take you up on that offer..." he began with a false laugh.

Yes, she'd watch them. She'd be happy to.

--It was good they'd already met her. They wouldn't be on edge. And they'd go to kindergarten tomorrow morning, which would mean she'd only have half a day watching them.

--Don't be silly, Sean. A half day or full day makes no difference. They're beautiful boys. Danny and Bobbie.

--No, Robby. He thinks Bobbie sounds like a girl's name. Don't know why.

After arranging a time to pick her up in the morning, he told her he had to go fix dinner for them. When he hung up the phone, something akin to relief washed over him. But it was the same kind of relief he'd felt after a battle in the war. He was glad to have survived, but he knew there was more ahead.

He pulled out a pot and a package of hot dogs from the icebox. Then he popped his head around the corner of the kitchen door to ask the boys what they'd had for lunch.

They were on their bellies, elbows on the floor, heads in their hands, transfixed by the flashing black-and-white images on the set. Robby didn't have any socks on, and the soles of his feet were black with dirt. Danny's trouser hems were frayed, and both boys needed haircuts.

What a selfish lout he was, thinking of what he wanted and nothing else. The boys needed a woman in their lives. He and Brigitta got along okay in one important way. What the hell else did he expect? Another Mary?

Chapter Eighteen

HE CAME IN JULIA'S OFFICE looking like the cat that had swallowed the canary, a broad grin on his face, his hands behind his back. Her immediate reaction was fear of embarrassment. Will was quite a joker, and often his idea of humor wasn't sophisticated or even polite. What was he up to now? Linda said hello, asked him how things were going, and he just nodded to them, not saying a word.

He walked to her chair. He knelt in front of her. He held out a small velvet box, the kind that only contains one kind of jewelry. He said the words he'd already uttered, this time with an audience. *Will you marry me, Julia Dell?*

Linda cooed. He opened the box. Inside was a gaudy diamond surrounded by lesser stones that Julia suspected were paste. She even had doubts about the diamond, she thought with a pang of guilt.

In front of an audience, she couldn't begin to articulate what had escaped her in the privacy of her room with her sister Helen. She blushed. She even cried, but not for the reasons Will and Linda were thinking. She wished she could run from the room.

"It's...it's too big." This was true. Her finger was swimming in the large ring. "I'll lose it if I wear it like this."

"Aw, honey," Linda chimed in, standing over her shoulder. "It's easy as pie to get these resized." She looked at Will. "You just take Julia to the shop with you, and they'll fit it to her finger."

Will beamed. "How about tonight, Jules?"

"Oh, I don't know. I have to visit my father...."

"You can show him the ring!" He was grinning from ear to ear, like a child proud of an accomplishment. She couldn't crush him now, not in front of Linda.

"Yes, and Mutti, too..."

Linda congratulated her, asking when they were setting a date, and before Julia could answer, Mrs. Wilcox saved her by appearing in the doorway. Her stern look sent Will scurrying back to his office and Linda back to her desk.

"I have some good news," Mrs. Wilcox said. "The vaccine trials are moving forward. Dr. Bodian found the problem."

❧

Sean rubbed his head and flipped listlessly through pages of the NYU yearbook. So many things were wrong about this morning that he couldn't bear to dwell on one over another.

First, there was the physical pain of a hangover. After fixing his boys' dinner last night, he'd cracked open a bottle of bourbon and drank a few stiff ones to forget his troubles. The booze had accomplished only one thing. It had made him so drowsy he'd fallen asleep on the couch, wrinkling his clean pants and making his neck ache.

Now his head throbbed at the temples, and his mouth felt like sandpaper even after two cups of coffee. He usually held his liquor well. But when Mary had taken sick, he couldn't afford to be woozy or sleepy. He'd cut back to the occasional shot or the beer after work. His body was no longer used to a lot of alcohol, and it was rebelling at his drinking the night before, first the wine with Brigitta, then the whiskey on his own.

Worse was his feeling of guilt about Brigitta. She'd taken a cab to his house that morning—he'd insisted on paying the fare when she'd insisted he not pick her up. And she'd looked so eager and cheerful that it had pierced him to realize he didn't feel the same way. He was happy, sure, that a decent woman was helping him out. But seeing her in the cool morning light had just made it all stand out in stark contrast—that is, his lack of feeling for her.

Well, that wasn't true. He had some feelings. She'd worn blue trousers that had hugged her ample hips, and a white sweater that had embraced other curves. Those things stirred feelings. But, good lord, those were feelings he was trying to quell as far as she was concerned. Sal's sister. Shit. If it were anyone else, maybe...

No, not maybe. Who was he trying to kid? He wasn't that kind of guy, the ones who ran off after women like dogs in season. Unbeknownst to anyone but himself, Mary had been the only woman Sean'd ever lain with. During the war, when buddies had gone off to brothels or started "seeing" French or German broads, he'd stayed true. He and a bunch of other married saps had formed something like an unnamed club, playing cards, reading, writing letters home when other guys were out carousing.

Brigitta was a nice woman, more attractive than most, smart, talented, sexy as hell, but there was something about her, an edge, that didn't call out to him. That, in fact, repelled him a little when he wasn't being tempted by her other charms. That made his loneliness without Mary ache even more. That was it—seeing Brigitta this morning had made him miss his Mary in new ways, had pricked open still-raw wounds. He couldn't stay with a woman who did that to him, no matter what he told himself.

"Big news," Sal said as he wandered in. He hung up his hat as their boss O'Brien stood at the corner of his door, looking pointedly at his watch. Sal glanced over to him. "Interviewing witnesses!" he yelled, loud enough for the whole floor to hear. Sean cringed. O'Brien frowned and went back to his desk.

"What big news?" Shit—had Brigitta told her brother the two of them had gone at it?

"I stopped by Jansen's house."

"Talked to him again?"

Sal chuckled. "Hell, no. But his door was ajar...."

Sean smiled.

"...so I let myself in." He took off his jacket and draped it over the back of his chair. "Did a quick search and discovered that our fine doctor was married and divorced."

Sean sat up, reached for the file on Jansen and gave it a quick once-over. "That's not in his personnel file. They usually list those things."

Sal continued. "He has a couple photos of his ex-wife. Didn't see any pictures of kids, though. And I came across the divorce decree in a case in his closet."

"That just happened to be open?"

"Yeah, imagine that!" Sal handed Sean a slip of paper on which he'd written the particulars. Irene Brodie Jansen. Married June 1934. Divorced January 1936. New York.

"That didn't last long," Sean said, pointing to the dates. "Wonder if we can reach her."

"I was going to try the New York operators, check for her under her maiden and married name."

"Hope she didn't remarry."

"Yeah, well." Sal reached for the phone.

"We've got something else big, too. Richard Hill is our victim's real name. Not Lowenstein."

Sal's eyes widened and he grinned. "Brigitta helped you get through to Patelson."

"Yeah. There's no record of a Lowenstein's will in Patelson's office. There is one for our Richard Hill. He left everything to the March of Dimes."

Sal pointed to the yearbook. "You find anything in that?"

"Nothing but the wrong Dr. Lowenstein." He flipped back to the beginning. He forced himself to focus on the black-and-white photographs before him, formal pictures of serious-looking doctors all aligned as mug shots across the page. Sal glanced over at it.

"What about the students? You look at their photos?"

"There are hundreds of 'em," Sean groused. And they all looked alike, too, staring at the camera the same way as their professors....

And because of their similarities he hadn't noticed the very ordinary name under the very ordinary man the first time through. But this ordinary man had a familiar face. And now a familiar name. Richard Hill, smiling benevolently at the camera, a man who looked untroubled and optimistic. Sean jabbed at the picture.

"Here's our victim," he said excitedly, looking up at Sal. "Richard Hill, M.D. Specialty: virology." He slid the book over to Sal.

"Wow — that's him all right." Sal held the receiver to his ear, waiting to be connected to an Irene Jansen in Great Neck.

"Missed it the first time."

"I would have, too," Sal said. A voice cut over the line, and Sal went to work as Sean flipped more pages, taking his time, really studying each photograph. What else was in here?

And this, too, yielded results as another doctor's photograph, this one a senior-level student, pricked his awareness. Jansen. Sean stared at the younger, happier version of the now pinched-looking man, reading the small type next to the photo, something some yearbook editor thought sounded jaunty. "A Nobel prize might lie ahead/But first this man will soon be wed." And so he had been, that very June. He heard Sal thanking an Irene for her time, an obvious wrong turn.

"Here's our Dr. Jansen," Sean said to his partner, scooting the book to him.

"He sure looks different."

"Yeah. Nicer."

"Funny how people change," said Sal.

"Wonder what made him so angry — his divorce?"

"Getting hold of his ex-wife would be nice." Sal started to dial again. "I guess we can always ask the doc himself where his ex is."

"Let's keep trying to find her first on our own. I'd rather get to her before he has a chance to contact her."

Sean went back to the yearbook, scouring each message next to students' names for a reference to a "Buck," the name Julia had overheard the morning of the murder. The yearbook felt like a treasure trove now. His heart raced as he leafed through pages. Maybe the killer would reveal himself here?

But he found nothing more. No more familiar names. No "Buck."

Finished with that task, he decided to try the NYU secretary again, to get more information on Richard Hill. But that call, like his first to NYU, yielded nothing. Maureen O'Donnell was out. He left a message and stood.

"I need to return a file to the lab." Sean tapped the file Julia had given him. "And I'll talk to Wilcox some more about our Dr. Richard Hill."

"Need any help?" Sal covered the receiver.

"No, no." He didn't want Sal to come, because he didn't want to risk him asking about Brigitta. "You stay here in case the NYU gal calls back, okay?" He reached for his hat and coat before Sal could protest. Sean's phone rang as he reached the doorway.

"Get that for me, will ya, buddy?"

❧

Julia spent her lunch hour at her father's bedside. It was a corporal act of mercy to visit the sick, but Julia felt as if the visit was as much for her own good as it was for her father's. She needed to be away, away from the possibility of seeing Will again.

Julia's mother sat, looking small, scared and tired, in a hard wooden chair by her father's head. She had no book to read, no knitting, no sewing to occupy her time. Her job was waiting, and she'd applied herself to it with no distractions. Julia patted her arm.

That first night her father had been in the hospital, Julia had stood at the foot of the gurney in the emergency room and forced herself to speak, just the way she'd consciously moved muscles in her bad leg. His skin had been the same starched white shade as the pillows, but overlaid with a waxy sheen that couldn't possibly mean anything good. And his chin had been covered with an unfamiliar stubble—her father prided himself on his appearance and shaved every day of his life, but he'd not shaved that day. Why hadn't she noticed it that morning at breakfast? His eyes had been the only thing about him that had reassured her that evening. They had still glowed with mirth. And, in fact, he'd made a feeble attempt at a joke when she'd first seen him, something about not "having the heart" to get up.

He was on the road to recovery. Now Julia realized her job was just as much about comforting and supporting her mother as it was seeing to her father's needs. The doctors were enthusiastically optimistic, so much so that even she, at her most skeptical, believed them. Her father just needed rest and continued care. If he cut back on smoking, working, and drinking, he should certainly be out of crisis for a long time to come.

Her mother, though—there was another story. Julia smiled at her, and her mother responded with a close-lipped nod. Mutti wouldn't disturb Father with even a whisper because he'd complained of not getting enough sleep with the nurses coming and going, waking him up at all hours. Her mother's vigil was a gift, a way of giving him rest.

Mutti is hopelessly in love with him. Still.

Her mother, Julia knew, had found it difficult to adjust to America at first. She'd hardly spoken any English when she'd first arrived and had regaled them all with stories of miscommunications with store clerks, doctors, neighbors, priests, and nuns. She'd come to America on a ship crammed with other women from Europe, French, German and even British brides whom the "doughboys" of the Great War had picked up. She was pregnant at the time of that journey, and Julia always suspected this was the reason for her parents' marriage. But they'd lost that baby, a boy, and the next one, too, another boy, before having the three girls in quick succession.

She looked at her mother's soft eyes, so lovingly focused on her husband as he slept. If something happened to him, Mutti would no longer be whole. And not just because he was the financial support of the family. No, Mutti would suffer through deprivation if it meant her beloved Howie could stay with her even a day longer.

Her parents were not outwardly affectionate except for kisses on the cheek, but the way they looked at each other communicated everything, from who should discipline the girls to when to go up to bed. Because language had been a barrier when they'd first met, they'd built their love on deeds and few words, on suppositions and speculation. They'd not disappointed each other.

Tell me what this is, Julia wanted to say. *Tell me what it feels like to love like this. How does it start? Did you ever think of other men, Mutti, when you were getting ready to marry Father? Was there a young German lad whose heart you'd stolen? Did you ever think of him and the touch of his kiss? How did you turn from that to doing what was right?*

Now wasn't the time for that conversation. She had to think of her mother, whose effervescence had begun to fade years ago and was becoming as fragile as the lace collar around her floral housedress. Julia selfishly wanted it back. When she was younger, her mother's laughter was like sunshine lighting up the house and, by extension, Julia's own heart.

Julia remembered her days as a young girl as if she were Eve before the fall. Her mother singing and telling stories about her youth. During those years, she was proud of her foreignness. It had set her apart, made her special.

The three girls had always been best friends. They'd played together, shared toys, even shared a bedroom for a while until Beth got to move to a separate room when she'd turned ten.

Warm summer days had been spent in the shaded backyard, lolling on a blanket reading and eating peanuts or grapes or pieces of a donut stolen from the kitchen when Mutti wasn't looking. School was at the convent school under the protective eye of the Sisters of St. Francis. Sunday dinners consisted of pot roast and potatoes—oh, Mutti always had to have her potatoes—and a bakery pie for dessert. Sunday evenings found them by the radio or around the piano, Beth and Helen playing the latest popular songs while Julia danced strange Isadora-Duncan-like movements with many scarves and a look of rapt seriousness on her face.

And now this. She looked at her father who breathed easily, then at her mother. She'd wanted to tell her about Will giving her the ring, ready to gauge her mother's true reaction in the subtlest blink of an eye or flicker of a muscle. But her mother was still and silent, unwilling to disturb Father or leave the room.

"Mother," Julia whispered at last. "Tell Father I was here and I love

314

him. I have to get back to work."

Her mother patted her on the arm and smiled but said nothing.

Julia would have to think it through on her own.

She hobbled back to her office, the long walk through corridors and staircases exhausting under the best of circumstances. But she was mentally tired as well. Maybe it had been a mistake to work at Hopkins after all. She'd met Will here and now she was....

"Miss Dell."

She looked up and saw Sean Reilly standing in the hall outside her office, file folder in hand. Warmth cascaded from her head to her feet. "Julia," she said. Was it a bad sign that he wasn't calling her that?

"I know your name," he teased, "and I think you know mine."

She walked toward him, composed now, able to look him in the eye. "Is that my file?"

He tapped it on his chest. "It's Dr. Jansen's file."

She frowned. "Shh..."

"Don't worry. He's not in. And your office mate appears to be on a coffee break."

"Hmm...Linda's not supposed to leave the phones unattended." She stood in front of him, close enough to smell his aftershave. "Could I have the file now?"

His face crinkled into a smile. "Nope. Have to give something up first."

Her eyes widened. Did he expect another kiss—here, in the hall? She opened her mouth to protest, at the same time hoping it *was* what he wanted.

"I need to know if you ever heard of a Dr. Richard Hill."

She stood straighter. "That's a very common name."

"A virologist. Worked at NYU while Dr. Jansen was there."

She shook her head. "The name doesn't ring a bell." She tried to remember if she'd seen it on research papers, journal articles, but her mind was blank. "I could ask Dr. Jansen."

"No, I'd appreciate it if you don't."

She tilted her head to one side, studying him. He was clearly pleased to see her, his face a smile, his attitude flirtatious. And he was taking her into some kind of confidence.

"Why not?"

"I'll tell you later, all right? Promise." He smiled again. "Dr. Jansen's family is from Detroit, you said. What about his wife?"

"He's not married."

"He was." When she didn't comment, he continued. "You didn't know?"

"No, he never mentioned it." It shouldn't have surprised her. After all, Dr. Jansen, like all the researchers, was a private man. But she hadn't noticed anything in his personnel file about being divorced, or children, if there were any. This discovery of a new secret just added to the suspicions.

Reading confusion on her face, Sean went on: "It wasn't in his file. I got it from another source."

She nodded, still troubled by her march toward judgment of Dr. Jansen. To add balance to the picture she'd painted of him, she offered Sean the information Mrs. Wilcox had passed along to them earlier.

"We had some news," she said. "You remember how I told you that there was a problem with the polio vaccine in Detroit?" She emphasized the city's name, so that Sean would know she was ultimately talking about Jansen.

"Yeah. Might be sabotage, right?"

She shook her head. "Our Dr. Bodian went to the National Institutes to go over the problem with other scientists — "

"Dr. Bodian?"

"He's a specialist. He's now mainly interested in the pathology of neurological diseases."

His smiled broadened. "You sound like a scientist yourself."

She ignored him and continued. "It makes him particularly suited to investigating whether the monkeys at the Detroit plant had polio. He met with other doctors at the National Institutes of Health to go over the problem."

"Did they?"

"No. Most of them didn't, anyway. Mrs. Wilcox told us that Dr. Bodian looked at tissue slides and determined they had something else, some wild infection probably passed from monkey to monkey. The one monkey that had polio — they figured out the problem with the vaccine and have fixed it."

Sean's smiled dropped. "Fixed it how? How can they be sure kids won't get sick, too?"

"They've tightened up the vaccine production process, put in place more safety checks."

She guessed what he was thinking. He had two boys. If he knew the vaccine they'd get could cause polio instead of preventing it, it would be hard to take that chance.

"Look, the chances are so small of catching it from the vaccine," she said.

"How do you know?"

"I..." Yes, how did she know? Because she believed in the doctors' work? Because famous researchers were involved? Because she wanted to believe? "I think there's risk in everything," she said. "There's risk in letting your children go swimming during the summer. They could catch it then. And how would you feel if you could have had them vaccinated but didn't?"

He didn't respond at first, and she wondered if she sounded too much like all the nurses and doctors who'd treated her. Too full of assurances that were nothing more than wishful thinking.

"Just because they fixed the problem doesn't mean there wasn't something fishy going on in Detroit," he said at last. "When's the last time your boss was out visiting family?"

"I'd have to check." She already knew. She'd looked at her old calendar and been shocked to discover Dr. Jansen had been in Detroit in recent months. But to get into the plant, to do something that would bollix up the vaccine—as she'd thought of each step necessary, it seemed more and more outlandish.

Some noise down the hall made them both turn their heads. Linda was coming back to the office, talking to a secretary from another floor, sandwich wrapped in wax paper in her hands, her face turned toward the other woman in friendly conversation. Julia felt a pinch of betrayal. Linda rarely went to lunch with her.

Sean turned his attention back to Julia. "Any more threatening calls?" he asked, loud enough for the others to hear. He was making sure they didn't think she was "tattling" on Dr. Jansen. Again, an act of kindness.

Before she could thank him, another figure appeared at the end of the hall walking fast. It was the detective's partner, the shorter, skinnier man.

"Sean," he called out, motioning him over. Sean nodded a farewell to Julia and joined Sal. Although he talked softly, she could hear what he was telling Sean.

"That call. It was from a hospital. I think we found Susan Schlager."

❧

"She's in a small hospital in Fallston," Sal said as they drove north of the city toward Harford County where the Susquehanna River divided Maryland from Pennsylvania. "In some kind of car accident near the dam. Busted up pretty bad."

"You sure?" Sean asked. "About the accident, I mean?" Had she used that as an excuse when checking herself into the hospital or had someone found a wreck and gotten her help?

"Don't know anything but what I told you, partner. She was checked in a day ago, but it's a slow-moving place and whoever took your first call didn't check around much."

"She gonna make it?"

Sal shrugged, slipping a cigarette into his mouth as he steered the car on to Pulaski Highway, Route 40. "Busted up bad," he repeated. "They didn't know who she was—had her in as Jane Doe. She didn't have no identification on her. If we peg her as Susan, they'll call the husband."

They didn't talk much as they traveled the hour out of town. A slow mudslide of feelings buried his good cheer at seeing Julia. He should have tried harder to find the Schlager woman. Maybe he could have found her before...

Before her husband beat her? Beat her and then let her have the car? Maybe. Maybe that's why the fellow hadn't seemed upset about her taking off, knowing the marks he'd left on her.

These dark thoughts were followed by more practical ones, deflating his mood all the more. It was now afternoon. By the time they got to the hospital, talked to Susan, found out what had happened to her, drove back into town...Jesus, he'd be lucky if he was home by eight that evening. Mrs. Buchanan...

....wasn't there. Brigitta was. Okay, that was good. Good to feel good about her.

❧

It was impossible to tell if Susan Schlager had been beat up by her husband, by a car wreck, or by someone else out to do her harm. Her right arm and both legs were in casts, stretched by wires and pulleys into what looked to Sean like a modern version of the rack. Scratches and bruises covered her neck, arms and face. Her eyes were puffy and dark, making her face look contorted and painful.

A nurse showed them to her bed, and Sal closed the screen while Sean sat down next to the woman. The police had found her, the front end of the vehicle smashed tight into a tree. She was lucky to be alive.

"Only a few minutes," the nurse said. "She can't talk much."

"Mrs. Schlager," Sean whispered. "Susan."

Her swollen eyes twitched as she struggled to open them. Finally, her right lid managed to lift a crack. She peered his way and groaned from the effort. He stood so she wouldn't have to strain her eyes his way.

"I'm Detective Reilly. I spoke with you before. This is my partner, Sal Sabataso." He gestured toward Sal who stood, holding his hat with both hands in front of him, at the foot of the bed.

"Mrs. Schlager," Sean repeated. "Did someone hurt you?" He decided to start from the premise that she'd been beaten before the accident. The beating, in fact, might have dulled her senses, leading to the accident.

Susan blinked her one good eye. Her cracked lips moved, but nothing came out. Sean leaned forward to listen.

"Take your time, ma'am," Sal offered.

She whispered something. Sean leaned farther in. "Who was it? Do you know?"

She moved her head oh, so slowly forward, a faint nod. "She..." she murmured. "She..."

"The nurse?" Sal said, growing impatient and worried.

Sean grimaced, figuring it wasn't the nurse. What other "she's" were in Susan's life?

"Your aunt?" Sean asked her. She moved her head slightly to the right. No. "Mrs. Wilcox?" Another slow painful half shake. "Linda?" No.

There was only one other "she" in Susan's orbit.

"Julia Dell?"

A hiccup of pain escaped her lips as she nodded.

૭ઝૂ

It was impossible to get much else from her. After an hour of struggling with a game of twenty questions, all they had was Susan's anger with Julia—a tear had rolled down her swollen cheek when Sean had pressed her again on the name—and something about a "note." That had been the only word that either of them could make out as Susan had tried to articulate through a jaw that barely moved. Eventually the nurse had ushered them out of the room. If they wanted more from Susan, they'd have to wait until she recovered sufficiently. Sean called Brigitta from a payphone to tell her he'd be late, and they left.

It was the time of long shadows as they drove back into the city, right after the worst of end-of-day traffic when a sense of peace descended over all families, gathering around tables for dinner, saying their Grace, telling each other stories about the day. Sean's peace was rattled. Julia Dell, that sweet little secretary, surely wasn't capable of...this. It was as if someone had accused his Mary of starting the war. She was an innocent with a pure heart.

But still, there was always that sense Julia was hiding something, her true self, from the world. It came out in flashes of bitterness.

"She could have used her cane," Sal said after a long silence. They were passing Chesaco Avenue just northeast of the city. They'd be downtown soon.

"On Susan?" He tried to sound disinterested, not disappointed.

"On both of them, Lowenstein and Susan."

"What's the motive?"

"Dr. Lowenstein—or rather, Dr. Hill—isn't working on polio. She's a polio. She wants them all working on her problem. Susan worked for the slacker doctor, so..."

"That's a lot of rage for a pretty slim reason. Why now? And what about the blackmail?" Sean gazed out the window. They weren't that far from his home where Brigitta was probably opening cans of soup for the boys, as he'd instructed her. He was relieved she was there with them, but the good feelings he'd conjured up earlier had somehow turned as flat as his disappointment about Julia.

"Maybe now that things are getting closer, the vaccine and all, she got madder?" Sal mused. "She's been upset about the investigation slowing things down, hasn't she? And we don't know about the blackmail angle for sure, buddy. Could be the good doc was using the money to give to his church or something. Anonymously. Just like his last gift."

Sean said nothing.

Finally he spoke. "If she'd used her cane, it would show some damage, don't you think? I'll check it out."

Chapter Nineteen

"YOU TOOK THAT TURN TOO WIDE. You almost ran into that poor old lady in the Ford!" Beth pointed to Helen's left where a blue-haired woman was hunched over the wheel of her old car, looking aghast as she veered to avoid Helen.

"Sorry. I'm still getting the hang of city driving."

"And doing a good job, too!" Julia sat in the back, her hands glued to the edge of the seat as she looked ahead to the next stop sign, wondering if she should point out to Helen that it was there. Next to her were Beth's three kids who yelled "whee!" every time they turned a corner. Up front, next to Beth, was Mutti, who had just murmured a soft *"Mein Gott!"*

Julia wanted to ask Beth how she'd make it home in time to fix dinner for Stu, but she was afraid to distract her when she had to help Helen navigate.

When Beth had arrived at the hospital that evening and announced that Helen was driving them all home, Julia had been shocked. She'd assumed that Beth had badgered Helen into doing it and had started to say that if Helen wasn't comfortable, they shouldn't force her. But Helen had interrupted, telling them all it was her idea. She wanted the experience, and the best way to get it was on the road, doing the kind of driving she'd have to do once Father was home. She'd taken the keys and slid behind the wheel with serene determination. As Beth had barked out instructions, she'd nodded and complied, jolting them away from the curb almost into the path of a blaring truck heading up Broadway. Julia had comforted herself by thinking that Beth wouldn't have allowed Helen to drive if she thought it was endangering her own children. Would she?

As soon as they were out of the heart of the city, Helen seemed to relax and the drive was smoother. Or maybe it was the rest of them who relaxed. Julia looked at the back of her sister's head, straight and regal, softly curling locks overlapping her sky-blue sweater collar. There was something about Helen now that she was learning to drive. In the space of a few days, she'd become more confident.

When she finally nudged the car into a parking spot in front of their home, Helen was silently victorious. Handing the keys to her sister, she asked, "When do you think I can take the driving test?"

Their mother got out of the car, dramatically exclaiming, *"Gott in Himmel!"* But Julia smiled because her mother's voice held as much amusement as fear. Beth's kids scrambled up to the front door, and Julia made her way around to the curb, tailing them all. Helen lingered with her, taking slow steps.

"Helen, I'm so proud of you." Julia used her good arm to pat her sister on the shoulder, but the movement caused her purse, which was dangling from her wrist, to open, spilling its contents on the glistening sidewalk.

"Here, I'll get it." Helen bent to retrieve the items, lipstick, handkerchief, wallet, compact and...the ring. Helen picked it up, shooting a glance of surprise to her sister. Julia didn't smile. In the afternoon sunlight, the ring looked even cheaper and gaudier. Helen' gaze held a question.

"Will finally got a ring," Julia explained. "It's too big, though."

Helen didn't respond at first. She stood slowly, thinking about something. Was it her own engagement to Tom? If so, the dark mood passed quickly, replaced by the same calm determination she'd exhibited in the car, as if she were setting herself to a task that carried both risk and reward. She snapped Julia's purse closed and handed the ring to her sister.

"Even so, you should wear it. I'm sure Mutti has a chain," she said in a pleasant but firm voice. Julia opened her mouth to ask why Helen was now pressing her to wear an engagement ring when just the other night she'd urged her sister to give up Will if that's what she really wanted. But Helen gave her no chance to talk. She took Julia by the elbow and called out to the others. "Julia has a happy surprise for you!" They didn't hear, though, as they went in the house.

Inside the front door, bedlam. The three boys pestered their mother for something to eat while Beth insisted they wash their hands and settle down. Mutti took off her scarf and coat, asking Helen if she had thought to get something for dinner. Helen told her she'd bought some chops and was going to make them.

"But first, listen to Julia's surprise," Helen said. Her eyes crinkled into a smile. There was no malevolent jealousy there. But no sheer joy either. Something else.

"What surprise?" Beth asked, breathless as she shooed Andy away.

Before Julia could answer, Helen winked at her. "Show them!" And then she walked back to the kitchen to start dinner, her task accomplished.

Julia opened her hand. The ring rested on her palm like a garish circus prize. She frowned.

But Beth cooed. "My gosh, Jules, that's wonderful! I was wondering when that fellow of yours was going to get a ring." She gave Julia an affectionate hug, her large stomach bumping against Julia's cane. "Well, put it on, for crying out loud!"

"It's too big. We have to have it resized."

"I just want you to try it on. You don't need to wear it. Here, let me." Beth took the ring from her hand and slipped it on Julia's finger, pulling Julia's hand out flat for them to admire.

"That is some ring," Beth said. "At least you'll know you can always pawn it if you run into money trouble!"

"Elisabeth!" their mother said, swatting Beth on the rear, another sign of good cheer. Helen's driving, a good report from the doctor, now this ring — they all seemed to be making Mutti "come back." Julia should be grateful.

"So when are you going to get it made smaller?" Beth asked. Before Julia could answer, however, Andrew ran up to his mother again and grabbed her legs. "Donny won't let me go outside." Beth turned her attention to the boy, taking his hand and heading to the back of the house. "Let's go talk to him," she said.

That left Julia alone with her mother in the hallway. Mutti came over to her, slipped Julia's scarf from her hair and helped her out of her raincoat as if she were still a little girl. As Julia pulled her hand through the coat sleeve, her fingers straightened, causing the ring to drop to the floor. Her mother retrieved it, looking it over, before handing it back to Julia.

"What do you think?" Julia asked her in the quiet hall. In the background, they could hear Beth scolding Donny and Helen throwing chops into a sizzling hot pan.

"It is a nice ring."

This was faint praise from a woman who usually liked glittering things.

"Just nice?"

Mutti shrugged and then smiled at her. "He is your boy, so whatever he gives you is nice."

"But really, do you think—" The doorbell buzzed behind them, and she stopped, her heart sinking to her stomach. Was Will stopping by to take her to the jeweler's? She'd tell him she was too tired, even sick. She'd retreat to her bed for the night...

Helen breezed back into the hallway, tying an apron around her waist. "My goodness, I didn't think anyone was here to answer it," she said, giving Julia and Mutti a look. Helen opened the door a crack, and they heard the low voice of a man.

"Julia, it's for you." Helen opened the door all the way to reveal the tired figure of Detective Sean Reilly.

Her mood, so blue a moment before, now lightened. She walked to the front door as her mother and Helen went back toward the kitchen.

Sean stood, holding his hat at one side, staring at her cane. Her smile faded.

"How can I help you?" she asked in the bright voice of a secretary, a good girl, a model patient.

"May I look at your cane?" He nodded his head in its direction. When she went to hand it over, he stepped forward. "Here, lean on me."

She did as he requested, feeling the tight muscles of his strong arm through the thin suit jacket. He held the cane up to the light and turned it around and around.

"Have you had any trouble with this, any need to replace it?"

"Not since last year. They're made to last. This one's pretty scuffed, though. I should take better care of it." She looked at the scratches and dirt around the tip. Really, this was embarrassing. Yet, still, she liked standing next to him, leaning against him.

When he handed the cane back to her, she lost her balance as she shifted her weight from him to the cane. He caught her before she fell, and once again, she was in his arms, her head resting against his chest. She heard him take a trembling breath, then he pushed her away and stared in her eyes.

"Do you know anything about a note to your buddy Susan? Did you write her one? Did someone else? A note that was upsetting?"

Julia stepped back, now warm from a different emotion, anger. Silly Susan. Always blubbering about something. Now what?

"I'm the one who should be upset," she blurted out and told him how she'd learned Susan was after her job.

"But you don't remember a note," Sean said, his brow creased and an odd look in his eye, a sadness.

Julia sighed with impatience. "There are lots of notes, lots of things the doctors write, that we type for them. Notes to colleagues, to other labs, to drug manufacturers..."

"Something different from that," he snapped.

She closed her eyes and wished she could tap her foot. There was only one note she could think of, something only slightly out of the ordinary. It had troubled her. And her reaction had troubled her. Oh God. As soon as she started telling him about it, she felt awful.

"There was a personal letter Susan wrote to Dr. Lowenstein. It came back to the office when she wasn't in – not enough postage – so I put it in another envelope and sent it to her home." She tried to sound businesslike, as if she'd only been doing the right thing. But it was obvious she'd known. A personal letter from Susan, always so goofy-eyed around Dr. Mike, sent to his home...

"You don't know what was in it?"

"No." But she had known, hadn't she? She'd guessed. Or maybe she'd even hoped... *Dear Lord, what was the matter with her, deliberately stirring up trouble. Was it because Susan was able-bodied?* She felt the need to run but couldn't. She felt...guilty.

She was discovering something about herself, something spoiled and withered, just like her leg, and it felt as if polio had done this to her, another handicap. She felt like crying.

"When did this happen?" he asked.

"Around when Dr. Lowenstein died. I... I put the note in the mail to Susan some time around then...." And felt victorious doing it. She'd suspected what was in the note. She'd seen how Susan mooned around Dr. Lowenstein, how she'd looked like a lovesick puppy. She was married! She had two good legs and a husband and a home!

"You didn't think she'd be in the next day?"

"I didn't know. I was in a hurry, trying to take care of lots of things." That part was true. She'd had a lot to do, and it had been easier to act on impulse than to think it through. She could have left the note for Susan on her desk.

He asked her a few more questions about Susan, about Susan's husband, but Julia was so tired by then, the weight of all her sins pushing her to a low spot, that even the detective could see he was wearing her out and would get no more valuable information from her. He left, and now she did retreat to her room, forgoing supper, curling up and falling asleep, wishing everyone would leave her alone and wishing, most of all, she could throw her blasted cane away.

✥

Stephen Schlager did something odd when Sal broke the news to him that his wife was in a hospital. His eyes welled. He was angry at Sal for delaying his departure to visit Susan. If he was acting, it was an award-winning performance.

Schlager was so eager to leave, in fact, that he brushed past Sal on the steps muttering a curse in German and not bothering to shut his door tight.

Damn, thought Sal, looking at him leave. Someone could go in and rob the fellow clean. Sal should make sure that wouldn't happen. But he should check the back door, too, to be absolutely positive the house was locked up tight.

He made his way into the now-dim, neat house and didn't see much out of the ordinary until he came to the bedroom. He would have missed it, too, if he hadn't remembered his partner telling him to always check the trash bins. There it was, a woman's lavender stationery, a note folded in two and ripped into a dozen pieces. He gathered them all, did his duty by the locks and left.

✥

Brigitta had dinner for Sean when he arrived home, some Italian soup with lots of vegetables that set his mouth watering as soon as he crossed his threshold. Instead of making him feel welcome and happy, though, it only dragged him down more, reminding him again of what he missed with Mary and of his lack of strong feelings for Brigitta in that way.

You can't fool yourself or anyone else when you're tired. And he was dead on his feet by then.

The boys had come out to him and hugged him with no screeches of joy. It was hard getting used to someone new. They looked good, though, with clean faces, neatly combed hair, even spotless shirts and trousers. She'd kept them in their good clothes just so he would see them.

"I didn't know if the boys liked minestrone," she said, ladling big portions for herself and Sean a few minutes later.

"Did they eat much?" he asked, remembering how he'd told her to open canned soup for them and irritated that she'd overruled his command.

"Oh, a little. It was something new, after all!" She smiled as if proud of this, but he saw no reason to be proud of forcing children to eat what they didn't like.

She asked about his case, and he gave her perfunctory answers, refusing her offer of a whiskey before dinner or even wine with the meal. He knew that only weakened his resolve.

After she was finished cleaning up, he told the boys to "hop on down to the car, we have to take Mrs. Lorenzo home now." She raised her eyebrows at that but got her purse and sweater and trundled off after him.

He walked her to her door after driving her home, but didn't want to stay long because the boys were in the car. *Just let me go home to what I know. The memory of Mary.*

"Did I do something wrong?" she asked, searching for her key.

"No, nothing wrong. You're a great sport, helping me out."

"You seem, oh, angry." She found her key and prepared to unlock her apartment door.

He *was* angry. At himself. "Naw, it's just the case." *Not just the case.* "And I feel bad asking you to help out with the boys like this. I'll find somebody real soon."

She opened her door, smiling at him. "Don't be silly, Sean. I have the time. You worry about your case first. When it's all wrapped up, you can think about getting somebody for the boys." She kissed him lightly on the cheek.

کرچ

She fell into bed exhausted. Looking after those boys had been more tiring than any of her office jobs. She'd had to constantly clean up after them, making them change twice before Sean came home so they'd be in spotless outfits when he arrived. She'd finally told them they had to play on the rug in their room and nowhere else until their father returned. That had worked.

Then there had been the boredom as well, sitting and listening to them prattle about things she had no interest in—that is, when she could understand them. Danny—had it been Danny?—mispronounced quite a few words and had trouble remembering others. At least he had talked to her. Robby had been so silent she'd thought he was mad at her half the time.

She rested for the briefest moment before getting up and changing into cleaner clothes. Then she sat at her tiny kitchenette table, leafing through a magazine, searching for the article she'd remembered while at Sean's house. Here it was: *The Rules All Good Wives Know.* She nodded her head as she read through each one, pleased that she'd followed some already.

Make sure the children are as spotless as the house when he comes home....Turn off the washing machine and other noisy appliances so he's greeted by soothing quiet.....Freshen your makeup and hair before he steps through the door....

She'd not had the chance to follow these rules with Ernie. They'd been so young, so....unaware. She closed the magazine. It was simple, really. Just like a real job.

Chapter Twenty

SEAN LOOKED ANXIOUSLY at O'Brien's closed door when he slipped into his desk chair. He'd overslept, dead tired from the day before, and he'd had trouble getting the boys dressed in time to go fetch Brigitta. He had to set his alarm earlier. On top of it all, he'd seen a story in the morning's paper about the investigation, some human interest crap written by a turd reporter probably itching to move up. Just interviews with folks at the hospital, all of whom were wondering when this thing would wrap up and some worrying about how it would affect the lab's work.

Sal gave him the news that the NYU secretary had called back.

"I didn't know what to ask her," he said, throwing a pencil on the desk. He was clearly unhappy with Sean's tardiness. Even Sal had his limits. O'Brien must have said something. "So I just threw a bunch of questions at her about Hill and Lowenstein...."

"And Jansen?"

"Hell, no. What was I supposed to ask about him?"

"About his ex, where she is..." Sean flipped through notes, trying to find his focus. No headache today, but he was beat and confused and mad at himself again. Sal knew about the babysitting Brigitta was doing and probably figured the two of them were really hitting it off. Crap.

"Yeah, I been working on that. Can't find his ex anywhere. Maybe she remarried." Sal crossed his arms over his chest. "O'Brien was on my back, by the way. Wondering where you were, what was up with the case. He stood over my shoulder when I got the damned call."

That must have been bad. O'Brien's imposing hulk casting a shadow over you while you try to sound like you know what you're doing. Sean shouldn't have left Sal without going over things. It was his job to shepherd the guy along.

"What did you find out?" He couldn't undo what was done. Might as well move forward.

"Not much that I could see is worthwhile." Sal opened his notebook and scanned his scribbled notes. "She just repeated what she wrote in the letter about Lowenstein, how he went to Germany, how some folks there had a few letters from him, thought he was coming back, and then boom, nothing until '46 when some survivor of his family came over and let them know he'd been killed." Sal spoke flatly, as if Sean didn't deserve to hear what he'd found out.

"What about Hill?"

"She said he was a quiet man. Not many remembered him because he stayed in the background a lot. Worked a bunch of different things."

"Polio?"

"Not so much. She said he had worked on it, was in the thick of it back in the '30s she was told. But that was before the—" He checked his notes—"the vaccine trials, she said. She said most of the people who knew him weren't there any more."

"Vaccine trials? You mean the ones being planned now?"

"No. Some other deal."

Sean said nothing. So, not many people knew Hill well. Just like at Hopkins. He kept to himself, was quiet. Sean heaved a sigh and pushed in closer to his desk.

"We have to do some telephoning, buddy." He smiled at Sal and was relieved to see his partner give him a grudging flicker back. "Did she tell you where Hill came from, where his family was from?"

"Yeah. A little town in upstate New York. Cresskill or something like that."

"Near the cabin he rented." Sean pointed to the phone. "Call the police there. See what you can find out about the Hill family."

"You mean *families*, don't you? There's gotta be a dozen of them."

"I was thinking two dozen." He grinned, and now Sal responded with a broad smile in return.

"All right. What am I looking for?"

"Living relatives. Someone who can tell us something that might help us figure out why Hill changed his name."

"What about you?"

"I'm going to keep trying to find out who Dr. Jansen married and what happened to his wife."

Sal pulled a taped-together note from a file and held it up as if it were a prize catch in a fishing derby. "I found something else, partner."

The note. Susan had said something about a note. Julia had mailed it back to her.

"....so when Schlager takes off, I walked in and there it was," Sal was saying, but Sean was remembering Julia's confused and sorrowful look the night before when she'd confessed to sending the returned note back to Susan. She'd probably guessed its contents.

"I found that other gal's letter with it. Julia Dell—she wrote Susan saying the postman couldn't deliver it so she thought she'd send it back to Susan." Sal looked Sean in the eye. "That's odd, don't you think? Why not just give it to the woman? It's like she wanted the poor gal's husband to open it."

Yes, she probably had wanted that. Susan was whole and Julia was not.

The returned note was sad and sweet at the same time. Susan Schlager was expressing her affection for her boss, hoping he might return it. She thought they could meet for dinner one night, or coffee. She admired his dedication to his job, but she thought he looked lonely, just like her. She wasn't happy in her marriage and he shouldn't feel guilty about "luering her away." She must have been looking for the note in Lowenstein's house, not realizing Julia had sent it back to her.

"So Susan's husband opened the note..." Sean said.

"And socked her in the face is my guess," Sal answered. "My guess is this was a pattern. He knocks her around. She leaves for a few days, maybe holes up at a hotel, or maybe she does have some aunt we couldn't find. That's why hubby ain't worried when she goes missing. But he did look blue when I told him about the accident."

Sal paused when Sean didn't comment. "It still could mean her husband was jealous, could mean he was jealous enough to—"

Sean cut him off. "He didn't see the note until after the murder."

"Maybe he suspected something."

"Then why wait to beat up the wife? More likely he would have offed the doc and then punched out the wife that night. She didn't show no signs of that." Sean swallowed. His throat was dry as he considered another possibility.

"Or maybe," Sal said, articulating what Sean didn't want even to think, "it was that cripple. She's all torn up inside. She's mad at the doctor for not working on her problem. She finds out her pal Sue is keen on the fellow. It all boils over and..." He raised his arm as if wielding a weapon, a cane.

"Her cane was clean," Sean murmured.

"Could have been new."

"No, it looked used. Just not used in that way." But she had said they were strong. Strong enough to beat a man to death and show no mark? What were they made of? He scraped back his chair, impatient to do something. "I'm going to look at her boss again. That Dr. Jansen. Try to find his ex. She might know something about Hill."

He left before Sal could protest.

※ ※

"Thank you for the telegram about Dr. Hill's death. I'm very sorry to hear he's passed, and to hear of the terrible way in which he died. It must be very upsetting to you and everyone at the lab. No time is a good time for these things to happen, but this is worse than most. I've read the hopeful news of Dr. Salk's work....

".... It seems as if almost everyone is gone now from the old group. Of course,

I'm sure you heard the horrible rumors about my cousin by now. It's really cruel the way some people speculate — as if they hoped he killed himself instead of being felled by a heart attack...."

Sean found the note in a pile of recently opened mail on the corner of Jansen's desk. Or rather, Julia led him to it. Another note pointing to guilt. In Susan's case, the guilt of loving a man other than her husband. And in Jansen's case, the guilt of hiding his relationship with the deceased.

Yes, Sean was glad to find it but unhappy that Julia was the one to lead him to it. Did she even realize what she was doing — setting people up? Exposing their sins, putting them in jeopardy?

Most of the mail was related to the research, but this letter, on pretty linen stationery with a bluish hue, stood out, and Sean had reached for it first from the group when Julia had let him into the office. He even wondered if she herself had placed it on top after finding it in the doctor's materials. She'd shown no discomfort when letting him in. If anything, her mood was eager, as if she wanted to please him.

The note was signed simply, "Irene." The envelope was gone. Sean looked around the desk, under it, even in the trash can. Nothing. The cleaning crew must have recently emptied the bin. Shit. He was so close.

He needed to ask Julia some more questions about her cane or find someone who could tell him about such things. That had been the real reason for his visit despite what he'd told Sal, but she'd assumed he'd come to talk to Dr. Jansen, had told him he was out, and offered to let him in the doc's office, so eager-like, so helpful.

Ah, Julia. He rubbed his hand over his face. He wanted her to be...like Mary. Sweet and innocent.

All right, then. There was still Jansen to pursue. Just because Julia was pointing to the doctor's guilt didn't mean Jansen was free from stain. The man was still keeping secrets. He'd let his ex-wife know of Hill's death. He must have known the doctor's name and never let on. Enough was enough. Sean was going to bring him in for questioning.

Mrs. Wilcox had never heard of a Dr. Richard Hill, but she promised to make inquiries about him and about "Irene Brodie."

Before leaving Hopkins, Sean stopped back at the lab one more time to see if Jansen had returned, but his office was still empty. Julia hadn't heard from him either. Where was he? Julia couldn't reach him on the phone, his housekeeper was away — nobody knew where he'd gone. Damn. Had he run?

"You ever hear of an Irene Brodie?" he asked.

She shook her head no, blushing and looking down. She'd seen the "Irene" on the signature.

All right. Nobody knew the doc's ex. And now he was gone. Running was a sure sign of guilt. An odd sense of relief flooded him as he said goodbye to Julia that day. If Jansen were guilty, she was off the hook.

He hurried back to the station where he gave his info to Sal, who offered to check out the doc's house. After Sal left, Sean had to spend a good hour talking alone to O'Brien, convincing him to let Sal head up to Cresskill, New York to investigate the vic's life.

O'Brien thought Sal was too "green" and was even willing to okay both their fares so Sean could show Sal the ropes on such an outing. Sean couldn't leave his boys, though, so he had to offer multiple assurances that he'd coach Sal through what he should look for and stay in touch often.

"Jesus Christ," O'Brien said at that, "I'll probably end up spending more on toll calls than the train fare would have cost the department."

Back at his desk, he was ready to leave for the day when his phone rang, his partner's voice coming over the line and what sounded like a two-way radio squawking in the background.

"Where are you?" Sean asked.

"Hampden Cab Company. I ran into some neighbor of Jansen's who told me the guy took off kind of in a hurry last night, with a suitcase like he was going away. Got one of these taxis."

"Where'd it take him?"

"They just pulled the sheet for me—to his housekeeper's house and then to the airport. He scrammed, for sure."

"But why the stop at the housekeeper's?"

"I'm heading there now. You wanna join me?"

Sean looked at his watch and sighed. "Yeah. What's that address again?"

❧

Sal might have wanted Sean to accompany him so he wouldn't botch the interview, but there really was no need. The elderly Negro woman, the housekeeper's mother, had no interest in covering for Jansen, even if he was innocent. She looked beyond Sean and Sal, checking to see if any big-shouldered cops were waiting to drag her away. Not that it would have taken more than Sean himself. She was only a little over five feet and frail as a bird.

"I know your daughter's boss came by here last night. What for?"

"He picked up something. Something he had left with my girl."

"What was it?"

"I don't know. I mean it was just papers. Files and such. I didn't look at it."

"Why didn't you tell us about that when we questioned you before?"

"You didn't ask about no papers. You just asked about where Dr. Jansen was at such-and-such a time and the like." She had recovered her poise and looked him directly in the eye, daring him to bother her when all she was doing was what she was told.

"When had he left these papers with you?"

She thought for a moment, crossing her arms across her chest. "I don't remember exactly. Last few days or so."

"Did he say why he needed you to keep them?"

She shook her head. "Just said he couldn't be leaving them about the lab or his house."

"If he comes back, you call me. You get to a neighbor's phone and you call me." Sean handed her a card with his number on it.

Before he headed home to pack his bag and catch an overnight train to Cresskill, Sal told him he'd get the station to put some black-and-whites out looking for Jansen.

≈≈≈

"There you go, ma'am."

"Now it feels too tight." Hope rose in her throat as the ring caught around her knuckle.

"Let me see." Will twisted the ring so hard she cried out, but he managed to push it into place. He held out her hand and smiled broadly. "That's a beaut, if I do say so myself."

He looked up at the jeweler, an older man who owned his own shop on Belair Road. They'd caught him just before closing, and he'd worked on the ring while they waited. Julia didn't want to look at the proprietor. She was afraid she'd see his true opinion of the ring in his eyes.

"I don't know, Will. My finger might get swollen." She pulled her hand from his and rubbed the knuckle.

The jeweler took another look. "Hmm...no, looks fine to me. That's a heavy ring. Don't want it loose. Could fall off easy."

"Thanks a lot, Bennie," Will said.

Bennie? The man's name was Benjamin Schoor, and Will had never met him before this evening. Will always assumed a nickname when talking to people he hardly knew.

"How much I owe you?"

While Will settled with "Bennie," Julia walked to the front of the shop and stared out at the street, busy with cars, lit by the piercing late-day sun. It was almost Easter. Soon, she and Helen and her mother would go to Holy Thursday and Good Friday services, and on Saturday they'd take food to be blessed.

Will wanted her to come to his house for Easter dinner, but she'd avoided giving him a definite answer. If her father was home from the hospital, she'd want to spend that Sunday with her own family. Besides, Mrs. Beschmann was a nice enough woman, but she made Julia uncomfortable with her relentless insistence that Julia not lift a finger to help. Julia was never sure it was the woman's excessive brand of hospitality or her desire to keep a cripple from overtiring herself. Either way, it grated.

And she couldn't possibly go to Easter dinner at the Beschmann household this year if she was thinking of ending her engagement with Will. She laughed at herself. She hadn't even had the courage to fend off this visit to the jeweler's. How on earth would she find the fortitude to beg off the marriage entirely? She was a fraud.

"C'mon, honey." Will looped his arm around her shoulder and lightly kissed her on the cheek. "Let's go show your sister and mother. Let me see it again—it looks great!"

ოჳ

An hour later, she bade Will farewell at the door. Her face ached from pretending to smile so much, smile when her sister and Mutti had admired the ring, smile when Will had joked about pawning it for a down payment on a new house, smile when he'd suggested they have a "real big engagement party." Smile, smile, smile.

She begged off sitting up with Helen and Mutti while they watched television, and went to her room where she sat on the bed, staring into the twilight, wondering what to do and how to do it.

She wanted to start fresh on something. On what? What was she even capable of doing that was fresh and different? She'd used up her share.

It hadn't been that long ago that she'd been excited about starting her new job, about finding a beau, even, yes, having him propose to her. These had been accomplishments, just like going from bed to wheelchair and wheelchair to cane.

When she'd first come out of the hospital, nearly a year after contracting polio, she'd felt born again, as if God had given her a second chance at life, and she'd never take anything good or sweet for granted again.

It had lasted for quite a while, that feeling. In fact, nearly every small happiness at that time—from a mild, sunny day to her mother's smile—had brought tears to her eyes. She had been so, so grateful just to be alive, and to only have the cane and brace.

But over time, that thankfulness had faded. The brace rubbed and hurt, the cane was awkward, every task was harder, requiring accommodation and thought.

It seemed cruel to have the good feeling fade, one more bitterness to swallow, her consolation disappearing. She couldn't pinpoint when it had happened, but she'd lost her sense of new beginnings and become who she was now, a determined but often-frustrated polio.

Yes, she was defined by the disease. It would forever describe her. She wasn't just Julia Dell. She was the polio, Julia Dell.

She looked at the ring and thought of taking it off. But Helen and Mutti would notice if she didn't wear it to work the next day.

Damn it.

She blinked and looked again at the ring. She'd break with Will. She didn't need an argument to do that. She just needed courage.

She didn't want to enter a marriage knowing it would end in divorce. That was a humiliation as well as a sin against the church. Why, even Dr. Jansen had hidden his divorce from everyone. No one had known he had a wife. Irene Brodie, her name was. Julia wondered what she was like, what kind of woman would have married cranky Dr. Jansen.

Brodie. The name was so familiar....

A faint memory teased her thoughts. She grabbed her cane and walked to the hallway, calling down to her family.

"I'm going to make a phone call," she said, heading for her mother's room where she sat on the edge of the bed, reaching for the telephone directory her parents kept on a shelf below the phone. She quickly found what she was looking for and dialed, cheered by the sound of her former boss's voice when he himself answered after only three rings.

The conversation with Dr. MacIntyre was friendly and melancholy. Here was yet another example of something Julia had failed to adequately appreciate until it was gone. Dr. MacIntyre had been a good boss, his only quirk his unwillingness to confront her directly when he was displeased.

They made pleasant small talk about the labs, and he asked about a memorial for "Mike." She broke the news to him that Dr. Lowenstein was really a Richard Hill. The name had no significance to him, and he was quite taken aback by the knowledge that a colleague would have lied to his fellow doctors like that.

"There's another name I wanted to ask you about," she said. "Irene Brodie. I remember you telling me something about polio research that a Dr. Brodie was involved in...."

The name "Irene Brodie" didn't mean anything at all to him, but as soon as he started talking about the Dr. Brodie he knew of and the vaccine trials of 1935, the story came back to her.

Her dark mood lightened. This was important. This would move the case forward. She would call Detective Reilly in the morning.

Chapter Twenty-One

HE WAS LATE FOR WORK. Really late. He and Brigitta had had an argument over Danny's show-and-tell at kindergarten.

Danny had gotten into his head that he'd take in his old "blankie." Only problem was that his "blankie" had been a square of cotton bed jacket that had belonged to Mary. Sean was surprised the boy had chosen it. Surprised and knifed to the core. He'd had to spend a good twenty minutes trying to persuade Danny to take something else, eventually getting the boy to settle on a felt cowboy hat Sean'd bought for him at Gwynn Oak amusement park the previous summer.

But it hadn't been the talk with Danny that had thrown his schedule off kilter. No, the culprit had been the argument with Brigitta *before* his talk with Danny.

Sean had picked Brigitta up, and the kids had still been in their pajamas. She'd commented on that, said something like it wasn't "good for them to be in their nightclothes riding around town." He'd offered an apology, then thought better of it. The weather was mild today, and the pajamas were just as warm as the light cotton shirts and pants they'd don at home. Brigitta had then remarked that she'd been cleaning out some things the day before and had thrown away a few items that were too "full of holes to mend." At his house. Not her things. His. The boys'.

That had set him on edge, but he'd said nothing. It had only been when Danny insisted on the blankie for show-and-tell that the truth had come out. Brigitta had found the garment fragment stashed in a corner of the boy's dresser drawer, and into the trash it had gone.

"I didn't know what it was!" she'd protested when Danny had started crying. "I wasn't sure if...if it was something inappropriate."

"Jesus Christ, Brigitta, do you think you could have asked me? We better find it."

"I put it in the trash, Sean. It's going to be all dirty and greasy now."

"It doesn't matter. You can wash it."

"*I* can wash it?"

"All right. I can. Just find it, will you?" Sean had marched off to the boys' bedroom to look for another item for show-and-tell, eventually coming upon the hat which Robby had said made Danny look like a "real cowboy." That had been the selling point.

Brigitta hadn't found the "blankie," but that was because she'd hardly looked. Sean had come upon her staring in the trash bin out back but not moving an item to see where it might have gone. He'd poked around until he found it, mussing up his just-laundered shirt. When he'd gone to change, Brigitta had muttered, "I guess I'll wash that one, too."

This isn't working.

Over and over that had gone through his mind on the way to the stationhouse. He had to do something about it. He had to stop putting it off.

Now he sat at his desk, staring at the note O'Brien had left on it. "See me at ten." That meant O'Brien had noticed he was late.

Great—one more worry.

Brigitta Lorenzo might be a good woman, a kind woman, a sexy-as-hell woman. But she wasn't the woman for him and the boys. His natural optimism plus his desperation had led him to use her in a way that normally would have sent him to the confessional. Now that the sex was out of the picture, it was clearer than ever that he had to break it off with her.

He picked up the phone and asked the operator to ring through to his church's convent. A woman answered. No, she wasn't a nun, just the housekeeper who came by in the morning. Yes, she could take a message. He carefully spelled his name and gave his office number and told her what he needed—a recommendation or two for a babysitter for his boys.

"I'm sure they'll know of someone, Mr. Reilly," the woman said. "I know of a Mrs. Creed myself...."

He took down the number, feeling like it was God himself telling him to move on with it and get a real sitter. As soon as he hung up the phone, it rang. He expected it to be Sal, reporting in before his search begin in earnest, so Sean answered the phone with a jaunty accent to confuse his partner.

"Oh...I must have the wrong number...."

Julia.

"No, uh, it's me, Sean. Is your boss back?" He already pushed back his chair, ready to leave.

"No. But I have some information...I thought might be useful."

∾∾∾

He didn't need to go in to talk to her. He could have stayed at his desk and taken it all down. But he craved movement, anything that kept him from stewing about Brigitta and his kids.

They sat in the cafeteria which he'd suggested so Linda wouldn't overhear. She started off by telling him that Susan's husband had called in sick for her, saying she might be out for a while. He nodded but didn't reveal what he knew about that part of the case.

"Dr. Jansen had been married, to an Irene Brodie," she said, telling him what he already knew.

"Yes."

"The name sounded familiar, but I couldn't place it. But last night..." She waved her left hand in the air in a nervous gesture.

He noticed the ring. Her face reddened, and her mouth dropped open. She didn't speak. But why should she? They were nothing to each other.

Still, something deep inside caved in. Just a little. Just a little tumbling of grief that, left unchecked, could lead to an avalanche. *Well, ain't that a surprise, Sean. You were hoping....*

He was still staring at it. He forced his gaze away.

She must have just gotten engaged. He hadn't seen the ring yesterday. It had happened last night. Even she, a cripple, had found somebody. Maybe he would, too, someday....

"When I worked for Dr. MacIntyre," she continued, "he used to tell me things about polio research, about its history, what the doctors were trying to do, what they knew and didn't know. I remembered Dr. Mac mentioning a Dr. Brodie."

Sean straightened and leaned forward, his eyes narrowing. Did she just remember this or had she saved it, throwing out these clues like breadcrumbs down a path. Would this get someone else in trouble— someone she resented?

"The vaccine trials that are about to begin weren't the first attempts to make a polio vaccine. There have been others. In fact, years ago, there was a disastrous trial. I might have mentioned it to you. It was in 1935...

"The main doctors involved—Brodie and Kolmer—were reviled by their colleagues at a Public Health Association Meeting. They were practically accused of murder in speeches at the meeting. Apparently, Dr. Kolmer said at the meeting he wished the floor would swallow him up. Dr. Brodie—well, he died very young...."

"Since Jansen was married to a Brodie, would it ruin his career if anyone knew?"

"I don't know," she said, shaking her head. "It's not something he'd be bragging about. You see, the trials were horrible. Children were infected by the vaccines. Some died. But it got worse. Some came down with other terrible infections because the vaccine was mixed with monkey tissue. This caused abscesses in some children, whole body infections in others, awful allergies...."

Sean's lip curled up in disgust.

"Here's the sad part about Brodie—he wasn't responsible for the worst of it, Dr. Mac said. His experiments were more sloppy than harmful. He became something of a scapegoat, though, because of his involvement.

Dr. MacIntyre said the man was never the same again, a promising career wiped out. No one wanted to work with him."

Sean thought for a moment. "What about Dr. Hill? Dr. MacIntyre know of him?"

"No. He was quite taken aback by his deception."

"What if Hill were involved with those earlier trials? Would doctors have worked with him?"

"Dr. Hill wasn't involved in polio research," Julia reminded him.

No, he wasn't. Not at Hopkins anyway.

He stared at her as she sipped her coffee. She seemed happy. Was that because she was engaged, or because she was helping him? Or...did she revel in getting other people into trouble, crippling their lives in some way?

It doesn't matter, he reminded himself. She'd provided valuable information. She didn't need to be a saint for it to be worthwhile.

∾∾

Brigitta rubbed her temples and put her feet up on the small ottoman in front of the chair. If she had a cool cloth...

"Danny, darling, could you go in the bathroom and wet a washcloth for me?"

The boy looked up from his blocks, scattered on the living room floor, and silently nodded.

"And push those blocks back on the rug, will you, honey?" She'd nearly twisted her ankle on one walking into the kitchen earlier. She wished they'd keep their toys in their room and leave the living room clean and tidy. Sean had explained to her that he allowed them to play wherever they liked, and he didn't mind straightening up if need be. But she would straighten up before he came home, so that the house was as spotless as a church.

While Danny dragged himself off to the bathroom, she looked over at Robby. He was making choo-choo noises while running a metal train across the hooked rug. She worried it would snag and tear the carpet and wondered whether she should restrict him to only playing with the metal trains and cars outside on the sidewalk. Not a fight she wanted to deal with right now. Her head ached too much, and her stomach was beginning to feel uncomfortably cramped.

Danny returned, a dripping wet washcloth in his hand. When he handed it to her, it left big splotches on her pale blue trousers.

"This is awfully wet, sweetie," she said with as much cheer as she could muster. "Could you wring it out some?" But he had gone back to his blocks. And she wasn't sure he understood what "wringing it out" meant anyway.

She stood, but her head didn't follow. The room spun, and she sat back down. Dammit. She was sick. Probably picked up that nasty flu the boys had just gotten over.

This wasn't working, she thought miserably, sliding back into the chair and letting the cloth drip over her blouse as she placed it on her forehead.

She liked Sean well enough. She still thought she could even learn to love him. But she didn't like…this.

She didn't like being a mother. She wasn't even convinced that would change with her own children. She hated the forced idleness, the sitting around just watching, trying to schedule the day so that she had something to do—ironing or dusting or even reading—in their presence just to keep an eye on them. She didn't like listening to them talk—she wasn't interested in their stories. She had nothing in common with the other kindergarten mothers with whom she waited outside the school. She especially disliked the lack of order, the fact that she couldn't count on things staying clean or in place or even quiet for when Sean returned from work.

In a sad way, she felt she was betraying her Ernie with these thoughts. If Ernie had lived, she would have been a mother and housewife...and discovering what she was learning now, that it didn't suit her. Her life with Ernie would have changed from passionate idyll to...this. These thoughts...they were akin to abandoning him, and they shook her deeply.

Maybe, she sighed, Sean could afford to send the boys to boarding school if she worked, too. She knew some of the lawyers had done that with their children. She now saw the wisdom of it. And then, she didn't need to have children of her own. Sean might not even want them. The two boys were a handful.

What was the matter with her? She was contemplating marriage with a man she hardly knew, a man who'd gone from hot passion to cool kisses on the cheek in a few days' time. And she wasn't even sure she liked his children. All because she'd made a stupid mistake on her job. She had to shake out of these blues. They were clouding her judgment.

"Ow! Stop it, Wobbie!" Danny smacked his brother on the arm.

"I didn't do nothin.' Get your stupid blocks out of the way!"

She watched them fight but said nothing to stop them. She was too tired. She closed her eyes and tried to block everything out.

Chapter Twenty-Two

HE HURRIED TO GRAB HIS PHONE, pleased to hear his partner's chipper voice. After filling him in on the Brodie info, Sean eased into his chair. Poor Sal must have been bushed, traveling all night and then getting right to the task at hand in the morning.

"What you find out?"

"Everything and then some."

"Spill it, partner."

"Well, after talking to every goofball Hill in and around Cresskill, New York this a.m., I finally hit on something."

"A family member?"

"Nope. Just dumb luck. I got a Rebecca Hill. She's not related to our dead doc, but she knew of the family, remembered hearing something about them years ago. A pharmacy shop owner. His store burned down."

"When?"

"She didn't remember—sounded like she had trouble remembering a lot of things. But I figured – "

" – the local firemen should know."

"Which is why I checked with them. A shop belonging to Gustav Hill burned down in 1936 or '37. Pretty sad."

"Where was our Hill?"

"At NYU apparently. They were proud as the dickens of him, according to some old codger with the fire department. And he was a good son, says this fellow. Sent his parents money regular. Visited every chance he could."

"So he was a good guy."

"You sound surprised."

Sean scratched his head. "He had something in his past worth blackmail money, something he was tryin' to hide."

A fellow detective walked by, placing a note on his desk: *Brigitta called. Call back.*

Sean mentally cursed. "Anybody else in the family?"

"The fireman says there was a brother. Didn't know what happened to him."

"But you found out?" Sean drummed his fingers, studying the note to call Brigitta.

"The fireman put me in touch with some old biddy named Abendschoen. Means 'beautiful evening' in Deutch. And the reason I know that, pal, is because she was some German version of that gal in Homeland who'd known our vic as Mike Lowe."

Despite his impatience, Sean chuckled. "You charm them, Sal."

"Yeah, well, I spent nearly an hour with her and would have spent more if her nurse didn't tell her she had to go to the doc or something. I think I'm gonna marry that nurse."

"You're still not telling me what you got."

"The fireman was a little off, but not by much. Richard Hill was the apple of his parents' eye. That's true. They scrimped and sent him to medical school, and then he got work as a researcher for some Rockefeller Institute, real big, real honor and all that. They had a newspaper story about it in their store window and everything, apparently."

"The store that burned?"

"Yeah, that's right. But turns out the parents weren't killed in it. Just wiped out."

"So good son helps them out?"

"Yeah. Even buys them a shiny new car. Only problem is, they were in an accident...." Sean could hear Sal flipping through notes. "Killed both of them."

"Geez. Bad luck."

"This guy was a magnet for it. Little while later, younger brother comes to New York to visit his successful doctor brother and...gets hit by a bus and is paralyzed. Was in and out of hospitals until about '48. Then he died. Rumor is he drank himself to the grave."

Sean thought for a minute, his fingers grabbing the note to call home.

"The old lady—she know anything else about the family's relatives in the old country?"

"I think she would have told me the history of the Holy Roman Empire if I'd've sat there long enough. Yeah, she knew the Hill family's story. During the war, a bunch of them got shot as traitors."

"They *were* Jewish?"

"No. Just in the wrong place at the wrong time." Sal cursed. "That was the worst of it. She gave me an earful about how awful things were in Germany before the war and how nobody here really understood what was going on. She made it sound like it was our fault they all let Hitler take over."

"What's your nose telling you?"

"To tell the truth my head's so full of this woman's gab I have a hard time hearing myself think right now. But I guess my gut feeling is Dr. Hill did something that made him a target. His parents' house burns down. They die in an accident in the car he gave them. His brother is paralyzed in an accident visiting him. If it was all bad luck, that's a shit load to have happen to you. If it was deliberate — if someone was after him, say, and got his family in the crosshairs — well, I can see why he'd run away."

"When you headed back here?"

"I'll be in in the morning."

When Sean got off the phone, he called Brigitta immediately, his hands sweating and heart thumping, expecting bad news.

Nothing was wrong, though. She just had a spare moment and thought she'd see how his day was going. That was an excuse. He could hear again something tense in her voice, as if she were about to snap. He told her he couldn't stay on, had to get to something, and felt guilty as soon as he hung up. Get to what? He looked around the office at other desks, other policemen, at O'Brien's door. If he went home, would his boss notice or assume he was out on the case?

All right, he would work the case. He'd talk to Julia again and see if she knew anything about this Dr. Hill stuff now that he had more. Maybe her memory needed a little shove. And he'd double-check the hotel where Dr. Jansen was supposed to be staying in California. Maybe the fellow left early for that conference.

He dialed Hopkins and waited, then heard Linda's voice on the line.

"I'm afraid you just missed her. Her father's being discharged."

❦

"You get on the other side of him. I'll stay on his right."

"Mutti, he doesn't need us carrying him to the house."

"You're darn right I don't. One of the reasons I had to get out of there was all the swarming those folks do." Howard Dell waved a hand in front of him, but Julia noticed it shook just a little. She sidled up next to her father and looped her arm through his.

"Then you can help *me*. How's that?"

Helen relinquished her position and ran in front of them to unlock the door. "I'll get his bag in a sec," she called over her shoulder.

"Beth is on her way over," Julia said to her father as they ambled up the walkway.

"With the children? They will be too noisy!" her mother exclaimed.

"I'd like to see them," Howie said.

"You get into bed and rest. We'll wake you up when she arrives." Julia smiled at her father but quickly looked away. He was still so pale. They entered the house where already the smell of coffee filled the air. Helen had set up the percolator before they'd left for the hospital. She appeared in the hallway, laughing and pointing to a smear of red on her yellow dress.

"I opened some tomato soup. I'm afraid there won't be as much as I'd planned."

Julia looked into her sister's laughing eyes. Helen had driven them home so smoothly that no one had even thought about it. Now she was cooking in a haphazard way, without the meticulous apron she usually wore. She'd changed, quickly and for the better. If Helen could do it, so could Julia.

Mutti insisted on getting her husband settled in bed on her own. While she fussed over him, Julia joined her sister in the kitchen.

"You're not wearing your ring." Helen pointed to Julia's hand with a wooden spoon.

"My god, you're observant." She had taken it off after her talk with the detective.

"About some things."

Julia breathed in deeply, as if about to jump into a pool. "I think I'm going to tell Will I can't marry him."

Helen looked at her in silence, then walked over to her and hugged her. "When?"

"Probably next week. He called me right before we got the news about Dad getting out. He's taking his Mom to Lancaster to visit some relatives over the weekend."

"So you won't see him until next week?"

"That's right. I told him I'd talk to him on Monday."

"Oh, Jules, I know it will be hard."

"I think waiting to do it will be harder."

"No, it won't. This weekend, we'll be busy taking care of Dad."

"I think Dad would prefer it if we weren't so busy at that."

Helen smiled. "Then we'll be busy making sure Mutti and Beth don't overwhelm him."

The sound of children's feet clomping up the front porch steps carried through the hall. Then Beth's booming voice calling out hello followed the yammer of the children.

"If you want to talk about it later," Helen said, indicating the hall with her eyes.

"Thanks. I think I'd rather not tell many people now." She helped Helen set the table and put together a tray for their father.

The rest of the day and evening was consumed with the happy relief of a return to normalcy. Their father might still be ailing, but he was home. Home where they could take care of him. Where they didn't need to study the looks of doctors and nurses and examine their words as if they were secret codes holding the key to happiness.

Beth's children were on their best behavior that night, and they all made happy plans for the coming holiday, all three girls together with their mother in their large living room. Helen sat on the edge of their mother's chair, paper and pencil in hand, taking down the Easter menu.

Beth lounged on the sofa, an arm around her children who nestled nearby. Julia perched on an ottoman. They laughed. They talked. They even sang—when Beth insisted she knew the words to "Easter Parade."

Julia's mood lightened with every happy note. She wasn't thinking about Easter or her father or special menus, though. She was thinking of how Detective Reilly might look when he noticed her ring was gone, and she could explain she was free.

✌✎

He was beat, physically and emotionally. As he dragged himself out of the car and walked up his front steps, O'Brien's words still stung.

"Show some focus, Reilly. Show me you're back."

O'Brien had been irritated, not pleased, when Sean had gone over the latest info with him. O'Brien hadn't said much about Sal's great detective work. He'd focused instead on Jansen. He couldn't understand why they hadn't staked out the man's house and followed his every move when all indicators were that he was guilty of something. After all, if they knew the man had been in Lowenstein/Hill's house the morning of the murder and they knew he had made arrangements to flee, what the hell had they been waiting for?

There'd been no point in arguing about all the other leads they'd tracked down. The way O'Brien had said it, Sean had to agree. Jansen should have been the prime suspect from the first day. Now he was gone, and they were left with nothing.

O'Brien had then asked him his plans for the evening, and Sean knew exactly what he'd expected him to say—that he would be watching Jansen's house, talking to more neighbors, chasing down more colleagues. Instead, he'd mumbled that his boys were still ailing, and he had to get home.

Show me you're back.

Sure, I'll do that, boss. How do I get "back?"

He opened the door and threw his keys on the table. The house was quiet, and for a moment, Sean closed his eyes and remembered Mary sitting and reading softly to the boys in the backyard when the sun would glint her hair into spun gold.

"Sean, are you okay?" Brigitta appeared from the kitchen, and although she was the one asking after his health, she looked like she wasn't faring so well. Her hair was tousled, and a brown stain marred her white blouse. Her face was white as paste, and he noticed no smell of cooking.

"Are you all right?" he asked, ignoring her question.

Her hand flew to her head. "To tell the truth, I think I might be coming down with whatever the boys have. I can't seem to keep much down and was feeling a bit woozy earlier."

Oh, Christ. Maybe she wasn't sick. Maybe she was…

He'd thought of it, but pushed it out of his head.

Mary had complained the same way those first months carrying the boys, even before the doctor had confirmed her intuition. Like Brigitta, she'd been dog-tired and green at the gills.

It would be months before they'd know for sure. Better to not mention it. Maybe it *was* what the boys had had and nothing more. But she had to be thinking it, too.

A quick roll in the hay and he ends up with a woman for the rest of his life. His boss was right. He had to focus. He had to come back. He had to get himself back.

He rubbed his hand over his face and stared at her.

"Maybe this is too much for you...."

"No, I'll be fine. Really. I'm strong. I just need some rest. I'm sure that's all."

It sounded as if she was trying to convince herself as much as him. Crap, she was worried about it, too.

"Let me take you home," he said, pointing to her purse on the sofa. "Are the boys out back?"

"They're napping."

A nap this late in the day. It hadn't been a good day, then.

He went to rouse them, and in a few seconds they were all bundled up and in the car but not before Brigitta used the bathroom. She tried to hide it by flushing the toilet twice, but he could tell she was puking her guts out.

Chapter Twenty-Three

LATE AGAIN. Both boys had taken ages to get to sleep last night. It was that damned nap. And it turned out they'd not had anything to eat either, so Sean had treated them to burgers at the White Tower on the way home. It had been good fun, and he'd enjoyed seeing them smile and laugh. But he'd paid for it with their wakefulness. He'd washed out their school shirts after that, and cleaned up and worried that he wouldn't have anyone to watch them the next day.

But Brigitta had been ready when he picked her up. Pale but ready. She'd hardly talked to him on the way back to his house, only telling him she was sure she was getting over whatever she had, and she'd find time to rest while the boys napped that day. It was an act and he knew it.

O'Brien glowered at him as he came in, so he raised his hand in an over-friendly wave, as if he were scheduled to come in late. Sal would be back late morning.

As he threw his notebook on the desk, O'Brien stepped on to the floor. "Reilly, come here!" He didn't wait for Sean to respond before heading back into his office.

Sean thought of excuses he could offer for his tardiness and settled on a faulty alarm. He'd not used that one. He mentally rehearsed it, thinking of the jaunty tone he should strike to make it appear that he knew O'Brien would understand. As he stepped over the threshold, though, his boss was on the phone, finishing up a phone call.

O'Brien grunted out a goodbye to his caller and didn't bother to tell Sean to sit down.

"Jansen's back in town," he said simply. "Picked up at the airport. Should be here within the hour."

Sean nodded. "I'll question him. Sal's on the train."

O'Brien looked at him as if waiting for more. When Sean didn't offer anything else, O'Brien spoke without taking his glance off the detective. "We got the first call about eight," he said, "but you were nowhere to be found."

The alarm clock story wouldn't do. Sean just frowned and swallowed, acknowledging his guilt. "Won't happen again."

๛

Brigitta wasn't sure why she'd not begged off today. Her stomach would absolutely not stay still. She was overwhelmed with the desire to retch, but she had nothing left to spit up. Only a strong dose of bicarb that morning had kept her reasonably serene when Sean had picked her up. And she'd made a good show of it, she'd thought, only hinting at some distress. "Nothing to worry about. Probably what the boys had."

As the day wore on, she realized she'd been trying to fool herself as much as Sean into thinking this wasn't what most women would suspect after making love to a man. My god. All those years as Gavin's lover and not once—but they'd been so careful. With Sean, it had been impulsive, no time for care.

It didn't seem fair to have to worry about this so soon. Sure, she'd thought about it after both of their encounters. But there was no use fretting too much until her time of the month rolled around. Besides, she and Ernie had never been careful, and they'd certainly done enough lovemaking to start a family ten times over before he'd had to leave.

A tear rolled down her cheek and her chin trembled. Her stomach was still turning over. Her head throbbed. Was she warm, too? Or was it the house on this spring day? The boys were arguing in the other room, and she just wanted them to be quiet. She needed quiet to think of where she'd gone wrong.

A memory flooded her. Ernie in his brown Army uniform looking so dapper and young, throwing her a kiss from across the dining room at her mother's house. She'd proudly risen from her seat and gone to him, draping her arms around his shoulders and kissing him fully on the mouth, to jeers and cheers from her siblings. "We're married. We don't need to pretend," she'd told him.

Being his wife had made her feel bold and impulsive. Grown-up. It had given her "standing" in the world. And then when the telegram had come...

She had thought of dying herself. Walking to the harbor and throwing herself in the dirty gray water. She'd thought "my life is over now." She would never feel so strongly about a man again.

And she'd been right. She hadn't felt like that again. There is no second "first time."

Oh, she knew people looked at Brigitta Lorenzo and thought, "There's a woman with courage, with strength." But they had no idea how she'd struggled at first, forcing herself to go outside her secure world of family and neighbors, to push herself into situations where she knew she wasn't wanted, but daring people to reject her, staring them in the eyes. And as she'd succeeded, she'd felt...safe. She'd felt she'd found the way to keep life from hurting too deeply. Stare it down. Grab what you want.

She'd filled her life with purpose, with direction. She'd accumulated a small degree of wealth — at least compared to her family's standards. She'd done everything right.

And yet here she was, aching in body and spirit, and the pain she'd suffered years ago at Ernie's death seemed as fresh as the day's sun. She'd never be the same again. And she'd never fully protect herself from being hurt like that. She'd been a fool to think otherwise.

"Anything the matter, Mrs. Lorenzo?" Danny stood in front of her. He'd pronounced her name correctly. That was a small blessing.

But she couldn't tell him so, because suddenly she was sobbing and wishing she was alone so she could cry in peace.

"Maybe I should call Daddy," the boy said. "Do you want me to call Daddy?"

≈≈

"You simply don't understand." He said it calmly, with a touch of condescension, a schoolmaster lecturing a slow student. "The scientific community is divided over Dr. Salk's approach. It is a legitimate point of view to disagree with him. It isn't an anomaly or an aberration, something out of the ordinary, that is, something that indicates wickedness. Or worse."

Doctor Jansen attempted a fleeting smile. His face shone with sweat, and he clasped his hands together so tightly that the knuckles had turned white.

"I think I do understand, doc. That's the problem."

Sean placed his keys in his pocket and looked at his watch. He was hoping Sal would show up and join him, but his partner was probably only now pulling into Baltimore on the train from Cresskill.

He'd already been with Jansen in the small airless interview room for more than an hour. Uniforms had picked the doc up as he'd come off the plane. He'd been to Cincinnati, he'd told Sean, to see Dr. Sabin about a job. He didn't feel Hopkins was the place for him any longer.

Sean had pressed him on why he'd run away, and instead of getting answers, he was getting a lecture. Every time Sean tried to turn the conversation back to his murdered colleague, Jansen would spout off about the research and his disagreements with the powers-that-be, as if trying to lay out a case for his anger being legit, just not directed at Lowenstein/Hill.

"No, you can't possibly understand. Dr. Salk — and the entire National Foundation - that's the National Foundation for Infantile Paralysis, Basil O'Connor and his team…" His voice contained the whiff of a sneer. "They made promises to the American public, to people like you, people who have been waiting for a cure. You give us your dimes and pennies and dollars and we'll give you a nice, tidy vaccine faster than you can say poliomyelitis. And the quickest kind of vaccine is made with a killed virus.

It's not even true science. It's pure drudgery. Mechanics. Nothing skillful or creative about it."

"Okay, so they're working on this killed virus. And the rest of you fellows, including that Sabin guy you mentioned, are working on a live one. You told me this already, doc. Sounds to me like it's all you can think about. The kind of thing that drives a man crazy."

"Oh, for heaven's sake." Jansen shook his head. "Do you think I would have come back if I was guilty of killing Dr...."

"Dr. Hill. Richard Hill. You knew him. That's why you were so careful when you told me you didn't know Lowenstein at NYU, isn't it? It's because you knew Hill, not Lowenstein. C'mon. Save us both some time." He'd mentioned this to Jansen already, and gotten no response.

Dr. Jansen glared at him. "If you already know, then why bother asking me about him?"

"You and Hill were in on that bad experiment in '35. Hill gets out of town, changes his name, starts over. But you hang on to your moniker. Can't give it up after you've spent so much time building up your reputation as the 'live virus' champion of the world."

Jansen seethed out a sigh. "I'm not a champion of anything but...science. Pure science. I told you, but you simply don't understand. A live virus vaccine is more difficult to come by. It takes more than skill. It takes art...."

"Do you think I care about this baloney?"

"I'm trying to explain to you what *I* care about! So you'll see it wasn't about...about..."

"Murdering your pal Dr. Hill."

"I didn't murder him!" Jansen visibly shook with rage but immediately calmed himself, closing his eyes and breathing slowly.

"Okay, maybe you didn't mean to murder him. Maybe you just got so riled up—like you are now talking about your science stuff—that you got into a fight. One thing leads to another, and bam, the fellow's on the floor with a banged-in head. Is that how it happened? It would go easier for you that way. Everybody gets pushed a little too far sometimes. Maybe you were pushed over the edge. It's understandable. We all have our moments. C'mon, doc, tell me the story."

Jansen remained still. Eventually he opened his eyes, and it was as if he'd not heard a word of what Sean had just said.

"Determining what strain to use, which one will trigger the body's antibodies without giving the inoculated the disease itself, it's very difficult work. How to make that strain absolutely safe so that it will have virtually no chance of real infection. You can't rush this work, you see. It could take years. Decades! If I'm angry about anything, it's that!"

Decades—while little ones suffered, while the likes of Julia lost part of their lives. What an arrogant S.O.B.

Sean gritted his teeth and stared down at him. The man was a nutcase, in his opinion. Why wouldn't he just give it up? Tell him what happened?

"Science is what it's all about, huh?" Sean said, prodding him now to keep his ire punched up. Maybe if the doc got mad enough, he would spill.

Jansen didn't catch the sneer in Sean's voice and wholeheartedly agreed. "Yes. Yes. Science is what's important. Looking into the very heart of life itself, seeing how organisms grow and die, what affects them, what changes them. It's like...like..."

"Playing God?"

Jansen's head shot up. His eyes narrowed, and his lips pressed together into thin angry lines. Sean stepped forward and leaned on the table.

"Or maybe not God. God, after all, is merciful. Whereas you and your smarty-pants friends don't give a shit about the suffering of little ones. Don't care at all if another child is struck down tomorrow while you get jacked up over what you can discover if you get to take your time." He spit out his words. "No, you're not playing God. Just the opposite, in fact."

"How dare you..."

Sean slammed his fist on the table. He was tired of this man, always bringing the conversation back to what he cared about and to hell with anything—and anyone—else. He'd let him go on too long, figuring he might spill something useful.

"How dare I?" He leaned in even farther until his face was inches away from Jansen's. The man's eyes now bulged, his forehead beaded sweat. Sean dropped his voice to a near whisper.

"How dare you, Dr. Jansen. How dare you inject children with some witch's brew of monkey brains and virus and God knows what else just so you could write numbers in a ledger."

Jansen wiped his face with his hand. "I didn't...it wasn't me...I didn't run that..."

"That's when you met Dr. Hill, wasn't it? As part of that experiment in 1935?"

"It wasn't what you think."

At last, an admission of sorts that he'd known and worked with Hill.

"Then tell me what I should think."

"They were trying to help. They did have compassion. They thought it would work. They thought they had the answer, that they were going to save thousands, millions. They thought..."

"—that you'd be heroes. Just like Dr .Salk is now, right?"

"No, not like that. We thought..."

"So you admit you were in it? Don't matter if you do. I knew you were. Through your wife's connections. That ain't all I know. You took the papers on that experiment from Dr. Hill's house and you gave them to your housekeeper to hold. You knew what they meant. Dr. Hill could expose you. He was out of the polio game, but you're still in it, trying to make a name in it. Trying to get the world to see just what a great doc you are."

Jansen heaved a trembling sigh. Here, at last, Sean had found something that touched him. Jansen was tired, too, and Sean went in for the kill.

"What—your wife kick you out because you weren't big enough in the university? You think you had to prove something to her?

"My marriage was over after that experiment. Irene and I..."

"Her cousin was the one who got you in on it, right?" An educated guess.

"Yes. A distant cousin..."

Jansen hung his head. "She was so excited. Thought it was a great opportunity." He spoke with some bitterness. "I wasn't so sure. But I had no other prospects at the moment. I was just out of school, just married. I started to believe her."

"Don't give me that. You probably jumped at the chance. You with your shiny new degree and wanting to show the world how great you were. You probably couldn't wait to get going. Don't be laying it on her. When you gonna stand up like a man and take your lumps? You shot up those kids with poison!"

Jansen didn't respond at first, didn't even look at him. When he did speak, it was so softly that Sean could barely hear him.

"I was just a lowly technician. Just the fellow who gives the injections and records the data. I didn't plan the experiment. I didn't have anything to do with that. But they thought they were doing good. I thought so, too. I really thought..."

He looked up, and in his eyes Sean saw the ghost of something. Not the ghosts of those hurt children. The ghost of what Jansen thought he could have been and never would have the chance to be.

"I really thought we were enhancing the public good," he whispered. "And that's when I learned what a mistake it was to think that way. The road to hell..." He sucked in his lip, gathered his wits and spoke more strongly. "Pure science. That's the only way to work. Focus on the science. Not the good. That comes from the science."

"Where were you when your wife's cousin died?"

Jansen's head shot up again. "What?"

"Some think he killed himself. Were you around?"

"My God, man, you are insane. No, I wasn't around. Nowhere near. Dr. Brodie died of a heart attack." He sighed again, as if losing patience with Sean. "Call my wife. My ex-wife. She'll tell you I hadn't seen the family in years. She's remarried now. Irene Peterson. Here, I'll even give you her number...." He pulled a slip of paper and a pen from his pocket, wrote on it, and pushed it toward Sean.

"But if he were out of the picture, there's one less fellow around who knew about your involvement."

"I told you, I was hardly involved at all."

"Then why not tell us about Dr. Hill earlier?"

"I was honoring the dead!" Jansen stared at him wild-eyed. "I don't expect you to understand. Dick was a good man, unfairly treated. Dick didn't want people to know...."

"Why'd he leave polio research if he was such a good man?"

"Dick was troubled by the '35 incident, even spoke of quitting research altogether. He was talked out of it by some doctors at NYU. But he was never really comfortable staying in. Then in '37, his parents' house and store burned down—his father was a chemist, a pharmacist, in upstate New York. It left them penniless. Just a month later, they died in a car accident." Jansen swallowed. "And then his brother..." He looked up at Sean. "And other relatives, in Germany."

"Were you out to get him and his family?"

Jansen barked out a laugh as if Sean were crazy.

He tilted his head and stared at the detective. "Do you really think I'd go to the trouble of learning the arsonist's trade, then find a way to place Hill's family in harm's way in automobile traffic...oh, *and* travel to Germany to dispatch his relatives there? Good God, man, if I were that diabolically smart..." He swallowed and turned serious. "No, it was a string of bad luck. Awful luck. But Dick didn't see it that way. He saw it as...something more."

A horrible picture presented itself in Sean's mind. Dr. Hill being stripped of every person he loved, even distant family. And in the case of his parents and brother, he would have felt partially responsible. He'd bought his parents the car. And he'd invited his brother to visit him.

He thought he was being punished, Sean thought grimly.

That was why his home had been filled with religious tracts about atonement, forgiveness, the Prodigal Son, the story of Job. Hill had felt like that, like a man gone astray and needing to be welcomed home, into the kingdom. God, Sean hoped he had been.

"That's why he abandoned polio research," Jansen continued, calmer now, "even though his heart and soul was in it and he had a brilliant mind for it, too. He gave it up completely. As a penance. But he was constantly being pressed to return. What was worse, though, were those who thought he shouldn't continue in research at all, thought his hands were so dirty he should go away somewhere and never be heard from again. But this was all he knew, all he really loved. When he left the university, I had no idea where he went, what happened to him...."

"Until you ran into him here, as Lowenstein."

"Yes."

"But you didn't tell us you knew who he was."

"I just told you why—I was honoring Dick's wishes."

"Bullshit. He was dead. You didn't tell us because you couldn't have anyone finding out you were involved in that 1935 disaster. You came to Hopkins a year ago, discovered who Lowenstein really was, and saw he was a changed man. But you weren't. And you didn't want him ratting you out, so you came up with a plan. Sure, you're scared, but Hill is even more scared. So you blackmail him. Say you won't tell if he just pays you to keep quiet. You get some extra cash at the same time you keep the lid on things, letting him think you could turn over that stone and let the ugly truth crawl out just like that." Sean snapped his fingers, causing Jansen to jump a bit in his chair.

"That's absurd...."

"You get a nice tidy sum every month until he decides to stop paying. What, did he tell you he wasn't going to hide anymore? Is that what got you so angry that you smashed his head in? Or maybe he said a few bad words about that hero of yours, that Dr. Sabin...."

"No! I didn't hurt him. I didn't...kill him. Oh, God." Jansen's voice shook. He ran his fingers through his hair. He looked as if he was struggling to control himself, to keep from showing his true feelings.

"Look," he said in a monotone, "I knew he was going to tell. He was getting old and tired. Tired of pretending to be someone he wasn't. He felt particularly bad about pretending to be a Jew after...after everything that happened over there. People were always asking him if he lost family in the camps. It felt wrong to him...."

"But you didn't want him to say anything. Your game was up."

"Yes! I admit it—I didn't want him to say anything. That doesn't make me a murderer." His voice turned to a whisper. "It just makes me a coward."

Jansen looked at his hands on the table before him. "I was respected. I was making headway. Albert Sabin himself complimented a paper I'd written. I couldn't just throw all that away on the chance that someone would misunderstand my involvement. I begged Dick...I pleaded with him to wait. Just a little while longer. We were supposed to meet that morning to talk about it...I called to tell him I'd be late..."

"But talk didn't work. So you took action."

Jansen slowly shook his head. "No, no, no. I didn't kill him. I didn't do it." He looked up at Sean, eyes frantic. "Don't you understand? I wasn't blackmailing him! Someone else was! Someone who's been following me. I feel it. I know it. I'm the one in danger, you fool. That's one of the reasons I want to leave Hopkins. One of the reasons I bought a gun."

❧

"I think we should call Daddy."

"You're a scaredycat. Scaredycat, scaredycat, can't even kill a rat."

Robby shoved Danny's shoulder and ran into the living room. But now he was the scaredycat. The woman whose name he couldn't pronounce was sitting in the chair with her mouth half open and her eyes closed and she looked....

...like his mommy when Daddy had taken him to the hospital to say goodbye...

He started crying. Then he ran into the kitchen, pulled the chair to the wall, climbed up, and dialed his father's number at work, the number Daddy had made them both memorize.

✎✎

Call Robby.

Sean hurried from the room, crumpling the message paper in his hand, not stopping to tell the officer on duty where he was going or the clerk who'd brought the message why he was leaving. A message from Robby — that was bad, really bad. They never called him. They knew only to use the number in emergencies. He'd drilled them on that.

He reached for the nearest phone, on someone's desk near his, and dialed. Danny answered. Mrs. Lorenzo was sick, real sick. They couldn't wake her up. And Robby had gone to fetch Dr. Spencer...

"No, tell him not to do that, Danny. Has he left already? Can you still see him? Go after him, son. Tell him to come back!" Sean's voice was as firm as he could make it while panic crawled up his throat imagining Robby wandering on the streets by their home, lost. "Listen very carefully, son. You tell Robby to stay put or I'll get the belt on him. Do you understand? That's good. Just stay put. I'll be home in a few minutes. I'll call Doctor Spencer."

"Daddy, is she going to die like Mommy?"

Jesus Christ.

"No, son. She's just a little sick, that's all. Just like you and Robby. You go talk to your brother now. Tell him what I said. I need to call the doctor."

As soon as he hung up, he phoned Doc Spencer, got his answering service, and left a hurried message about an emergency at home. And then he left, no thought of Dr. Jansen or Dr. Lowenstein or Dr. Hill in his head. No instructions for the officer on duty about what to do with Dr. Jansen....

✎✎

"My goodness, such a fuss over nothing." Brigitta blew her nose. Despite her words to the contrary, she looked pale and weak. When Sean had arrived home, she'd been asleep in the chair. Asleep, only asleep, he'd reassured Danny and Robby. Doctor Spencer had arrived within a quarter hour and was just now finishing his examination.

"Can't say I find anything out of the ordinary," he said, a touch of irritation in his voice. He was wearing golfing pants. It was obviously his day off. He looked at Brigitta. "You're married, Mrs. Lorenzo?"

Oh, shit. Even Doc Spencer was thinking....

"Widowed."

"Sorry to hear." Dr. Spencer closed his bag. "Must be a touch of the flu." He stood. Sean noticed that this time he didn't offer any free medicine bottles. "I can write you a prescription..."

"I'm sure if I rest I'll be fine," Brigitta said. She looked at Sean. "I'm sorry to be such a burden. I was supposed to be helping you."

"It's not your fault."

Dr. Spencer moved to the door, put his hat on, and held out his hand to Sean. "She should rest. You might want to get her home." He looked at Brigitta. "You have someone to take care of you?"

"Um...my mother can stop by."

Doctor Spencer nodded. His hand on the door, he stopped. "How's that investigation going? You find the culprit?"

Sean's thoughts raced a hundred miles a minute to the present. Yeah. He'd found the culprit...and had had to leave him to come home. "We have a suspect," he said. "Hope to wrap it up soon."

After Dr. Spencer left, Brigitta donned her coat and Sean helped the boys find theirs. They were just scurrying to the car when the phone rang.

"Go on along," he said to them. "I'll get it and be out in a sec."

He rushed to grab the ringing phone, still holding a toy Danny wanted to take in the car.

"Sean?"

"Sal, you're back! Look, I'll be right in. Had something of a family problem." He didn't want to tell Sal about Brigitta not feeling well.

"Sorry to hear that..." Sal sounded tired. He was practically whispering.

"I'll be in soon to fill you in and spell you. You should go home and rest." Then he remembered the boys. What would he do with them? Call that Mrs. Creed? Why hadn't he made those arrangements? He'd think of something.

"Maybe you can go talk to Jansen some more. I got some good stuff..."

"Jansen's not here."

"What?" Sean straightened, his nerves on edge.

"He walked."

Oh, no.

"I left him with..."

"He told the officer you said he was free to go." Sal didn't sound angry, just bushed.

"Since when do you take a perp's word for anything?"

"Him being a doctor and all..." Sal said, yawning. "He's a smooth talker."

Sean closed his eyes and shook his head. Would he have a job when he went in? Would he be sacked then and there?

"Look, Sal, you didn't have nothing to do with this. It's all my fault. I'll tell O'Brien."

"I appreciate that, buddy, but here's how we're gonna play this. You got called home on an emergency, so you better stay put or else it looks like you were shamming. I'll talk to O'Brien and give him my New York report. I'll be real good about it. I'll tell him one of your boys was hurt and I called you from the train station and said I was on my way, but only problem was the train had been late, so I didn't make it in right away. I'll tell him you didn't think you needed to tell some greenhorn uniform that he shouldn't let a suspect being questioned go. I'll handle it."

"I don't know…" Sean didn't like Sal taking all the heat.

"Listen, it's best for both of us if I do. I'll call you later. You take care of your boys."

&⁓

Sal handled it as best he could. But late in the day, just as Sean was cleaning up after dinner with the boys, Sal called him from his home. O'Brien wanted to see him first thing Monday. Sean was off the Lowenstein murder. And he might want to check how his old uniforms fit.

"Beat cop?"

"He might not go through with it. Could be a threat," Sal said.

"He's been wanting to do something like this for a while," Sean said, depressed.

"He's threatening me with probation."

"You didn't do anything wrong!" Sean exclaimed. "Except get chained to me as a partner."

"Oh, he had a few items I done wrong."

"I'll talk to him about it."

Sal chuckled. "No offense, buddy, but I don't think it would help."

Sean thought of a beat cop's schedule. No flexibility, bad hours. How could he do that?

"I don't know, Sal. I might not be able to keep on the force."

"Look, he's not firing you." Then Sal got his meaning. "What—you're gonna quit?"

"I don't know."

"Hold on tight, buddy. This case ain't over yet."

"Who's he handing it to?"

"I think he's taking it over himself while they look for Jansen again."

"Well, once they get him, the case is over."

"You think it was him?"

"Nobody else fits." But still, now that the interview with Jansen had settled in his mind, Sean didn't feel he'd been talking to a murderer. A coward, yeah, just as Jansen had said. But a killer? Naw, not a messy, beater kind of killer. Not Jansen. He wouldn't get his hands dirty. And besides, he'd admitted to having a gun. Why hadn't he used that on Hill?

&⁓

Sean thought he'd have a weekend to calm down and figure out what to do. A weekend of peace with his boys when he'd force himself not to worry about Brigitta or about his job. Just pay attention to them, take them for a walk, maybe fly a kite in the park. Push thoughts of everything else away for a little while.

But the Saturday morning paper changed that.

Accident claims prominent doctor, a headline at the bottom of the city section read.

Dr. Jansen was dead. Died in a fall at his house Friday evening.

Chapter Twenty-Four

HE DRESSED THE BOYS in last year's suits and took them to church on Sunday where they listened to the prayers and heard the good wishes of other churchgoers on the steps as they left. He'd not gone to Communion. He still hadn't found time to get to confession and he needed to be absolved for...for everything. For Jansen. For Brigitta. For messing up his job. Next week was Palm Sunday, he told the boys, and after that Easter.

What had he done last Palm Sunday? He tried to remember as he walked the boys home through glorious sun. He remembered a Sunday—had it been Palm Sunday? He'd driven Mary and the boys to a beach on Middle River, and he'd taken them fishing while she'd sat on the shoreline, arms looped around her knees, looking pale and drawn and trying to pretend she was having a good time. He'd made them all dinner that evening, undercooking the chicken, overcooking the potatoes. She'd eaten two spoonfuls exactly—he'd watched her eating habits like a hawk at that point—telling him it was "lovely," before collapsing in bed, too tired to even undress.

"What we doing today, Dad?" Danny asked him, kicking a stone up the street.

Sean had no heart for taking them fishing. He couldn't pretend like Mary had that everything was all right.

"Momma put palms behind the cross," Danny said, looking at his feet.

Yes, when they'd come home from church on Palm Sundays, Mary had immediately taken the boys' palms and put them behind the crucifix that hung in their bedroom, behind the Sacred Heart of Jesus picture in the hallway, and behind the picture of Our Lady of Lourdes, a recent purchase at the time, in the living room.

"We can do that," Sean said.

Robby looked up at him. "Will she have palms, too? In heaven?"

He didn't know if there was a heaven anymore, and, despite what he'd said to Dr. Jansen, he didn't know if God truly was merciful.

They walked in silence the rest of the way home. When they reached the house, beautiful things waited to pierce his heart. Purple crocuses and red tulips were blooming, from bulbs she'd planted the first fall in the house. He'd not noticed them on their rush out that morning. And inside, with no cooking smells to obscure it, was the faintest scent of her rosewater perfume, brought out by the warmth of the day. *Oh, Christ.*

"Go to the bathroom, boys. We're taking a drive."

He took them out to the little cemetery off Taylor Avenue and laid some of her tulips on her grave. They all stood straight and silent, hands grasped before them, lost in their own thoughts and prayers.

Mary, I've gone and made a muck of things. I've gambled away my future and the boys,' too. I didn't know it'd hurt so much to miss you. I didn't know it would cloud so many things, my sweet. It's made me crazy. Dear lord, I don't know what to do now.

It was a slow day after that, like walking through water. He played catch with the boys in the yard. He made a pot roast, according to directions Mrs. Buchanan had left him months ago. He told them he'd buy them new suits for Easter, and teased them about the Easter Bunny and what he would bring.

He sat down that afternoon and called the woman the nun's housekeeper had mentioned to him for possible sitters and arranged for her to come by the next day.

He also called Brigitta to see how she was faring—"better, thank you"—and to let her know he'd found another sitter and she need not worry about helping him out. He apologized for "taking advantage of your good nature" and assured her he'd call her that week to talk about going out the next weekend. If things were as he suspected, he better start building a real relationship with this woman.

By the time he put his sons to bed that night, after a bath and a story, he was empty, feeling his face muscles ache the way they had after visiting Mary in the hospital. It wasn't from the effort to smile. It was from the effort not to frown, not to let his face and body collapse into the wailing grief he felt deep inside.

He sat alone that night in the living room, drinking a whiskey and listening to the radio, feeling the joy in his life drained away. *And you thought that had happened after Mary was gone. But there was still more pain to feel, more loss to experience.*

He was about to turn off the radio and go to bed when Walter Winchell's report came on. Here was a pleasant memory. Mary and he used to listen to Winchell, sitting quiet on a Sunday evening, content in each other's company. So he stayed, hoping to grab some of that peace back.

"Good evening, Mr. and Mrs. America and all the ships at sea," the familiar voice began. "Attention everyone. In a few moments I will report on a new polio vaccine—it may be a killer..."

Sean sat up, waited through the commercial, and listened to the rest.

"Attention all doctors and families. The National Foundation for Infantile Paralysis plans to inoculate one million children this month. The U.S. Public Health Service tested ten batches of this new vaccine. They found, I am told, that seven of the ten contained live — not dead — virus. That it killed seven monkeys. The name of the vaccine is the Salk vaccine..."

જિજ

By Monday, he'd talked himself into taking whatever came at him. He deserved a demotion. Deserved it because of Jansen, because of everything. Was lucky that was all he was getting.

"As far as I'm concerned, the case is closed." O'Brien looked up at him, his eyes red-rimmed and puffy. Either he'd had a hard night or allergies were bothering him. "Jansen was the killer. Jansen is dead."

"It was an accident then?"

"He was found at the bottom of his steps by his housekeeper, his neck broken in a fall."

"No evidence of foul play?" He remembered Jansen being afraid someone was after him. Had he been right?

O'Brien didn't respond. Just stared at him, breathing out a quick, angry sigh. He'd begun the meeting by reminding Sean of how understanding he'd been when his wife had been sick. At length, he spoke.

"What the hell do you care?"

Now it was Sean's turn to remain silent.

"You let the guy go," O'Brien continued. "If he'd have stayed in custody, he'd still be alive. You're better off not knowing if it was foul play, buster."

This was true.

"I've talked to Kaminsky," O'Brien said. "He can take you if you're willing to start on the night shift. Cherry Hill and that side of town."

Back on the beat. With no Mary to admire his uniform. The boys would like it. And they'd not know what it signified. There was comfort, at least.

"Yes, sir." He had to provide for the boys. He was lucky to have his job. "When do I start?"

"In a week." O'Brien put his hand on his phone, a sign the meeting was ending. "In the meantime, keep your nose out of trouble. Type up other detectives' reports for them or something. I noticed you're good at typing."

જિજ

Julia came in at noon that day. Mrs. Wilcox had called her at home on Saturday and told her she should feel free to take the entire day off after the shock of Dr. Jansen's death. But she couldn't do that. She had an appointment that evening...

She twisted the ring on her finger. She'd worn it just so she could take it off and return it to Will. She didn't want him asking where it was. She just wanted to get it over with. Her head was in a muddle, as confused as the day she'd discovered Dr. Lowenstein's body, lighting on one thought that would scamper away as quickly as she comprehended it.

Dr. Jansen was dead. She'd thought of calling Sean after reading the news, but what in the world would have been her reason? To ask for reassurances?

Yes, she did want that. She wanted to know what had happened when he'd talked to Dr Jansen, and if...if anything, even a small crumb of information she had divulged, had led to his death.

It had hung over her Sunday like a thundercloud waiting to burst, weighting her down more than the leg brace.

It had been supposed to be a day of celebration, her father's first Sunday at home since the heart attack. Beth and Stu were there with the kids after church, and Julia had helped Helen prepare a dinner that would rival Easter's feast. They'd gone straight to the kitchen after Mass where Helen had rolled out biscuits and instructed Julia on how to prepare the chicken for roasting. Then they'd come up with a brilliant game for the children — Find Grandpa's Cigarettes.

Since coming home, Howie Dell had wanted nothing so badly as a smoke, and both Helen and Julia had caught him taking a drag in secret, snatching the smoke from his lips before he'd had a chance to get more than a few whiffs. He had them stashed somewhere. Donny had found a pack between mattress and box spring. Even little Andy had come up with some, stuck behind a flowerpot in the kitchen.

Those moments of lightness, when they'd teased their father about his energetic pursuit of smoking, had lifted her for brief periods from her blues. She'd needed desperately to talk to someone about Dr. Jansen.

And that someone, not surprisingly, had ended up being Helen. As they'd washed the dishes together, Helen had brought it up.

"You must be pretty shaken up," she'd said, handing Julia a dish to dry at the table. They'd all offered similar condolences on Saturday after reading the news, and then no one had spoken of it, so wrapped up in the planning for Sunday's celebration. "I imagine it's hard not to dwell on it."

Julia had looked up at Helen and realized how wrong she'd been to assume that Helen had turned into a cipher after Tom's death. She'd retreated, yes. But she'd not stopped thinking and observing.

"It has been hard," she'd said, placing a dried plate on a pile of others. She'd sat while she dried, too afraid she'd drop something while standing and balancing herself on her good leg. "I told the detective some things about Dr. Jansen and I thought he was going to be questioned. I don't know if that happened. I wonder sometimes if..." If his death wasn't accidental. If he'd killed himself, or worse.

"Oh, Jules, don't torture yourself like that. If you had information related to the case, you would have been remiss for not turning it over."

"I suppose."

"You should take off tomorrow," Helen had said. "We could do something together. I don't have to be at the shop until three."

"Mrs. Wilcox called to tell me I could take off."

"Well, there you go!" Helen had handed her another dripping plate. "We'll go to the market for Mutti together. Or just take a drive."

"Listen to you — 'just take a drive' — Helen, you've changed so much."

"Necessity is the mother of invention...." She'd rinsed another plate and handed it over. "So you'll take the day?"

"I don't know. I really need to talk to Will, and he'd made this plan, before the news about Dr. Jansen, of course, that we could grab a bite to eat after work tomorrow since we didn't see each other this weekend."

"You're going to break the engagement then."

"Yes."

"I think that's wise, to do it in a public place. Less chance of a big scene."

"I hope so."

So now here she was at work, her thoughts a universe away from the tasks at hand, just waiting for the moment when she could tell Will she no longer wanted to be his wife two days after learning of her boss's death. She felt as if the nerves in her body were firing rapid signals to each other, creating a static that wouldn't let coherent thoughts penetrate the crackle.

"Dr. Morton's taking a vacation," Linda said, her voice seeming to come from afar. "After the funeral, of course."

Julia looked up from the reports she'd been arranging on her desk. "I can understand him wanting to get away."

"I'm surprised *you're* here."

"I couldn't sit at home."

So the afternoon passed. Julia was in a daze and kept hoping that routine would comfort her. But at this point, the only thing that would make her feel better would be if Will would show up to say quite cheerfully that he had found another woman and wanted to release Julia from her promise to marry him. So she plodded along, watching time crawl by on the clock, taking phone calls about Dr. Jansen's death and the funeral arrangements, feeling like her life had crumbled away under her feet, and she was left with nothing to stand on, no firm, sure place to press her cane.

◈◈◈

"He do it?"

"Yup. Busted me back." Sean looked up at Sal who stood in shirt sleeves and no jacket and tie at his desk.

"Crap. I was hoping he was just talking big." Sal plopped a thick pile of files on Sean's desk, explaining, "It's the stuff we collected on the case. I took it home Friday night, figuring I'd go over it with a fine tooth comb over the weekend. Had a theory. No point in that now."

"What was your theory?"

Sal twisted his mouth to one side. "What I said before — that crippled secretary. I started thinking how she was a troublemaker, always getting folks in the soup. She's angry deep down, and it comes out that way."

Sean heaved a sigh. Julia was hiding her anger, sure, but did she have enough to kill? He didn't think so.

Sal continued, "Maybe she got angry at our Dr. Hill. She had reasons. He refused to work on *her* disease."

Sean had seen fierce determination in her eyes, had heard fomenting anger in her voice. But, like Jansen, she'd been timid with her rage, not showing it off to the world.

"Anybody talk to Jansen's neighbors — see anybody coming to visit him Friday night?"

Sal shook his head. "Doubt it. I think the case is closed."

"Yeah, I guess it is." As O'Brien had just told him. This was a fool's errand in every possible way to keep pursuing it. It could only mean trouble for Sean.

Sean changed topics. "What's your sentence?"

"Two weeks' probation," Sal said. "O'Brien let me know Friday night before I left. I'm not supposed to be here." He smiled. "I'm going to the beach right before Easter. Got some money saved."

"Hope it won't be too cold."

"I don't care, man. I just want to sit in a bar drinking a National Bo and thinking about nothing related to doctors and the like." He rocked on his heels. "Your beat days are only temporary, right?"

Sean shrugged. "He's not saying."

"Ain't nothing you can do?"

Sean leaned back in his chair. "I'd always thought of opening my own shop one day. A PI agency. Something all on my own. But I can't do that now. Have to support the boys."

"My guess is O'Brien will make you walk the beat for a month tops and then reel you back in."

Sean smiled at Sal's optimism. "I think it's more likely he'll be glad to be rid of me."

The man himself appeared in the doorway to his office, shooting them a dour look that made them both realize there was worse their boss could do to them still.

"I'll be talking to you," Sal said before leaving. "Best of lucky, buddy. You'll land on your feet."

After Sal left, Sean spent a humiliating day typing reports as O'Brien had directed. One of the other detectives kept ribbing him about it, calling him "Miss Reilly," as if he were a secretary. No wonder that Julia was filled with rage, he thought as he rolled out the last page of the day. Just the typing alone was enough to send you over the edge.

He leaned on his elbows and wiped his face with his hand. If she'd had something to do with the murders, he should find out. It didn't matter if O'Brien thought the case was closed. Their job was to take killers off the street.

My god—Sal had thought Julia Dell was the killer. It turned his stomach. But maybe he'd just wanted her to be innocent. He'd wanted to see that in her because...because he'd seen a wee bit of his Mary in her, something soft buried underneath all that pretend cheer.

To hell with O'Brien. He was working the case. He wouldn't be able to live with himself otherwise. He picked up the phone and dialed Julia's number.

کوکٹ

Why'd you send that note to Susan's house instead of just handing it to the girl?

You knew I'd see the letter from Dr. Jansen's ex-wife. You must have seen it yourself when you went in his office. Why didn't you just give it to me outright?

"I—I don't know," she said, and he could hear the tears in her voice. "I—I sent the letter to Sue because I was afraid I'd forget it...I..."

"Why were you so eager to let us know about Jansen—giving me his file and all? You're not a detective, Julia. Did you think he did it?"

"I..." Again, she stumbled. He was hitting a nerve. She must have been realizing how bad she looked, at best a mean-spirited tattler. "I wanted to help."

Just like Jansen had wanted to help, to do good.

"All you did was get your friends in trouble. Why'd you want to do that? Were you trying to take the focus off yourself?" He swallowed hard, forcing himself to keep pressing.

"No! Really, detective, I...I only wanted to be helpful." She sniffled.

"But you didn't like your boss, did you? He was a hard man to work for, right?"

"He's dead!" she said, and her meaning was clear—she wouldn't speak ill of the dead, even if Sean was right about him.

"But that don't make him likeable. C'mon, you know he was a tough one, a real dictator. And that attitude of his—how'd you put up with that? It must have made you real mad some times, didn't it? Do you often get mad like that?"

"Please, stop this. I didn't do anything wrong. I told you the truth about things, that's all. I didn't...I didn't do anything bad. I'm sad Dr. Jansen is dead. I'm..."

"But you thought he did it, didn't you?"

"I don't know." She blew her nose.

"You thought he bashed in the good Doctor Lowenstein's head, didn't you? You've seen him mad. You know what he can do."

"No! I mean, yes! I've—I'd seen him angry. But he...he...why would he kill him like that?" She was weeping now.

"You mean not stick a needle in him nice and neat? Well, when you're mad, you don't take time to do things neat."

"No! I mean...why didn't he just shoot him! He had a gun!"

He straightened. She'd known this?

"Dr. Jansen had a gun...." And then she told him of how she'd startled him in his lab one day, and he'd pointed a gun at her.

So it hadn't just been a story Jansen had made up in the interrogation room. Julia had known about the gun and Jansen's fears, too. Why hadn't she given him that with all the other stuff, goddammit?

He cursed under his breath. "Why didn't you tell me about that?"

"I don't know," she said, sniffling. "I thought it made him look...guilty."

"And you didn't think he really was?"

A long pause before she answered. "No."

"Where were you Friday night?" he asked her and heard her suck in her breath.

"At home with my family."

"They can vouch for you?"

"Yes! You can call them right now. Please, do!"

"Anybody besides your family see you?"

"Oh, my god, you think I—I couldn't even get to Dr. Jansen's house Friday without help! I didn't hurt him. I couldn't have done it. I'm not strong enough. For God's sake, I'm a cripple!" And then she hiccupped a huge sob, and Sean felt like a heel.

He calmed her down and got off the phone. It was a relief to feel in his gut she wasn't guilty, but he still believed the killer was out there. Jansen had known it. He'd gotten a gun to protect himself. He'd told Julia he was afraid.

Heaving a sigh, Sean scooped up the papers Sal had brought in and left. He'd head to Jansen's house and take one last look-see before calling it a day. If O'Brien missed him, too bad.

Chapter Twenty-Five

THE BRIGHT COFFEE SHOP with its smell of onions, cigarettes and coffee, its uncomfortable booths with rubbery seats, its chrome-edged counter and cracked tile floor all combined to make Julia feel tawdry.

It was a fitting place to end an engagement that had never glistened with joy, she thought as she slid awkwardly into a booth across from Will. Staring at her "betrothed" over a spaghetti-stained menu in this joint made her realize just how much she didn't love him and never had.

Will looked up at her and smiled, then noticed she had her ring hand in her lap, out of sight.

"Now, Julia, are you embarrassed or something?" He laughed. "If I didn't know you, I'd think you were ashamed of it."

Ashamed — that's precisely how she'd felt whenever anyone saw it. And she felt even more down now, after the troubling conversation with Sean earlier.

The waitress stood over them, pad and pencil in hand.

"Did you see, Jules? Blue plate special is liver and onions."

Her stomach turned at the thought. "Just coffee," she said, smiling at the waitress.

Will made a show of frowning. "You have to put some meat on those bones, honey." Turning to the waitress, he said, "Bring her a piece of cherry pie. And I'll take the special."

"I've never liked liver," Julia said after the waitress left. "My mother doesn't like it either. She'll fix it for my father and fix something else for us."

Will chuckled. "Well, there you go. You probably just picked up her dislike for it. Maybe you just need to try it again. I was reading an article about how eating liver is good for your blood. You need your strength, Julia. When you're cooking for me, you'll be making liver, so maybe you'll develop an appetite for it."

He asked about her weekend, but it was just an excuse so he could talk about his own. While they waited for their food, Will excitedly described the drive over the Conowingo Dam to Lancaster and the many farms he and his mother had passed along the way. She let him prattle as her thoughts wandered.

They wandered to an image that brought a sour taste to her mouth—she at a stove, frilly apron around her waist, frying up Will's dinner of liver and onions while she waited for him to return home. It was a nice home, the one-story rancher that she coveted, in a good neighborhood, and it was filled with furniture she liked and things she cherished, but she was sick to her stomach as she cooked because Will would be coming home soon...

"I can't do it." She had both hands on the table and was nervously stroking the nail of her index finger.

He looked perplexed at first and then blurted out his misunderstanding.

"Oh, c'mon honey. My mom'll show you how to fix it. Maybe your mother doesn't cook it right—"

"No, I mean I can't get married." She closed her eyes, opened them, looked up. She saw his face change from uncomprehending to angry. His mouth slackened, then set in a straight bitter line. She expected him to ask her why not, but he stared, unblinking, daring her to continue. She took a deep breath before going on.

"I've thought about it, Will. I'm not ready to get married." She was surprised at how forceful she sounded. It was easier once she'd started.

"Not ready? Christ, Julia, you're practically thirty!"

"I'm only twenty-five."

"Most girls your age have been married and had two or more kids by now." His voice rose. She saw a man in a booth up ahead glance at them.

"My sister Helen's not married."

"Your sister Helen is a freak."

She sat up as if slapped. It was one thing to insult her, but Helen...Helen was a sweet soul who wouldn't hurt a fly. "Helen is as normal as you or I. She was engaged during the war. Lots of girls lost—"

Their food arrived, forcing silence upon them while the waitress arranged the heavy porcelain plates. Julia wrapped her hands around the mug but pushed the pie to the side. She was surprised when Will picked up his knife and fork and began eating.

"Your sister's shut herself up like a nun." He talked with his mouth full. Julia couldn't stop her upper lip from curling up in disgust. Will pointed his fork at her. "Is that what you want to be like?"

"Let's not talk about Helen," she said, leaning into the table and speaking low, hoping he'd follow her example. "The fact is I'm just not ready to get married." She twisted the ring off her finger with some effort. Now that they'd had it resized, it was too tight, and it took her several painful turns to get it over her knuckle.

"Here," she said, placing it on the table in front of his plate when he made no effort to take it. "I can't keep it. Maybe you could get your money back."

He snorted and reached for his coffee, then scooped up the ring with his other hand and deposited it in his shirt pocket. When he sipped his coffee, he sloshed some liquid on his shirt.

"You seeing someone else?" he asked through gritted teeth before picking up his fork again. He speared a piece of meat and jammed it in his mouth. "Is that what this is all about?"

"No!" Looking at him now, she wondered why she'd even gone out with him, let alone agreed to marry him.

He shook his head. "Course not. Who would you find? Christ, the fellas in the office—they couldn't figure out what I saw in you. A one-legged gimp. How you gonna...."

She couldn't believe the stream of filth that poured from his mouth. She didn't hear it. Once he'd said the word "gimp," his voice receded to the background, and all she saw was his mouth, opening and closing, saying things, eating things, a disgusting dirty orifice that she once let kiss her on the lips. She thought she was going to gag.

"I have to go." She scooted to the edge of the booth, but it took her a while because of her bad leg. "I'm sorry, Will." She stood, leaned on her cane and buttoned her sweater.

"Is it someone else?"

"I told you. No."

"I mean a woman. Is that what it is? I've always wondered about that sister of yours, Helen. She introduce you to one of her friends?"

She wanted to slap him. But she sucked in her breath, stared and said nothing. Then she left him, eating his precious liver and onions that she would never—thank god—have to fix for him.

ᔕᔓ

Sean sat in Jansen's home at the dead man's kitchen table, poring through papers. Jansen hadn't done it. Sean was sure of it. The man had been afraid—justifiably so, it seemed. And just as Jansen had stopped feeling like the perpetrator to Sean, so, too, had Julia faded as a possibility. Holding back on the info about Jansen's gun sealed it for Sean. She'd been quick to give over lots of lesser info that pointed to guilt. The man having a gun would have made him look as if he was on the verge of using it and had only resorted to a beating when opportunity had collided with motivation.

No, if Julia herself had been guilty, she'd have rushed to hand over that little tidbit. She might be mixed up inside, but she wasn't guilty of murder.

When he'd arrived at the Jansen house, he'd spent a good half hour looking for that gun and not found it. This troubled him. If Jansen had been killed, and hadn't died of an accidental fall, had his murderer taken the victim's gun? Had Jansen tried to protect himself with it, only to have it knocked from his hands before being knocked out himself?

Maybe the gun was at the lab?

He'd check on that soon enough. Right now he wanted to finish looking through the papers he'd brought from the office, the ones Sal had scooped up before everything went bad, the ones Jansen had coveted.

At first, as Sean flipped the pages, he'd been bewildered why the man would hang on to them. They were records of the 1935 experiment, the very event he'd wanted to distance himself from. But as Sean reviewed page after page of meticulous data, names and dates, outcomes and conclusions, he understood why. As damning as these might be for Jansen, the man hadn't been able to bring himself to destroy them because they still represented science. Yes, a scientific error. But still...science. He couldn't wipe out the results of the experiment, no matter how horrible it had been.

Sean took a drag from a cigarette from a pack he'd picked up on the way over. He'd also picked up the police report on Jansen's death. No evidence of alcohol. No evidence of foul play. "Suicide?" one cop had written in the margin. No, not a suicide. Throwing yourself down a flight of steps wasn't a sure way to die. You could end up worse than dead—in a wheelchair the rest of your life. If he'd had a gun, he'd have taken the quickest, surest route with the pistol. But where was it? No record of it in the police report. Not stashed in a drawer or under a mattress. It had vanished.

He stopped turning pages.

A familiar name. Vaguely familiar. Something dancing around the edges of his mind. Something...someone he'd met.

There. On the list. Children inoculated in '35.

Dagley, Earl. Followed by Dagley, Weston.

Earl Dagley.

Sean stuck his cigarette in his mouth and reached for the files on the case. Sal had interviewed someone, one of the Hopkins workers. A cleaning man? No, but on the same level. He found it. The chimp tender...

His eyes widened, his blood pumped fast.

Now in a rush to discover more, Sean shuffled through his other notes. What else had he missed?

He found the letter from Ethan Pendleton to Dr. Lowenstein/Hill telling him the deal on the cabin had fallen through. Sean had never actually read that note. Now he ripped it from the envelope.

"....*Mr. Dagley has retracted his offer so the cabin is now available....He's a polio victim and was asking quite a bit about you. I hope you don't mind but I told him you were at Hopkins...*"

Dagley. Earl Dagley had been in Hill's cabin. The cabin where Hill had burned some records. Not all of them. Dagley must have found the remnants. Enough to connect Hill to...

Dammit. He should have read this when it came in. He should have...

Sean stood, pushed his cigarette into a saucer, and reached for the phone, quickly calling Mrs. Creed to tell her he'd be late.

∾∾

She'd made no arrangement for a ride home. Her family assumed Will would bring her home, of course, because they didn't know she was breaking the engagement. Only Helen knew, and she was at the shop this evening.

She made her way across Broadway back toward the hospital feeling pressed into the earth, ground down by both Sean earlier and now Will. What kind of person was she? Why had she debased herself by agreeing to marry a man like Will? Why had she taken pleasure in getting her coworkers into trouble?

She couldn't think it all out. Her mind was muddled. She'd talk about it with Helen. She'd call Helen and ask her to come fetch her, and they'd talk about it on the way home.

Her hand trembled as she leaned on her cane. She couldn't stop thinking of the awful things Will had said to her. They made her stomach turn.

Agreeing to marry a man like Will told her something about herself she didn't want to face. Would she have settled for someone like him before the polio? God, no. This brought tears to her eyes. She'd ignored his obvious faults because she'd thought he was all she could get. She'd lied to herself, of course. Had told herself that the best men were gone in the war or promised to other girls. But that wasn't the real reason. She'd been afraid a good man wouldn't want her. He'd want someone whole.

She stared at the steps to the grand lobby of Hopkins and decided she was too tired to tackle them. She headed for a side door instead, one for which she had the key because of her lameness—"the staircase has a banister there," Mrs. Wilcox had said her first week on the job. In defiance, Julia had rarely used this entrance. Tonight she didn't feel like a rebel.

She let herself in. The hallways were brightly lit and quiet, the rooms along the hall dark. The only noise came from the monkey room where a light still shone. Earl was probably feeding the animals before going home for the night. She hurried past, not wanting to run into another living soul. As she rushed by the slightly opened door, she heard him talking to the chimps.

"That's it, girls. That's the way. Now stop that fighting. Stop it right now, I tell you!" His voice was elevated, angry, as he tried to get the animals to quiet down and feed. There was something familiar about it....

"Buck won't hurt you now. Take it easy."

Despite herself, she gasped. Buck? Earl. Early Dagley.

Sucking in her lips, she raced as quietly as she could past the closed door and up to her office. Once there, her hands shook as she reached for the phone, ready to dial her sister, the police.

But before she'd even begun to call, a cane fell across her phone, knocking the receiver out of her hand. She jumped, almost falling.

"I warned you, Julia. I told you to stay away from the case."

She looked up to see Earl Dagley pointing Dr. Jansen's gun at her heart.

❧❧

He tried the lab first, and his hopes rose when he saw that the door to the monkey room was open and the light on. Dagley must still be around.

Then he'd trudged upstairs and found another light on. Julia's office, the one on her desk. But her phone was knocked off the hook, and, more ominously, her cane leaned against the chair.

❧❧

"What makes you think they're any better than the Nazis? They experiment on children, for Christ's sake! Helpless children. Children like my brother, in the Taconic School for the Feeble-Minded. He didn't have no say in what happened to him. None! And they injected him like he was a monkey! Hah! They treat the monkeys here better than they treated him. They didn't care whether he got sick or died. They cared even less if he suffered. And he did suffer! We all did. Still do!"

"They don't do that sort of thing anymore...." She didn't know where they were headed. She only knew it was awfully hard trying to walk without her cane. She had to balance by holding her hand out to the wall. If she moved too slowly, he jabbed the gun in her side.

Earl knew hallways and passages in Hopkins that she'd never discovered. If she saw another soul, she'd cry out. But he was too adept at mapping the route, too good at avoiding contact. Her heart pounded out a thousand regrets. She wished she'd been happier with her life. She wished she'd appreciated what she had, even the use of one leg. She wished....

He waved the gun near her face, and she took in a sharp breath. She picked up her pace.

"The Polk School up there near Pittsburgh. You know what I'm talking about." He nodded as he caught her flicker of recognition. "You're like me. You lap up any crumb of information about this disease. You know as well as I do. That doctor in Pittsburgh..."

"Dr. Salk..." she panted.

"Dr. Salk injected kids at the Polk School for the Feeble-Minded."

"He got permission first!"

Earl laughed. "Right. Permission from the state of Pennsylvania. What kind of mother is that? Didn't take much to get them to say go ahead. The murdering bastards."

"The tests were good. They...they led to the trials...the ones they're starting..." She could barely speak from the effort at walking, but she wanted to keep talking to him, to keep him rational. Maybe she could reason with him eventually? Oh, God, could she?

"How do you know the 'tests were good?' Because they told you, the doctors here? Hill? Your boss? Lying bastards."

They wouldn't lie. She trusted them. They were trying to do good, to save lives, to prevent crippling... They wouldn't lie. Would they?

As if reading her mind, he continued, "In '35 the doctors all said they were doing it for the public good. They all said they were going to keep us from getting polio." He shook his cane at her. "But they didn't. They did the opposite. And worse!" He continued to prod her through darkened hallways where researchers and technicians had left for the day.

"They didn't know...."

"They don't know now. They knew enough back then to know that using monkey brains and the like was inviting trouble. Oh, yeah, I read about it, too. Just like you. Reading newspapers and magazines and whatever to find out anything we can about this project." He grunted in disgust. "Do you know why we do that?"

She shook her head, willing herself to stay strong, trying to figure out what to say.

"Because we think we'll read something that will give *us* hope! Something that will let us believe we'll be whole again once they get this puzzle solved."

"That's not true," she whispered.

But it was. It was an awful truth, one she'd refused to face, happy in the knowledge she was working for men who were making progress on the disease. But it was progress that would never benefit her or Earl. If anything, a vaccine would kill hope for them entirely.

Once the disease could be prevented, who would care about victims any longer?

They would become lost to the world, forgotten.

Earl had already hit one target without firing a shot — her misplaced hope.

"Keep walking." He held the gun steady now and his voice changed.

"Where to?"

"Straight, then right up ahead."

She did as he said. He was forcing her toward the front of the hospital. He seemed to know every cul-de-sac and back stairwell. He led her up and around and over and up again, doubling back sometimes, always avoiding the actual hospital wards, taking her past darkened offices, closed doors, and shadowed corners. She was breathless and sweating from the effort. She noticed his breathing coming faster. Even with a cane, he found all this walking hard, too.

"Where are you taking me?" Her throat was dry, and her leg ached from all the stair climbing. Her hand trembled on the banister. He noticed.

"People don't realize how much effort it takes to make up for lost muscles."

"You must be tired too." She tried glancing over her shoulder, but when she did, he scurried up behind and jammed the gun into her rib cage.

"I'm hardly breaking a sweat. You're hurting, though, aren't you?"

"I'd like to rest." Maybe if they paused, she could reason with him. He was, after all, like her, a fellow polio. They'd shared a few moments of understanding before.

He laughed. "Bet you don't admit that to most folks, do you? You keep up the cheerful face, the happy-to-be-alive face, don't you? The one they expected everybody to wear in the hospitals."

Yes, she did those things. "Where are we going?" she repeated.

"Same kind of place I took your boss."

Ice cold fear prickled up her spine. "What do you mean?"

"Now, really, Julia. I can't allow you to tattle on me. The way you tattled on your boss."

"I didn't..."

"Of course you did. That's how I found out about him. When the cops hauled him in for Dick Hill's death, I heard the gossip. I didn't know he'd been involved, too, back in '35. Here I thought he was a decent fellow...."

Julia stopped. Dear lord, her trail had led Earl to him. Dr. Jansen had been hurt because of her. Susan had been hurt because of...

"Keep moving!" He shoved the gun again into her rib cage.

"No, no, I can't. I'm too tired." She wanted to curl up and close her eyes. She wanted everything to stop.

She'd been selfish and confused and lacking in the courage she arrogantly thought she had. She should have broken with Will and let Sean make a pass at her and then maybe, maybe she wouldn't have used Dr. Jansen as an excuse to have contact with the detective...she should have...done a hundred things differently.

"Do you want it to end right here?"

✌୨

"Earl Dagley. He tends the animals they're using for research!"

"No, sir. I haven't heard of him. Did you check in? Visiting hours are over."

Christ almighty. The nurse was driving him mad.

Sean had run into this nosey Florence Nightingale while double-stepping it up a staircase. When she'd asked him what he was looking for, he'd thrown the question about Earl back at her.

"You really need to check in. Otherwise, I'll have to report you to security."

"Dammit, woman, I *am* security." He pulled out his badge and flashed it at her, glad he'd not handed it in earlier that day. Without waiting for a reply, he rushed past her, panicked now that he'd be too late for Julia as he'd been for Jansen. He ducked down a darkened hallway and called her name. No answer.

He couldn't have gotten far. Not with a bum leg. Not with her bad leg.

❧

"Why did you do it?" She was moving again. If she kept him talking, maybe he'd get distracted, and she could reach for the gun?

"I was making good money off of Dick. But the arrogant bastard decided he'd had enough of hiding. Thought he needed to 'come clean,' he told me. Make 'restitution.'" Earl laughed. "Like that would wipe everything away."

"He did atone! He gave all his money to—"

"The fucking March of Dimes. Yeah, I figured that one out, too. That doesn't make things better. It makes them worse!"

She could tell from his breathing that he was growing much more tired now, too. They'd climbed several staircases. They must be on the fifth floor or higher, and she thought they were headed toward the front of the hospital.

"It was an accident," she improvised. "Killing Dr. Lowen—Dr. Hill. People will understand. You were upset. You had a right to be upset." She saw a door up ahead and knew now where they were—at the top tier of octagonal balconies that overlooked the lobby with its statue of Christ the Healer. Why would he take her here?

"No, *you* don't understand." He directed her to stay still while he backed open the door and glanced through. No one must have been about, because he waved her through the door ahead of him. "Once I killed Dick, I decided to give Dr. Jansen a go-round, see if he'd pay up. He wasn't too happy about it. Tried pulling this on me..." He waved the gun. "But he was a might nervous about it, and I know how to use this cane."

"Then that was an accident, too, Earl. People will understand. You didn't mean to—"

"Shut up! I damn well meant to. I was happy to see him tumble! I'm glad he's gone."

He'd enjoyed killing a man. Why did she think she could stop him from doing it to her?

"Poor Doctor Jansen," Earl said sarcastically, urging her forward, toward the balcony. "Broke his neck."

She couldn't look over the edge. Even before the polio, she'd been afraid of heights. Her head swam, and she gripped the railing with both hands behind her.

❧

He took whatever hallway or staircase was darkened or empty. Earl wouldn't lead her around other people. He wouldn't risk her calling out. He himself called her name at every intersection, ever corner. Nothing. Stone silence.

❧

"Earl...I'm not going to say anything. I swear it. It will be our secret. Between us polios."

"You have two choices," he said in a voice as cold as death itself. "You jump or I push you."

"People will know you did it...."

"Yeah, how? Nobody knows who the hell I am. Me and my brother were just numbers in a book, not real people. Even Dr. Jansen didn't recognize me. Didn't know I was one of the kids he'd poisoned."

"But they'll know I wouldn't...wouldn't do this." Her back was to the balcony. Far below was the statue of Christ the Healer, his arms extended, welcoming the sick and their loved ones to this place of healing. She prayed to Christ now, desperate, inarticulate prayers. *Help me, help me,* beating in the back of her mind like an ostinato. *I'll appreciate life now. I won't give up.*

"They'll just figure you gave up at last. You stopped trying."

"But my family and everyone here..." She nodded toward the hospital beyond but couldn't bring herself to release her grip on the railing, "they all know I'm a fighter, that I wouldn't give up..."

"Stop it, Julia. You can't fool me. I know what it was like. I've got a second-degree burn on my back from one of them hot packs. Oh, yeah, I remember it like it was yesterday. Getting pushed and pulled this way and that and hell to pay if you don't do exactly what they want. That's not fighting, Julia. That's giving in." He narrowed his eyes and pointed the gun at her chest. "Admit it."

When she said nothing, he shouted at her. "Tell. The. Damn. Truth."

"It was hard but..."

"Stop. Pretending!" he yelled, and she hoped someone would hear. "Admit it was awful. Tell the fucking truth!"

"All right, all right!" She was so afraid. And he was right. It had been horrible. She was sick of pretending it hadn't been, sick of trying to look happy. Tears ran down her cheeks. "Yes. It was awful. It was...."

"Tell me what you remember," he sneered. "The truth. Not the shit they showed to the world in movie reels. How long were you in?"

"Nearly a year."

"How did they treat you? Gently? Like a baby learning to walk?" he asked, waving the gun.

"No."

"Tell me!"

"They...." She stopped, swallowed, struggled for control. She remembered how alone she'd felt, how she'd wanted to tell her parents, her sisters how awful it was, but she couldn't. She couldn't because she knew she was supposed to feel lucky to be alive and every other patient was trying so hard. Surely there was something wrong with her, mentally, if she wasn't happy to be trying, no matter how hard it hurt. "They made me pick myself up..."

"After you'd fallen. Yeah. How many times?"

She didn't need him to explain. He was asking the most number of times she had fallen in one therapy session. "Twenty-two."

"And they probably would have let you lie on the floor in your own shit rather than help you up."

Messy tears stained her blouse. The therapist was cruel. And so damned happy about it. *Now, Julia, nobody will be around to help you once you get out of here. You need to learn to cope...*

She'd been black and blue that night, aching in body and spirit. Humiliated, she'd sobbed herself to sleep.

She was sobbing now.

"And you probably thought that maybe dying would have been easier." His voice was lower now, but harder, too.

Yes, she had thought that. On that night, she had wondered why she'd been so stubborn about living. It had seemed like a vice, not a virtue, and living as a cripple would be penance for that sin, the sin of clinging to something too hard when it had been meant to be taken away.

"Yes, I did," she said, her voice trembling.

"You wanted to die," he repeated, victorious.

She cried, nodded, looked at the floor where her withered foot served as a constant reminder of her stubbornness. Not an asset at all.

"Yes, yes, I did." She was sobbing now. "Are you happy? Yes, I had moments when I didn't want to live!"

"Drop the gun, Earl!" Sean's voice, strong and safe, came from below.

❧❧

He'd heard it all. The confession. Julia's admission of despair. And he somehow felt responsible for this, too, for putting her in danger and forcing her to voice these thoughts that she'd hidden from the world. If he'd kept Jansen in custody...

He stood on a balcony below them, his gun pointed toward Earl. It was too far. He couldn't risk the shot. Julia might get hurt.

"Let her go, Earl. Let's you and me talk."

"You're the one who should go. Or I'll plug the girl."

"It's over," Sean called. "A squad's on the way," he lied. "All that's left is you dropping the gun."

Silence.

Then a blur of action. Earl was forcing Julia somewhere else, out of range.

"Earl! They'll understand. I read the records. I know what they did to you and your brother."

He heard the movement above him cease. And then Earl's face appeared over the edge. His arm was still pointed away from the balcony. He had the gun on Julia.

"They're going to do it to thousands more in just a few weeks!"

"You can warn them, Earl. You can't do that if you're dead."

"Winchell already warned them."

"But it's not the same as someone who's been through it."

"You got children?"

"Two boys."

"Will you take them for the shots?"

After what he'd heard, what he'd read...he didn't know. But he said nothing.

"The government's ordered thousands of little white coffins," Earl said. "Did you know that?"

"I heard rumors...."

Julia's voice now. "That's not true. There are no coffins! That's a ridiculous lie! Earl, stop it, what they're doing now isn't what happened before..."

Dammit, shut up, Julia.

But her interjection made Earl turn his head away from Sean. Just a split-second chance, the only chance. Sean took it and squeezed the trigger.

Earl dropped his gun over the side and groaned, grabbing his arm. Sean had winged him.

"Run, Julia!" Sean called out to her and aimed again for Dagley.

But she couldn't run. She'd never be able to do that, whether it was a murderer or a child on her tail.

Earl reached out and grabbed her by the shoulder, trying to wrestle his arm around her neck.

Sean froze, not knowing whether to stay where he was or run up to help her. He was about to take the latter course, when he heard her scream. He watched in horror as they struggled by the railing, her back pinned perilously over the edge, the slightest push able to upset her balance. Dagley yelled something to Sean about letting her fall if Sean didn't leave. He couldn't leave. He couldn't do anything.

Dammit. He couldn't *not* do anything. He held his gun with both hands, aimed it, and...

And then with a mighty shove, Julia pushed Earl to the side. Now he was the one leaning back against the rail. He reached out for her, grabbed her by the collar, but she would have none of it. She pressed both hands against his shoulders and pushed with all her might away from him, grunting with the effort.

In a moment that seemed to stretch for hours, his body teetered on the railing, and he tried to balance himself with his grip, unable to counter the weight of his upper body. It was too late. He twisted backwards over the edge and fell, a rush, a blur, an image neither would forget.

He didn't scream. He didn't utter a sound. He just fell, landing with a hard thud at the feet of Christ the Healer.

Blood pooled around his head, but his legs lay perfectly straight as if they'd never been crippled, as if he was healed at last, a final sacrifice offered at the altar in this temple of science.

Sean heard her whisper "oh, no," and saw her at the edge, covering her mouth with her hand, and then sinking slowly to her knees, her hand grasping the railing. He ran back through the door and up the stairs, racing to her side, until he knelt by her, cradling her in his arms.

She was hysterical with shock and grief. She kept muttering "I didn't mean to..." and he stroked her hair and kissed her forehead.

"It wasn't your fault," he whispered, thinking, *No, it was mine. All mine. I'm the guilty one.*

"Julia, Julia," he said to her. "I'm here. I'll take care of you. Don't fret, my sweet. I'll take care of you."

Epilogue

A WEEK AFTER HE'D RESCUED Julia Dell from Earl Dagley, Sean looked at himself in the mirror and adjusted his cap. He remembered the first time Mary had seen him in his blues. She'd been standing on the corner of Broadway and Patterson, out shopping with her aunt. Her face had been drawn down with fatigue, but when she'd realized he was standing there in his neat uniform, a smile had transformed her into a delighted child. She'd even raised her hands together as if to clap. He'd never felt so proud, not even later in his Army uniform on parade.

What would Julia think of him if she saw him like this? He didn't want to know. Had to push that thought away.

Danny came in the bathroom and hugged his leg. "You going to get bad guys?" he asked, fingering the heavy buttons on the jacket and yawning.

It was evening, and the boys would be going to bed as soon as Mrs. Creed arrived. He wished he could go to bed, too. This night shift was running him into the ground. And he wasn't sure how much longer the Creed woman would stand for it.

"Going to try," he answered, straightening the hat. It didn't look right. Maybe it was the wrong size. He looked down at Danny and rubbed his head. "You should be settling down."

The phone rang, sending a pang of fear and guilt through Sean. Maybe she couldn't sit with them tonight. Damn. Or maybe it was...

"Brigitta, I was going to call you first thing tomorrow," he lied, standing in the kitchen. He'd told her he would call her this week. But every time he'd thought of it, his gut had twisted.

He listened as she told him she was hoping they could go to the movies that weekend, but what he heard was this: *I don't know yet, Sean, so we have to keep going...*

After some strained small talk, he told her he had to go. Where was Creed?

He hung up the phone, but his hand lingered on the receiver. A dozen times he'd felt the pull to call Julia, to ask how she was doing. Once he'd even dialed her number and was relieved when no one answered.

He heard a car door slam outside. That would be Mrs. Creed at last. He took a deep breath and strode toward the front of the house.

≈≈

When the vaccine trials began, Julia was curled up in bed under the treatment of a doctor. Nervous exhaustion, he called it. To her it just felt like despair.

She read the papers every day and listened to the radio. The reports wouldn't be written for a year, but she knew, deep down, that this was it. Her disease would be gone from generations to come.

And so, too, would any attention on people like her. *Lost to the world, forgotten – she and the other polios.*

The phone rang, and her heart leapt, her nerves on edge as she listened and waited...Mutti's muffled tones carried through the floorboards, and Julia closed her eyes and wished. Wished. Prayed. Hoped.

Please let it be Sean. He said he'd take care of me. Don't let him *forget...*

Author's note

The crime and those involved in it in *Lost to the World* are pure fiction, as are references to an "Irene Brodie." Drs. Jansen, Lowenstein, Spencer, MacIntyre and Rollins are all fictional.

Information about the polio vaccine trials, however, is based on fact, including the references to previous trials and the impact these trials had on the researchers involved in them. Dr. Brodie, for example, did die at a young age, his death a suspected suicide. The reference to the Walter Winchell broadcast of 1954 in which he warned America of the "white coffins" ordered before the vaccine trials is true and quoted exactly.

The most prominent researchers of the time, Drs. Jonas Salk and Albert Sabin, were Jewish, and researchers did receive some anti-Semitic hate mail complaining of a Jewish conspiracy. Dr. David Bodian of Hopkins, who is referred to in this novel, was involved in the research and did help solve a mystery related to why monkeys at a Park, Davis lab seemed to be afflicted with polio after being inoculated with the new vaccine. Drs. Salk and Sabin did have an intense rivalry, and Dr. Sabin lobbied the research community to forgo trials on a killed vaccine and wait until a live vaccine was ready. Some members of the research community believed, as does Dr. Jansen in this novel, that the March of Dimes had reduced the search for a vaccine to a "circus" and resented the organization's influence even as they took its money.

Ultimately, the vaccines saved generations from being affected by the scourge of polio. I am a member of the generation that received the vaccine, at school, on a sugar cube. I had an aunt who'd had the disease as a youngster. She wore a leg brace her entire life. Those who didn't live in those times, prior to many of the wonderful vaccines that now save lives, don't adequately understand the fear and impact of diseases now faint memories in many people's minds.

Sources for this book include:

A Splendid Solution: Jonas Salk and the Conquest of Polio by Jeffrey Kluger
A Summer Plague: Polio and its Survivors by Tony Gould
Polio: An American Story by David M. Oshinsky
A Nearly Normal Life by Charles L. Mee
Small Steps: The Year I Got Polio by Peg Kehret
"What Ever Happened to Polio?" Smithsonian Institute exhibit

Because I am a graduate of a music conservatory, I have a hard time resisting art song as a source for book titles. This book's title is from the title of a poem by Friedrich Rückert, set sublimely to music by Gustav Mahler: *Ich bin der Welt abhanden gekommen.* The first lines, roughly translated, are: *I have become lost to the world, with which I used to waste so much time...*

About Libby Sternberg

Libby Sternberg is the author of several young adult mysteries, the first of which (*Uncovering Sadie's Secrets*) was an Edgar finalist. Her first historical women's fiction, *Sloane Hall,* a retelling of the Jane Eyre story set in old Hollywood, has been praised by Bronte experts. Writing under the name Libby Malin, she is the author of several humorous women's fiction books, one of which has been optioned for film. Before becoming a novelist, she studied voice, earning both bachelor's and master's degrees from Peabody Conservatory of Music.

Visit her website at www.LibbySternberg.com

If you enjoyed these or any books you read,
consider leaving a review at book blogs or major book retail sites –
they mean the world to writers and can help boost sales
of your favorite authors!

11/16

1X 1/17 (7/17)

1X 1/17 (7/20

We are the only
library in Sierra
that has this
book